Reviews for Beyond the Gateway

Reapers reset the bar for Bryan Davis books, with a tight plot, a protagonist I fell in love with on page one and his equally loveable friends, a dark world with a thin veil between natural and spiritual, and intricately woven themes of life over death, sacrifice over selfishness, and the quest for light in the darkness. This trilogy is the *Esther* of the Davis canon, and I've waited patiently (most of the time) for book two.

Beyond the Gateway picks up immediately where we left Phoenix, Shanghai, and Singapore, takes off running, and doesn't stop. If anyone had any doubts about the spiritual content and themes of *Reapers*, they can be assured of utmost satisfaction and then some in *Beyond the Gateway*.

We have met the best this world has to offer, and he is not enough. Righteous heroes are not born overnight, but are forged, hammered, and fashioned in the deepest of sorrow. With Phoenix, I have experienced hate, love, fear, cravings for the fruits of good and evil, confusion, longing, despair, and hope.

Everything I loved about *Reapers* is magnified in *Beyond the Gateway*. Mr. Davis exceeds expectations and brings a few highly unexpected twists before the end. I look forward to the final installment.

— Kaci Hill, Co-author of *Lunatic* and *Elyon*

D1496265

The path is unclear, people are treacherous, and Phoenix's own heart is torn. With so much against him, can he find the light glimmering *Beyond the Gateway*? This story is the perfect second-step in The Reapers Trilogy, answering just enough questions to make me want more.

— Cadi Murphy, Editor for Geeks Under Grace

Beyond The Gateway miraculously managed to be even more thrilling and captivating than the first novel, *Reapers*. Again I was up late, reading for hours straight, unable to stop consuming this amazing story. It is by far the best sequel I have ever read, and I am already itching to read the third installment.

— Natasha Sapienza, I Am Resistance Productions

Wow! I thought *Reapers* was a marvelous read, but *Beyond the Gateway* topped it in so many ways. I loved how the story progressed, the characters developed, and the tension increased. And the ending. I loved the ending. The twists were amazing. Mr. Davis never ceased to keep me on the edge of my seat and my tear ducts ready to open. Well done. Bravo.

— Christian Johnson, Student

BEYOND THE GATEWAY

OTHER BOOKS BY BRYAN DAVIS

Dragons in our Midst® series
Raising Dragons
The Candlestone
Circles of Seven
Tears of a Dragon

Oracles of Fire® series
Eye of the Oracle
Enoch's Ghost
Last of the Nephilim
The Bones of Makaidos

Children of the Bard series
Song of the Ovulum
From the Mouth of Elijah
The Seventh Door
Omega Dragon

BOOK 2 OF THE REAPERS TRILOGY

BEYOND THE GATEWAY

A NOVEL BY

BRYAN DAVIS

Beyond the Gateway

Book 2 of The Reapers Trilogy

Published by Scrub Jay Journeys
P. O. Box 512
Middleton, TN 38052
www.scrubjayjourneys.com
email: info@scrubjayjourneys.com

ISBN: 978-0-9898122-4-5

First Printing – October 2015

Printed in the U.S.A.

Library of Congress Control Number: 2015951631

CHAPTER ONE

Phoenix's Initiation Ceremony

"PHOENIX, I BROUGHT ghosts with me." Hanoi's breath reeked of stale whiskey as he draped my cloak—made of my own hair interwoven with flax—over my shoulders. "You need to prove yourself."

I pushed my arms through the sleeves and glanced at my Reaper-training graduation certificate on a nearby desk. "I already passed the tests. The initiation doesn't call for—"

"A Council member asked for a demonstration."

"A Council member?" I pointed toward the floor's braided rug. "Here? In my house?"

"Merely an observer, though I understand your anxiety. If the Council is taking an interest in you, the Gatekeeper must have his eye on you. That's enough to make anyone uncomfortable." He fastened the cloak's clasp and plugged it into my sternum valve—a metallic adapter that looked like a double gate joined by two hands, the fingers of each hand curled around the other's.

When he locked the clasp in place, a stinging sensation pinched my gut. The surgery that embedded the valve and attached it to my heart had been too recent to allow for complete healing.

"Don't worry," he said. "I brought two easy ghosts. You won't have to dematerialize to reap them. Make it quick, for your mother's sake."

I nodded and eyed the door to this cramped den. In the living room, everyone waited for my entrance, including Misty. I had to make her proud. With my mother being held captive because of her resistance to my upcoming departure, and my father holding a grudge against everything associated with being a Reaper, Misty remained as the only person in the room who really cared about what I felt. She cared about the real me hiding under the cloak.

I pulled the cloak's hood over my freshly shaved head. "Let's go."

Hanoi opened the door. Chatter and the odor of beer and pizza filtered in. Keeping my shoulders back, I walked into a mass of people holding plastic cups and plates.

A curtain of silence fell. At least thirty heads turned toward me. My father stood near a punch bowl, his eyes the only pair staring somewhere else—aloof, as usual. I spotted Misty to his left. Her fiery locks made her easy to find, and her bright smile lit up the room. A tall woman stood next to her. Blonde hair draped her cloaked shoulders, and a white tribal-like mask covered her face. Black lines outlined the mask's facial features—expressionless, as if hiding a secret.

I avoided eye contact. She had to be the Council representative. They always kept their identities a secret.

Misty called with her distinctive Scottish accent,

"Ah! You look dashing—" She glanced at my father, then quickly turned her gaze downward and rubbed a pewter ring on her finger.

I read his expression—firm lips, plunging brow— utter disapproval of this "foster-home wench," as he once called her. But no matter. Reaper service would keep me away from Misty for twenty years. He had nothing to worry about.

As I walked to the center of the room, the crowd parted and lined the walls. I scanned the faces and spotted pairs of glowing eyes—a stooped man in tattered military garb, a teenaged girl wearing a bloodstained prom dress, and a scar-faced man clutching a bottle.

I blinked and counted again. Three ghosts? Hanoi said two.

Hanoi stepped in front of me. "Raise your right hand."

I did so, though I shifted my gaze from one ghost to the other. Since ghosts were often unpredictable, I had to be ready for anything.

Hanoi cleared his throat. "I, Phoenix, do solemnly pledge to uphold the principles of the Reaper's Code."

As I opened my mouth, a woman called, "Wait."

I turned toward the voice. The masked Council member stepped forward and pointed at me with a long, rigid finger. "Why should I believe your pledge when you have ignored the souls in our midst?"

I squinted. "You can see them?"

"Of course." She drew her cloak's hood over her head and closed in, her steely eyes, visible through the mask's holes, locked on me. She whispered, "Reaper, I detect fear within you, but do not pay heed to it. Remember that your mother waits in captivity for you to complete this initiation, and your success here is the only way to guarantee her safe return home."

Behind the woman, the scar-faced ghost stalked closer to Misty, his glowing eyes trained on her. I had no experience with hostile souls. I had been taught that they could do physical harm only to Reapers, though they sometimes invaded the dreams of normal humans and drove them insane.

I shouted at the ghost, "Get away from her!"

The guests looked around, whispering, some with fear-filled expressions.

The ghost sneered. "I am her next nightmare." He leaped on Misty's back. She gasped, and her face paled.

I lunged and whipped my cloak over the ghost. When the fibers adhered, I wrenched him to the floor. He plunged a hand through my sternum valve. His icy fingers grabbed my heart and squeezed with a compression that felt almost physical.

Cold shot through my body. Every limb stiffened. I looked at Hanoi and squeaked, "Help!"

Hanoi took a hard step forward, but the masked woman raised her arm, blocking him. "If a level-two ghost can kill him, his district will be better off without an inferior Reaper. Let him stand or fall here and now."

Misty dropped to her knees next to me. "You can do it, Phoenix!"

Her words brought a surge of warmth. One of my arms loosened, and my hand disembodied. I curled my phantom fingers around the ghost's throat and pushed him away, drawing his frigid hand out of my body. With my physical arm, I wrapped him in the cloak again and focused on the energy coursing from my sternum valve and through the cloak's fibers.

As the material clung to the ghost and absorbed him, he screeched. His face elongated, and his glowing eyes exploded into dark mist. Seconds later, every particle vanished into the fabric.

The nightmarish screeching continued, though muffled by my cloak. I unplugged the clasp from the valve, silencing the noise.

Misty crossed herself and rose to her feet. Her eyes offered silent congratulations, and her trembling smile expressed pride in my victory.

Sitting on the floor and heaving shallow breaths, I looked up at the masked woman. "Now for the other two ghosts."

"In a moment." She crouched and spoke in a low tone. "Very impressive, Phoenix. Most Reapers your age would have failed this test. In fact, I have never seen a thirteen-year-old conquer such an antagonistic ghost."

"Then why did you—"

She set a cold finger on my lips. "Never mind." As she lowered her hand from my mouth, her metallic eyes drilled into me. After a few seconds, she nodded. "Yes, I think you do have the gift. I will watch you closely." She reached into her pants pocket, withdrew a tiny cloth bag, and dangled it from a string in front of my nose. She blew across it, sending a syrupy sweet aroma into my nostrils. "Soon, you will not remember meeting me." She rose and hurried out of the house.

When the door closed, Misty reached to help me up, but my father stepped in the way, grabbed my wrist, and hauled me to my feet. "Now that you've proven yourself, let's get on with it."

His words felt like the ghost's icy grip. Although he never physically abused or directly insulted me, coldness made him as loving as a frozen statue. Without a doubt, he loved my mother. If only he had spared a few embraces and kind words for his son.

After reaping the other ghosts, I stumbled through the ceremony—reciting my pledge, then receiving a weapons belt for protection in a remote city, far from my parents... and from Misty.

Hanoi escorted me outside to a limo waiting at the curb. The door opened, and the masked woman called from the backseat, "First the Gateway to deliver the souls, then the airport. There you will be able to say good-bye to your mother, and we will send her home."

I slid in next to the woman and looked back. Misty waved from a window, her expression hopeful. I managed a weak wave in return.

A large hand snapped the drapes closed, hiding her from view.

I shut the door. The limo pulled away, and my house faded from sight. I sighed and fingered my own pewter ring. Separated from Misty and my mother, twenty years would feel like an eternity.

CHAPTER TWO

Nearly four years later — After the corrections-camp escape

GHOSTS RARELY SHOCKED people anymore, especially Reapers. We were accustomed to seeing the souls of the dead. We carried them in our cloaks, conversed with them, comforted them, and, at times, even scolded them. Nothing in the invisible realm surprised us.

Yet, when the phantom image of Singapore hovered over my hand as I clutched her photo stick, my heart pounded. She was just a hologram, not even a ghost, but she still haunted me far more than any ghost ever could.

Sing posed with her hands folded in front and her cloak's hood raised. Her eyes pierced deeply—intense, determined, focused. The whites around her brown irises stood in contrast to her milk chocolate skin, black cloak, and dark mood. She was a Reaper on a mission.

Shanghai stood next to me below my apartment. Early morning sun shone on her from the alley opening. The light revealed rips and bloodstains at the elbows and knees of her Reaper ensemble—forest green pants, black shirt and running shoes, and cloak, its hood pulled back, revealing an oozing gash on her forehead. The damage, along with the surrounding broken beer bottles and other alley trash, made her look like she had been in a bar brawl.

As Shanghai stared at the hologram, she whispered, "Sing looks so serious."

"She does." Pain still ripping through my body from the recent corrections-camp battles and near-total loss of energy gas, I leaned against the staff Shanghai had given me. "I think she's about to talk. Listen."

"Phoenix," Sing said, her tone somber, "since you have my photo stick, I assume that I am now dead. Of course I don't know the circumstances of my death, if you killed me or if I killed myself, but if you did kill me, I know you did it under pressure, probably to save other lives, so I bear no anger or resentment."

I glanced up at my apartment's window where the fire-escape landing loomed one floor up from the alley. No one was looking. Since Sing's message likely held closely guarded secrets, I couldn't risk anyone eavesdropping.

She brushed a tear away before continuing. "You see, I sent my mother, Tokyo, to the Gateway, thinking that a Reaper as powerful as she might be able to return. She wanted to learn the Gateway's secrets and come back to tell the world what she discovered. Unfortunately, she has not returned as quickly as we hoped, so I volunteered to go myself to check on her. There is a theory that one soul can bring another back from beyond the Gateway, though the retrieving soul must stay behind forever. Of course, returning from beyond might simply be impossible, and my own journey could be a fool's errand. Yet, for my mother's sake, I decided to try."

Sing lifted a metallic disk, no bigger than a small coin, from behind her shirt and let it dangle from a thin chain around her neck. "This medallion was anointed with Reaper blood, so it is genetically encoded. Soon, if the Eagle is correct, Alex will show you how she plans to track you with a specialized device. Pay attention to how she uses it, and you will learn how to track me with a similar device my father gave you."

Shanghai cocked her head. "Her father gave you a tracking device?"

I pressed a finger to my lips. Hers was a great question, but it could wait.

"You see," Sing continued, "even if my mother is able to return, we don't know where she will emerge, so I need you to follow Erin and learn where they are taking me to be reaped. At least, I assume Erin will have this task if all goes according to the Eagle's plans."

The mention of Erin brought her face and form to mind—a trim redhead, around thirty years old. As a Gateway Depot entry clerk, she seemed harmless, but when she started ferrying the souls of innocent execution victims to the Gateway, she became much more sinister.

Sing set a hand on her chest. "My hope is that Erin will take my body to the Gatekeeper's domain. When you get there, try to locate my mother's soul and carry her to safety. If you are not able to find her, then maybe you can search for my soul. I have no idea what they will do with it, so I can offer you no guidance."

Sing took a deep breath and let it out slowly. A smile emerged, a sad sort of smile. "I assume Shanghai will accompany you, and I am glad of her alliance. She is strong, courageous, and beautiful in every way. I trust that she will be a loyal companion who will never leave your side, a life-long friend that I had hoped to be but could not."

Shanghai curled her arm around mine and leaned her head against my shoulder, whispering, "Singapore, you're so wonderful."

Sing brushed away another tear. "Phoenix, this might be inappropriate at such an urgent time, but I need to tell you this. I deceived you in a number of ways, and I still have not told you all of my secrets, so I understand if you don't believe me now." She looked straight at me. "I love you, Phoenix, and I always will. I'm sorry I can't fulfill the promise of love, but, as I said, I'm sure Shanghai can be to you what I cannot, a friend to lift you up, an ally to fight at your side, an abode of warmth to soothe your pain whether it stabs your body or your soul."

Sing fanned out her cloak, revealing her narrow frame. The surrounding aura from the hologram made her look like a dark angel, beautiful and mysterious. "Phoenix, there is a crucial reason for my secretive ways, but even now I cannot reveal it to you. Too many steps remain in your journey. Too many storm clouds loom on the horizon. Yet, I have prayed for a Sancta to come to your aid. She will be a mysterious woman wearing a scarlet cloak. If on your path to the Gateway you meet one, listen carefully. The Sanctae are often cryptic, but they provide wisdom that is beyond normal understanding."

Sing blew a kiss. "Until we meet again, my dear friend. May the God of the true Gateway guide your steps and show you the love with which I love you, a love that doesn't die when the body perishes. True love never dies." The hologram faded until it vanished.

Shanghai breathed a quiet, "Wow."

"Yeah. That was…" I swallowed through a tightening throat. "Intense."

Shanghai waved her arms. "We have to help her. Follow her right away. She has no idea that the Gatekeeper plans to throw her soul into the abyss. She couldn't bring Tokyo back even if someone *could* return from the Gateway."

"You're right." I opened my hand. Sing's photo stick lay in my palm. So many mysteries surrounded her, and her hologram raised new ones. "What was that about Sanctae? Do you know what it means?"

"Not really." Shanghai touched the photo stick as if prodding it for more information. "I heard it in a song my mother used to sing when I was little, but I never understood it."

"How does it go?"

"Let me think." Shanghai looked upward and began humming. Then, she added words.

Our bridge is lost to fairer lands;
O Sanctae find the crossing home
And greet my soul with open hands,
No more to wander nor to roam.

When her tune faded, I whispered, "Kind of melancholy, isn't it?"

She brushed a tear away. "The tune is sad, but it's hopeful at the same time."

"True." As Sing's words echoed in my mind, I stroked my chin, now covered with stubble. "Sing mentioned meeting a Sancta. That's probably the singular form of Sanctae."

Shanghai nodded. "That was my guess."

I gazed into her reddened eyes. She looked so tired,

yet so determined. Her loyalty and love sparkled like sunlight on the sea. "Okay," I said, "we'll put the Sanctae mystery aside for now. The first step is to figure out how to use the tracking device." I slid the photo stick into my pocket, withdrew the watch Kwame had given me, and popped open the brass-colored cover. "This is the only gift I ever received from Sing's father. Just before she died she said to search the watch, but I'll probably need watchmaker tools to open it."

"Maybe you'll get a clue when you talk to Alex." Shanghai looked up at my apartment window, then turned to me again, her voice lower. "But here's the part I don't understand. Why does she want to track you?"

I pinched a thin chain around my neck and lifted the coin-shaped medallion Alex had given me, stained with my blood. "When Alex was trying to get me to execute Sing, she whispered that she wanted to conquer the Gatekeeper, something about me having a special talent."

"Your talent is resistance," Shanghai said, nodding. "You already overcame the Gatekeeper's direct influence. Alex thinks you're strong enough to get past his defenses."

"Maybe. But I have no idea what his defenses are." I pushed the watch back to my pocket. "No sense putting it off. We'd better talk to Alex."

"We?" Shanghai prodded my arm. "She told *you* to come to your apartment, not me."

"I'll tell her I need your help. We both need an energy recharge, so you'd better come along."

Shanghai rolled her eyes. "If it's that joy juice she gave us before, we'll have trouble staying on the ground. That stuff would make bricks float."

"But we got used to it. We might be immune to the

side effects now." I took her hand. "You're coming with me to find Sing, right?"

She looked at our hand clasp. "Of course, but—"

"Then Alex might as well know about it up front. She'll eventually hear that we're together anyway." I led Shanghai toward the alley opening. Just before we exited, a gray-haired woman wearing a tattered black dress stumbled in. She fell and spilled something from her hands. Two pill bottles skittered across the alley's uneven pavement. Her eyes wide, she lurched for them with clawing fingers, but they had rolled well out of reach.

I dropped to my knees and grasped her arm. "Let me help you up."

As she rose with my pull, she looked at me, her mouth agape. "A Reaper?"

"I'll get the bottles." Just as Shanghai stooped to pick them up, a girl shouted from the sidewalk beyond the alley opening.

"Hey, Reapers! Come here!"

I turned toward her. The girl, maybe ten years old, barefoot, and dressed in an ankle-length white nightgown, waved. "Help me! Hurry!"

Her eyes glowed—a ghost, not quite level two. Something greenish-yellow stained the front of her nightgown, perhaps vomit.

"I'll check her out." Shanghai scooped up the pill bottles, handed them to me, and limped toward the girl.

I brushed gravel from a scrape on the woman's elbow. "Are you all right?"

Trembling, she folded her hands. Tears streamed down her dirty cheeks. "Please. I beg of you. Don't report me."

I looked at the pair of finger-length bottles—medications of some kind. "Are these from the shroud?"

She nodded. Her quaking face shouted wordless pleas.

"Who are they for?"

"My son." She swallowed hard. "He has radiation sickness. My husband died of it last month and my daughter last week."

An image of a family came to mind, each member fading as time elapsed. Radiation sickness wasn't unusual in Chicago, but having so many close relatives suffer from it back to back certainly was.

"I'm sorry to hear about your losses." I glanced at Shanghai, now on the sidewalk speaking to the ghost—most likely the daughter. "I assume no Reaper took your daughter's soul to the Gateway."

The mother's brow lifted high. "How did you know?"

"Because she's here, trying to distract me so I won't report you." I slipped the bottles back into her hands and closed her fingers around them. "You need not fear."

"Oh, thank you!" She kissed my knuckles, then looked into my eyes. "I'm sorry I have no payment."

"Payment for what?"

"For your kindness. Reapers always expect payment, don't they?" She held up a pill bottle. "I could give you one of these. You could use the pills yourself or trade for something else. I have plenty for now, and I can get more."

I waved a hand. "No need. Kindness is always free."

"Kind Reapers like you are few and far between." She wrapped me in a full embrace, then drew back, again looking into my eyes. "When my daughter died, I sent a messenger to call our Reaper, but bandits ambushed him."

"Ambushed him? The messenger or the Reaper?"

"The messenger. Our district's Reaper is a female. Singapore. By the time she heard about my daughter and came to us, it was too late. Her soul was gone."

"That happens. Some souls don't stick around very long."

She looked from side to side. "You say my daughter is here?"

I nodded in Shanghai's direction. "Right over there."

The woman smiled. "I thought I saw her a few times before. Just a flash of her face at night. But now she is clear."

"She's probably just learning how to control her visibility." I set a hand on the mother's back. "Would you like to speak to her?"

Her smile widened. "Oh, yes! Please!"

I hobbled with her toward the sidewalk. When the ghost saw us, she spun and ran away.

"Deanna," the mother called. "Come back."

Shanghai looked in the direction Deanna had fled. "She's frightened. She loves her mother, but she's afraid she'll scare her."

"No! No!" the mother said as her eyes darted. "Seeing her gives me hope that death isn't the end."

Shanghai crossed her arms. "That doesn't matter to a ghost who isn't level two yet. She's confused. One moment she knows she's dead; the next moment she doesn't. It might take a few more days for her to acclimate."

I enfolded the mother's hands in my own. "Just go and take care of your son. Even confused ghosts find their way home. I'm sure you'll see her again."

"What about reaping? Is it all right if Deanna stays with me for a while?"

I glanced up at Sing's apartment, across the alley from mine. "Your district's Reaper is being replaced. When that happens, you'll hear about it. Until then, enjoy your time with Deanna."

"Thank you. Thank you so much." As she hobbled away on the sidewalk, she looked around, apparently searching for her daughter's ghost.

I kept my gaze on her. "She lost a husband and daughter to radiation poisoning, and now her son is sick."

"Maybe a genetic issue." Shanghai looked upward and scanned the sky. "Or maybe the level in the air is getting worse, but I haven't heard any warnings."

"They probably don't bother giving warnings in this part of town anymore."

Shanghai returned her gaze to me and huffed. "Death is good for business. Fuel for the furnaces. Fewer mouths to feed."

"It figures. No radiation warnings. A crackdown on the black market medicine. And when the supply gets pinched, prices go up, including the cost of the radiation-inhibitor shot. Not many people can afford it anymore."

"That's true in my district. A lot of people are just taking their chances. Staying inside as much as they can. On a day like today, I don't blame them."

"Like today?" I looked up. The ever-present layer of haze seemed thinner than usual, and the sun, without its normally dense foggy filter, was almost too bright to view. "It's like the shield is shifting downward. The lower levels of the atmosphere have to be getting soaked with isotopes."

"Nothing we can do about it." Shanghai gestured toward my apartment building. "Let's get going. It feels like we're stalling. We have to do this with a healthy dose of swagger. No hesitation. No fear."

"Agreed. Let's go in full Reaper mode." I plugged my cloak's clasp into my sternum's valve and raised the hood. Shanghai did the same. Two district hounds walking together always raised eyebrows, but no one would ask questions if we appeared to be seeking souls.

A shimmer ran along Shanghai's cloak—Colm Fitzpatrick's soul within the fibers. "It's time to visit the witch who killed you," she said to him. "Remember, since she's a former Reaper she can hear anything you say."

Colm replied in his usual tempered manner. "Thank you. I will listen in silence."

As my cloak energized, Crandyke... Albert... spoke up. "You plugged in. Are you getting ready to reap someone?"

"No. Just going to see Alex. Figured I'd look like a Reaper as much as I can. We're pretty beat up."

"Be careful. Alex is a force to be reckoned with. Don't let that Owl sink her talons into you."

Alex's piercing eyes came to mind. Sometimes she seemed able to read thoughts. "We all have to be careful. Like Shanghai said to Colm, Alex can hear you."

"Okay. Shutting up. But I'll be listening. You might need my advice. Always pay heed to dead guys who hang around in your cloak for way too long."

"And girls," a female added.

"Right, Tori. You tell him. Phoenix doesn't always listen to me. He gets his cloak wet way too often."

I smiled. Imagining the souls of a middle-aged man and a young girl commiserating over the discomfort in my cloak was amusing. "Yeah, yeah. Keep complaining. I need the laughs."

Again using the staff for support, I walked with Shanghai into my apartment building's vacant lobby. With electricity back in service for the day, we rode the elevator to the second floor and exited onto the hallway's frayed carpet. Now close enough for Alex to hear us, I pressed the staff down softly as we made our way to my unit near the end of the corridor.

The door stood ajar. Alex was expecting us.

CHAPTER THREE

I EXTENDED THE STAFF to Shanghai and whispered, "We have to look stronger than we really are or she'll take advantage of us."

When she took the staff, we nodded at each other. We could do this.

Every bone aching, I straightened my body, opened the door fully, and walked in. Each step hurt, like walking barefoot on needles, but I managed to keep my face calm. Shanghai followed close behind.

Alex sat in my reading chair, her gaze fixed on an open book in her lap—my copy of *1984*. Her blonde hair pulled back in a ponytail, she wore the black leather jacket typical of Death Enforcement Officers. The jacket's open zipper exposed a form-fitting white T-shirt and a sonic gun in a shoulder holster. Next to the chair, a silver gas tank stood upright in a wheeled carrier, a nozzle and tube attached at the top. At the base of the tank, a first-aid kit sat on the floor.

Without looking up, she read out loud, "For the first time he perceived that if you want to keep a secret you must also hide it from yourself. You must know all the while that it is there, but until it is needed you must never let it emerge into your consciousness in any shape that could be given a name." She set the book on the chair's arm and stared at me with her metallic eyes. "Phoenix, you're too weak to hide secrets from me. I know how much pain you're in, so feel free to support yourself with the staff."

I huffed a sigh. Somehow I had to guard my thoughts from this mental vampiress, but I had no strength to build a wall.

As I reached for the staff, Shanghai pushed it into my hand. I leaned on it and gave Alex a hard stare. "If you're reading my mind now, I guess you're not too pleased with the plot."

Alex rose from the chair and strutted toward me, her dark pants clinging to her long legs. "I don't read minds, Phoenix. I read body language, attitudes, and intentions." She caressed my cheek, letting the pewter ring she had stolen from Misty rub against my skin. "You cannot deceive me. You cannot manipulate me. And you cannot find the souls of Singapore and Misty without my help."

I tensed. She knew our plans. She had already taken control of our meeting.

Shanghai stepped forward. "Of course he needs help. He's desperate for an energy charge. He can barely walk."

Alex lowered her hand and hummed a laugh as she turned toward Shanghai. "The ever-loyal friend trying to cover Phoenix's real need. I find your effort to be both honorable and praiseworthy, though entirely futile."

"*Real* need?" Shanghai asked.

"He needs energy, to be sure, but he also needs direction from me. He knows this, you know this, and I know this. So shall we drop the pretense that he is independent?"

Alex walked back to the chair, again with an obvious strut, and set a hand on top of the gas tank. "I will provide an energy charge and blood refill for both of you. I need your mental faculties to be fully engaged before I explain your task. There is a lot you will have to remember."

Shanghai gave the tank a skeptical stare. "What kind of energy is it? The pure stuff that sent us flying on the clouds?"

"It is the *pure stuff,* as you call it, but you should be able to endure it without an undue amount of flying. One of the reasons I exposed you both to it earlier was to allow you to acclimate to the hormonal effects, to build up a resistance. You will need the pure form in order to complete the journey that lies ahead." Alex lifted the tank's tube. "Who would like to go first?"

A siren blared outside, a two-second blast. Another blast sounded, then a third ended the sequence, signaling an audio bulletin from city broadcasting, maybe a relay of a worldwide announcement. As always, listening was mandatory.

"Where is your radio?" Alex asked.

"In the bathroom." I retrieved my portable, battery-operated radio from the bathroom vanity, set it on the living-area windowsill, and turned it on. The broadcast usually started about five minutes after the siren, so we had some time. I unplugged my clasp and walked to Alex. "I guess I'll go first."

"Blood drawing before energy recharge." While Alex retrieved the necessary items from the first-aid kit, I rolled up my torn sleeve. She wrapped an elastic band around my upper arm and swabbed the crook with an alcohol-doused cotton ball. Grime smeared my skin and adhered to the cotton, forcing her to use three balls to clean the area.

After she slid the needle into my skin and began drawing blood, she looked me in the eye, silent, searching. Her irises seemed to glitter, though the light in the room stayed constant.

When the syringe filled, she pressed a fresh cotton ball on the insertion point and slid the needle out. While I held the ball in place, she inserted the needle into my clasp and began infusing blood. "Freshening the blood supply won't boost your reaping abilities until after you receive the energy boost."

I crossed my eyes to watch the infusion. Alex's bedside manner was surprisingly pleasant, though it seemed strange that she would tell me Reaper facts that I already knew.

After finishing, she grasped the tank's hose, fitted its nozzle into my sternum with a click, and opened the tank's valve. "The trial with this gas proved that it provides a greater ability to transition efficiently into the ghost realm. Being invisible to non-Reapers will be essential if you hope to make it safely to the Gateway."

As the energy flowed, warmth spread from the entry point to my arms, abdomen, and legs. It seemed that every cell heaved a sigh of pleasure. My muscles flexed. My brain cleared. My body straightened. Everything felt great.

I looked at Shanghai. Although dirt marred her Asian features from chin to scalp, and tangles mussed her ebony hair, she radiated beauty from the top of her lovely head, down her athletic, toned body, to her sleek legs. She was the model of feminine perfection.

I wanted to shout how amazing she looked, but a niggling whisper told me to fight the energy's intoxicating influence. I had beaten it before; I could beat it again.

Alex eyed a tiny meter embedded in the nozzle attached to my valve. "I want to make sure you're at one hundred percent. It might be a while before you can get another dose." After several more seconds, she shut off the gas and detached the nozzle. "Fully charged."

Now feeling like a young buck ready to prance, I glided out of the way and laid the staff on the floor. "Shanghai, your turn."

She narrowed her eyes. "Are you able to control it?"

"It feels pretty amazing." I gave her a reassuring nod. "I'm handling it, though."

"If you say so." She stepped in front of Alex. "Let's do it."

After going through the same blood-and-energy infusion with Shanghai, Alex closed the first-aid kit and wrapped the hose around the top of the tank. "You are now both registering one hundred percent."

Shanghai turned toward me. Her eyes flashed as bright as strobes. She seemed ready to say something but bit her lip and folded her hands in front.

The radio let out a shrill beep, followed by a short anthem played on an organ. "Attention, Chicago residents." The announcer's voice was sweet and feminine. "The Gatekeeper, as benevolent as always, has sent us an extra allotment of cheese, heating oil, socks, and blankets for the approaching winter. Go to your assigned warehouse within the next three days to pick up your gifts. Be sure to bring an ID card for each family member. Remember, identity fraud is a serious offense. The Gatekeeper wants to be sure that everyone receives their fair share."

The organ anthem returned, followed by another beep, then silence.

Alex flashed a half smile. "It's a good thing you two are Cardinals now. You won't have to stand in a long line to get a brick of moldy cheese and a threadbare blanket from the oh-so-pleasant clerks working for the *benevolent* Gatekeeper."

I picked up the radio and turned it off. "When I visit him, should I tell him what you think of his benevolent gifts?"

Alex laughed. "You do that, Phoenix. But capture the moment with a camera. I want to see your surprised expression when the benevolent Gatekeeper executes you on the spot."

"I'm sure you do." I set the radio on the floor next to a wall. "Back to business. You mentioned a tracking device you wanted to show me."

"Yes, both of you come with me." She walked to the kitchen portion of my studio apartment where I kept a circular table and a folding metal chair.

On the tabletop, a wristwatch sat in an open jewel box. The wristband seemed ordinary—a narrow dark leather strap with a metal buckle. The analog face displayed two hands pointing toward standard clock numerals.

Alex lifted the watch and laid it over her wrist. When she buckled it in place, she spoke to it with careful enunciation. "Alexandria."

The two hands converged and became one. Three tiny

windows opened on the face, one below the twelve, the second next to the three, and the third above the six. "This device will track your position. When it is calibrated, the hand will point in your direction. The digital displays will tell me how far away you are as well as your energy level. If it gets too low, I might be able to send someone to help you."

Pinching the necklace chain, I lifted the medallion she gave me at the corrections camp. "And this sends the signal, I assume."

"Correct. It also has a sensor that reads the data in your sternum valve's microchip, so the energy-level data I receive should be accurate." Alex pressed a button on the side of the watch. The face glowed for a moment, then darkened. The hand drifted counterclockwise and pointed toward the window that opened to the alley.

She bent her brow. "This is strange. It isn't supposed to point until I activate your medallion."

I leaned to get a better look at the watch. "Do you have medallions on other Reapers?"

"A few, but this watch was pre-programmed to track your DNA." She nodded at my medallion. "Press it between your thumb and forefinger."

I pinched the disk.

Alex stared at the watch's face. "Do you feel anything?"

A tingle penetrated my fingertips, then a sense of warming. "It's heating up."

"Good. You can let it go now."

When I released the medallion, the watch's combined hands drifted again and pointed directly at me.

"Excellent." Alex nodded toward my reading chair. "Now stand over there."

I glanced at Shanghai. She stood with her arms crossed, monitoring everything with suspicious eyes.

Taking slow steps, I walked toward the chair, now no longer able to see the watch, though both Alex and Shanghai kept their stares focused on it.

"Perfect," Alex said. "The hands followed you. The display indicates that you're eight feet away."

I estimated the distance. "That sounds about right."

"In case you're wondering, these devices use the ancient units because Reapers are trained in them." She squinted at the watch. "Your energy level is ninety-nine-point-nine percent."

I touched the tingling medallion. "Will it transmit while I'm in ghost mode?"

"In theory, yes, but we haven't tested it." She waved a hand. "Transform, and we'll see."

I shifted to ghost mode in a flash, faster than ever before. "Done. What does it say?"

Alex drew the watch closer to her eyes. "Energy level and distance are the same as before. And a third display tells me how connected you are with the physical realm. It stands at eighty-one percent."

"Connected? You mean how hard it would be to transform back?"

"It's related. In your training, I'm sure Hanoi told you about the need for getting into and out of ghost mode as quickly as possible."

I nodded. "We have only a few minutes before we get locked in and lose focus."

"Exactly. If you were fully locked in, as you say, you would register zero percent on this meter. Eighty-one percent means you are far from danger. With the new energy, you will be able to stay in that mode for a long time."

I shifted out of ghost mode. A slight wooziness washed through my head. Nothing serious. "What happens if I lose the medallion? Or if someone else carries it?"

"The locator will no longer function, and the energy display will fall to zero." She crossed her arms, concealing the watch. "The medallion connects with you because of the DNA match between your body and the blood on its surface. If the display drops to zero, I will know that you and the medallion have been separated. Or perhaps you have died, because death will cause it to lose its connection. If such a drop occurs, I will investigate."

I walked back to the kitchen area. "Is this device being tested on non-Reapers? I mean, is the Gatekeeper hoping to track everyone?"

"Not yet. Experiments with non-Reaper blood have failed to this point, but I wouldn't be surprised if universal monitoring is the Gatekeeper's ultimate goal. Being the tyrant that he is, he wants to make sure no one can get close to him without his knowledge. He's paranoid about assassination attempts, which is why all Council members, including me, have a tracking chip embedded in our scalps. Although it has no ability to transmit energy or connection levels, it does provide location information, so the Gatekeeper knows where we are at all times. No Council member can sneak up on him."

"You call him a tyrant," Shanghai said. "Quite a surprise hearing that from one of his Council members."

Alex raised her brow. "Hasn't Phoenix told you about my own ultimate goal?"

"He told me." Shanghai narrowed her eyes. "But what

happens if he succeeds? Will we just have a new tyrant sitting on the Gatekeeper's throne?"

A wry grin crossed Alex's face. "Only if you consider Phoenix to be a tyrant."

CHAPTER FOUR

"ME?" I TOUCHED my chest. "You want me to take the Gatekeeper's place?"

Alex's smile thinned. "Of course. Did you think *I* wanted that position?"

"Well... yeah. You've been kind of... forceful, I guess."

She opened her jacket, exposing her sonic gun. "Contrary to my forceful ways, Phoenix, when it comes to being ruler of the world, I prefer to stay behind the scenes. Someone as principled and unassuming as you would make a more suitable figurehead. A dashing young man. Princely. Charming. The rabble are easily hypnotized by idols."

I frowned, intentionally deepening it for show. "So you'll consider me a figurehead. Just a pawn in your game."

"A pawn. Such an appropriate word. The Gatekeeper often refers to chess pieces. But I don't consider you a puny pawn. You are strong, and I need your strength. Your stamina. I don't have your ability to resist the Gatekeeper's influence, nor did Peter. Only you are able to usurp the Gatekeeper's seat, and only you are able to keep it."

"And if I refuse?"

Alex let out a humming laugh. "As if you actually could refuse."

I glanced at Shanghai. She gave me a curious look. When Alex noticed, she nodded in a knowing sort of way. "Shanghai, it seems that Phoenix neglected to tell you something about his genetic disposition. You see, he inherited his grandfather Maxwell's ability to resist the influence, though the poor man died while facing the same obstacles Phoenix will soon encounter. Fortunately for me, Phoenix also exhibits the same weakness that Maxwell had." Alex showed Shanghai her hand and the finger with Misty's ring. "I control Phoenix. He has no choice but to do what I tell him."

Shanghai set a fist on her hip. "What is that? Some sort of daydream concocted by a confirmed man hater? You said Phoenix is strong, but now you're saying he'll bow to your every whim."

Alex chuckled. "Scoff all you wish, dear Shanghai. You will witness reality soon enough. Phoenix will risk death to find the Gatekeeper, destroy him, and take his place. Then he will carry out my wishes as the new Gatekeeper."

"And what are those wishes?"

Alex's tone turned condescending. "Now don't you concern yourself about that. You have enough worries of your own. You'll be busy helping Phoenix locate the souls of two girls he loved more than he loves you. That motivation will spur him on until he reaches the Gatekeeper's abode."

Redness flushed Shanghai's cheeks. She looked away for a moment, swallowed, and took in a deep breath before returning her stare to Alex, her tone now softer.

"Okay. Keep living in your fantasy world. Just give us a starting point. Where should we go? What are the obstacles that killed Maxwell? How do we get past them?"

Alex zipped her jacket. "Start at the Gateway depot where you normally take souls and follow the exiting energy line. It will take you to the terminus of the Gateway feeder system. The line is invisible in most areas, but being Reapers, you should be able to feel its presence. If you come to a checkpoint, don't hesitate to tell the attendant who you are. I made a change to Phoenix's security clearance that should provide access to most areas. If you are turned back, you will have to come up with an alternative plan."

I drew a mental picture of the depot station. We had always stayed on the prescribed path, so the surrounding forest was a mystery. "I'm guessing checkpoints aren't the only obstacles."

"You are correct. You will run into opposition—bestial threats and even antagonistic ghosts. I am not familiar with how the Gatekeeper has equipped these ghosts to harm Reapers. I have only heard that they can, so you'll just have to be ready for anything."

I blew out a long breath. "Ghost gangs with Reaper repellent. Perfect."

"Also, I heard the Gatekeeper acquired a new species of guard called illuminaries. I don't know much about them besides the fact that they're deadly. When you leave, I will conduct more research. If I learn something significant that will help, I'll try to get the information to you."

"How far away is the terminus?" Shanghai asked. "Will we be able to go on foot? Will we need to find a car?"

Alex picked up her watch's box and walked toward

the energy tank. "I know only that it is on this continent. You will have to figure out its exact location."

"This continent?" Shanghai followed her. "That could be hundreds of miles. Maybe more than a thousand. We can't walk that far."

"No, but you can walk to the first checkpoint. At the depot, the energy line runs east-west, and the first checkpoint in either direction is fifteen miles away. When you arrive, you can use your elevated status and your ingenuity to acquire alternative transportation."

I joined them in the sitting room area. "Like what? I learned how to ride a DEO motorcycle in training, but I've never driven a car."

"Necessity is an excellent tutor." Alex grasped a handle at the top of the energy tank. "I have no worries about your ability to adapt. My primary concern is what you will encounter if you find that you must travel west. The Boundary River and the Western Wilds are not far beyond the first checkpoint. I'm sure you've heard about the radiation levels there. I hope you can avoid suffering through that."

I drew my head back. "Wait a minute. I thought you were on the Gatekeeper's Council."

She nodded. "I have been a member for five years. Why?"

"And you haven't been to the Gateway?"

"You call it the Gateway, but it's really a misnomer. When you arrive and learn its secrets, you will understand. Now that everything is coming out in the open, I prefer to call it the network's terminus. In any case, I have visited the place. In fact, I expect to be called to the next meeting there quite soon, perhaps at any moment.

I just don't know the physical location. Whenever the Gatekeeper wants to meet with Council members, we are taken there without the ability to see where we're going."

"What about the people who transport you?" I asked. "Since they know the way, aren't they a liability?"

"A remote-controlled flying vessel carries me. It has no windows, so I am unable to see outside during the journey, and I have no way of knowing how far I travel. About fifteen minutes after the vessel starts, a gas puts me to sleep. I am not awakened until I land in a forested area near a large building, and I walk from there."

"If you're going to a meeting soon, maybe Shanghai and I could stow away on your transport. That would save a lot of time and effort."

"Impossible. There is nowhere to hide on the craft. Besides, I have no guarantee that a meeting is imminent. It could be weeks away or only hours away. You need to start your journey toward the Gateway now."

"Have you seen the actual Gateway? I mean, the physical place where the souls go?"

"I have seen the earthly equivalent that leads to the heavenly Gateway." Alex gestured with her hands as if drawing a picture in the air. "As you already know, souls travel from the various depots around the world through an energy line that traverses the planet, but you don't know what happens at the terminus. The two ends of the line enter the building at separate points. Then they combine and channel to a chamber that has a domed ceiling. The energy in the line acts as a medium for the transport of souls, and they gather under the dome, which is the terminus point.

"At the proper time, the Gatekeeper sends a surge of

energy through the line to flush souls to make sure that all who have arrived are under the dome. Then he opens it and releases the souls to the heavens through a hole in the radioactive shield." She inhaled dramatically. "And that release is exhilarating! Every time I witness it, I can feel the emotions of every departing soul. Freedom. Ecstasy. Deliverance. At that moment I always wish I could go with them."

"Okay." I resisted the urge to sarcastically lengthen the word. This woman who casually murdered my beloved Misty couldn't fool me into thinking she cared about anyone's soul but her own. "Back to our mission. How will you know if we succeed in taking down the Gatekeeper?"

"I will know when you carry out your first duty as the new Gatekeeper. In his abode you will need to find a reservoir of energy, a large tank he houses somewhere. I don't know the location because it's a recent addition, and I haven't had an opportunity to search for it. Since he can track my location, I have to be careful where I go."

"Okay. Then what?"

"Release the stored energy into the atmosphere. It should dissolve the shield that surrounds the world. When the shield vanishes, the souls of the dead will no longer need to travel to the terminus. They will leave our world as they did for millennia before the meltdown, which will confirm both your power and your benevolence. You will not need threats or punishment to maintain rule. Once the shield is gone, I will know you succeeded, then I will follow your medallion's signal and join you, assuming I haven't already come for a Council meeting."

Shanghai tugged on my sleeve. "Let's get going."

I met her gaze. She seemed anxious about something.

"All right." I picked up the staff. "I guess we're ready to get started."

"Not quite." From her pants pocket, Alex withdrew a key ring with a brass key and a plastic DEO insignia. "This is to the condo I promised. The address is on the insignia. There you will find food, new Reapers' clothes that should fit you perfectly, and updated belts with fresh weapons." She laid the ring in my hand. "Wash, eat something, and pack for your journey. Perhaps even get some rest."

"Let's go. Now." Shanghai curled her arm through mine. Half dragging me, she led the way to the bottom of the stairs and out to the sidewalk.

I pulled back my hood. "Why the big rush?"

She lowered her own hood. "I got this creepy sensation that every moment you spent with her, she was locking in a connection to you, like she was digging fish hooks into your hide."

"A sensation? Maybe the joy juice is making you think—"

"No, it's reality. She spent a lot of time explaining things, you know, slowing down the process and lengthening our meeting. As soon as we got all the information we needed, I decided to bolt."

"Whatever. I don't feel any hooks in my hide." I looked at the key ring's DEO insignia and read the address imprinted in the plastic. "The Fife Tower. Tenth floor."

Shanghai pointed toward the northwest. "The business district. A little past the corrections camp."

"Right. We'd better start hoofing it. It'll take an hour to walk. Or maybe we can hitch a ride."

"Not likely for two Reapers walking together. There's no hurry, though. We have to wait for the next depot train."

"I'd better check the time." When I reached into my cloak pocket, my fingers struck something plastic. I grabbed it and pulled out a pill bottle. "How did I get this?"

"From Deanna's mother?" Shanghai asked.

I rolled my eyes. "Her payment. She probably dropped it into my pocket when she hugged me."

Shanghai read the label. "I've heard of this drug. It reduces the effects of radiation poisoning."

"Yeah, she told me. Too bad I can't get it back to her." I returned it to my pocket, withdrew the watch Kwame had given me, and read the hands—9:35 a.m. The high-speed train would leave at noon. We had plenty of time to get to the condo.

As we walked toward the camp, I gave the staff to Shanghai and laid the watch in my palm. "So I guess I'll just say Kwame's name. It was his watch."

"Go for it."

I spoke directly at the watch's face with clear enunciation. "Kwame." The hands stayed in place. After several seconds it still hadn't budged. "That didn't work."

Keeping her walking pace steady, Shanghai studied the watch. "I wonder why Sing didn't give you more to go on. She could've told you exactly what to do."

"Maybe she didn't know." I touched my pocket where the photo stick lay. "Her hologram must have been recorded quite a while ago. She might have been shooting from the hip."

Shanghai looked straight ahead. "I don't like this, Phoenix. Obviously the Eagle kept Sing in the dark about a lot of things, including the truth about her father. What else didn't Sing know?"

"My thoughts exactly. And the craziest part is Sing didn't even recognize her father, but she did recognize the watch when I showed it to her."

"There has to be a rational explanation. Sing's as smart as a whip."

A new lump swelled in my throat. "You mean *was*."

"Yeah." Shanghai's voice lowered to a whisper. "She was."

I heaved a sigh. "We'll just have to solve that mystery later."

"Back to the watch." Shanghai nodded toward it. "Maybe feel around for a tiny button or a switch."

I ran a finger along every surface. "Nothing."

"Then let's try other names. Maybe Sing's."

"Since her real name was engraved on the cover, I'll try that." I stopped and spoke to the watch again. "Akua."

The two hands drew together into one and began drifting, as if searching for the correct direction to point. Yet, no digital displays appeared. Apparently this model wasn't as advanced as Alex's.

Within a second or two, the combined hands pointed to the southwest. We both looked that way. Ahead, the road we were following intersected with a main thoroughfare at a ninety-degree angle, and the river lay beyond that, running parallel to the highway.

"The Gateway depot is the same direction," Shanghai said as she began walking.

I kept pace at her side. "It's all coming together now. Kwame told me Sing's real name out of the blue. It didn't really fit into the conversation." I showed Shanghai the engraving on the watch's cover—*From A.* "I think it's supposed to be 'From Akua,' but Kwame knew that the rest of the name had worn off, so he wanted to make sure I heard it."

"So you could activate the tracker."

"Right. I don't think Sing knew about the tracker when Kwame gave it to me. He was keeping secrets from her for some reason, but it looks like she figured it all out later."

"At least we'll have directional help. Alex said we *should* feel the presence of the energy line. I got the impression that she isn't really sure, so the watch will come in handy."

"Definitely." I closed the watch and slid it back into my pocket. "We're going to the depot, so we'd better collect more souls to make quota. Since I have Tori and Albert, I'll need maybe three more if they're young, four or five if they're older."

Shanghai shook her head. "The executions won't be till midnight. Way too late."

"We'll find plenty of ghosts at the camp."

"True, but it might be slow tracking them down and reaping them. Some were level threes."

"Then let's pick up the pace." We jogged to the main thoroughfare, turned right, and followed the sidewalk. As cars and trucks passed, I looked at the drivers to see if any might glance our way, hoping I could signal a request for a ride. But, as usual, they all kept their eyes forward. To most people, giving a Reaper a lift felt like inviting death itself to hop aboard.

Less than a block ahead, a red light stopped the flow of traffic. A pickup truck idled near the end of the line of vehicles.

I pointed. "Let's jump in the back."

We dashed to the truck and leaped into the payload

bed, careful to land without a sound. I sat on the bed's upright on the driver's side, and Shanghai sat on the other, holding the staff with both hands. When the light turned green, the truck accelerated, and the breeze made our cloaks flap.

The driver, a bearded white man in his fifties, lowered his window and yelled, "What are you Reapers doing on my truck?"

"Hitching a ride," I shouted back. "Just drop us off at the prison camp."

"You're not after my soul?"

"No." I winked at Shanghai. "Unless you're donating."

"Uh-uh! Not me!" He closed the window, set both hands on the steering wheel, and drove faster.

We grabbed the truck's frame and held on. Shanghai grinned. "You be nice."

"I *am* being nice." I returned her smile. Her face seemed to shine, though the glow was probably just my perception. The effects of the joy juice might last quite a while yet.

When we stopped at another traffic light within sight of the camp, the driver lowered his window again. "Is this close enough?"

"Yep. Thanks a lot." We leaped out and jogged toward the camp. The gate lay broken, as we had left it, though the bodies of the two executed prisoners and others who had been shot while trying to escape were gone.

Inside the grounds, a woman stood in front of the observation tower. Wearing a gray smock, flat shoes, and a red bandana around her dark hair, she looked like a factory worker. A glow around her eyes gave away her status as a ghost, and a bloody gash across her forehead along with no apparent concern for her wound told us even more. She was lost and confused.

I whispered to Shanghai, "Looks like a level two. Two point two max."

"Agreed. Let's see what's up."

When the woman saw us coming near, she lifted a hand. "Stay back! The stone is spinning! It's dangerous!"

We halted within a few paces. I leaned close to Shanghai. "The stone? Could she be Tori's mother?"

She replied in a whisper. "I see a resemblance."

I bowed my head toward the woman. "We'll be careful to stay away from the stone, but we're looking for the mother of a seven-year-old girl named Tori. Do you know—"

"Tori?" She clasped her hands. "Where is she? I've been looking everywhere for her."

I altered my voice to a soothing tone. "If you'll allow me to come closer, I'll let you talk to her."

Her eyes flared. "But the stone!"

"The stone isn't here," I crooned as I stepped closer. "Look around. You're not in the assembly room."

She glanced from side to side. "Where did it go? I haven't finished the lenses yet."

"What's your name?"

She gazed at me as if dreaming while awake. "Lillian. My friends call me Lily."

"I'm your friend, Lily." I plugged the cloak's clasp into my valve. As the fibers energized, the gentle sound of weeping filtered into my ears, likely Tori's reaction to seeing her mother.

I stepped within reach of Lily, slowly raised a hand, and transformed it to ghost mode. As I caressed her cheek,

I looked into her hungry eyes. "Would you like to speak to Tori?"

Her mouth opened, as if begging for a morsel of bread. "Yes, please."

I directed my voice toward the cloak. "Tori, have you been listening?"

A trembling *yes* came through, followed by, "Phoenix, she's bleeding. There's a horrid cut on her head."

Shanghai stepped close and began whispering to Lily, realizing that I had to disengage and speak to Tori for a moment.

"The cut isn't hurting her, Tori. She's dead. Some ghosts display their fatal wounds for a long time, but they don't feel them at all. She's confused, not even aware that she died, so we need to help her. She has to trust us completely. Tell me something only you and your mother would know."

"Okay." Tori sniffed. "Um… she gave me a candy cane on my birthday and said I was just as sweet. I don't think anybody knows about that."

"I'll try it." I turned to Lily and Shanghai. "Did you get anywhere?"

Shanghai shook her head. "She's zoning out. Thinks she's back in the assembly room again. We need to bring her to her senses."

"I'll go into full ghost mode and add some force. I shouldn't need an anchor, but keep a close eye on me."

"Will do."

I concentrated on the energy coursing through my cloak, willing it to flow into my body. My arms transformed into phantom appendages, and the change spread to my entire frame in seconds.

While Shanghai turned fuzzy around the edges, Lily clarified. Her shoulders sagged, and her eyelids hung low. She seemed ready to faint.

I grasped her wrist. "Lily. Tori told me something about you."

Her eyelids fluttered. "Tori? What did she say?"

"That you once gave her a candy cane and said she's just as sweet."

Lily's face brightened. "Yes. Yes. I did say that."

"I can take you to her." I grasped an edge of my cloak and draped it around her shoulders. "Just trust me."

Lily breathed, "I trust you."

I mentally guided my energy flow into her shoulders. Her upper torso dissolved into mist. As my cloak absorbed her, the rest of her body transformed as well. Within seconds, she vanished. Unlike similar ghosts, Lily left no film lining the cloak's interior. The fibers soaked up every particle without causing her or me any pain. The purified energy had worked well again.

"Mommy!"

"Tori!"

The cries emanated from my cloak. A happy reunion was taking place, a rare occurrence within the fibers of sorrow.

I willed myself out of the ghost realm. As my body solidified, the world spun in a dizzying circle. When I leaned against the spin to get my balance, a sense of falling took over.

"Whoa there, tiger!" Shanghai grasped my shoulder and looked straight at me, the staff in her free hand. "Focus on my eyes. Get your bearings."

I blinked, then stared at her face. Fuzzy at first, her

features slowly clarified. The dizziness faded to a vague sense of unsteadiness, like walking on the deck of a boat. "Thanks. I think I'm all right now."

"That reaping looked easier than usual for a level two."

"Yeah. It was quick."

"Then let's go ghost collecting." Shanghai scanned the prison yard. "Where should we check first?"

"The sleeping quarters. I saw quite a few last time I was there."

"One problem." Shanghai withdrew a photo stick from her pants pocket. "We have passage keys for Albert and Colm but not for Tori or her mother. And we won't have them for any ghosts we find here."

"They have to be somewhere in the compound. We'll ask the ghosts we collect."

"Sounds like a plan." She pushed the stick back to her pocket. "Let's go."

We hurried to the building that once housed the prisoners and found four level-one ghosts, six level twos, and two level threes. We had to transform to ghost mode to corral the level threes, but they didn't delay us more than a few minutes. Once we recovered from the dizziness, Shanghai carried eight souls in her cloak, including Colm's. My cloak also held eight, including Albert, Tori, and Lily. Making quota would be no problem.

Fortunately, one of the level threes knew where the guards kept the photo sticks—a metal lockbox in the tower. After finding a hammer to break into the box, we dug through the haphazard pile of sticks until we matched their labels to the ghosts' names.

When we finished, we walked out of the camp, our cloaks flowing behind us in the cool breeze. The exit march felt surreal. Just a few hours ago, Liam's van crashed into the gate to free the prisoners, and they ran out in a hail of gunfire. Now we walked through the exit in the midst of relative silence. Only nearby traffic noise blunted the effect.

I spotted a clock at a bank—10:45. We had only an hour and fifteen minutes to make the train. We ran the rest of the way to Fife Tower, a twelve-story high-rise that loomed at least three floors taller than the surrounding buildings. After taking the elevator to the tenth floor, we located our condo at the end of the hall.

Using the key Alex had given me, I unlocked the door. When we entered the foyer, lights in the ceiling flashed on. Shanghai looked up, her mouth open. Motion detectors were unheard of in the shanty-town areas. This relative affluence would take some getting used to.

The foyer led to a sitting area straight ahead, populated by a sofa, loveseat, and coffee table, each piece polished and free of scuff marks. A short corridor to the left led to a closed door, most likely the bedroom. To the right, the corridor ended at a kitchen, though only a refrigerator stood in view.

A few steps toward the kitchen, a large footlocker abutted the wall in the corridor. "No time to gawk, Phoenix." Shanghai leaned her staff against a wall, knelt in front of the footlocker, and opened it. Folded Reapers' uniforms lay inside. She lifted a tunic and let it fall open. It looked just like ours except for an insignia embroidered in scarlet on the breast—the clasped hands of the gateway.

I ran a finger along the red threads. "The symbol of a Cardinal. I didn't think of it till now, but Peter didn't have one of these, did he?"

"Not that I recall. He said he's been a Cardinal here for two years, so he should've had one."

"Must be a new designation." I pulled out trousers and a tunic that looked my size. "Let's get cleaned up. You want first shower?"

"Sure. I smell terrible."

I smiled. "I didn't notice."

Flashing a smile of her own, she picked up her new clothes and walked toward the end of the corridor, a swagger in her step. When she opened the door, she looked back at me and winked. "See you soon, Phoenix."

When the door closed, I shuddered. That smile—piercing, intoxicating. Heat radiated through my body. The new energy's effects spiked. I would be traveling with Shanghai on a journey that could last for several days... and nights.

I rubbed the pewter ring on my finger. Even though Misty was dead, something kept my mind in check, like a whispered warning. Although Shanghai was beautiful and alluring, entangling my heart and body with hers would be... wrong?

Wrong. Somehow that word felt different, as if a new meaning had come to life. Knowing the difference between right and wrong was sometimes easy. Killing innocent people was wrong. Saving victims' lives was right. Yet, sometimes a moral decision felt like the flip of a coin, a roll of the dice. Like deciding whether or not to keep Albert's soul in the cloak instead of sending him through the Gateway depot. I had to sacrifice his desires in order to aid another cause, that is, gaining vital information from him for my quest to learn the truth about the Gateway.

But was I right in making that choice? Who had the authority to decide? Taking a deep breath, I closed my eyes. So much introspection. The joy juice was having its way with my mind. Or had it opened my senses to hear other voices, like that odd inner whisper? In any case, I needed a distraction. Maybe I could make sandwiches for our journey.

I wandered to the kitchen and found roast beef, mustard, and sub rolls in a well-stocked refrigerator. These items, along with cabinets filled with cooking implements and utensils, as well as a faucet with decent water pressure, proved an important truth—fulfilling Alex's wishes brought a bounty few in the city could afford.

When I finished making a sandwich for each of us, Shanghai emerged from the bathroom. With her hair wet and shining, her clothes clean and form-fitting, and her smile unabated, she looked dazzling.

I hurried through a shower and shave, put my uniform on, and flexed my rejuvenated muscles. The clean newness felt great, like coming out of a smoke-filled room and breathing fresh air. Whatever obstacles we might face, I was ready.

After transferring the watch from my old clothes and putting on my cloak, I walked out. Shanghai met me at the door and pushed a brown paper bag into my hand. "Thanks for making our lunches. I packed your sandwich in here with a bottle of water." She showed me her own paper bag, then grabbed her staff. "Let's go catch a train."

CHAPTER FIVE

S HANGHAI AND I walked at a brisk pace toward the station while eating our sandwiches and drinking our water. Once we finished, we slid the empty bottles into a belt pouch for refilling later.

When we reached the train platform, we entered the Reapers' car at the tail end and sat together on a rear-facing bench, Shanghai next to the window with her staff under her seat. Soon, four other Reapers—three males and one female—entered, separated by short intervals. They each sat alone on other benches scattered about the car, their hoods raised and pulled low over their eyes.

Although the males were unfamiliar, I recognized the female—Saigon, a thirtyish black woman who once saved my life back when I was first assigned to my district. When five stiletto-wielding bandits surrounded me, she charged in and helped me fight them off, then accompanied me to the train station. She didn't say much, except to comment on my age—thirteen at the time—and that I needed to be more careful. Afterward, I saw her on the train every few months, though she stayed aloof. That never bothered me. Standoffishness was normal Reaper behavior.

Noon arrived, and the train departed the station with a

familiar squeak of metal wheels on metal rails. As it accelerated, the car swayed side to side as if trying to rock us to sleep. The Chicago skyline whisked past, a long stream of blurry buildings that melded into its own train of dirty bricks and mortar.

After a few minutes, I leaned close to Shanghai and whispered, "When we finish at the depot, the others will notice that we didn't come back to the train."

She nodded. "I've been thinking about that. Any ideas?"

"Let's give them an excuse ahead of time. Like one of us is hurt or sick, and we have to rest. They'll assume we'll catch the next train."

"That should work." Shanghai laid a hand on her stomach and groaned. "This rocking car is gonna make me puke."

I leaned over her and opened the window. Air rushed in and swirled about the car. "Lean out and let it fly."

She shook her head. "It'll just splash back in my face."

"Suit yourself. Just don't puke in here."

She closed her eyes and inhaled deeply. "Maybe I won't have to. The fresh air's helping."

Most of the other Reapers gave us cursory glances and resumed their detached poses, though Saigon stared at us, her dark brow low.

I gave her a nod. "She's not feeling well."

"Looks like Shanghai's not as invincible as she thinks." Saigon pulled her hood over her eyes and leaned against her window. "If she keeps her pie hole shut for a change, maybe she won't heave her guts."

One of the other Reapers laughed, then coughed to cover it.

Shanghai continued the charade with closed eyes and grimacing face, though her reddened cheeks gave away a flush of anger.

I whispered, "Ignore her. Probably just jealous."

"Maybe not." Her facial muscles relaxed. "I've made a few enemies. Saigon's one of them."

"What happened?"

"Well…" Shanghai leaned her head on my shoulder and lowered her voice further. "When I first became a Reaper, I was really full of myself. I had the highest training scores in the history of the program, and I was assigned to a huge jungle district right away. I reaped six souls my first day, including a rapist and a level-two wanderer."

"So Saigon wishes she had your skills?"

She opened her eyes, her voice still whisper soft. "Maybe, but that's not the issue. Because news was spreading about me, a reporter asked me for an interview. She said, 'By the time you're finished with your term, people might be comparing you to Tokyo.' That's when ego got the better of me. I said, 'I'm going to be better than Tokyo. Maybe I already am.'"

I winced. "Ouch."

"Yeah. I know. The Mount Everest of arrogance. And my dumb quip spread like wildfire. I'm surprised you never heard about it."

"No surprise. I don't listen to the grapevine unless I feel a death alarm. You never know what to believe."

"That's for sure. Anyway, my shining example of verbal stupidity put me on a lot of hate lists, and once you get on those, it's hard to get off, especially when reports of my accomplishments started spreading. The more I succeeded, the more other Reapers hated me. What was I supposed to do? Not be a good Reaper?"

"Of course not. You had to do your job."

"I know, but I still felt like an outcast. I still do."

We remained quiet for several minutes, her head staying against my shoulder. The gentle pressure felt good, as did her confession—the pinnacle of trust.

Several minutes later, the city scenes shifted to farming communities and fields bearing sickly brown cornstalks. Colm and Fiona had told me a couple of weeks ago that the crop this year was worse than ever. I needed to be ready for a rash of deaths, some from starvation, but more from government purging to avoid human stampedes. Soon another city would burn, maybe Chicago.

I pictured my district in flames—children screaming in parents' arms as throngs fled from burning buildings only to be blocked by a wall of fire set by the authorities. Hemmed in on all sides, they huddled trembling as the killing walls converged.

I shook my head to cast away the vision. I had to change the subject. Maybe go back to the previous one. "Shanghai," I whispered, "do you know if Tokyo heard your comment?"

"Huh?" She blinked. "Sorry. I was falling asleep."

"I was just wondering if Tokyo ever heard about your Mount Everest comment."

She yawned. "Probably. People wait in line to tell juicy gossip like that. She might have heard it fifty times for all I know."

"And she died, what, about two years later?"

"Something like that." Shanghai inhaled deeply.

"Let's drop the subject. It's making me sick. And we both need sleep."

"You're right."

We rode in silence, our heads leaning together as we tried to sleep while the car continued its gentle rocking. I dozed at times, though dreams of fires startled me from slumber every few minutes.

Our resting position raised reminders of how Sing and I slept in the same pose, how her curls tickled my skin, how her whisper-soft breaths made me wonder what she was dreaming. She was so vibrant. So pulsating with life. So much like Misty.

But now she was dead. As was Misty. With these lovely ghosts haunting the quiet moments, enjoying Shanghai's close company seemed impossible.

Whenever I woke up, I stealthily looked at the watch. The hands continued pointing toward the depot. It seemed clear that we had made the right decision. Soon the next step of the journey would begin.

The squeal of the decelerating train and a wet, stinging feeling on my face broke my slumber. We pulled apart and looked out the window. Rain pelted the side of the car, sending acidic droplets through the opening.

While the other Reapers disembarked through a side door at the rear of the car, I rose and closed the window. Shanghai remained on the bench, again taking on a sickly grimace as she wiped moisture from her face with a sleeve. When Saigon filed out at the end of the line, her head low and her eyes out of sight, I shifted to the aisle and helped Shanghai to her feet.

We exited the car arm-in-arm to the station's raised wooden platform. The others had already descended the two steps to the path and were hustling through a steady drizzle into the forest.

When the train pulled away, Shanghai shielded her eyes with a hand and watched the other Reapers until they passed out of view. "Perfect. The rain's making them hurry."

"No wonder. It stings quite a bit." I pointed with my thumb toward a pair of outhouses standing close to the platform. "We'd better take advantage of those. We might not get another chance for a while."

"Good idea."

After using the outhouses, which were smellier than usual, we crossed the tracks and walked along the gravel path toward the checkpoint. At this time of day, Erin usually worked the station, but since she had been appointed to higher-level duties with the Gatekeeper, including carrying the souls of Sing and Misty to the Gateway, she wouldn't be there.

Soon, the black wrought-iron gate came into view as well as a uniformed male attendant—tall, muscular, and clean cut. His thin lips and prominent cheekbones gave him a Russian appearance, and his navy-blue coveralls fit snugly, accentuating a twenty-something athletic form.

As usual, Bill sat on a stump less than a stone's throw from the front of the gate, his gray hair matted by the rain and his hands clutching a protest sign—*Reapers Beware. The Gateway Leads Souls to Torture.* A short stack of wet pamphlets sat on the ground at his side.

"Where's your umbrella, Bill?" I asked as we drew near.

"Broke." He peeled a pamphlet from the top of the

stack and extended it to me. "Newest edition. You're both mentioned."

"Shanghai and me?" I took the limp, tri-folded paper and pushed it into my pocket. "Thanks. We'll read it later."

"I'm sure you will." Bill nodded toward the man at the checkpoint. "Rumor has it that Erin's flying pretty high."

"Yeah. I saw her with the Gatekeeper. She's his attendant or something."

"Big feather in her cap, I guess." Bill waved a hand. "Well, be on your way, Phoenix. You have souls to torture."

Not bothering to answer that zinger, I walked with Shanghai to the checkpoint. The attendant stared at us without expression, his hands folded at his waist. A sonic gun sat in a holster at his hip, an unusual accessory for a checkpoint attendant. Erin never carried one, at least not where I could see it.

I offered him a friendly nod. "Phoenix and Shanghai from Chicago. We won't need an energy boost or blood refill. We've been here recently. Erin collected blood samples then, so we're good to go."

The attendant's expression remained stoic. "Let's see your birthmarks." His nasally voice pitched higher than expected. "I'll check the database."

I leaned over and rolled up my pant leg, exposing my calf. The attendant set a silver pen-like probe close to the brown splotch an inch or so above my ankle and pressed a button. A thin beam emanated from the pen and washed over the mark until it glowed with a purple hue.

"Identification verified." The attendant walked to a computer tablet hanging from the fence next to the gate and tapped on the screen. "You do have a blood sample in your account, and..." When he looked at me again, his face turned pale. "I apologize, sir. I didn't realize who you are."

Although I had no idea what he meant, it would be best to play along. "All is forgiven. But kindly tell me what my records say. I want to make sure they're up to date."

He unhooked the tablet from the fence and brought it to me, reading the screen as he walked. "I don't see anything you wouldn't already know. Supreme Cardinal, of course. I should have recognized your tunic's emblem, but I thought you were too young to be a Supreme." He bowed his head. "Again, I apologize for being so... terse, I suppose."

"You're just doing your job." I lifted my brow. "What's your name?"

"Grigory."

"Well, Grigory, be sure to show kindness to all Reapers. Even the rookies deserve it."

"Yes sir." Grigory scanned the screen again. "I see you're being monitored. Since you have a medallion, I guess you know that, too."

"Yes. Go on."

He shook his head. "Just the usual. Name. Age. Place of birth. Parents' names. Again, nothing you wouldn't know."

"Is my parents' status updated?"

Grigory's face reddened. "Yes sir. My condolences."

I swallowed hard. Condolences? Trying to keep my body from trembling, I opened my mouth to speak, but Shanghai broke in. "Grigory, Phoenix is still shaken up over his parents' deaths, so let's move on to getting me processed. I'm not feeling well, and we're already running late."

"Of course."

Every limb numbed, I watched as Grigory read the birthmark on Shanghai's neck and entered her information into the tablet. When he finished, he opened the gate and gestured for us to pass through.

Shanghai hooked her arm with mine and whispered, "Be strong, Supreme Cardinal."

"Right." I cleared my throat and nodded toward Grigory. "Good day to you."

"And to you, sir."

We strode through the opening and followed a trail of flattened grass. Thoughts of my parents dominated my mind—Mom's quiet love, Dad's honesty, even when his blunt words hurt. Although the Council took me away at an early age and I saw them only during sanctioned visits, Mom wrote to me every week, and Dad signed every letter.

Of course, the letters stopped when I became a district hound, but Mom probably kept writing them. She and Dad both had faults, but those seemed minimal now, not worth remembering. Almost four years had passed since the day I last saw their faces, and now I would never see them again.

CHAPTER SIX

S HANGHAI STAYED QUIET, likely sensing my dark
mood. The grass and trees slid by in a blur, and the
sting from pelting raindrops barely pierced my numbed
shell. Soon I would have to break out and be Phoenix
again, but for now I just wanted to walk in the shadowy
memories of better days when a naïve boy's blinders kept
him from seeing death, darkness, and deception in the
heart of nearly every person on earth.

When we arrived at the top of a crest, the depot came
into sight at the center of a clearing where overarching
trees provided a sheltering canopy. The four other Reapers
had just finished their extractions and were stepping out
of their holographic duplicates and off their pedestals.
The moment their feet touched the surrounding marble
floor, their holograms vanished.

The semi-transparent image of the Gatekeeper
remained atop the central pedestal—a larger-than-life man
with arms spread as if inviting souls to enter the shimmering representation of the Gateway behind him. As always,
his dark hair flowed back as if blown by a gentle breeze,
and his eyes shone too bright to view. His godlike visage

incited a round of nausea. I couldn't look at this disgusting tyrant for another second.

"I don't see Bartholomew or Thaddeus," Shanghai said. "We can leave our belts on."

"Good. Casual is always better."

We walked down the crest and onto the marble surface. Our own holograms appeared on pedestals, Shanghai's to the Gatekeeper's left and mine to the right.

The other Reapers pulled their hoods over their eyes. As they walked past us, Saigon gave me a brief glance but said nothing. Her expression seemed softer than before. Maybe getting a new dose of energy boosted her spirits.

Since the depot attendants were nowhere in sight, we could go through the extractions quickly without the formality Bartholomew insisted on when a rookie Reaper was present. He and Thaddeus were likely playing cards in their cabin behind the Gateway mockup while watching us on a monitor.

In front of the Gatekeeper's image, a plastic-covered computer tablet lay on a raised lectern-like stand. It was time to download our photo sticks into the system… and time to ask Albert a crucial question.

I plugged the cloak's clasp into my valve and spoke into the fibers. "I'm ready to send you through the Gateway. You know what that means."

His shaky voice reached my ears. "Decision time. And you can't ask me directly because you don't want the depot attendants to know if I decide to stay behind."

I imagined the attendants listening in remotely. Fortunately, being non-Reapers, they couldn't hear Albert. "Exactly."

"Well… in keeping with your secretive ways, do you mind if I speak in code?"

"Uh… I suppose it's all right. I'm not sure I'll understand, though."

"You will. I've been preparing for this moment for a while." He cleared his throat. "A clerk was scared of staying put on earth's terrestrial grounds. But now he's scared of other worlds and how the trumpet sounds."

After a few seconds of silence, I asked, "Is that it?"

"That's it." Albert groaned. "Come on, Phoenix. I thought you were smart enough to figure it out."

"Sorry. I'm a little preoccupied right now."

Shanghai tugged on a shimmering part of my cloak's sleeve. "Cool it. Phoenix just found out his parents are dead. Give him a break."

"Oh." Albert's voice fell to a whisper. "I didn't know. I'm terribly sorry to hear the news."

"And I'm sorry, too, Phoenix," Tori said. "I know how awful it feels."

"Thanks, Tori. I know you do."

"Anyway," she continued, "I figured out Albert's code. He's scared to go through the Gateway, and he doesn't want to scare me. But I'm not scared. Mommy and I want to go and see my daddy."

I let a smile break through the gloom. "Well, Albert, I guess you don't have to talk in code anymore."

"Yeah, but now I sound like a coward. A little girl has more courage than I do."

"You're the only one who thinks that. I wouldn't have made it this far without your help."

"Well… true." Albert sighed. "All right. All right. You can skip me. I'm coming with you."

Colm's voice emanated from Shanghai's cloak. "Unless my help is sorely needed, I would like to be with Molly. If the Gateway is not what we have been taught to believe, then she surely needs me to be with her."

"We'll manage," Shanghai said. "I'd probably do the same."

"Let's get this done." I withdrew photo sticks from my cloak pocket, leaving Albert's behind, easily identified by touch since it bore an embossed DEO emblem.

When I plugged the first stick into the tablet's port, Bartholomew's voice emanated through the speaker. "My condolences, Phoenix."

"You heard about my parents' deaths?"

"Considering that news of every death passes through my office, you shouldn't be surprised." As we downloaded stick after stick, Bartholomew continued. "As you know, your father was a good friend of mine years ago. I am greatly saddened by his passing. He was a fine man. I never met his wife, but he wrote to me about her. By all accounts, she was a splendid woman. Again, my condolences."

I downloaded my last stick. "Do you know how they died or when? No one told me anything. I heard about it from the checkpoint clerk."

"The council often keeps such deaths quiet." Intermittent raindrops tapped on the tablet's protected screen, making him hard to hear. "No word on the cause. Only that it was quite recent. Perhaps yesterday. The Reaper who carried their souls here left only moments ago. You could ask her for more information."

"Her?" My cheeks flushed hot. "Saigon?"

"Yes. Since you know her, I'm surprised she didn't speak to you about it on your way here."

"But why was Saigon carrying them? My parents didn't live anywhere near Chicago."

"My understanding is that they were in the area on a business trip, but I have no details. I assume you can discuss it with Saigon during your return to Chicago."

"Definitely."

Shanghai gave me a questioning look but stayed quiet.

"According to my records," Bartholomew said, "you still have Albert Crandyke in your cloak, and you have not downloaded his information."

I stiffened. "Well... I... that is—"

"You thought I wouldn't notice." He let out a sigh. "Phoenix, I am a compassionate man. Just tell me why you're holding him. Is he providing information about your parents?"

"Not yet. But I just learned that they died. I'm hoping he'll remember something."

"Very well. You may keep him for one more cycle. But please don't test me again. Full disclosure is always your best option."

I let my muscles relax. "All right. Thank you."

"Get into position. I'll make the extractions quick."

I stepped up to my pedestal and connected the depot hose's adapter to my cloak and sternum valve. Shanghai copied my actions at her position. The vacuum pressurized, securing the hose in place. Within seconds, my sternum valve grew warm. The usual tingling sensation followed as the shimmering souls rode the cloak fibers toward the valve.

As the souls funneled into the hose, my heart pounded

hard. My joints ached. Yet, the pain was nothing compared to the excruciating torture the extraction process usually caused. Could the new energy be the reason? If so, I had to put on an act for the observation camera.

I grimaced tightly and added a low moan. Across the way, Shanghai did the same. Within a few minutes, the system withdrew every soul from my cloak except Albert's. When the vacuum pressure eased, we disconnected and hopped down from our pedestals.

"Let's go." I jogged toward the path to the train station. When we got out of earshot of the depot, Shanghai caught up and ran alongside me.

"We can't get back on the train," she said. "We have to follow the energy line."

I maintained the quick pace. Rain stung my cheeks, worse than before. "We'll stay here, but I need to talk to Saigon before she boards."

"Then she'll know we stayed behind on purpose. Everyone will know. Someone will get suspicious and come looking for us."

As I stared down the path, I let out an exasperated sigh. Saigon was my only shot at finding out what happened to my parents, but since their souls were now in the Gateway system, it made more sense to follow their trail. They might be in danger.

I slowed to a walk. "All right. We'll check out with Grigory so the system thinks we've left. Then we'll come back in ghost mode. Just remember to act sick."

As we continued over rain-slickened turf, I imagined the planned scenario. We couldn't let anyone see us transform into ghost mode, so we would have to get out of Grigory's sight and avoid Bill as well.

His name raised a reminder—the flyer he had given me. I fished it from my pocket and peeled the damp paper open. A headline on the front page blared the news about the corrections-camp rescue and how Shanghai and I had risked our lives to set the prisoners free. The story badly skewed the facts, making us out to be superheroes with inhuman strength and speed, which probably helped our cause. No one outside of the Resistance sympathizers would take the report seriously.

After Grigory processed our exits, we walked toward the train station. I slid an arm around Shanghai's waist and helped her hobble along the path. Puddles had formed at the grassy sides, but the gravel remained free of standing water.

Metal wheels screeched at the station platform. The train was arriving. Bill scooped up his pile of pamphlets and shouted toward Grigory, "I'm outta here, Ruski. See you tomorrow. Same time, same place." He passed us and walked ahead, glancing back. "You two are up to something, aren't you?"

I gave him a smile that I hoped looked innocent. "Up to something? Here? What could we possibly do here?"

"Well, if you are, just a warning. The woods are filled with cameras and guard dogs." He turned away. "So be careful."

As soon as we came within sight of the station, I halted our march. The train waited on the tracks, the last car standing between us and the loading platform. Saigon stood on the platform's edge and peered around the back of the car. Whether or not she spotted us, I couldn't tell.

I whispered, "Pretend to be sick."

Shanghai dropped to her knees and dry heaved.

"Oooh," Bill said as he pivoted toward us. "She sounds awful."

I knelt at Shanghai's side. "Yeah. I think we'll have to wait for the next train. If you see any other Reapers, let them know."

"Will do." He turned and walked toward the station.

Now low enough to avoid Saigon's gaze, I whispered, "Ghost mode."

Shanghai began dematerializing. I concentrated on my energy flow and followed her lead. Within seconds, a windblown mist streamed across the surrounding world. The rain stopped, and my cloak felt lighter, as if completely dry. We were now ghosts and would probably remain that way for a long time.

Bill pivoted and raised a finger. "One more thing." He blinked as his eyes darted. "Where did you go?"

"Good. We're invisible." I grasped Shanghai's hand and helped her rise. We jogged together toward the checkpoint. The misty world breezed by on both sides, bringing a feeling of disorientation. Moving quickly in this state would take some getting used to.

When we reached the gate, we walked right through the bars while Grigory stood nearby with an umbrella over his head. He stared as if lost in thought, apparently unaware of our presence.

As we walked, Shanghai's face twisted into a frown.

"What's wrong?" I asked.

"I just remembered that I left my staff under our seat."

"That's too bad. It's a great weapon."

"Yeah, it would've come in handy." Her frown melted into a smile that seemed forced. "It would probably get in the way. You know, feel as heavy as a tree after a few miles. Right?"

"Definitely. Traveling light is always better." I offered a confident smile, but mine probably looked forced, too. Still, we had to keep our spirits up somehow. Striding into the unknown brought a foreboding that was hard to shake.

A few minutes later, we crested the first hill and began descending the slope. Shanghai released my hand and looked at her fingers as she wiggled them. "How long should we stay like this?"

"We'll follow the depot's energy line till we get out of the compound and past the cameras. Then it should be safe to change back."

"That'll be quite an energy drain. And once we're physical, we'll need some recovery time."

"We'll just have to deal with it. Not much choice." As we continued at a quick marching pace, the misty landscape blurred, though now it felt more normal. Yet, becoming accustomed to this mode presented a danger, as Alex had mentioned. We had no anchor to pull us back to reality. If we stayed ghosts for too long, getting stuck was a real possibility.

After another minute, we descended the final slope to the depot, walked onto the marble floor, and stopped directly in front of the shimmering Gateway—a manifestation of vibrant energy in the shape of a double gate that towered over our heads and stretched several arms' lengths to our sides. The bottom edge floated a foot or so off the ground, and attached channels of light extended into the forest to the right and left.

"I've never been this close before," Shanghai said as

she set a hand near the latch. "Alex said we'd be able to sense the energy, but I don't feel anything. Maybe because we're in ghost mode."

"Could be." I withdrew Sing's watch from my cloak pocket and flipped it open while Shanghai looked on. The combined hands wavered erratically, as if the guiding beacon were jumping all around.

"The watch is in ghost mode with us," Shanghai said. "The needle can't find anything to point to in this realm."

"I could go back to normal for a minute, but the cameras would see me."

"And you'd be disoriented. We'd get caught."

"Then we'll have to guess." I looked at the hazy sun as it hovered low in the western sky. When we were in Chicago and while we rode the train, the watch's hands pointed toward the depot—southwest of the city, so it made sense to continue in the same general direction. The energy line to the left led that way, making it the better choice.

I pointed. "Let's follow the sun for a while."

"Maybe a long while. It's a big continent."

We walked along the energy line. The marble floor ended, giving way to grass and then to matted leaves in a forested area. The radiance ran straight through trees and bushes unhindered, as did we.

After traveling about a hundred yards, we came upon the chain-link fence that encircled the compound. It, too, proved to be no obstacle as we followed the energy line through it. On the other side, the forest thinned to a tree-dotted meadow. In one tree, a camera rotated slowly. For a moment, it seemed that it followed our movements.

Shanghai kept her eye on it. "Cameras can't see us, right?"

"Not if we're invisible."

"What if a Reaper is monitoring the feed?"

"I hadn't thought of that." I lowered my head and increased the pace. "All we can do is keep moving."

Soon, a wolf-like dog appeared ahead, walking straight toward us while sniffing the ground. When it drew near, it halted and looked around, its pointed ears perked. We stopped within a couple of steps and looked it over. A DEO insignia had been attached to its collar as well as a small electronic box, maybe a monitoring device.

The dog let out a whine and panted. A dripping tongue protruded over sharp teeth within a set of powerful jaws. After looking around for another moment, it continued sniffing and passed through us.

"It knew we were here," Shanghai said as she watched it amble away. "A dog's sixth sense."

"No telling how big their patrol area is. We'll have to stay in ghost mode until we're out of range."

"We'd better set a time limit. Let's say if we don't see a dog or a camera for an hour, we'll switch to physical."

I nodded. "That should be safe."

As we walked through the ever-present mist, I glanced at Shanghai now and then. Although her eyes stayed focused straight ahead, her expression shifted frequently—distressed one moment, content the next, angry the next. Obviously many thoughts percolated within.

I sidled closer to her. "Want to tell me what you're thinking about? It'll help pass the time."

She smiled. "You sure you want to hear it? I'll probably start venting."

I shrugged. "You've been Mount Everest. Why not a volcano?"

"Okay, but if you get tired of my whining, just say so."

"That's not likely. Go ahead."

As we walked on, her brow dipped, as if she were contemplating how to begin. After another minute, she took a deep breath and spoke with ease. "A little background first. I'm sure you remember when I got transferred to a different trainer and had to leave you. We were both a month shy of ten years old, just kids with only one friend. Each other. Although we were close, we kept stiff upper lips, believing we would find new friends.

"Well, when I arrived at the facility, things changed a lot. I was the new kid, and I looked different. Everyone else was Anglo or Latino, and I was the slant-eyed little girl with strange-colored skin. To make matters worse, I stopped growing, while the other kids got taller and taller. The sparring matches got harder. I just didn't have the same reach. Since I had to fight boys as well as girls, I got beat up pretty badly—bruises, black eyes, even a concussion."

I winced at the mental image but stayed quiet. She didn't seem to expect any interjections.

"Not only that, I got called every name in the book—bug-eater, slant-eyes, slit-face, and even Chink, which is pretty stupid because I'm not Chinese. They were too ignorant to know the difference. Anyway, they poured rice in my hair, soy sauce in my water, and crumbled fortune cookies in my bed. They never stopped tormenting me."

My hands curled into fists, but I continued staying quiet.

"As you can imagine, their abuse made me feel

smaller than ever. After about a year of enduring it, something new hit me in the head, worse than any karate kick. I heard my parents were killed by gangsters."

My throat caught. "What? You never told me that."

She shook her head. "That's because I didn't see you again until we met in the bandits' park just a few months after I transferred to Chicago."

"I assumed they were alive. You told me about a daydream you had, the one about going home to be with them. Your brother killed himself, so you wanted to be there to fill the void."

"That's true. I did have that daydream before they died, but I didn't tell you more because I didn't want you to feel sorry for me. But now that your parents are dead, I thought we could…" She shrugged. "I don't know. Commiserate."

"We can. When two people are down for the same reason, they can lift each other up."

She looked at me and smiled. "Like you're lifting me up just by letting me bend your ear."

"Keep bending it. What happened after you heard the bad news? I'll bet you were lonely."

"Worse than lonely. I was alone." She focused straight ahead again. "The name calling made me grow a chip on my shoulder. I worked harder than ever to be the best. That's when I started getting my swagger, more of an act to hide my tears than anything else.

"But it worked. By the time I was twelve, I had broken the noses of several girls at the training camp. Then I started growing again and catching up, and a month before my thirteenth birthday, I broke the nose of the biggest boy, a six-foot-four brute named Dennis. I kicked him in the face so hard, everyone heard the crack. They had to take him to the hospital to get the nosebleed to stop."

"I can picture you doing it. A three-sixty jump?"

She grinned. "My trademark."

"Let's just hope I never see it up close and personal. I don't want a broken nose."

She shook a finger. "Just stay on my good side, Reaper boy. Spoiling a face as handsome as yours would be a crime."

"Trust me. I will."

"Anyway, that kick did nothing to stop the abuse. It just got worse. I ate alone. I walked alone. I even played board games alone. My swagger was my mask, my protection from pain. Fortunately, my thirteenth birthday ended the torment. It was time for me to leave training and go to a district. The administrator hated me, so she made sure I got assigned to the most dangerous district in the city, hoping I'd get killed by bandits."

"Who had that district before you came?"

She held up a pair of fingers. "Two guys you wouldn't know. They always traveled together for safety. The administrator busted them to roamers to make room for me. They were guilty, but most Reapers are into something they can get busted for. Some get away with it. Some don't. It just depends on whose bad side they're on."

"So a thirteen-year-old girl took the place of two men. You were set up to fail."

She nodded. "That's why I made my Mount Everest comment. I had to set my foot, let the bandits know they couldn't intimidate me. I had to show my swagger. But I was too immature to know that swagger didn't have to be so cocky. I didn't have to alienate people." She let out a long sigh. "But deep down, maybe I wanted to alien-ate people. Push them all away, like an ultimate defense mechanism. Because if everyone stayed away..." She blinked through welling tears. "Maybe no one would call me names. Being alone meant no one could hurt me."

I grasped her hand. "I'm sorry, Shanghai. I wish we could've stayed together. You know I would've been your friend. No one would've called you names while I was around."

"I know, Phoenix. I know." She lifted my hand to her lips and kissed it. Tears flowed as her voice pitched higher. "Now you know why I latched on to you when we got back together, why I wanted us to live together. I know I was really forward, but I wanted to make sure you knew my feelings. You're the only friend I ever had, the only person who didn't care that I have slanted eyes or banana-peel skin or anything else. You loved me for who I was, a lost and lonely little girl who just wanted someone to talk to." A trembling smile graced her lips. "And now here you are. Letting me vent. Talking about it helps a lot."

"I'm glad to listen anytime." As we continued walk-ing, I pondered her words further. She was more wounded than I ever imagined. Maybe I could do more than just let her talk it out.

I drew her hand to my lips, returned the kiss, and reached deep for all the passion I could muster. "Shanghai, I was excited to see you again. I admit you kind of sur-prised me with the living-together talk, but that didn't change my mind about one Mount Everest fact."

Smiling, I paused for effect until she nudged my ribs with an elbow. "C'mon, buster. Don't make me wait for the punch line."

I stopped our march and faced her. With a gentle touch, I ran a finger along the outline of her perfect Oriental eyes, then a hand through her dark-as-pitch hair. I whispered, "Only a fool would make fun of your features. It would be like cursing the rising sun."

She grinned. "Rising sun? That's kind of overboard, isn't it?"

"Not at all. You're a beautiful woman, Shanghai, but that's not why I think you're amazing. You're a great friend, and now that we're together again, I've never been happier. I hope nothing ever separates us."

As her eyes misted, she sniffed. "Do you really mean that? Or is the joy juice talking again?"

Her tears reflected her fragile heart. Mine was also fragile… broken in pieces, really. People I loved were dying all around me. Only the two of us remained. "Shanghai, I…" My voice quaked. "I'm not sure what's going on between me and you. I just know I need you right now. To be at my side without thinking about the future. Can you do that until I get my head straightened out?"

"With all my heart." Her face contorting, she walked into my arms and laid her head on my shoulder. While she wept, I rubbed her back, battling my own tears. Mist flowed around our embrace, two bodies stripped of physical shells, two minds stripped of emotional boundaries. All fear had melted away. We were two ghosts on a deadly journey who had found heaven's door. If only we could stay here and never let this moment end.

But it had to end. Many miles lay before us, maybe hundreds. And many mysteries needed to be solved, including a new one. Our parents getting killed seemed like too much of a coincidence. A conspiracy wasn't out of the question.

After staying in our quiet embrace for nearly a minute, we drew apart and walked on. Soon, we arrived at another forest. As the energy line continued deeper into the woods, it faded until it disappeared in the distance. I grasped Shanghai's arm and stopped next to a large oak. "I haven't seen any dogs or cameras. We should shift to normal."

"Okay. Be ready for a kick in the head."

We sat together at the base of the oak and leaned against it. As I willed myself out of the ghost realm, the mist slowly evaporated. The forest swayed from side to side as if tossed by ocean waves, though the ground beneath remained firm. No falling drops pattered on leaves above or the surrounding soil. Either the rain had stopped or I hadn't fully transitioned.

Shanghai groaned. "I think I might really get sick."

"Just close your eyes. It'll pass." I followed my own advice and shut out the tempest-tossed woods. Although no rain fell, my cloak felt moist and heavy. Our hours in ghost mode had given it no chance to dry. "Do you think we're back to reality yet?"

"Not sure," Shanghai said with a groan. "Check the watch."

I opened my eyes. A woman wearing a scarlet cloak stood in front of us. A raised hood revealed only her lovely face. The cloak's sleeves ended with wide white cuffs that loosely encircled her hands, folded at her waist.

As her sparkling stare locked with mine, my limbs froze. I opened my mouth, but I couldn't speak. I could barely even breathe.

CHAPTER SEVEN

THE WOMAN CROUCHED close and lowered her hood. Soft brown hair spilled past her shoulders and across a white blouse, buttoned high to reveal only her tawny throat. Her lips, glistening as if glazed by pink sugar crystals, parted as she looked me over.

Her head tilted. "You are a Reaper." Her voice carried a melodic lilt, like a song.

I ached to look at Shanghai, but my head wouldn't turn. I barely managed a nod.

"Why, pray tell, is a Reaper in this forest?" She caressed my throat with her fingers. The touch sent a wild tingle across my skin from head to toe. "I loose your tongue from its bonds."

My muscles relaxed. I glanced at Shanghai. Her eyes were still closed. "I'm on a journey."

The woman kept her stare fixed on me. Although she said nothing, I knew she wanted more information. I couldn't help but continue.

"I'm searching for a soul. Two souls, actually. Friends of mine. I heard they're going to be thrown into the abyss."

She nodded. "You seek the terminus of this energy line."

"Yes. Do you know where it is?"

"I do."

"Where?"

She waved a hand toward the line. "At the terminus."

"Right. I guessed that. How far away is it?"

"I do not know."

"But you just said you know where it is."

"I did say that." She tilted her head again. "You speak as if my words are contradictory."

"Aren't they?"

"No, young Reaper." She looked at the western sky. "Do you know where our guiding star is?"

"Sure." I nodded toward the sun. "It's right there."

She turned her gaze back to me. "Do you know how far away it is?"

"Uh… no. I probably should remember that from school, but… no."

"Are you contradicting yourself by saying you know where the sun is while not knowing the distance to it?"

"I guess not."

"Then you have taken a strong step toward understanding." She looked into my eyes more deeply than ever. "You have much turmoil within, young Reaper. I sense that you have learned a great deal of wisdom, but you lack intimate knowledge of the Higher Powers."

I tried to look away, but my eyes wouldn't move. "That's what Sing said."

"Sing said?" She laughed merrily. "What a lovely phrase. A song often says more than mere prose can communicate. A melody weeps or laughs or ponders, and the hearer understands at a level too deep for words alone."

"That's true, but Sing is a person. Short for Singapore. She's one of the souls I'm looking for."

The woman's smile wilted. "I rejoiced over your phrase because it carried the wit of wisdom, but I see now that your wit was accidental."

My cheeks warmed. "Sorry."

"No harm done, but let us return to our topic. I am evaluating your understanding of the Powers. I concentrate better when I avoid distractions."

"Okay." I looked toward Shanghai. Her eyes were still closed. "Should my traveling companion be involved?"

The woman peered at Shanghai. "Considering that she hasn't stirred at the sound of our conversation, she is either asleep or unable to comprehend my presence. I suspect the latter. Her spiritual cognizance is low."

"What do you mean?"

"Exactly what I said." She blinked. "Did I use a word that is foreign to your understanding? Perhaps *cognizance*?"

"No, I'm just wondering why she wouldn't be able to hear us. Is one of us still a ghost?"

"Do you not realize that you are not a ghost?" She tapped her chin with a finger. "You are a more complex case than I first realized."

"No. I know I'm not a ghost. I was in the ghost realm for maybe two hours, and I'm not used to being there for so long, and I didn't know…" Her curious stare, deep and beautiful, melted the rest of my sentence.

"I think I understand." Her stare remained unmoved. "Are you not curious about who I am?"

The heat in my cheeks spiked. "Actually, I didn't think about it. I just…" Again her sparkling eyes destroyed my thoughts.

She pointed at herself. "Sancta sum." She then leaned closer. Her breath, warm and sweet, caressed my cheeks. "Do you know what that means?"

An urge to retreat seemed overwhelming, but the tree blocked my way. "Uh... Sing mentioned possibly meeting a Sancta, but she didn't say what it means."

"I said 'I am a Sancta.' A Sancta is a temple. A dwelling of the Highest Power. The language is ancient. Only a few still know it."

"Phoenix?" Shanghai opened her eyes. "My dizziness is almost gone. How about yours?"

"Uh... I'm okay."

The Sancta whispered, "I will do what I can to soften the hearts of those you meet, though some might be hardened beyond relief." She breathed on me and drew back. "You will find water over the next rise, young Reaper. I look forward to seeing you again." Her body stretched out and streamed into the energy line. Sparks erupted from her entry point with a loud snap.

Shanghai flinched. "What was that?"

"Some kind of energy disruption." I rose and walked closer to the splash point. A tingling sensation crawled across my skin, similar to the Sancta's touch, and damp fibers scratched my neck. Although the rain had ended, my cloak was still pretty wet.

I rubbed a sleeve to quell the tingles. Shanghai noticed the sparks, but maybe the splash really was just a disruption, and the sound woke me from a dream. In any case, she had no knowledge of the mysterious visit. It might be better to keep it to myself until I could figure out what was real and what wasn't.

I withdrew the watch and opened the cover. The hands

pointed in the direction we had been walking. "Looks like we guessed right."

Shanghai set her palm inches from the energy wall. "I feel it now. We'll be able to track it when it turns invisible."

I stretched my arms. "I feel strong. How about you?"

"I'm fine." She peered into the forest. "Just thinking about food and water. I can go a few days without eating, but we'll need water pretty soon."

I pointed ahead. "I think we'll find some over the next rise."

"What rise?" She looked that way, blinking. "I don't see a rise."

"Trees are in the way." I strode onward, staying within reach of the energy wall. "Come on."

Shanghai caught up and looked at me while she walked. "You're acting kind of strange."

I glanced at her. "Strange? Why do you say that?"

"You're acting distant and talking about a rise that isn't there. What's eating you?"

"I fell asleep and had a dream. At least it might have been a dream. I'm not sure. It was kind of… disturbing."

"Maybe it's because you're grieving." She looped her arm with mine. "It's normal."

"Yeah. Maybe so." Her words dredged up a shovelful of sorrow. My parents were dead. I hadn't given them more than a passing thought since we left the depot. Entering the ghost realm must have twisted my mind more than I realized.

We marched on side by side. The energy field faded from sight, though the tingle continued, like static electricity dancing across our bodies.

After a mile or so, we broke out of the forest and into

another meadow. The ground bent into a grassy incline, forcing us to lean into our steps. When we reached the crest, we stopped to survey the land.

I set a hand to my brow to shield against the sun— hazy and reddish, still well above the western horizon. Ahead, green grass spread out as far as the eye could see. About a hundred yards away, a shallow stream flowed from right to left. "There's our water."

"How did you know? There's no way you could see it from where we were."

"I guess it wasn't a dream after all. I'll explain on the way." As we descended, I gave her a summary of my encounter with the Sancta, though I skipped the part about Shanghai lacking spiritual cognizance. That would raise questions I couldn't answer. I just assumed she had fallen asleep and couldn't hear the conversation. I also omitted the Sancta's words about softening hearts, mainly because I wasn't sure what she meant. Maybe the meaning would come to light as we journeyed on.

Shanghai agreed that knowledge of the water source proved the reality of the encounter. Yet she seemed unhappy about being left out of the loop, even after I explained that the Sancta's presence paralyzed me. I couldn't alert her, at least not right away.

When we arrived at the stream, we washed our faces, filled our bottles, and continued walking across endless fields of grass, always feeling the energy line to our right.

Afternoon slipped into evening and evening into night. A gibbous moon provided sufficient light, so we continued our relentless march without need of our flash-lights, speaking only to warn each other about a stone or gulley in our path. A gentle breeze dried our clothes and eased the weight on our bodies, a welcome comfort.

About an hour past dark, Shanghai spoke up. "Did the Sancta say anything about transportation?"

"No. Are your legs getting tired?"

"Not yet, but I was thinking we must be closing in on the checkpoint. We've hiked at least ten miles, haven't we?"

"I'm not sure. Ghost mode kind of skewed my bearings."

"I suppose if we miss it, we'll eventually hit a dead end at the Boundary River. Then we'll know we've gone too far."

I looked straight ahead. Although I had never seen the Boundary River, the name conjured troubling images. According to the maps, it began well north in the Lakes and flowed south to the Gulf of Texas. Beyond it lay the Western Wilds, a desolate region that stretched from the Texas border northward, a land where only crazy explorers journeyed in search of precious metals. Most never returned. "Let's hope for the best."

Shanghai touched my cloak. "Maybe Crandyke… I mean, Albert… has some insight. Sometimes the pencil pushers know more than the head honchos."

"Good call." Still walking, I plugged the cloak into my sternum valve. As soon as the fibers energized, Albert spoke up. "What were you doing? Wading through a river?"

I winked at Shanghai. "Through a deep marsh. Alligators. Pythons. Mosquitoes the size of hawks."

"Har, har. You really crack me up. A comedian with a soul-sucking scythe."

"Sorry to get your dead dander up. It rained on us for a while. Nothing I could do about it."

"All right. All right. So you plugged in. I suppose you need my help."

I locked on a shadow far ahead to keep a straight course. "We're following the energy line westward from the depot. Any idea how far it is to the Gateway?"

Albert laughed. "Phoenix, a guy like me could get killed for knowing the location."

"You dodged the question. And you're already dead. So spill it."

"Well... I've made some deductions based on purchase orders I processed over the years. Quite a number of acquisitions approved by the central command were delivered to rural transfer locations that form a line along the highway that runs north to south just east of the Boundary River. Since there was never a record of other trucks picking up the transfers, and since delivery trucks can't cross the river in that area, I suspect that the purchases were ferried across by boat and picked up by someone on the other side."

"If you plotted the center point of these deliveries, about where would it be?"

"As a matter of fact," Albert said, "I wondered that myself. I looked at a map just a few days before I died. The center point would be almost due west of the depot."

"And what's across the river from there?"

"A high-radiation zone, but that's the norm in the Western Wilds."

"High radiation. Not exactly what I wanted to hear."

"How recent was your last anti-radiation shot?"

"A month ago." I turned toward Shanghai. "You?"

She looked upward for a moment. "I think three months. I should be fine."

"Fine for Chicago," Albert said, "but we're talking about the Western Wilds. Workers near the border get their levels boosted every two months."

I touched my cloak's clasp. "Thanks, Albert. I'm going to unplug to save energy. I'll check back with you in a while. Keep your spirits up."

"Spirits. Another funny one, Phoenix." Albert huffed. "Okay. Unplug me. Just stay dry, and I'll be fine."

"I'll avoid the marshes." After I disconnected my clasp, Shanghai and I walked on in silence. Since our only knowledge of the Western Wilds came from history books that had proven themselves unreliable at best and little more than fairy tales at worst, we didn't have much to say.

At what seemed like around midnight, dark boxy shapes appeared at ground level about half a mile away. As we drew closer, the shapes clarified—one-story buildings, maybe farm houses or small town businesses. A lone figure walked in front of one building, first from left to right, then from right to left, as if marching a circuit, though the slouched form indicated boredom pacing more than diligent sentry walking.

"First checkpoint," I whispered. "Coming this late at night, the guard will be suspicious."

Shanghai smoothed out her cloak. "Hoods up. Let's milk the persona for all it's worth."

We raised our hoods and walked at a slow pace. When we came within several steps, the guard stopped and aimed a flashlight at us. The beam shifted from my chest to Shanghai's.

"Halt." The voice was low and sharp, though feminine. "Who are you?"

We stopped at a boundary between the meadow's grass and a narrow road that ran perpendicular to our path. The guard stood near the middle of the road. "Two Reapers," I said in a solemn tone.

"Well, I can see that." She turned the light off. "What are you doing here? No one's ready to kick the bucket." She glanced at the buildings behind her. "At least not that I know of."

With the beam doused, my eyes adjusted to the darkness. A big-boned woman maybe thirty years old and at least an inch taller than either or us stood just out of reach. I gave her a respectful nod. "We are Cardinal-level Reapers on a special assignment. I am Phoenix from Chicago. My companion is Shanghai, also from Chicago. If you look up my profile, you'll see that I have clearance to continue."

"Continue? Why you'd want to get this close to the Boundary River is beyond me." From her pants pocket she withdrew a computer tablet and tapped on the screen. "Let's see… Phoenix from Chicago."

Shanghai whispered, "I see a motorcycle. Looks like the only vehicle around. Probably no chance she'll let us borrow it."

I bent to the side and looked behind the guard. The grounds appeared to hold a barracks, big enough to sleep three or four people, and another building that might house a kitchen and latrine, but it was too dark to be sure. A motorcycle stood close to the side of the barracks, leaning on its kickstand.

"Ah. Here you are." The guard's brow rose. "Cardinal Supreme. Priority two. I'm practically hobnobbing with royalty." She lifted the tablet to eye level and glanced between it and me. "Definitely looks like you, but I'll need to check your thumbprint. Not that many people come by here impersonating big-shot Reapers."

"Sure." When she turned the tablet toward me, I pressed my thumb within a box on the screen.

She looked at the tablet again. "You're verified. But how does such a young Reaper get that high of a clearance?"

"Because of the special assignment."

She slid the tablet into her pocket. "Why all the hush-hush? Is the assignment too secret to tell me why you're on foot and traveling off road?"

"We have no other transportation, and the route we took was the most direct. If we had a motorcycle, I'm sure we could make better time, but..." I shrugged. "I guess we'll have to keep hoofing it."

The guard pivoted her thumb from side to side. "Are you turning north or south from here?"

"Whichever way is the closest bridge over the Boundary River."

Her eyes widened. "Over the river? Do you have a death wish?"

CHAPTER EIGHT

"NO DEATH WISH," I said. "Just doing what we have to do."

The guard bobbed her head. "Oh. I get it. You're going to collect ghosts over there."

I raised a finger to my lips. "I hope you'll keep our mission quiet. It's important to ensure that the identities of the deceased stay under wraps."

"Say no more. I'm just worried about you two getting cooked. The radiation spikes like crazy just three miles into the Western Wilds."

The mention of radiation brought the pill bottle to mind. I withdrew it from my cloak pocket and showed it to her. "What do you know about this medication?"

She set the beam on the label. "Potabal. That's the pharma name for a blend of potassium iodide and marsilla salts. We use it here if our radiation levels get too high."

"How much do you take?"

"One a day until my levels drop. If you're in the Western Wilds, the pills will help, but it's like trying to put out an inferno with a water pistol. Don't go there thinking that medicine's going to keep you alive."

I slid the bottle back to my pocket. "Thank you for

your concern, but we don't have any choice. We Reapers do what we must."

She glanced at the motorcycle, then at us, worry lines etched in her brow. "If you had wheels, how long do you think you'd be gone?"

"Impossible to say. We never know for certain where death alarms will lead us."

"I suppose you can't be over there more than three days, right? You'd get cooked for sure."

"I certainly hope we'll be back by then. Getting cooked would keep us from transporting the souls to the Gateway."

She glanced at the motorcycle again. "Listen, I could get busted for this, but you can take my bike. It'll hold two. But be back in less than three days. That's when my husband and I go home on relief."

I kept my expression solemn. "I am grateful for your offer, and I accept. We will certainly do everything we can to return in time."

She pointed north. "The closest bridge is two miles that way. It's the first left. The bridge is blocked, but a motorcycle can squeeze between the barricades. Once you cross, the road heads west and becomes a bigger highway. The pavement has potholes, and it's washed away in some places, but our motorcycle can handle almost anything."

I gave her a thankful nod. "We appreciate your kindness."

From her shirt pocket, the guard withdrew a key attached to a shoelace and handed it to me. "If you leave the headlight off, the battery's charged enough to go about a hundred miles. You'll have to stop before dawn and let it charge by solar when the sun rises. There's an outpost not far into the Wilds, last safe shelter going westward.

I don't know if anyone's manning it these days, but I'm sure no one stays overnight. So maybe you can stop there and grab some sleep before you get to the higher radiation zone."

I added the key to the items in my cloak pocket. "Are warning signs posted letting you know you're entering the zone?"

She shook her head. "Wouldn't do any good. The radiation boundaries shift. You'll just have to watch your meters."

"Meters? We don't have meters."

The guard blinked. "You're traveling to the Western Wilds and you don't have meters?"

"When we left Chicago, we weren't sure how far we would have to go."

"Then you really do have a death wish. Lucky for you I have an extra one. I'll be right back." She turned and hustled toward the barracks.

Shanghai crossed her arms in front. "I'm impressed. Your new security clearance is really helping."

I opened my mouth to agree, but the words caught in my throat. Like a song riding the wind, the Sancta's voice came to mind. *I will do what I can to soften hearts in your path.* The memory warmed my own heart and raised a chill along my skin at the same time. "The new clearance is great, but I have a feeling something more is going on."

Shanghai cocked her head. "Like what?"

"Not sure yet. Something... something invisible, I guess. When I figure it out, I'll let you know."

She wiggled her fingers. "Oooh. Mysterious. Reapers aren't supposed to be spooked by stuff like that."

"Like I said, I'm trying to figure it out."

She smiled. "Fair enough. Just trying to lighten the mood a bit."

When the guard returned, she wrapped a plastic watchband around my wrist and fastened its buckle. "The glowing number reads two right now. Three is safe. Four is borderline. Five is risky. Six starts the real danger zone. Anything higher than that, and you're getting fried."

I looked at the face at the center of the band as if reading a wristwatch. The numeral 2 glowed light green on a black background. "Got it."

She gazed at us, her eyes darting from me to Shanghai and back to me. "Is it all right if I ask you a personal question?"

I nodded. "Sure. Go ahead."

"You're not brother and sister, and you look too young to be married." She shifted from foot to foot. "Do unmarried Reapers often travel together like this? Overnight journeys, I mean?"

"Not often. We're usually loners. Why?"

Hazy moonlight illuminated her lips, one pulled in under a bite. "Never mind. It's none of my business." She gave us a friendly smile. "I hope your journey is blessed with safety."

"Thank you again." I walked past her with Shanghai following. When we reached the motorcycle, I looked it over. It appeared to be similar to Alex's model, though the seat was longer, obviously built for two riders. "Do you want to drive?"

She shook her head. "You be the pilot. I can take over if you get tired."

I kicked up the stand, straddled the bike, and settled onto the padded seat. Shanghai sat behind me and set her hands on my waist. When I inserted the key and turned it, the motor hummed. I twisted the handlebar accelerator and guided the cycle onto the road and then north.

The headwind blew back our hoods. When we passed through the Gateway's energy line, the tingling sensation spiked, then faded just as quickly. Once we crossed the Boundary River, we would have to head south again and find the line, an easy task if the path was clear.

As I guided the motorcycle along the dimly lit road, dodging occasional potholes, Shanghai tapped my shoulder. "What was all that about?" she asked. "Us not being married, I mean."

I raised my voice to compete with the breeze. "Did you take the ethics course in training school?"

"Let's say I didn't. Humor me."

"Some people believe a guy and a girl should be married before they... well... become intimate. Since we're traveling together overnight, maybe she assumed we're an intimate couple."

"I guess that's a reasonable assumption." Shanghai stayed quiet for a few moments before speaking up again. "Not many people believe that way anymore."

"I can think of three married couples in my district. Two, now that Colm is dead. I guess that's not many, like you said."

"I like the idea. Promising to stay together forever no matter what. It's quaint, but it feels right." After another few moments of silence, she added, "I'll just follow your lead, Phoenix. I know your heart's still broken over Misty."

Heat rose to my cheeks. Once again Shanghai assumed that Misty, like a haunting ghost, was keeping us apart. Yet Shanghai's words raised new questions. In her mind, why was it acceptable to let heartbreak over a dead girl stop us from becoming intimate? Earlier, she expressed concern about her being too forward, as if assuming that I might protest cohabitation. But if there was nothing morally wrong with pre-marital intimacy, why would anyone object?

I blew out a quiet sigh. Once again thoughts on morality had cropped up, thoughts I had no real capacity to process. Being a loner for so long had kept relationship issues at bay, and the ethics training class taught nothing about personal morality, only what to expect with regard to the people in our district.

In any case, the sudden exposure to these thoughts felt as if someone had opened a door to a part of my mind I had never explored, a portion filled with cobwebs and question marks that wouldn't go away.

When we reached the first left, I made the turn and scooted along a narrower, pothole-filled road at a slower speed. Considering all the ruts, probably no one had traveled here in decades.

Shanghai tapped my shoulder again. "I see the river. Moonlight's reflecting on it."

A silvery disk shone at ground level about a hundred yards in the distance, rippled by the current—the Boundary River, the edge of the Western Wilds.

Within a minute, we came upon a ramp leading up to the bridge. Concrete barriers bordered each side, and a line of barrels blocked forward progress. As the guard had said, I was able to squeeze the motorcycle between two barrels and continue on.

When we reached the crest of the bridge, I stopped, set my feet on the pavement, and looked out over the river and the surrounding land. A warm breeze blew from the south and cast ripples across the dark water below, as if trying to push back the southward-flowing current. On the western side, the land was flat and dark with only a few spindly trees interrupting the monotony.

I glanced at the wrist meter. A 3 glowed on the face. "It seems strange to be heading into a place we've only heard about. A dangerous place that'll flay us to the bone."

"And we're going voluntarily," Shanghai said. "I guess we're either crazy or stupid."

"Maybe both." I withdrew Sing's watch and looked at the face. "The hands point straight ahead. My guess is if we stay on this road, we'll run parallel to the energy line."

Shanghai peeked over my shoulder. "Not if Sing and the Gateway are in different places. Then the hands would be pointing one way, and the energy line would lead another."

"I think we can risk it for a little while. We'll find that outpost the guard mentioned and get some sleep. Then we'll figure out what to do when we have more light."

Shanghai pointed toward the western horizon. "That looks like quite a storm."

Illuminated by the moon, a north-south line of clouds boiled in the distance. Lightning bolts of red and orange flashed to the ground all along the cloud bank. Thunder rolled across the river and shook the bridge.

I lifted my feet. "Let's go." We rode to the end of the bridge's descending ramp and continued westward on what soon became a divided highway. The approaching storm sent clouds across the moon, dimming the tree-less land.

"If we don't find that outpost soon, we'll have to

turn around. Get under the bridge, or maybe go back to the checkpoint." I turned on the motorcycle's headlight. "Let's have a look around."

Shanghai unclipped her flashlight and searched each side with the beam. "Did she say how far the outpost is?"

"She said it's safe, and the radiation spikes in three miles, so it has to be closer than that."

A raindrop splashed on my face. The wetness stung worse than usual. A deluge might be painful or even dangerous.

"I see something." Shanghai's light stabbed the darkness just to my left. "At about ten o'clock."

The beam struck a one-story building not much bigger than a roadside fruit stand. A radio tower rose to the sky at its side, maybe fifty feet high. "Hang on." As soon as Shanghai flicked off her light and tightened her grip on me, I angled the bike toward the building. We bounced along rutted terrain and tufts of grass, while raindrops, more numerous now, continued splashing our faces and biting into our exposed skin.

When we reached the building, I stopped under its overhang on the east side, sheltered from the westerly wind, and engaged the motorcycle's kickstand. We both detached our flashlights and turned them on. I aimed mine at a narrow door and followed the beam to a lift latch. "She said no one's here at night, so…"

I pushed the door open and pointed my beam into the one-room shack while Shanghai looked over my shoulder. At that moment, lightning flashed, gunshot thunder banged, and rain pounded the ground.

We bustled into the room and closed the door. Shanghai swept her beam across the walls, illuminating a curtained alcove. I pushed the curtain to the side, revealing a reasonably clean latrine pot sitting on the floor, a frayed hand towel hanging on a wall bracket, and a half-empty roll of tissue lying close to the pot.

When I closed the curtain, she shifted her beam across a metal filing cabinet, a single wooden chair, a cot with a pillow, and a desk. A digital clock sat atop the desk. The time shone in dim red numerals—1:14 a.m.

A thick book also sat on the desk, open to a page near the back, and a stubby black pencil lay nearby.

"Probably a log book," Shanghai said. "Maybe someone takes radiation readings here."

I shone my light on the page. Rows and columns ran from margin to margin. Numbers written in pencil by a careful hand filled each cell. Most readings ranged between four and five, though a few recent entries were above six.

Shanghai set a finger on the page. "Six point three. That's the last reading."

I looked at the wristband. A 5 glowed on the surface. "Higher than it is right now, but it's still too hot for my liking."

"And the fallout rain might make it worse. That stuff is sizzling."

I continued scanning with the beam. "I wonder where they read the level."

"Here." Shanghai set her light on a box attached to the wall and leaned close, squinting. "Looks like five point one." When she stepped back, her gaze followed the wall up to the ceiling. "This is where the tower is. The sensor is probably up top."

"Or maybe multiple sensors, and it calculates an

average." Lightning flashed again. More thunder boomed, and the sound of cascading rain washed through the cramped room. Water dripped from the ceiling in one corner, safely away from the cot. "Obviously we're not going any farther tonight."

"Nope." Shanghai turned off her flashlight. "Best to get some sleep and start again in the morning."

I sat on the chair and pointed my beam at the cot. "You can sack out there. I'll take the floor."

She shook her head. "No way, Sir Chivalry. I'm not some Miss Flower Girl who needs her petals pampered."

I laughed under my breath. "That cot is hardly pampering."

"Compared to the floor, it is." She removed her cloak, folded it, and laid it on the floor. "Besides, you had a harder day than I did."

"On one condition." I sat on the cot. "If we have another situation like this, you get the better bed."

"Suits me. Fair is fair."

After we each used the latrine and cleaned up the best we could using the towel moistened by water from our bottles, Shanghai lay on the floor with her head on the cloak and closed her eyes.

I turned off my flashlight and settled onto the cot. The pillow emitted a musty odor, but as tired as I was, it wouldn't bother me. Troubling thoughts might pose a bigger problem.

Closing my eyes, I let the storm's noise carry my mind toward sleep. Every time a temptation rose to think about my parents, I brushed it away. Yet, haunting images of their faces resisted my efforts. What could I focus on to replace them? It would have to be something captivating. Maybe the Sancta?

I probed my memory for her image—the red cloak, her soft brown hair and smooth skin. Yet, her physical appearance was only part of her overwhelming presence. If only I could hear her voice, that melodic, mesmerizing voice, then I could ignore the calls to grieve and instead fly away with her into the world of dreams.

I whispered, "Speak to me, Sancta."

In my mind, she cocked her head as if not understanding. I repeated my words, though I kept them whisper quiet to avoid disturbing Shanghai. "Speak to me, Sancta."

Although the mental image's lips stayed motionless, her voice entered my ears. "What do you want me to say, young Reaper?"

I opened my eyes. The Sancta stood at the foot of the cot, her face and cloak glowing. I glanced at Shanghai as she lay sleeping in the aura's wash. Lightning flashed in a window, followed by a roll of thunder.

Keeping my voice low, I asked, "Am I dreaming?"

Her humming laugh rippled through the aura. "No, but my denial is poor proof, is it not?"

"True." I rose and sat cross-legged. "Why are you here?"

"You called for me." She sat on the cot. Her weight pushed it down, proving that she was more than a spiritual presence. "You asked me to speak but provided no question."

My heart seemed to swell within. Her beautiful voice chased away every shadow of sadness. "Will you always show up when I call?"

"When I am able." She folded her hands on her lap. "There are places I cannot go."

"Like where?"

"Within the Gatekeeper's abode."

"Why are you appearing to me now? I've been a Reaper for almost four years and never saw you before."

"A worshiper of the Highest Power requested that I help you, so I have come to be your guide, at least for a while."

"A worshiper? You mean Singapore?"

The Sancta nodded. "I know her as Akua. We met before she became a Reaper."

"If you're my guide, then why do you come only when I call? I mean, I could be way off course by now."

"Perhaps. Yet you are not."

I blew out a sigh. "Good. I was worried about making it to the Gateway on time."

"I said nothing about your schedule. I indicated that you are not off course. A sojourner might never stray from his course and yet arrive too late to complete his task."

"That's true." I shifted my feet to the floor and sat closer to her. "Do you know if Sing and Misty have been thrown into the abyss?"

"I do not. The abyss is within the Gatekeeper's abode."

"Then you can't possibly know if I'm going to be late."

"Once again, not so. There is a time-sensitive issue that you seem to have forgotten."

"What is it?"

The Sancta's brow bent. "Have worries clouded your thinking? Have you so quickly abandoned pursuit of your beloved's regeneration?"

"Regenerate Misty? How?"

"Misty?" She shook her head. "I do not speak of Misty."

"You said my beloved."

"Do you have only one beloved?"

"Should I have more than one?"

The Sancta looked at Shanghai. "Do you not love this female who sleeps at your side?"

"Shanghai? She's my friend. My close friend, and I do love her, but—"

"If she were in mortal danger, would you cast your body down and die in her stead?"

"Well, yeah. I kind of already did that."

"Is it not love to sacrifice one's life for another?"

"Sure. I guess it is."

"Then Shanghai is your beloved." The Sancta straightened her back and looked me in the eye. "Young Reaper, what name may I call you?"

"You mean you don't know it?"

"I know both of your names. I am asking which one you prefer."

"Phoenix. My Reaper name."

"Phoenix, love is proven by one simple demonstration. If you give of yourself to someone with no thought of a return benefit, then you love that person. That is all that is needed for someone to qualify as your beloved."

I nodded. "Okay, then Misty and Shanghai are both my beloved."

"And?"

"And what?"

She again folded her hands on her lap. "Oh, Phoenix, must I spell this out as one might to a child?"

Her words pricked like a needle. "Look, I'm sorry I can't read your mind. Sing told me a Sancta might be cryptic, but…" I let the sentence die. Sing? Of course. She was my beloved as well. Now I felt really stupid.

The Sancta gave me a knowing nod. "I see the light of realization in your eyes and the blush of shame on your cheeks."

Although her comment made me feel three inches tall, her expression gave no hint of superiority. Her hands-in-lap posture seemed kind and unassuming. Yet I couldn't keep asking questions and feeling stupid afterward. I had to think before I spoke.

I backtracked through the conversation to her earlier question—*Have you so quickly abandoned pursuit of your beloved's regeneration?*

Then something Bartholomew said came to mind. He mentioned the possibility of preserving Mex's body while someone tried to retrieve his soul, but that option would require him to start the preservation process right away. I had thought of that soon after Sing killed herself but dismissed it, thinking Erin wouldn't do anything to keep Sing from deteriorating.

I gazed into the Sancta's patient eyes. "There's still a chance to regenerate Sing."

"A chance? Perhaps. Since I am not with Akua, I do not know. I was merely trying to reveal your loss of purpose." Her penetrating gaze stayed locked on me. "You have the knowledge to discern whether or not a chance to regenerate her remains. I do not have it. Therefore, you must seek your own counsel."

"Why would Erin make sure Sing's body is preserved?"

"Again, I do not know. Erin's mind and motivations are beyond my reach."

"Did she kill Peter?"

The Sancta nodded. "I was with Akua when it happened. Yet I do not know what became of Peter's soul."

I flinched. Even though Peter acted as an enemy, the thought of Erin killing him shook me to the core. Cold-blooded murder? Someone had to stop the madness. "Any advice on what I should do next?"

"Continue following your course. I cannot provide counsel beyond that, because the future is often unpredictable, and crucial events are taking place even as we speak." She laid a hand on my cheek and blew softly into my eyes. The sensation tingled, much like the touch of the energy line. "Sleep, Phoenix. Your mind has been in turmoil. In such a state you will not find the answers you seek... the deep answers... the answers that will restore this world. You must rest. Be at peace. Morning light will provide new revelations. All you need do is remember. Piece together your scattered memories. The result will serve you well."

When the Sancta rose, the cot creaked. She walked to the door and passed right through it without a pause. Lightning flashed, sending a burst of light through the window. Then all fell dark. The Sancta was gone.

As thunder rumbled in response, I lay back with my eyes open. How could I sleep now? So many new thoughts tumbled about as if tossed in the storm. Yet, the tingling sensation from her breath lingered, like a subtle numbness that drew my eyelids downward. The room's darkness seeped into my mind and pushed out the turmoil. Within seconds, I fell asleep.

CHAPTER NINE

"WELL, I DIDN'T expect to see a couple of Reapers conked out in my office."

I opened my eyes. A man wearing khaki everything from his pants to his cap stood in a shaft of dim light coming through the open doorway. Short, stocky, and sporting a reddish mustache, he gave me a half smile. "Did you hear a death bell, or are you on a ghost-hunting safari?"

"We're on a journey." I prodded Shanghai's shoulder and sat up in the cot. "I hope it was all right to stay here."

"I should say so. I haven't had company in eons." He sat in the desk chair. A few spider-web strands hung on his mustache, and dirt smudged his forehead, but he emanated no noticeable odor. "I'm guessing you're on a hunt. I've seen a few ghosts here and about, and I always tell them to head east. That's where the Reapers are. But I suppose they have to send Reapers into the Wilds every so often to collect the stragglers."

Shanghai picked up her cloak, climbed to her feet, and brushed dust from the seat of her pants. "What's your name, sir?"

He took off his cap, revealing closely cropped red hair.

"Sal, short for Salvador. I'm named after a place, just like Reapers are, but I've never been there. Have you?"

"To Salvador?" I shook my head. "Never."

"Same here." Shanghai draped her cloak over her shoulders. "We go where we're told."

Sal snapped his fingers. "Nobody's been there. I'm hoping someone'll tell me what it's like, 'cause I'm sure I'll never get there myself."

"I'm Shanghai." She touched herself on the chest, then shifted her finger toward me. "This is Phoenix. Neither of us has been to our namesakes either. Both cities were burned to the ground."

"Well, ain't that the bricks? Named after a pile of ashes."

I rose from the cot and straightened my clothes. "Well, it's been nice meeting you, Sal, and we appreciate the accommodations, but we should be on our way."

"Now don't you be running off so soon. I've been talking to lizards and scorpions to keep my sanity. Finally I got a couple of humans in my shack, and you're ready to ditch me."

I glanced at Shanghai. Grinning, she gave me an approving nod. I nodded in return and sat on the cot. "All right. We'll stay for a little while. Our motorcycle needs to charge anyway."

"Good." Sal settled back in his chair. "I saw the scooter. Sun's shining right on it. Should be ready to go in an hour or so."

I looked at the clock on the desk—6:17 a.m. "Okay. We leave in one hour."

"How far do you expect to go?"

"We don't know yet. Maybe as far as the scooter will take us."

"North or south?"

"We're heading west."

"West?" Sal's eyebrows lifted high. "Are you out of your ghost-chasing minds? You'll be a pair of shriveled skeletons before the end of the day. Buzzards wouldn't bother picking your bones. Not that there are any buzzards west of here, but you get my meaning."

"Is the radiation that bad everywhere to the west?"

"Not everywhere, but if you stay on the westbound road you'll hit some pockets that'll peel the skin right off your carcass."

"How do you know?" Shanghai asked.

"Because one of my jobs is to map the radiation zones in this region. I have my own scooter, and I take readings. I've found more than one lost wanderer lying in the ditch, let me tell you. And it ain't a pretty sight."

"How do you survive the dangerous pockets?"

"I dodge them. When I get to a high-level area, I skirt around the boundary and label that spot dangerous on the map. No one cares how high it gets inside danger zones. Folks just want to steer clear of them, so I go out there every day to keep the boundaries up to date."

I showed him my wristband. It registered a 5. "Will this wristband be enough to avoid those zones?"

He shook his head. "Too slow. Riding that scooter, you could be tasting air that's eight or nine before that band changes to seven. You need a sensor that will give you instant readings."

"How can we get one?"

"You're out of luck." Sal withdrew a small yellow box

from his pants pocket. "I have the only instant sensor for miles, besides the one on the tower here. You can't take either of them. I need mine for safe surveying, and the tower sensor's welded on."

"Will you come with us?" Shanghai asked. "Lead the way on your scooter. Warn us about danger pockets."

Sal stroked his chin. "Well, now that's a thought. A dangerous adventure with a pair of Reapers. That'd put some bounce back in my step." He turned his head toward the desk and looked longingly at the record book. "But it would be a shame to leave my duties behind. I'm the dedicated sort. Never missed a day of work in my life."

I rose and flipped the book's pages to the front. The first page's ratty edges flaked off with my touch. "Who looks at the log?"

"Lately? No one." He pushed the sensor back into his pocket. "It's been more than a year since an inspector came by."

I turned the book to the last-used page. "Then they probably won't care if a few entries are missing."

Sal eyed the door. "You just watch. The first time I skip a reading, the inspector will show up with a sharp pencil to fill out my pink slip. They never announce their visits ahead of time."

"Speaking of pencils..." Shanghai stepped to the desk and picked up the logbook pencil. "You could..." She looked at the desk for a moment before putting the pencil back in place. "On second thought, maybe not."

"Something wrong?" I asked.

"Nothing critical." Shanghai sat next to me on the cot. "I'll tell you later."

Sal intertwined his fingers behind his head. "While

we're waiting for our solar cells to sip some sun, let's have a little chat. First, you two tell me about yourselves, then I'll tell you about me."

I nodded. "Fair enough."

Shanghai and I gave Sal a summary of our lives—our training, duties, living conditions, and a few blow-by-blow accounts of reapings. He sat in wide-eyed awe as Shanghai told of a battle with the souls of two murderers who, while she was partially in ghost mode, tried to freeze her heart with their icy hands. Since he seemed to enjoy that tale, I related how we collected souls at the executions and sometimes had to fight evil ghosts in front of a blazing furnace at the crematorium.

When we finished, Sal whistled. "Well, you two sure have more exciting lives than mine, but maybe I can let you in on some secrets that you probably never heard in your training school."

I looked at the clock again—6:55. "Sure. Let's hear it."

"As they say, a picture is worth a thousand words." He pulled a photo stick from his pocket and closed his fingers over it. Glowing mist seeped upward between his fingers and formed into a building hovering above his hand. Smokestacks rose from each side of the structure and pushed billowing clouds into the air that vanished as they passed beyond the hologram's upper boundary.

Sal leaned closer and spoke with a storyteller's cadence. "Once upon a time, workers at a nuclear power plant began a dangerously stupid experiment. A mad scientist tested a crazy theory that was supposed to supply the world with energy forever. He thought he could duplicate the sun, put it in a box, and let it fuse atoms together for eternity." Sal snapped his fingers. "Boom! Instant energy."

In the hologram, light burst within the building. The walls melted, revealing a fiery yellow sphere. Flares erupted from the sphere's surface and whipped the surrounding air as if lashing out at anyone who dared draw near.

"As you see," Sal continued, "things got out of hand in a hurry. Those idiot scientists started a fire they couldn't put out, so what did they decide to do next? I'll tell you. Something even stupider. They dropped a nuclear bomb on that pseudo-sun to snuff it. But not just any nuclear bomb. It had a payload of materials that was supposed to smother the flames, like a blanket over a campfire."

An explosion ripped the fireball to shreds. Thick smoke shot upward in gray plumes that spread across the sky.

Sal's eyes grew wide. "Smoke... ash... dust flew everywhere, and radiation charged every last particle. It collected into one ginormous cloud that covered the entire earth." He looked upward. "And when we try to count the stars above like our ancestors tell us about in their tattered diaries, or watch for meteors streaking across the heavens, all we see is our dirty blanket. The fireball is out, but its smoke still chokes the life out of us."

He opened his hand. When the hologram disappeared, he breathed a long sigh. "And that radioactive blanket is why souls can't escape from this world, and why we need our friends the Reapers to take us to the Gateway when we die."

After letting his words settle for a moment, I gave Sal a nod. "I knew most of that story, but where was the power plant located?"

"West, young man. Farther back in the Western Wilds. The scuttlebutt says that it was smack dab where the

Gateway is now. The explosion created a hole in its own smothering blanket."

"Does that mean the radiation level will be highest there?"

"Probably, but I ain't anxious to bust through the boundaries looking for it."

"Can't blame you for that." I checked the clock once more—7:10. "It's time to go."

"I'll get my scooter." Sal put his cap on, leaped from the chair, and hurried out the door, leaving it open.

"Now that we're alone." I set a hand on Shanghai's arm. "I have something to tell you. The Sancta visited me again during the night."

Her brow lifted. "Oh? What did she say?"

I gave her a quick summary of the conversation. While I spoke, Shanghai's facial expression remained stoic, unreadable. When I finished with the Sancta's mention of Sing's possible regeneration, Shanghai clutched my wrist. "Have you figured out what she meant by having the knowledge?"

I shook my head. "I haven't had time to think about it. Sal kind of dominated our morning."

"Speaking of Sal, I wanted to tell you—"

"Hey, Reapers," Sal called from beyond the door, "let's get going."

"We'll talk on the road." I walked outside. Near the eastern horizon, a rising red sun pierced the usual haze. On a nearby dirt path, Sal sat on a single-rider electric motorcycle, one fist around a handlebar and the other clutching his radiation sensor.

"Adventure time," he said with a playful growl. "Let's head into the jaws of death and find those ghosts you're looking for."

With Shanghai at my side, I walked our bike behind Sal. When he took off to the north, we jumped aboard our saddle and followed. Within a half mile, the path intersected with the main road where we turned west.

Stunted trees with withered green leaves grew here and there. A dense cluster ran along a meandering line parallel to the highway where a muddy creek flowed swiftly eastward, most likely swelled by last night's storm.

I withdrew Sing's watch. The hands pointed straight ahead. So far, so good. I raised my voice over the hum of the motor. "What did you want to say about Sal?"

"Remember when I picked up the pencil?"

I pushed the watch back to my pocket. "Yeah."

"Dust covered the desk except where the pencil was. It hadn't been moved in a long time."

"Maybe it's just really dusty and it collected overnight. Or maybe Sal carries another pencil. The one on the desk looked ready for the trash can."

"Could be. I tried to read the last entry date on the log, but it was just a series of numbers, some kind of code. All the dates were like that, too."

I focused on Sal. He held his meter at eye level and scooted along at about 30 miles per hour. "What are you concerned about?"

"I just can't figure out why a man is stationed at this dangerous outpost keeping a record that no one cares about."

I laughed. "Since when do the powers-that-be need a good reason to do something? Most of them are bureaucrats who're trying to justify their jobs."

"True." After a few seconds of silence, she moved her hands from my waist to my shoulders. "Let's get back to

Sing. What knowledge do we have that'll help us figure out if she can be regenerated?"

"Well, we know her body has the medallion around her neck, and it's sending a signal that..." I peeked at my own medallion as it swayed on its chain. Alex had said if the medallion were to be separated from me, it would stop functioning. It matched the DNA in the blood it carried with my own DNA. How could Sing's medallion function if she were dead?

"Phoenix, you clammed up. What are you thinking?"

"I'm wondering how Sing's medallion could be working. She was definitely dead. No doubt about it."

Shanghai patted my shoulder. "That's our answer. Erin hooked her up to a preservation device, like what Bartholomew mentioned. It's keeping the signal going."

"Erin wouldn't do that unless she's on our side."

"Or Alex's side," Shanghai said. "When they were together at the portable depot, they seemed pretty cozy."

"Then why didn't Alex mention Sing's medallion? If she knew about it, I think she would've spoken up. She likes to show off what she knows."

"True, but I can't believe Erin's helping us on her own, not after seeing how callously she participated in those executions."

"Can't argue with that." I focused again on Sal. He continued puttering down the road in the same pose. Ahead, the highway appeared to be leading into a more hilly area. The chances of continuing in a straight westward line would soon fall.

"What does your meter say?"

I looked at my wrist. A 7 glowed. "It's a seven."

"Seven? That means we're already cooking. And if your meter is slow to increase, then Sal's might be even higher."

"Let's check." I accelerated. The road ascended into a long incline, but the scooter had no trouble catching up with Sal. As we rode side by side, I called out, "What does your meter read?"

He turned the box toward me. "Seven point two."

I showed him my wrist. "Mine says seven."

"Yep. Yours is keeping up pretty good."

"Isn't it getting risky? Should we get off the road and try to find a safer path?"

"Just about to do that. There's a persistent radioactive bubble coming up that I always avoid. We'll be in a safer area in a few minutes. Don't worry. I've done this a thousand times."

"Okay. I'm trusting you."

"Good. That makes two smart things I've noticed about you."

"What's the other one?"

He nodded toward Shanghai. "Hitching up with her. She's a winner, if you don't mind me saying so."

"I don't mind. Just remember, though, that Reapers are martial arts experts."

"Got it. Don't be fresh." Sal looked straight ahead. "Forget I said anything."

Shanghai laughed. "You have nothing to worry about, Sal. And thank you for the compliment."

Sal touched the bill of his cap. "Thank you for not knocking my block off."

I decelerated and pulled in behind him. "Looks like we have no choice but to keep following."

"What does Sing's watch say now?"

While Shanghai looked over my shoulder, I withdrew the watch again. The hands pointed to the left of straight ahead. "We're getting off course."

At that moment, Sal drove off the highway onto a narrow dirt road that angled left and continued climbing in altitude. While I followed, I kept glancing at the watch. Our new direction lined up with the hands.

"A coincidence?" Shanghai asked.

"Maybe not. People get to the Gateway somehow. Even the flying machines probably can't go through high radiation. There must be a safe path."

The trees thinned out until the surrounding landscape became nothing but cracked ground and solid rock, not even a sprig of grass.

"No vegetation," Shanghai said. "That doesn't bode well."

"The radiation must be spiking here." I looked at the wristband. It registered an 8. "We're really getting cooked now."

"Should we turn back?"

"Sal said to trust him, but this is getting ridiculous." I shouted ahead. "Sal, what does your sensor say?"

Just as we neared the top of the incline, he called out, "Nine point one!" Then his scooter crested the hill and kept ascending, as if launched into the sky. He punched the air, shouted, "Woohoo!" and vanished along with his motorcycle.

I gasped. Shanghai clutched my shoulder and cried out, "Sal's a ghost!"

CHAPTER TEN

W HEN WE REACHED the top of the hill, I stopped our motorcycle and looked up where Sal and his scooter sailed away. No sign of him anywhere.

We dismounted and walked to the end of the path. A cliff plunged into a bowl-shaped valley that appeared to be at least three miles across. Massive trees covered the entire valley floor with lush foliage—a blanket of green that concealed everything underneath.

I whistled. "How do these trees survive with such high radiation levels?"

"No clue." Shanghai stepped to the edge and looked down. "That's quite a drop."

"Any idea why Sal would lead us here?"

"Questions later. Let's get to a safer place."

I checked my wristband. A numeral 9 flashed red. "We'd better take a pill first. Then we'll head south and find the energy line. Maybe from there we can get into the valley and under the leaves." ·

After washing a pill down with what remained of our water, we remounted the scooter, turned south, and followed the lip of the bowl. At times we had to retreat to the east to avoid a crack or uneven rock, but the treeless terrain allowed for unobstructed turns. The sun felt stronger here. Exposed skin on Shanghai's hands and face dried out and took on a reddish hue. My hands looked the same, and my face probably did as well.

As the bowl's lip shifted gradually back to the west, I held a hand high to feel for the energy line's tingle. Although the air temperature stayed mild, the dryness, and probably the radiation, sapped our moisture. We had to find water soon.

After nearly a mile, the tell-tale sensation crawled along my palm. I stopped the scooter and set my feet. "It's here."

Shanghai dismounted, raised her hands, and waved them while sidestepping away from the cliff, as if she were cleaning a wall. After stopping, she reversed course, her hands still lifted. "Okay. I know how it's running." She stepped to the edge and looked down. "The energy line goes straight into the valley."

I withdrew Sing's watch and read the hands. They pointed in the same direction. "It must be at least a hundred feet to the bottom. We'd never survive a jump. Even if we grabbed a tree on the way down, we'd get ripped apart."

"Then we'll have to try it as ghosts, but I have no idea how gravity will affect us or how we'll adapt to the plunge. This is all new to me."

I nodded. "At least as ghosts we'll get out of the radiation. We'll fry if we stay here."

Shanghai touched one of the motorcycle's handlebars. "I don't think we'll be returning the bike to its owner anytime soon."

"Not likely." I dismounted and engaged the kickstand. "It's not like a horse that can find its way home."

"I suppose it can't be helped."

"A minor worry. Let's move." Taking a deep breath, I concentrated once again on the energy flowing within. Soon, the familiar mist congealed around us.

Shanghai sidled close to me and touched my arm. "Okay. Looks like we're ready."

I looked down into the bowl again. "So we just jump?"

"I suppose so. Sal didn't seem scared, though he might be half insane."

"Or he intentionally brought us here and showed us what to do."

Shanghai tilted her head. "Why would he do that?"

"I'm wondering if the Sancta whispered in his ear. If we went into the Wilds by ourselves, we wouldn't have gotten this far. The radiation levels would've turned us back."

"That's true. I was nervous long before it hit seven."

I extended a foot over the edge. "I guess I'll go first."

Shanghai leaped, calling out, "Last one to the bottom has to kiss Alex." She dropped and disappeared in the mist.

I jumped after her. During the first half-second, the plunge felt as fast as expected, but when I hoped for a slowdown, I decelerated as if I could control the descent. Within another second, I drifted more like a leaf than a human body.

Soon, I touched down next to Shanghai. Her grin proved that she was enjoying this new experience. She punched my arm. "This would be a breeze if not for the energy loss."

"And the recovery period." I scanned the area—nothing but the wall we had fallen from, leaf debris, tree trunks, and hovering mist. "We'd better go physical again. We can't find the right direction as ghosts."

"Over here looks good." Shanghai sat on the ground with her back against a tree. "That was a short stint as ghosts. Maybe recovery will be easier."

"Let's hope so." I sat next to her and started the transformation. Within seconds, the mist cleared, though dimness still permeated the area. The dense forest allowed only dappled sunlight through the canopy.

I looked at the wristband. Although it swayed in my dizzied vision, the 5 was clear. A second later, it changed to a 4. "We're at four. Much better."

"So we're in an oasis. A perfect place for the Gateway, but I wonder how they keep the radiation out."

I let my gaze wander through the foliage above. "The trees could filter it, but then they would suffer. Maybe they're some sort of resistant hybrid."

Shanghai rose. Blinking, she wobbled for a moment before standing straight. "I'll find the energy line."

Still sitting, I withdrew the watch. The hands pointed directly away from the wall.

Shanghai pointed parallel to the wall. "The line goes this way."

I rose and showed her the hands. "Sing's not in the same direction now."

"So do we look for the Gateway or Sing's body?"

"Her body. Sing is a concrete reality, and she wants us to find her. We can come back to the line later if we have to." I lifted a leg, but it felt like a saturated log. "We'll have to take it slow."

"Yeah, I feel like I weigh a thousand pounds."

Holding the watch in front like a compass, I trudged ahead. At times, my feet dragged, but I couldn't help it. Shanghai kept pace with me, though she winced with every step.

We dodged trees, plowed through fallen leaves, and stumbled over protruding roots, but we made steady progress as our legs slowly returned to normal.

After a few minutes, Shanghai grabbed my arm and stopped. "I hear something."

"What does it sound like?"

"Like an animal growling."

I rotated in place, focusing on the sounds in the air— the brush of the breeze in the tree boughs, the pops of twigs somewhere among the endless maze of trunks, but no growls. If we were being stalked, the animal was smart enough to stay quiet when we stopped.

"Alex mentioned bestial threats." I slid the watch back to my pocket and plucked a dagger from my weapons belt. "I can follow a straight line for a while. Just stay alert."

Shanghai withdrew a dagger of her own. "Lead the way. I'll watch and listen."

I plodded onward and kept my focus ahead, trusting Shanghai's keen senses. If a wild beast were to attack, we had the ability to defend ourselves, but if several pounced together, could we escape? With our legs still rubbery, maybe not.

An unearthly screech erupted from our left. A glowing cat the size of a leopard leaped from the woods. Shanghai slung her dagger. The blade pierced its head, passed right through, and kept flying. The cat dropped to the forest floor, screeching in pain.

I lunged at it and drove my dagger into its back. An electric shock sent me flying backwards with the hilt still in my grip.

After rising on wobbly legs, the cat slinked away into the forest. The radiance around its head and back wounds flickered like dying lightbulbs.

Shanghai found her dagger and picked it up. "I hear more cats."

I froze and listened again. Soon, the growls reached my ears—at least three, maybe as many as five.

"Let's move." I jogged ahead, urging my legs to pump faster, but they wouldn't obey. At my side, Shanghai ran with thumping footfalls. Again she winced in time with her steps.

Just as the growls began diminishing to the rear, a cat dropped from a tree and blocked our path. Like the other one, it glowed as if electrified. Although poised to pounce, it merely watched us, snarling.

I looked back. Four more cats weaved around the trees in a stalking march, all glowing eerily. They would be on us in seconds.

"Ghost mode," I whispered.

Shanghai nodded. "Good call."

I willed myself into phantom status once again. Immediately my legs felt light and strong. Within the mist, the cats, now no longer glowing, continued their approach from behind while the one in front kept its stare locked on us. "They can see us."

"I think these cats are ghosts," Shanghai said. "Somehow they're charged with electricity in the real world."

"Maybe a ghost dagger can kill a ghost cat." I charged

toward the cat in front. It leaped at me, and we collided chest to chest. Its momentum sent me stumbling back. As the beast dug its claws into my shoulders and I plunged my blade into its chest, I rolled into a backwards somersault and kicked the cat with both feet. It landed near Shanghai and lay motionless.

"Good job." Shanghai stood with her dagger poised to strike. "Now get off your butt and help me."

I leaped to my feet and stood at her side. The other four cats stalked closer, their bodies low and their hackles raised. "Let's see what our smoke can do in the ghost realm. If it makes a good screen, you take the two cats on the left. I'll take the two on the right."

Shanghai nodded. "Got it."

I popped four capsules from my belt and threw them at the cats. Shanghai followed with four of her own. When they struck the ground, smoke erupted and blossomed in eight expanding clouds.

"Now!" Holding my breath, I ran through the smoke and slashed with my dagger. The blade struck flesh. A cat squealed. My next slash cut flesh again. More squeals erupted. A third swipe hit only air. Nearby, cat shrieks pierced the smoke. Soon, all was quiet.

I reached toward Shanghai. "Where are you?"

She grasped my hand. "Here."

I pulled her out of the smoke and took a deep breath. As the haze dispersed, the bodies of three cats appeared, the one I had stabbed earlier and two new carcasses. The other cats had fled into the woods.

Shanghai prodded one of the bodies with the toe of her shoe. "How do ghost cats die? Aren't they already dead?"

"Good question. And I have another." I looked at my

dagger. No blood on the blade. "Can the cats kill us while we're ghosts?"

"We're better off believing they can." Shanghai sheathed her dagger. "At least the survivors will think twice before attacking us again."

"Let's hope they warn their friends to stay away." I slid my dagger to its sheath. "We'll stay in ghost mode. I don't think I need the watch for a while."

"Agreed. Recovery is too crippling."

"Double time." I jogged along the path I had set earlier. Shanghai caught up and ran abreast. This time avoiding the obstacles proved much easier as we hopped over roots and passed straight through trees. For now, the advantages of ghost mode outweighed the drawbacks.

After we had run for several minutes without tiring, the trees thinned, and a clearing came into view. I slowed to a walk. Shanghai did as well. Ahead, a circular expanse of grass stretched out at least three hundred paces, bordered by the forest at its perimeter. A shaft of light shone from above, its shape a cylindrical column with perimeter boundaries at the edge of the woods. Mist rose from the grass and towered into the sky through a bright hole in the blanket of clouds, apparently the same size as the column of light.

I stopped a step or two before the clearing's edge. The mist rose in streaming ribbons that painted an undulating haze throughout the entire glade. "Why didn't we see this from the cliff? It's too big to miss."

"Maybe because we weren't in ghost mode up there. We jumped as soon as we transformed." Shanghai raised a hand and set her palm inches from the boundary. "I sense the energy right in front of us. Even stronger than the line we followed."

"Could this be the Gateway?"

"Maybe. I always pictured a gate like we see at the depot." She extended her arm into the mist. Her hand stretched, and her body lifted off the ground. "Phoenix!" she called as she rose higher. "Help!"

CHAPTER ELEVEN

I GRABBED SHANGHAI'S LEGS and heaved backwards. She popped out of the current, and we tumbled together to the ground, her body sprawled over mine.

She rolled off and rose to her knees, breathless. "What just happened?"

"You were getting sucked into the air." I climbed to my feet and helped Shanghai to hers. "Sal mentioned a hole in the cloud shield. Maybe this is the place. Since we're in ghost mode, we can't walk under the hole without getting caught in the suction."

She brushed her hands together. "Then this is a dead end. One step more and we're inside a vacuum cleaner."

"We'll have to transform again and find a safe place to recover."

"Let's backtrack a bit. We're too close for comfort." Shanghai led the way to a tree, grabbed the lowest branch, and swung up to it. As soon as she climbed to the next branch, I followed. My body felt light and nimble, as if I were a small fraction of my real weight.

After a minute or two, we sat together on a wide limb

about twenty feet from the ground, our legs dangling. "Did you feel as light as a feather?" I asked.

Shanghai nodded. "Almost like I could fly."

"Maybe that's the reason the recovery's so hard. It's a gravity issue. The longer we're in this state, the more our bodies adapt to the feeling. Then when we return, gravity kicks in and our bodies react. Even our brains get whacked, so we feel dizzy. It takes a while to adjust."

"If it's as bad as the first recovery, we'd better tie in." She pulled a line from a spool on her belt. "Help me wrap this around the trunk. There's room for us both to sit on this limb with our backs to the tree."

Soon, we had pulled the line around the tree and our bodies as we sat side by side facing the clearing, each of us dangling a leg to the side of the limb. I attached the loose end of the line to my belt, securing us in place. "Okay. Let's transform."

I concentrated on the energy flow once again and guided myself out of the ghost realm. Within seconds the mist cleared, though the fog in my brain thickened.

The entire world rocked from one side to the other, then jerked back. Nausea churned, and my bones ached, especially my tailbone where my weight pressed against the supporting limb.

I shifted to ease the pressure. If not for the spool line, I would have toppled off.

Shanghai whispered with a weak moan. "I'm getting sick."

"Same here. This one's the worst. Probably a combination of low energy and high radiation."

As my vision settled, the area ahead clarified. The clearing was gone. Now trees extended onward without a break. Something white lay in the midst of the forest, a massive building of some kind. But we were in no shape to investigate.

Below, one of the cats prowled at ground level, glowing now that we were again in the real world. It looked up, its feline eyes radiant.

"A cat," I whispered. "It sees us."

Shanghai looked down. "We can probably handle one. If it brings company, we're sunk."

The cat turned and loped away. "It's gone. Let's hope you didn't give it any ideas about bringing more."

Shanghai clenched her eyes closed. "Sorry. I can't watch. I'm just trying not to vomit."

"We have to find water, but anything on the ground around here might be contaminated." I kept my eye on the spot where the cat went. At any second, we might have to fight again, but we needed more recovery time.

After a couple of minutes, a human figure dressed in Reaper's garb ran from that direction and stopped next to our tree. When he looked up, his familiar dark face came into view.

I called out, "Noah?"

Smiling, he scaled the tree and sat on our limb, facing us. "I'm Cairo now. Have you already forgotten?"

"No, Cairo. It's just... well... I knew you as Noah for so long." Grief stabbed my heart, throttling my voice. "I'm so sorry. My plan got you killed. And your poor mother. I don't know how I'm going to tell her."

"Yeah." His smile evaporated. "That's the worst part. I don't mind so much, 'cause I want to see Tanya again. But with me and my sister both dead, my mother will be alone. She still has Harold and Aunt Valerie, but they don't live close by."

Shanghai gave him a nod, though she winced at the effort. "Glad to see you, Cairo."

He nodded in return. "Likewise."

"So how did you get to the forest?" I asked. "The last I saw you, you hopped into the trunk of Erin's car. What happened after that?"

"Well, I stayed in the trunk because I knew Peter would see me if I tried to pass into the backseat. When the car stopped, I peeked out. Erin and Peter walked to a fly-ing machine, but I didn't know until later that it could fly. It looked like one of those helicopters in the history books, but it didn't have any propellers. Anyway, Peter was car-rying Sing's body. I figured he'd be distracted by that, so I followed pretty close behind. When they got to the flying machine and Peter put Sing inside, Erin shot him in the back of the head. He flopped like a fish for a second and then went limp on the seat.

"Then Erin got in, so I sneaked in with her. She pulled out a computer tablet and tapped on it. A few seconds later, the machine lifted off the ground. Then some kind of gas spewed from the ceiling, and Erin fell asleep. The machine flew really fast, and it landed in a clear spot in this forest. When Erin woke up, she got out and ran, like her house was on fire. I followed her to that line." Cairo pointed toward the area that used to be a clearing. "But just as I stepped across, something tried to suck me up. I barely jumped away in time."

"So she just left the bodies in the flying machine?"

"Not for long. She ran back, carrying a little box of some kind, and she got into the flying machine again.

Just as I was about to get in with her, she flipped a switch on the box, and a light flashed around the seating area. It stayed lit and shimmered. I tried to get in, but I just bounced back. Then the machine lifted off and flew toward that clear area where I can't go."

Cairo shrugged. "So I stayed here, thinking maybe Erin would come back. I wasn't sure what else to do."

"Staying here is dangerous," I said. "Did you see the cats stalking this forest?"

"Yeah. I ran away and hid in the trees. I think their eyesight's pretty bad. They tracked me, but when they looked up, they never saw me."

"I'm pretty sure one cat saw us up here. I'm guessing they can see us no matter what mode we're in." The bark pinched my backside, forcing me to shift to a more comfortable position. "I think the area that tried to suck you into the sky is the Gateway. You would have been drawn into eternity."

Cairo looked upward. "Where Tanya is?"

"I haven't figured it all out yet, but I think so."

Shanghai tapped my thigh. "I hear growls."

Deep in the forest, a massive glow appeared, shifting toward us like a living tide of radiance. The scout cat had returned with a horde.

I reached for the spool line. "Cats are coming. An army of them. Since they know we're up here, we'll be trapped if we stay."

Cairo hopped off the limb, dropped to the ground, and looked up. "I'll see if I can distract them." He ran toward the approaching cats.

"Shanghai," I whispered, "I'll anchor you. Go ahead and drop."

She slid off and dangled by the line while I swung my leg over the limb and held on. As she released line, she descended. When her feet touched, she sat cross-legged and looked up. "Your turn."

I detached her, wrapped my own spool line around the limb, and lowered myself in the same manner. The moment I landed, I unhooked the spool and reached for her hand. "We have to run."

"I guess crawling's out of the question." She let me hoist her up. "I'll do my best."

With a chorus of growls heightening behind us, we slogged toward the former clearing. As I shuffled, my legs felt like concrete.

Shanghai took a step, dragged a foot, then took another step. To the rear, Cairo sprinted toward us. At least twenty cats pursued, half of them only seconds behind. With so much electrical energy in those feline bodies, they could turn us into toast.

"Hurry!" I slid an arm around Shanghai and pushed with my legs, half carrying her. She, too, forced a burst of energy. The cats' approaching glow brightened the trees around us. The growls spiked. Cairo shouted a long whoop.

I tripped on a root and flew forward with Shanghai. As we fell, I jerked out my dagger and flipped over to face the onslaught. Shanghai turned with me. We slid to a stop on our backs and raised our daggers.

Cairo ran closer. A dozen cats chased him while several others stayed back. Electricity arced across their sleek fur and shot from their razor teeth. When Cairo and his pursuers raced past, the cats didn't seem to notice us. Their fierce eyes stayed locked on Cairo.

He leaped, but instead of falling, he flew straight upward and disappeared past the treetops. The cats tried to stop, but their momentum sent them sliding and tumbling into the upward vacuum. They shot into the air and vanished high above.

The trailing company of cats, at least eight, stalked toward us. We helped each other up, then backpedaled until we crossed the boundary where Cairo left this world. Dizzy and off balance, we sat with a thud.

Just two steps away, the cats stayed behind the boundary, pacing and snarling as their radiant bodies cast flickering light over us.

Shanghai mopped her brow with a sleeve. "Whew! That was close."

"Way too close." I massaged my legs. Every muscle burned, and nausea again stirred in my stomach—a cauldron of sickening swill. "How are you feeling?"

"Like a volcano of vomit ready to erupt. I think my bones are trying to tunnel through my skin."

"Radiation poisoning. Leaving ghost mode has never been this bad."

"Should we take another pill?"

I shook my head. "Too soon. Maybe the pill we took will work in a little while."

"Or maybe we got cooked too long for a pill to make any difference."

"Could be. The radiation is really strong." As a gentle breeze cooled my hot cheeks, I looked up at the hole in the clouds and whispered, "Good-bye, Noah. Thanks for everything."

"Well, we'd better not sit here on our duffs. Sick or not,

we have to keep moving." Shanghai grasped my wrists. "Together on three."

After counting to three, we pulled each other to a standing position. My calf muscles cramped. I raised and lowered my legs and tried to shake out the spasms. After a few seconds, the pain eased.

We turned away from the prowling cats. About a hundred yards in the distance, a white building stood in the midst of the forest. Although trees veiled the building's details, they couldn't hide its massive size—at least a city block wide and two stories tall.

"It's not a clearing anymore," Shanghai said.

"I noticed that earlier. The trees and building aren't visible in the ghost world."

"Maybe this area has some kind of cloaking mechanism that ghosts can't see through. Even Reapers."

"Another mystery." I exhaled. "Okay. Now the fun begins."

Shanghai's keen eyes scanned the forest. "No sign of guards. Maybe they think no one could get this far. Humans would die falling into the valley, those cats could kill humans or ghosts, and ghosts would get sucked into eternity from this point on."

"Let's hope you're right." I withdrew Sing's watch. The hands pointed toward the building. I forced my legs into a balanced stride. Every step felt like my feet were on fire. My muscles throbbed, and the swill in my belly sloshed. Shanghai's lips trembled as if she were ready to throw up at any moment.

As we drew close to the building, the middle portion took shape. Three stairs led to a semi-circular foyer that jutted out like a tongue. The main structure rose thirty feet high and spanned hundreds of feet to the left and right. Thick vines curled over the rooftops in spiral twists, like fibrous serpents constricting the arms of a prostrate man, forcing his tongue to stick out.

When we reached the bottom of the stairway, I slid the watch into my pocket and studied the building's structure. Made of ivory-colored bricks, it carried no hint of stain, mold, or mildew. It sparkled like freshly polished marble. Yet, since trees grew close all around and branches brushed the exterior, it seemed that the entire building had been constructed before the valley gave birth to these woods.

Above, tall steeples covered with leaf-green shingles crowned the rooftops, making the expanse above the building look like an elevated forest. No wonder I hadn't noticed it from the overlook at the edge of the valley.

I glanced at the sun. Since we had been traveling west for so long, it took only a moment to orient myself. The building's door faced due south, and the wings extended due west to the left and east to the right, as if the builder had planned a compass-like layout.

"Phoenix, look." Shanghai pointed toward the western wing. "The energy line."

To the west, a fence of shimmering radiance appeared out of nowhere, ran twenty feet or so, and entered the far end of the wing.

"And over there." She pointed in the opposite direction.

A mirror image of the western side, another radiant fence ran into the end of the eastern wing. I imagined our familiar depot and mentally traced the energy line as it traveled in opposite directions. To the west, the way we followed the line, it ran straight to the building's western wing. To the east, it traversed the entire world, running through other depots like ours, until it terminated at the eastern wing.

I whispered, "The terminus."

Shanghai nodded. "It's like walking into a fairy tale. We're finally at the Gateway."

"No use gawking. Let's go." We climbed the steps to the door. I turned its crystalline knob and pulled. The door swung open noiselessly. Inside, the foyer's marble floor extended to an intersection of hallways several steps to the north.

At the center of the intersection, a man sat at a table, his body turned toward us. His elbows leaned on the table, and his hands propped his head in a studious pose. Not moving a muscle, he appeared to be a statue of the Gatekeeper, perhaps a wax figure.

Since the anteroom seemed to be safe, we stepped inside, leaving the door open in case we needed to retreat in a hurry. To the right, water spurted vertically from a waist-high pedestal similar to a birdbath, an oasis of sorts, perhaps designed for visiting Council members.

"Think it's safe to drink?" I asked.

"Most likely." Shanghai leaned over the fountain, drank deeply, and washed her face in the flow. When she rose, she let out a long "Ahhh."

I drank and washed as well. The cool water felt and tasted wonderful. When I finished, I looked at the meter on my wrist. A numeral 1 shone in the display. "No radiation here." I took the band off and slid it into my pocket. "Let's go."

We walked across the anteroom and stopped at the

statue. The Gatekeeper's likeness studied a chessboard, its medieval-themed pieces in mid-game array. An empty chair stood at the opposite side of the table, as if inviting someone to sit and take part in the match.

Adjacent to the statue, one corridor led to a wing on the west side, another led to a similar wing to the east, and a third proceeded north toward a large chamber in the distance, each passageway wide enough for a half-dozen people to walk abreast.

On the ceiling, three-foot-wide swaths of white radiance hovered along flat panels, one swath coming from the west and the other from the east. The two joined above our heads and turned to follow the north-bound corridor's ceiling toward the rear of the building. Far to the north, the combined energy line exited through a gap between the ceiling and the top of a double door.

"The depot energy lines," Shanghai whispered.

"The terminus is past that door." I checked the watch again. The hands pointed toward the western wing. "To the left." Just as we took a step in that direction, two dark creatures appeared at the end of the corridor. Wearing black cloaks with hoods that shadowed their faces, they looked like living phantoms.

We ducked behind the statue and drew our daggers. As if floating, the creatures glided closer, though at a slow pace. A flash of light covered one of them for a full second, then it dimmed. Two seconds later, the other one lit up and dimmed in the same way.

I whispered, barely moving my lips. "Alex mentioned illuminaries. That must be what these two are."

When the specters drew near, details emerged within their hoods—skeletonized faces and bright red eyes. They each flashed again and turned toward the entry door, staying at the same, unhurried pace. Seconds later, they proceeded outside and out of sight.

I shoved my dagger to its sheath. "They acted like sentries on patrol."

"Not very observant sentries." Shanghai resheathed her dagger. "Let's look for Sing."

We rose and walked side by side through the westbound corridor and into an enormous chamber. Upright glass cylinders with domed tops filled the room, arranged in a matrix with gaps big enough to allow passage between rows and columns.

At the center cylinder in the closest row, we stopped and peered through the glass. A semitransparent girl, maybe ten years old, stood upright, hovering over a white disk—a foot-high pedestal the size of a manhole cover. Wearing blood-drenched jeans and T-shirt with an arrow protruding from her chest, she looked like she had been shot by an archer. Her closed eyes and motionless body indicated sleep or some other form of unconsciousness.

A hologram stood within her—a phantom superimposed on another phantom—the same girl dressed in immaculate jeans and T-shirt, shooting an arrow from a bow. She plucked another arrow from a quiver on her back and fired again, and the sequence continued in a loop, arrow after arrow, while the girl's spirit slept on.

"A ghost," Shanghai whispered.

"I've never heard of a sleeping ghost."

"Maybe they're sedated somehow."

"The hologram is probably from her photo stick." I ran a finger along the glass. "Now we know another reason they download the images into the Gateway system.

Whoever operates this room might not be able to see the ghosts, so the hologram identifies them."

I crouched and touched a rectangular meter on the pedestal. A glowing blue number read 96%. "I wonder what this means."

Shanghai leaned over and looked at it. "No clue."

"Maybe a visibility measurement." I lifted a flexible tube that ran between the pedestal and the next one. Another tube connected that pedestal to the next and so on. At the end of the row, the final tube merged with those at the ends of other rows into a single tube that attached to an adapter in the wall.

I rose and touched the pedestal with the toe of my shoe. "These are the same as the ones the corrections-camp prisoners were making."

"So that's why it was such a big secret," Shanghai said. "The pedestals were coming here."

I studied the watch's hands. They pointed directly into the gap between the girl's enclosure and the one to its right. "Sing's in here somewhere."

"I suppose she could be." Shanghai set her hand on a glass enclosure. "But these are ghosts, and Sing was wearing the medallion on her physical body."

"Then her body and her soul might both be in this room."

"And maybe your parents, too."

"Right." I scanned the ghosts within view. No faces seemed familiar. "Do you know what they look like?"

Shanghai nodded. "I saw the photos you kept in your room back when we trained together."

"Good. Let me know if you recognize anyone."

With Shanghai following, I walked along the gap toward the western end of the wing. Men, women, and children stood in quiet slumber, all with solemn expressions, though their superimposed holograms frequently displayed them running, eating, or dancing, a stark contrast... and a morbid one.

As we continued down the line, the ghosts appeared more and more haggard—withered, thin, wrinkled. Even the children looked progressively gaunt and prune faced.

After at least thirty rows, the ghosts seemed barely human, nothing more than twisted wisps with hollowed eye sockets and open mouths. Thin, skeleton-like hands and bony feet protruded from clothes that hung like limp rags over their dwindled frames. In the final three rows, the enclosures stood empty.

I halted at the end, a step or two from a blank wall. "This setup's draining them until they wither away."

"Souls in specimen jars." Shanghai clutched her stomach. "I think I'm getting sick again."

I backtracked and crouched at the pedestal of one of the most emaciated ghosts. The meter showed 4%. "It's measuring how much is left of them."

"But what is the system sucking out of them? Their vitality? Their energy?"

"The conspiracy theorists have long said that the Gatekeeper consumes energy from the souls. Maybe this is how he harvests it."

"By draining them to nothing."

"Let's see if these things move." I grasped the sides of an empty enclosure while nudging the pedestal with my foot. The entire unit slid easily along the smooth marble floor. "Not hard at all."

Shanghai touched another empty enclosure in the last row. "I guess when they drain a row of souls, they take the pedestals to the front, fill them with new souls, and start again. It's like an assembly line... or a disassembly line."

"Let's see if we can find where the souls come in." I walked with Shanghai to the northwest corner of the chamber where the swath of energy entered through a square gap near the ceiling, like a transom over a door. The gap's lower edge was a foot or so above my head. "Feel up to giving me a boost?"

"For a few seconds." She interlaced her fingers and set her hands near my knee. "Ready."

When I set my foot, she boosted me to the gap. I grabbed the edge and muscled up until my forearms rested on a two-foot-wide ledge—the sill of a window to another room. Now that I was bearing my own weight, Shanghai straightened and tapped one of my dangling legs, whispering, "Remember those sentries might come by soon."

I acknowledged with a nod and focused on the new room. At the far wall, the energy line entered as a vertical fence and passed through an upright glass flywheel that looked like a revolving door. With each turn, the flywheel extracted a ghost from the line and threw it to the right into a huge tank with transparent walls. Inside the tank, a tangled mass of ghosts squirmed about, their size reduced by the compression.

An illuminary opened a door to the tank, pulled a semi-transparent woman out, and set her on a pedestal. Stunned and confused, she wavered in place while the illuminary set a glass enclosure over her head. The illuminary stooped at the pedestal and tapped on a computer tablet. A moment later, a hologram of the woman appeared, superimposed on the ghost. A high-pitched noise emanated from the pedestal. As it quieted, the ghost drifted into an unconscious state.

The illuminary pushed the pedestal-and-glass combination into a gathering of several others and returned to the flywheel. After a few more souls flew out of the energy line, the illuminary repeated the process of putting a ghost in an enclosure, apparently not concerned that its rate of removing souls from the tank could never keep up with the rate that souls were being stuffed into it.

As I watched the imprisoned souls squirm in the tank, I winced. How many could that tank hold? Since they weren't physical, no theoretical limit existed, but they appeared to be uncomfortable as the containment shrank their size.

I returned my focus to the incoming energy line. After it passed through the flywheel, it twisted ninety degrees and rose to the ceiling, ran over my head, and into our room.

I dropped to the floor and gave Shanghai a quick summary of what I had seen. When I finished, she looked to the east. "Probably an identical process on the other end."

"Probably. This entire setup is a torture chamber. It's worse than anyone in the Resistance ever imagined."

"It's like a drainage farm, a field of ghostly crops."

"Good analogy, but here's what I don't get. Why does the Gatekeeper need so much energy? He's just one person. Why drain so many souls?"

"No idea. Another mystery to solve."

"They're piling up." I looked at the watch again. The hands had reversed and now pointed in the direction we had come. "That's strange." I showed the watch to Shanghai. "I didn't see Sing, but she must be here somewhere."

Shanghai peered down the column gap we recently traversed. "We'll just follow the hands until they pinpoint her."

"This way." I walked eastward. When I passed the halfway mark, the hands swept around and pointed in the opposite direction. I stopped and turned toward Shanghai. "She has to be right around here somewhere."

For the next minute, we checked every pedestal in the area. With each sad, withering face I looked into, my own sadness grew, and my body aches seemed to heighten.

When we reconvened near the center of the room, I spread out my hands. "No sign of her."

"Same here." Shanghai glanced around for a moment, then looked up. "The watch's hands can't point in three dimensions."

I followed her gaze. The ceiling lay about ten feet above our heads, much lower than the height of the building. I turned the watch vertically. The hands pointed upward. As I rotated it clockwise, the hands moved along the face, constantly pointing toward the ceiling.

"We have to find a stairway. But first let's check every pedestal for her soul." I slid the watch back to my pocket. "She hasn't been dead long, so if her soul is here, she should be in that tank in the other room or on a pedestal in the first few rows."

Shanghai nodded. "You take the left half of the room. I'll take the right."

We hurried to the eastern side of the room and walked back westward from pedestal to pedestal. Near one end of the second row, I came upon an enclosure that held a girl wearing a leotard. I set my eyes close to the glass. Although her face was pale and thinner than usual, her identity was clear—Molly Fitzpatrick. Her hologram, dressed in a ragged ballerina tutu, danced and twirled within her ghostly frame.

"Shanghai. Over here. It's Molly, Colm and Fiona's daughter."

Shanghai joined me and looked into the enclosure. "I saw this one earlier. I've never met Molly, so I didn't recognize her."

"I wonder if I can wake her up." I tapped lightly on the glass. Molly's eyes opened. She looked at me and blinked as if confused. Then, her face ablaze with alarm, she set her nebulous hands on the glass. She seemed to be shouting, but no sound came through. Her lips formed "Help me, Phoenix" as well as other words, though I couldn't make them out.

I wrapped my arms around the glass and lifted the enclosure an inch. Something hissed. Molly's body stretched toward the gap. When I set the glass back in place, she returned to normal.

Molly dropped to her knees and wept, her hands covering her face as her projected self danced over her head.

"What do you make of it?" Shanghai asked.

I shook my head. "It's strange. A special glass ghosts can't penetrate. I've never heard of such a thing."

"Why don't we lift it and let her out?"

I pointed upward. "In the ghost realm, we're under the hole in the shield, so I'm worried she'd get sucked into the sky. Since the system partially drained her, she'd go to eternity in a crippled state."

"If it's the wonderful place it's supposed to be, maybe she'd get restored."

"Maybe's not good enough. We have to be sure." I crouched and waved my hand in front of Molly, but her eyes were still covered. "There has to be another way to get her out."

Shanghai crouched with me. "How?"

I ran a finger along the bottom edge of the enclosure where it met the pedestal. "If one of us lifts the glass, maybe the other could reap her and absorb her in a cloak before she takes off."

"No way. She's level three, and our energy's low. Even at full strength we can't do a level one that fast. Never mind a level three."

"Maybe disconnect the tubes to stop the bleeding." I shook my head at my own idea. "That might break a vacuum seal in the whole network, and everyone would get sucked out."

"The answer's not in this room, Phoenix. We have to find a way to shut the entire system down."

"I guess you're right." I tapped the glass again. Molly lifted her head. Tears dripped and disappeared inches from the pedestal floor. "Molly." I formed each word carefully. "I'll be back for you. I promise." I wrapped my arms around the cylinder as far as they would go.

As I rose and stepped away, she lunged and set her palms on the glass. Her wordless scream was easy to read. "Phoenix! No! Don't leave me in this awful place!"

"There's nothing we can do." Shanghai curled her arm around mine and pulled. "Staying will just make it harder."

I tore my stare from Molly and gave in to Shanghai's pull. As I drew away, Molly's terrified face flashed in my mind. She trusted me, and I rewarded that trust by sending her to this torture chamber. Even if I had to take this building apart pebble by pebble, I would get her out of here.

CHAPTER TWELVE

EVER WATCHFUL FOR the sentries, we hurriedly looked at each enclosure, nearly five hundred in all. Sing was not among the tortured souls. When we returned to the anteroom where we first entered, we stopped at the statue of the seated Gatekeeper and looked down the corridor that led to the north end of the building.

In a chamber a hundred feet away, a pair of staircases led to the second floor, one to the left and one to the right. I shifted my gaze to the eastern wing. If it held another drainage farm, as Shanghai called it, we had to search there for Sing's soul.

"This way." With Shanghai close behind, I hurried to the wing and into an identical room filled with deteriorating ghosts trapped in glass enclosures. Although we failed to locate my parents, we found Colm in the first row and Mex three rows back, all asleep. Colm appeared as normal as ghosts could look, but Mex had shriveled to a shadow of himself, thin and wrinkled. I didn't bother trying to awaken them.

Of course, we failed to find Tanya. She died long ago and probably would have been sucked dry long before now. Then again, maybe this system hadn't been put in place at that time. Alex intimated that things had changed of late, including the appearance of the illuminaries. Maybe Tanya skipped the torture and flew into eternity.

As we walked again toward the hallway intersection, I whispered to Shanghai, "That's nearly a thousand of those enclosures. Colm told me they had built about a hundred and fifty."

"Other corrections camps probably supplied the rest," Shanghai said. "It might be a worldwide effort."

At the statue, we turned into the corridor leading north toward the rear of the building. High columns rose against the sides of this marble-coated hall. Portraits of the Gatekeeper hung in the gaps between the columns. Each oil painting showed him in a different pompous pose, either speaking on stage to an adoring crowd, kissing children, or handing wrapped gifts to women dressed in rags. Yet with no one here to look at them, the statue and gallery must have been placed for the purpose of self-admiration.

Trying to keep myself from gagging, I walked on, following the line drawn by the combined energy streams running along the ceiling. If Alex was right, this route would take us to the dome room. With every step, a tingling sensation increased, as if we were approaching the line's most concentrated point.

After about fifty paces, we stopped in front of enormous mahogany double doors, carved with ambiguous faces and flower designs, the surfaces polished to perfection. Above the doors, the energy stream passed through the gap I had seen earlier.

To the west and east, each staircase—marble steps and oaken banisters—rose to an overlook with a waist-high wall that formed a three-sided balcony. A person on that level could walk around and peer down on this room from any point to the east, west, or south, or he could leave the area through a passage on either side that led southward, back the way we had come.

I set my ear against the door. The voice of a man penetrated but no distinguishable words. A woman answered. A few disconnected phrases made sense. "Preparations are complete... Still no sign of Tokyo... We can proceed when..." Then the voices lowered further.

With my ear still at the door, I whispered to Shanghai, "A man and a woman."

"The Gatekeeper and Erin?"

"Maybe. The woman mentioned Tokyo." Footsteps sounded, drawing closer. "Someone's coming."

Shanghai pointed at the stairway to the west. "That way."

Keeping our footfalls light, we ran up the stairs, hid behind the half-wall, and peeked over the top.

The huge door opened. Erin walked out with the Gatekeeper. Dressed in jeans, casual shirts, and athletic shoes, they looked ready to go to a picnic. The Gatekeeper's unearthly white glow accentuated his dark curly hair, making him look like a storybook angel, though his clothes failed to match the mold.

They stopped in front of the door and faced each other. The Gatekeeper extended a hand toward Erin's shoulder, but she dodged his touch and shook a finger, smiling. "No, Melchizedek. Remember your promise. Just three more days."

"I apologize." His voice resonated in the chamber like

echoing thunder. "But when we come together, you will be mine, body and soul."

"Of course." She ran fingers through her reddish mane in a seductive manner. "I can hardly wait."

Melchizidek folded his hands at his waist. "What will you do now?"

"I'm going to the control room to search again for Tokyo. She has to be in the grid somewhere."

"Might you use Singapore as bait?"

Erin shook her head. "Singapore's soul is already in the abyss, as you directed."

I clenched my teeth. That was the worst news possible.

"Oh, yes." The Gatekeeper sighed. "It's a shame to waste such talent, but we do what we must." Without another word, he walked to the eastern stairway and disappeared behind it.

Erin pushed the huge door closed. Blinking, she looked around as if searching or listening. Then she shrugged and walked toward the western stairs.

I whispered to Shanghai, "Let's move."

Staying low, we hurried away from the stairs through a passage leading toward the front of the building. Flat carpet and plaster walls guided our steps to a door on the right, but it was locked. We hurried on to the far end of the hall where a door blocked our way.

I opened it and peeked in. Nothing but darkness lay within. I stepped inside with Shanghai, turned, and pulled the door until only a narrow gap remained.

With Shanghai at my shoulder, we peered together into the hall. Erin stood at the top of the stairs, looking down as if talking to someone on the first floor. Her words drifted through the hallway. "They have to be here some-where. When you find them, bring them to me."

She nodded, then waved a hand. "Just be quiet about it." After nodding again, she twisted her face into a dis-approving scowl. "All right. I'll come with you. But your model is supposed to be equipped to deal with Reapers. You shouldn't need help." She stalked down the stairs and out of sight.

I whispered to Shanghai, "Could you hear who Erin was talking to?"

She shook her head. "Maybe one of the illuminaries. She referred to models, so maybe they're like robots."

"Maybe. They didn't seem very smart." I turned and scanned the room. In the dimness, it appeared to be empty. "See if you can find a light switch."

Shanghai ran her hands along the wall. Something clicked, and ceiling lights flashed to life. As my eyes adjusted, I blinked. The room, about a quarter the size of the soul-sucking chamber below, held nothing. Flat gray carpet extended to the four walls, all bare except for the north wall. To the left of the door we had entered, a hinged panel the size of a kitchen oven hung a few feet from the floor, a pair of pull handles protruding at the center.

I stepped to the panel and pulled the handles. Two doors swung out, revealing a blank computer screen with a recessed drawer that held a keyboard and electronic sty-lus. "Erin mentioned a control room. This might be where she was going."

"Then we don't have much time." Shanghai pushed a button at the base of the monitor. As a hum emanated, the screen brightened, showing a diagram that looked like a floor plan.

She picked up the stylus. "I'll try to figure this out while you get another read on Sing's body."

"Sounds good." I withdrew the watch and looked at the face. The hands pointed to the west. As I walked that way, the hands slowly turned clockwise until they aimed north, directly at the wall.

I ran a hand along the bare surface. "She must be in a room behind this wall, probably where that locked door leads."

"According to this building plan, there's an access panel right about where you are." Shanghai touched the screen with the stylus. "I think this should open it."

Something clicked. A door slid to the side, revealing a glass enclosure standing in a closet-like cavity. Veiled by shadows, a pale female ghost floated within the glass, semitransparent and motionless. "Shanghai," I whispered. "It's someone's soul. A female. Not Sing, though."

"Just a second." She touched the screen again with the stylus. The floor inside the closet shifted forward, carrying the enclosure and its supporting pedestal into the room.

When it stopped, I gazed at the ghost—Misty, still wearing the cloak Alex had used to disguise her. With her head drooping and her eyes closed, she appeared to be asleep. Her silky tresses hovered like a splash of orange around her beautiful face.

I swallowed, barely able to breathe.

Shanghai sucked in a breath. "Misty?"

I nodded.

Shanghai looked at the floor near the pedestal's base. "I don't see any hoses attached. They must not be draining her energy."

I cleared my throat and rasped, "Looks that way."

"Are you going to wake her up?"

"I'll try." My body shook, rattling my voice. "Do you see something that will allow sound to penetrate?"

She scanned the controls. "There are hundreds. I don't know which one is Misty's." Shanghai's eyes locked on something. "Here's a switch that'll turn them all on." Using the stylus, she again touched the screen. "That should do it."

When I poised my hand to knock on the glass, Shanghai said, "Wait."

"What?"

"Um…" Her eyes shifted to the entry door. "I'd better stand guard in the hall in case Erin comes." She exited, leaving the door open a crack.

As Misty slept on, I stared at her. Obviously Shanghai left so we could have some time alone, but her departure made me feel stripped naked. How could I face Misty now? I had failed to save her life. I had failed to protect her soul. And now she was trapped in a specimen jar with no way out.

I rapped on the glass. Misty's eyelids fluttered. When she raised her head and looked at me, a weak smile crossed her lips. "Hello, my dear friend." Her Scottish accent came through as lovely as ever.

"Misty…" A bitter lump swelled in my throat. I swallowed, but it wouldn't go away. "I'm sorry I couldn't save you. I tried. I really did."

She pressed a phantom hand against the glass. A ghostly copy of her pewter ring encircled her finger. "I know you did. I saw everything. You have a heroic heart, and I am blessed that you worked so hard to rescue me."

I set my palm against hers, begging the dividing glass

to melt away. How strange that her mind conjured the ring even though Alex stole it from her body. She also wore a thin chain with a crucifixion cross dangling at her chest. I had seen such manifestations before. Wishful remembrance allowed some ghosts to dress themselves in favorite outfits, though most wore the clothes they died in. "Do you know how you got here?"

"I am aware of bits and pieces of my journey. A young man named Peter reaped my soul. He was kind with his words and set me at peace. For a long while, he and a woman conversed, but I understood very little. Then Peter fell silent, and I didn't hear from him again. After that, I saw only darkness and felt only emptiness until you awakened me."

I nodded. No need to tell her about Peter's death. "Did he say what they did with your body?"

"The woman mentioned it. She located my half brother, Camden, and arranged to have my body sent to him to be buried."

My heart sank. No chance of restoring her. Not that there was much of a chance before. The rumors about keeping a body intact and reinfusing a soul were probably just that—rumors, regardless of what the Sancta believed about Sing's chances. "I wish I could let you out, but you would get sucked into eternity."

Misty's brow lifted. "What would be wrong with that?"

"Well, you'd be transported to the sky, the unknown."

"Is the unknown worse than the known?" She touched the glass. "The known is a prison. The unknown is freedom."

"You hope it's freedom. You can't be sure."

"All of life is based on hope. Without hope, we would

all be miserable wretches. A blind man with a tin cup hopes for a coin. A starving cat rubs against a leg, hoping for a saucer of milk. Where would they be without hope?"

I stared at her sincere eyes. When we spent time together, as short as that time was during my sanctioned visits home, she had never been so profound, so poised in speech. It seemed that wisdom had blossomed during the years we were separated.

Misty heaved a sigh. "If a blind man or a cat can have hope, then so can I. My hope is that my flight to the heavens will be a return to the one who created me."

"Created you?" An image of Misty rising through the clouds came to mind, but picturing her bowing before a creator seemed impossible. With all the suffering in the world, not many people bothered believing in a god anymore. Those who shoved us along the paths of life were too cruel. "I guess I'll hope for that with you."

"As you should. Hope blooms in the soils of suffering. Those who are prosperous in this life rarely long for the next. Comfort stunts hope, while pain makes us long for hope's fulfillment."

"Misty, that's... that's really profound."

Her smile grew. "You are kind, but the wisdom is from others who have come across my path, and suffering teaches unforgettable lessons."

"Suffering? What happened?"

"More than you might want to hear." Her expression turned dark. "Shortly after you left, my foster parents and my sister died in an influenza outbreak, so I went to live with an ailing elderly woman who gave me room and board in exchange for my aid. When I arrived, I found her living in squalor, and I turned the rats' nest into a livable apartment. When she died, I stayed there and paid the rent on my own, but I had to work at a laundry three miles away.

"At fourteen years old I was laboring twelve hours a day just to survive. I lived alone in a shantytown filled with drug addicts, winos, and hookers. Once in a while I took in a girl who wanted to get clean, thinking she might be able to share the rent or household chores, but the arrangements never worked out. One girl beat me up and robbed every penny I had. Another contracted an STD, and I cared for her without access to medicine until she died. A third came down with scarlet fever, and I caught it from her. I missed too many days of work and lost my job."

My heart ached. Why couldn't I have been there to help her? "I'm really sorry, Misty. I didn't know."

She raised a hand. "Of course you didn't. I'm not telling you this to make you feel sorry for me. I want you to understand why I am ready to leave this sea of suffering. You see, I was so distraught about the lack of medicine, I went to work for a smuggler in the shroud, hoping to make supplies more readily available for everyone, but a few weeks ago I was caught and later sentenced to death. Just two days before my execution, someone whisked me out of prison, blindfolded me, and hours later bound me to that chair in the corrections camp. I heard shouts and fighting but had only the faintest idea what was going on until the hood came off and I saw you." She bowed her head. "You know the rest."

The horrible moment flashed in my mind, an image of Misty jerking as the sonic gun popped. I stared at the floor. "I do."

"I sense that suffering has taught you many lessons as well."

"Too many. Sometimes I get everything confused. I don't know which way is up."

"Aye, I know that feeling. Suffering provides tools for living, but it often feels as if hammers and screwdrivers are being thrown at you."

Still looking down, I laughed in spite of the heartache. "That's a good illustration."

"It is not my own. I heard it from a Sancta. Have you ever heard of the Sanctae?"

I refocused on her. "Yes. Only recently. I met one while on my journey here."

Her smile returned. "Then we both know how wise they are. While I was in prison awaiting my execution, a Sancta came to me. She told me that I need not fear death. Since I have suffered for the faith passed on to me by my foster mother, I should have confidence that my hope in the next life will be realized. She set me at peace, and I was ready to die. But when I saw you, fear erupted again. Not for me, but for you. I saw no hope in your eyes, only fear."

"I feared for you, not for myself."

She nodded. "I can believe that, but what about hope? You have likely suffered as much as I have. Don't you look forward to leaving this wretched world?"

"If the Gateway leads to a better place, of course I want to go, but what about the people I would leave behind? I need to stay here no matter how wretched the world is. You talk about hope, but if I leave, what hope will the people who count on me have?"

"Ah, yes. You are right. The Sancta told me about people like you. You are a mirror. Those who suffer look at you and see the creator reflected in your love, and that glimpse gives them hope—hope that your kindness and sacrifice come from a heavenly source. They hope their last heartbeat will lead them to a better place, the abode of the loving God they see in you."

Heat rose into my cheeks. She was giving me way too much credit. "Well, I'm not sure about reflecting the creator, but I do want to be kind and sacrificial for the people in my district. That's why I don't think much about leaving. Or about hope. I just do what I have to do."

She nodded again. "Aye. You were always the dutiful one. Yet perhaps now hope will sprout in your heart, since leaving this world is the only way we can reunite." Her smile widened. "Together with me for all eternity wouldn't be so bad, would it?"

"No. Of course not. I always dreamed about being with you when I finished my term. It was the only thought that kept me sane."

She curled a hand around the cross at her chest. "Then hold to that thought. Someday it will happen. We'll finally be at peace with our creator."

I spread my arms. "How do you know? I mean, how can anyone know they'll go to a place of peace? No one's been there and come back."

She released the cross and laid a hand on her chest. "You ask how I know. Well, I ask how you know that no one has come back from eternity?"

"Tokyo tried. If she couldn't do it, who could? No Reaper is more powerful than she was."

"True. No Reaper is more powerful. But the Sanctae are more powerful. The one who spoke with me said she has traveled beyond the Gateway. She told me joy abounds to those who cling tightly to their hope."

"And you believed her?" I shook my head. "Sorry. Of course you did. I just—"

"You just want proof." Her stare took on a probing aspect. "I have only the Sancta's word, and that is enough for me. Isn't it reasonable to trust someone who demonstrates great power and love?"

I averted my eyes. "I suppose so. When we were low on water, the Sancta told me where to find some, and she was right."

"There. You see? Power and love wrapped in simple instructions. Yet even without an eyewitness account from a Sancta, I know there must be a creator. All of life sings of such a being."

"Life sings?" I shook my head. "I've never heard any singing."

"Oh, how tragic! The air is filled with song. As a Reaper, don't you have times alone to listen to the music of the city?"

"I listen all the time. I hear the cries of sick children, the wails of their mothers, the laments of their fathers. And when a final breath draws close, I hear them gasp for air. They choke through narrowed throats, because they can't get medicine to reduce the swelling. Why? Because the god of this world deems it so. The tyrant who wants them to suffer and die.

"Then when the gasp turns into a death rattle, I hear a death alarm. No melody. No tune to hum. Just a thud in my heart—heavy, dark, oppressive. I follow it until I find the suffering soul, and then I send that soul here to suffer even more. Whatever hopes they had are dashed. Their torment goes on and on." I gazed at Misty's face again. Sparkling tears dripped from her eyes and vanished. "I don't reflect hope. I bring darkness. I deliver souls to torture. If there is a creator, then I'm the worst reflector possible. Unless the creator is evil. Then I'm a perfect portrait."

"Ah, my dear friend, listen to your prose. It is poetic and lyrical. You have heard singing, but it is a song of shadows, hope stifled, longings unanswered." She offered a sympathetic nod. "No wonder you feel hopeless. Your experiences have infused darkness into your soul, as my own tortures did to my soul for a time. Yet, perhaps your journey through the shadows has prepared you for this end. You had to hear the laments and suffer with the brokenhearted so your passions would be stirred and your brave heart would be emboldened."

She set a fist against her chest. "Since your heart truly reflects that of the creator, a heart that weeps over the evils perpetrated in this world, you can be his instrument to bring this suffering to an end so that all souls will finally go to the glorious place he has prepared for them. You can sing the creator's song and fill their hearts with new hope."

I spread out my hands. "But I don't know the song. How can I sing something I've never heard?"

"You have heard it. You just haven't recognized it. For almost four years you have withdrawn the spiritual from the physical, stealing souls from the bonds of corruption, proving that life continues after death. Souls must escape the shackles of earth and fly away, because the song of the creator calls them into eternity. Since souls exist, they must have a spiritual destination. Your very purpose demands that this be true."

"Then why are souls trapped in this place? Why hasn't the creator done something about it?"

"The smothering hand of evil has stifled the song, and the creator *is* doing something about it. He sent you to cut off that hand."

"Me? Who am I to wield a blade for him?"

"Who is anyone to do so? Yet, the creator has chosen you, and I will tell you why. You are filled with love. You act with love. You live for love. You think you have no hope, but with every fiber of your being you emanate hope. Otherwise you would have no care for those who look to you as a light in this dark world." Misty set both hands on the glass and drifted as close to me as possible. "You have been guided here to liberate the song. The creator knows you can do it. I know you can do it. Let that confidence seep into your own mind. Embrace it, and let it strengthen you for the task ahead."

Her words fell like raindrops on a parched land. As I soaked them in, they filtered through my body and sent cooling refreshment to every cell. "Misty, did you learn all this from the Sancta? Even the way you talk has changed."

She nodded. "Listening to her altered my entire outlook on life, as well as how I think and talk. My experiences had embittered me, but now I am content and ready to face whatever comes my way." She stooped and touched the base of the glass, her eyes staying trained on mine. "And now my dearest friend, I wish to give you a visual spark of hope. Release me from this prison and let me fly to my creator. Then perhaps during your darkest days you will remember that I am waiting for you, and we can both look forward to our reunion in a place of light where we can be together for all eternity."

Tears welled in my eyes as my throat tightened further. "But that might be years. I'm not sure I can stand it."

"Aye. You will continue to suffer while I am in comfort. It isn't fair, to be sure." She slid off her pewter ring. The moment it cleared her finger, it vanished. "Death breaks our covenant, Ariel. I hope you will find comfort in the arms of a woman who loves you as much as I have."

Ariel. My real name. I hadn't heard anyone utter it in almost four years. My mind raced back to the day I left home, the moment my Council escort let me see my mother one last time. After hugging me, Mother said, "Ariel means lion of God. You will need spiritual courage to survive the path before you."

I laid my palms on the glass and looked into Misty's hopeful eyes. It would take about two seconds to lift the enclosure and let her escape. But escape to what? To a place of light and comfort as she hoped? Or into space where she would float in eternal loneliness or maybe disperse into mindless limbo? Either way, anything would be better than getting her energy siphoned off to be consumed by the ravenous Gatekeeper. And shouldn't I grant her final wish and accept the spark of hope she offered?

I glanced at the door where Shanghai waited in the hall. She peeked through the opening, likely wondering what was taking so long. No matter. She would understand what I had to do.

Using both hands, I shoved the glass. It toppled to the carpet with a thud. Misty streamed toward me with her arms outstretched. I reached around her phantom body, but she slipped from my grasp and flowed upward, calling, "I will be waiting for you, my love."

Then she passed through the ceiling and vanished.

I closed my eyes and wept. Misty, my first love, maybe my only real love, was gone.

Someone slid arms around my torso and hugged me. "I'm so sorry, Phoenix. Go ahead and cry. I'm here for you."

Shanghai's voice. I pulled her into a tight embrace, our cheeks pressed close. She felt so warm, so strong, so... real.

"You can pretend I'm Misty if you want. Just keep your eyes closed and pretend she's here."

"No, Shanghai." I opened my eyes and ran trembling fingers through her tangled hair. "I need you to be who you are. You're the only friend I have left."

"I won't leave you." She kissed my cheek and pulled away, her hands holding mine. Tears glistened in her deep brown eyes. "I'll stay by your side no matter what."

"Thank you." I caressed her cheek. "I'll count on that."

Her face reddened, warming under my touch. She grasped my wrist and pulled my hand down. "Yeah... um..." She cleared her throat. "While I was in the hall, I looked at that side door again. The lock is electronic." She walked to the control panel. "I'll see if I can unlock it from here."

While she studied the panel, I put the glass enclosure on the pedestal. With a tap of the screen from Shanghai, the unit drew back into the wall, and the door slid closed.

"I found the lock control." She turned off the monitor and closed the twin panel doors. "Let's go."

CHAPTER THIRTEEN

W E ENTERED THE hallway and stopped at the side door. I opened it and peered in. Darkness prevailed except for a series of pinpoint red lights on the wall on the left that likely abutted the control room we had just exited.

Erin's voice came from the stairway at the end of the hall. "If you find any sign of Tokyo, contact me immediately."

I pulled Shanghai into the room, closed the door, and leaned against it. Erin's voice, now muffled, drew closer. "If she's here, we'll find her." The sound of a door opening and closing followed.

After pushing away, I grabbed my flashlight and flicked it on. "If we use the ceiling lights in here, Erin might be able to detect it from the panel."

"True." Shanghai's flashlight beam joined mine. "She'll know someone's been in the control room if she checks on Misty's soul."

"Maybe not. Erin might think Misty's invisible." I set my beam on a control panel that held blinking lights, numeric meters, and rocker switches. Below the panel, a coffin-like box made of glass lay on a long table. Hoses and wires ran from the box to the wall panel.

I walked to the box and aimed the beam through the glass top. Sing lay inside, motionless. No sign of breathing.

Tightening my grip on the flashlight, I whispered, "It's Sing."

Shanghai rushed to my side. Her eyes fixed on Sing, she grasped my hand and held it without saying a word.

I passed the beam along Sing's body. She wore her Reaper's garments—cloak, black running shoes, forest green pants, and dark tunic, the tunic open below the neck to reveal her embedded valve and the thin chain that carried her medallion. The chain had slipped back, and the medallion, now out of sight, likely lay hidden behind her curly dark hair. A flexible hose led from her valve through the glass and into a wall port, probably an energy feed to keep her body intact.

I halted the beam on Sing's face—peaceful, motionless, lovely. A memory drifted in—Sing sitting across the alley on her fire escape's railing. Her feet, wearing the same shoes, swung into and out of the moonlight. Her opening words—Hello, Phoenix—began a new friendship and introduced me to a true heroine, beautiful in every way. But now it was over.

A tear crept to my eye. Sing had fulfilled her quest to guide us here, but for what purpose? We had been obsessed with finding her by using the directional watch hand, but now that we had done so, all guidance vanished. What should we do next? The horrors of this place injected hopelessness into every thought.

I brushed the tear away. Grief had to take a backseat and stop clouding my thoughts. We were here to conquer the Gatekeeper and end this madness. We would avenge this heroine's death.

Shanghai shone her beam on the wall. A meter labeled Heart Rate read zero, and another labeled Body Temperature read 37 C. "Her temperature is normal."

"I guess this setup explains why her medallion didn't shut off. Her plan worked."

"But how did she know anyone would preserve her body?"

I shrugged. "No idea."

Shanghai shifted her beam to the right. "Is that another coffin?" She walked toward a second box, also lying on the table. When she shone the light inside, she gasped. "It's Peter!"

I stepped over and looked inside. Peter also lay in full Reaper attire, his hands folded on his chest. His blond hair had been combed neatly, making him appear unruffled by his murder, though his clothes bore wrinkles and a couple of tears, and his now-deflated muscles no longer filled out his tunic. Wall meters displayed a zero heart rate and a 36.8-degree body temperature. He, too, had a feeder hose running from the wall to his sternum valve.

Shanghai ran a hand along the glass. "Final proof that he's dead."

"But we didn't see his soul anywhere."

"Maybe he's in the abyss, too."

I looked upward. "Or beyond the Gateway. Since he was a Council member's son, maybe they just let him go."

"But what does *beyond the Gateway* mean?" Shanghai asked. "Remember Bartholomew said Mex was on the eternity side of the Gateway, but he could still be retrieved by a Reaper. Then he said he *sent Mex on*, whatever that means. I thought he meant beyond the Gateway, but now we know Mex's soul is in that room with the others."

"Sorry. No clue."

She let out a sigh. "I feel clueless myself."

"One thing's certain; the next step is to find Sing's soul."

Shanghai nodded toward the control room. "I studied the layout map and didn't see any other drainage farms, but I did find the abyss. We can go check it out now."

"But if they threw her soul into the abyss, why would they preserve her body?"

Shanghai pointed at herself. "You're asking me? I'm the head of the clueless crowd."

"You have company." I looked at the door to the hall. "Okay. Where's the abyss?"

"Downstairs. In that room Erin and the Gatekeeper came out of."

I walked to the door and set my ear close. Shanghai joined me, and we stood face to face, listening.

A chime from the hallway penetrated. "Hello?... Yes, Alex."

Shanghai whispered, "It's Erin again."

I nodded.

"I haven't seen them," Erin continued, "but we have evidence that a pair of Reapers were in the forest. Abandoned spool lines and dead ghost cats.... No evidence that they made it inside, but if they did, we have energy ports throughout the building. Maybe they'll find one and use it. They can't possibly survive the abyss without a recharge... He's in the abyss with Sing.... I used a sonic gun while he wasn't looking.... Yes, it's a shame. He was a powerful Reaper.... All right. I'll see you at the meeting in three hours…. No, I have to go over some affairs of state with Melchizidek…. I agree. Good-bye."

Footsteps sounded, drifting toward the stairs.

I stepped back from the door. "You guessed right. Peter and Sing are both in the abyss."

"Yeah." Deep lines etched Shanghai's brow. "Really convenient for us to hear all of that."

"I get your point. Huge coincidence to stop and talk where we could listen in."

"She knows we're here. She's just dodging us for some reason."

"If so," I said, "she knows what we've found. I'm not sure what game she's playing, but I'd feel more comfortable if we stayed away from her."

"No argument from me."

"One thing we do know. We have three hours to get into that room and out again with Sing's soul."

"And Peter's?"

Sighing, I gave her a halfhearted nod. "And Peter's."

"Hey, it won't hurt my feelings if you want to leave him behind. He's earned his place in the abyss."

"True. I guess we'll cross that bridge when we come to it."

"Okay. First step is to find one of those energy ports and get charged up."

I gestured toward the coffins. "Probably over there."

Guided again by flashlights, we walked to the coffins. Besides the hoses leading to Sing and Peter, two others dangled from spare wall ports.

I lifted one. "It's like Erin made everything ready for us. She knew the watch would bring us here. The hoses are for us."

Shanghai touched the other hose. "Then why did she mention ports throughout the building instead of these specific ports?"

"Maybe because Alex doesn't know about Sing's medallion."

Shanghai cocked her head. "Are you thinking what I'm thinking?"

"Let's skip that game. What are you thinking?"

"Erin knows we're inside the building. She must've brought Sing to this room and preserved her body for the purpose of leading us here. But Erin, who is now Melchizidek's sweetheart, is hiding Sing from Alex. Alex is out of that loop."

"But why?" I asked. "We know Alex wants to conquer Melchizidek. Is Erin trying to protect him from her?"

"What else could explain what she's doing? He elevated her from a lowly depot clerk. She's obviously going to guard his backside."

"I'm not so sure. Did you see her dodge his touch?"

Shanghai nodded. "Not exactly an affectionate move."

"More than that. His touch can put you under his control. She wants to stay in her right mind."

"The only reason to do that would be to work against him." Shanghai shook her head. "I'm back on the clueless bus."

"Let me think a minute." I began pacing a short circuit. "It seems like Erin's the key to all the mysteries. Who is she, really? What woman can leap from being a depot clerk to the inner circle so fast?"

As I continued my back-and-forth march, a mental image formed, Erin standing at her station at the gate outside the depot grounds. All she did was check Reaper identities and log their data in the records, though during my most recent visit she collected a blood sample for the new tracking mechanism. She likely also collected Mex's body from the depot. Certainly Bartholomew and Thaddeus were too high and mighty to stoop to such physical labor.

My mental image shifted to Erin heaving Mex onto a wheeled cart. He wore no cloak or weapons belt because we had taken them, but Shanghai had left her staff as a symbolic gift for his spiritual travels. In my imagined scene, the staff lay over his body, tucked under his arm, as Erin pushed the cart toward the checkpoint.

I stopped. Shanghai found the staff in Liam's van while it was outside the corrections camp. Erin must have put it there. But why? How could she know that Liam was involved at all? Who else knew that we had procured his help? Shanghai and Sing, of course. Fiona. The people at the restaurant. And… I finished the thought in a whisper. "The Eagle."

"What?"

"The Eagle. Erin is the Eagle. She's the head of the Resistance. She's not on Alex's side or the Gatekeeper's side. She's on our side."

Shanghai growled, "No one who would let Misty and Sing die like that is on our side. She was so callous. I wanted to rip her throat out."

"I know what you mean, but think about it. Erin had Mex's staff. No one but the Eagle could've known to put it in Liam's van. It was a signal, a clue to let us know she's with us. She had to go along with the killings or she'd blow her cover."

Shanghai whispered, "That's why Bill said what he did."

"What did he say?"

"I've been thinking about it ever since. He said Erin's flying pretty high, and she got a big feather in her cap. He was giving us clues."

"That seals it. Bill knew, and now we know."

Shanghai crossed her arms. "Eagle or not, I'm not ready to trust anyone who'd let innocent people die."

"I get that. We'll just keep our distance for now and see if she drops more clues for us." I lifted one of the loose hoses again. "Ready to lock in?"

Shanghai picked up the other one and stared at it, her brow low.

"Is something wrong?" I asked.

She offered me a quick glance and returned her stare to the hose. "I'm not sure I should tell you."

"Why wouldn't you?"

"I guess I have to. It's not fair otherwise." She looked me in the eye. "You know this energy probably comes from the soul farm downstairs."

"From the farm?" My head grew dizzy.

She grasped my wrist. "You're wobbling. You really do need a recharge."

"I know, but..." I shook my head. "I can't take their energy. That would be..." The right word refused to come to mind.

"Hypocritical," Shanghai finished as she released my wrist. "Self-serving."

"Right." I dropped the hose. "So we can't do it."

"Phoenix, it makes me sick to my stomach, but we have to. Besides, we've both been taking it for years."

"You mean, all this time…"

She nodded. "Our energy can't come out of thin air. It has to come from the harvested souls. It keeps the Gatekeeper powerful, and it gives Reapers the ability to collect more souls for his ghoulish garden. It's a vicious, evil cycle, and we're trapped in it."

I lifted the hose again and stared at the valve on the end. Guilt pounded like a hammer. It seemed that everything I had known was crashing down. For almost four years I had been an accomplice to evil, guiding souls to a place where their life energy would be milked from their withering remains and sent back to me for my own consumption. I promised them peace and rest, but I was in league with an executioner who butchered them and fed me their leftover body parts. And I consumed them eagerly.

"Phoenix." Shanghai snapped her fingers. "Stay with me. We don't have much time. We have to find Sing's soul."

"I can't take the infusion. Not now. Not after—"

"If we don't, we'll eventually die, especially if we go into the abyss. We need the strength to return."

"But it's wrong. It's so wrong."

Shanghai's jaw firmed. "There's no difference between taking it then and taking it now."

"There is a difference." I spoke through clenched teeth. "Before, I didn't know. Now I do."

She gave me a hard stare. "Is it wrong to let the souls here suffer for eternity? Is it wrong to let the Gatekeeper keep his iron grip on the entire world and squeeze the life out of countless millions? Is it wrong to let Sing die in vain after she sacrificed herself to lead you here?" Shanghai pressed a finger against my chest. "Yes, those are wrong. Dead wrong. And if you don't get the energy infusion, you'll be doing all three, because without it we have no chance. We're both about to collapse already, and we have a long way to go."

"But if I do wrong to stop other wrongs, what good is that? It's still wrong."

"I'm done arguing, Phoenix." Shanghai crossed her arms. "I came here with you to save the world, but I can't do it alone, and I'm not going on this mission unless we both have the energy we need to complete it."

"Are you saying if I don't take the energy I have to finish by myself?"

A tear trickled down her cheek. "Don't make me say that." Her voice pitched higher. "Phoenix, I've always stayed with you, and I've never demanded anything, but I can't let you make this mistake. The whole world is counting on us."

I gazed at her pleading eyes. How could I turn my back on her now? "All right. All right. Let's do it before I change my mind." We connected the tubes to our valves, found control switches on the wall, and turned them on. As the energy flowed, my muscles seemed to breathe in and out as if luxuriating in the new infusion. Yet, with every second of pleasure, images of the dried-out ghosts flashed across my mind.

My heart ached. I was a hypocrite. A traitor. A cannibal. A thief. And there was nothing I could do about it.

When we finished, I disconnected and kept my eyes averted from Shanghai's. "We'd better get going."

After opening the door and checking the hall, Shanghai led the way to the stairs. We skulked down to the first floor and stopped at the entry doors where Erin and the Gatekeeper had emerged earlier.

I opened one of the doors a crack and peered inside. Dimness shrouded the enormous chamber. As my eyes adjusted, details came into focus. Near the center, seven perfectly spaced, high-backed chairs formed a semi-circle behind an eight-foot-wide hole in the floor. Flashing light emanated from it as if animated pixies were being held captive in the depths. That hole had to be the abyss.

"Looks clear," I whispered as I led the way inside.

After closing the door, we walked farther in. A domed ceiling covered the chamber, its apex directly above the abyss. Just as Alex had described, the combined energy lines ended under the dome where the radiance took the semi-spherical shape of the structure, as if filling a huge, upside-down bowl with luminescent soup.

We stopped near the edge of the abyss and looked down. Elongated humanoid shapes, radiant and flashing, swirled in a cyclonic spin around a deep void of blackness—a whirlpool plunging into apparent nothingness. Some of the trapped souls reached up with groping hands, their eyes wide and mouths agape, desperate for rescue from this nightmarish spin, only to be sucked out of sight and replaced by equally desperate faces and hands.

Tiny voices rose, tortured and garbled, too many blended together to decipher. It sounded like hundreds of panicked souls riding up and down on storm-tossed waves, their cries amplified for one moment, then drowned the next as a wave crashed over them, silencing their pleas.

"They look physical," I whispered.

"Not likely. They're probably level threes. We can't see that they're ghosts."

"Let's make sure." As I leaned to try to grab one of the hands, a suction caught my body and drew me dangerously closer. Shanghai jerked me back, breaking the hold.

"Did you feel it?" I asked.

Shanghai nodded. "It's like a vacuum. That must be how it keeps souls inside."

I extended an arm to her. "Hold tight."

While she clutched my wrist, I bent low and tried again to grab the closest groping hand. The moment my fingers touched it, a jolt sent me reeling into Shanghai's arms.

She pushed me upright and helped me balance. "What happened?"

"An electric shock." I shook the pain out of my hand. "The souls are charged, like those cats in the forest."

Shanghai peered into the abyss. "So we can't go in physical form without getting zapped. Ghost mode should be safe, though. That downward suction should keep us from shooting into the sky."

"Only one of us can go. The other has to stay here and wait. The diver will collect Sing and Peter in their cloak, fight their way back to the top, and materialize an arm."

"Then the other person grabs the arm and hauls the diver out." Shanghai nodded. "Makes perfect sense."

"And I need to be the one to go in."

Her jaw hardened. "Why you?"

"Why not me?"

"Because you're not the only Reaper who can do this." She gave me a long stare, one eye half closed. "Okay. You go. You gave in on the energy boost. I'll give in on this."

I plugged my cloak into my sternum valve. "Good."

"Should I stay close to the abyss or hide in the shadows for a while?"

As my cloak's fibers energized, I patted her shoulder. "I'll trust your judgment."

She slid her hand into mine, drew me close, and gazed into my eyes. "I won't be far. I'll be watching and listening."

"I know you will."

As she looked at me, her voice took on a troubled tone. "Phoenix, I can't shake this feeling that you're walking into a trap. I mean, it's the abyss, for crying out loud, and you're jumping right into it."

"Trap or no trap, I'll make it out of there." I forced a confident smile. "I remember a certain Reaper telling me, 'If you plan to die, you will die.'"

"Right. Swagger. No tails tucked between our legs." She smirked. "I also said when all of this is over, I'm going to plant history's biggest kiss on that gorgeous face of yours, and I mean to keep that promise."

"I'll look forward to it." I stepped to the edge of the abyss. The moment the downward suction took hold, I began transforming into ghost mode. As I dematerialized, beginning with my arms, my fingers elongated and stretched toward the void.

I bent over, let the suction take me headfirst, and plunged into the center of the vortex—a funnel that narrowed on the way down. Spinning ribbons of light amidst the darkness zoomed past on all sides in a whoosh. Screams magnified and pierced my brain like thousands of vocal needles.

As the central funnel tightened, hands grasped from the bodies spinning in darkness at all sides, some batting or clawing at my clothes. I tucked my arms to avoid the touches but to no avail. One of the hands caught my arm and dragged me into the spin. As if diving into a pool, I splashed into dark water and floated in a swiftly flowing current. Radiant human forms swam all around me. Thin and withered, they were no more than skeletons with leathery skin draped over their bones.

Most battled to rise higher in the spin, screaming with every jerk of a flailing limb. Their eyes—terrified and haunted—displayed the torture of vain attempts to survive this hopeless tempest. A few just floated limply in a downward draw, carried along in submissive misery. The torture of being here for days, months, or years had dashed their hopes. They had given up.

As I searched the sea of souls for a familiar face, the spin gradually pulled me deeper into the abyss. Waving my arms and kicking with my feet, I fought against the pull. Yet, was that the right strategy? Would Sing stay near the top? Or would she try to help those who had lost hope, maybe even search for the bottom of the abyss to learn more about it?

I reversed course and swam down. As I descended, the bodies grew denser, and the limp souls outnumbered the struggling ones. The screams subsided, replaced by a hush. Soon, I had to push bodies aside to swim deeper.

After several minutes, I arrived at a blockade—limp souls clogging the funnel in a tight, rapid spin. As before, every soul was emaciated. Since Sing didn't have time to go through the drainage process, she would still look normal, as would Peter, though I hadn't specifically searched for him.

I swam into the blockade, digging through the mass

until the bodies surrounded me and pressed close. Squirming, I pushed myself down until my extended hand broke through the bottom of the clog, but try as I might, I couldn't budge.

A voice rose from below. "It's Phoenix. I recognize his ring."

Something that felt like a hand grabbed mine and pulled. With my body paralyzed by the pressure around me, I couldn't resist. I inched forward until my forearm cleared the mass. Then another hand grasped my wrist. I slid through the clog and popped out into a clear area no bigger than a small closet.

Sing and Peter, both as radiant as the other souls, set me in a crouch. Sing, wearing her usual Reaper's outfit except for the cloak, lunged into my embrace. "You made it! You came for me!"

I held her close and ran a hand through her lovely curls. Her strong arms felt so good. My precious friend, once dead, was now alive. At least in a way.

She pushed back and gazed at me, smiling as tears streamed down her cheeks. "I kind of expected you to figure out how to track my body, but diving into the abyss?" Her smile broadened. "Phoenix, that's just… just…" She drew me into her arms again. "Oh, Phoenix, I love you so much!"

"I love you, too, Sing." I pulled away and looked around the tiny refuge, apparently the bottom of the abyss. Unlike in the upper portions, we huddled in air rather than the spinning liquid-like environment, as though the clog kept the liquid from filling this space. The radiant souls just above our heads, as well as an energy field that ran along the refuge's perimeter and floor, provided light.

Peter crouched close behind Sing. I gave him a genial nod. "Thanks for your help."

"No problem. It was the least I could do after..." He averted his eyes. "You know."

"Yeah. I know." I tried to read his stoic expression, but he hid his feelings well. "Has anyone told you how you died?"

"Erin did it, I'm sure." He refocused on me. "I figured out she's a Resistance leader, so she took me down."

Sing looked me in the eye. "Phoenix, Erin is the Eagle. I couldn't tell you that before. She said it was too dangerous to let you know. Anyway, she's on our side. You can trust her."

"Obviously she doesn't trust me." I looked up and imagined Shanghai waiting at the top. I had to get moving.

I forked my fingers at them. "Listen, Erin preserved your bodies. I think she plans to try to repair them and restore your souls."

Sing winced, likely thinking about the sonic blast that shattered her brain stem.

Peter pointed at himself. "Why would she want to restore me?"

"No clue. You'd have to ask her. Anyway, she led Shanghai and me to the abyss by dropping bread crumbs for us to follow. Now I have to get you out of here."

"Phoenix, look at this." Sing ran her fingers along a handle to a trap door. "The floor has some kind of barrier that won't let us pass through. The entire abyss is the same. I think if we could open this door, we could get out, but we're not physical, so we can't pull the handle."

I grasped at it, but my fingers passed through. "We can't be sure where this door leads. I could reap both of you and put you into my cloak. Then I could swim to the top."

"It's impossible to get out that way," Peter said. "We've both tried."

"I'm still alive, so I can materialize my arm, and Shanghai will pull me out. She's waiting up there."

"Then materialize here and open this door," Peter said. "It'll be a lot easier."

I glared at him. Who was he to tell me what to do? After taking part in killing Misty, Sing, and innocent prisoners, he had no right to assert himself. I let anger infuse my tone. "If this door leads out of the abyss, you'll just get sucked up into eternity. Trust me, I saw it happen to Misty, the innocent girl your mother murdered. The suction tore her out of my embrace and into the sky. She's gone forever."

Peter frowned but said nothing.

Sing grasped my hand. She, too, stayed quiet.

"Anyway," I continued, "if you ride in my cloak, you'll be safe. I already have one soul in there, and he hasn't been affected by the suction."

Sing ran a hand along my arm. "Can you at least see what's down there? Maybe you'll learn something about how the abyss works."

I let out a sigh. "Okay. I'll have a look. But when I go physical, don't touch me. Somehow you got electrified, so you'll give me a jolt."

Sing waved toward the surrounding wall. "We think that light made us glow, just like all the others." She pinched my sleeve. "And just like you."

"So I'm electrified now?" I looked at my hand.

Radiance emanated from my skin. "I wonder if I'll shock myself if I go physical."

"Better to find out here," Peter said, pointing upward, "than up there after fighting to get to the top."

"All right. Here goes." I curled my fingers around the handle. Past experience revealed that the physics of partial transformations were often unpredictable. I probably couldn't use my ghost legs to brace myself and lift a physical object with a physical hand. Yet, a physical person could grab a partial ghost by a physical arm and pull the entire person, ghost parts and all. In any case, to avoid the possibility of ripping myself apart, it would be best to transform completely out of ghost mode to make this attempt.

As I rematerialized my hand and arm, a sharp tingle coursed across my newly formed skin. Yes, this was going to hurt... a lot. I urged the process to hurry, but it seemed slower than before. Maybe pain skewed my perspective.

When I finished, a shock jolted my body. I jerked the door up, grabbed the edge of the opening, and lowered myself until I dangled over the unknown room.

The door dropped on my fingers. The pain of impact proved to be minimal, but the sting from the energy field still crawled along my hands. I wouldn't be able to hang on for much longer.

While recovery dizziness swam through my head, I scanned the area below. Light from the upper room peeked through the gap in the trap door and shone on a floor about five feet down. Something hummed nearby, like electronic machinery, maybe a device that kept this abyss charged and spinning. A stepladder lay on the floor, apparently a makeshift stairway to this access point. I could get back without a problem.

Above, the energy field from the abyss began streaming through the gap and across the ceiling. I called out, "I'll be back as soon as I can," then dropped.

CHAPTER FOURTEEN

W HEN I LANDED on the floor, I bent to a crouch and waited for the dizziness to subside. Since I hadn't been in ghost mode long, the woozy sensation passed in about a minute.

After rising, I detached my flashlight and flicked it on. I swept the beam across an array of machines that lined most of the room, each one a gray metal box about six feet tall and nearly the same width. In a gap between machines, a double-door panel, similar to the one in the room where we found Misty's soul, hung on the wall.

I opened the doors, revealing a monitor, a stylus, and a slide-out keyboard. After turning on the monitor, I picked up the stylus and tapped it on the screen. A message appeared—Enter Password.

"Password?" I asked out loud. How could I possibly guess the password? If Erin knew it and if she was really on our side, wouldn't she have sneaked it to me somehow? Maybe she wasn't aware of this machine room or if there was any way to halt the abyss. She probably just expected me to collect Sing and Peter and fight my way to the top.

In any case, maybe the people in the death industry

had a password-creation standard, and only one person would be able to help me with that. I checked my cloak's clasp, still plugged into my valve. Albert had been uncharacteristically silent. "Hey, Albert," I said into the fibers. "You've been super quiet lately. I nearly forgot all about you."

He replied in a resigned tone. "It's been a rough ride. Abysmally painful. I heard you talking about radiation exposure earlier, so I guessed that was the cause. I also guessed you didn't need to hear me complaining. I know you're doing the best you can."

"Um… thank you. I appreciate that. Really. What brought about this newfound… contentment, I guess you might call it?"

"Well, I could've gone to the Gateway. You gave me the choice. But I chose to go with you, so I lost my right to gripe. But if you want to hear what it's been like—"

"No. No. That's all right. I'll just try to make it more comfortable from now on."

"I heard you say password. Is that why you called me?"

"Yeah." I swept the beam around again. "I'm standing in a machine room in front of a computer. I think the computer controls these machines, and I'm pretty sure they operate the abyss in the Gatekeeper's fortress."

"The abyss? I heard you talking about it. So it's not a myth after all."

"It's worse than any myth. Right now I'm underneath it, and I'm trying to shut it down, but I can't get into the system." I slid the keyboard out. "Do you know of any standards for security passwords the Council uses?"

"I don't know about the Council, but passwords at our office had to be at least eight characters long, a mixture of upper and lower case letters, at least one numeral, and at least one non-standard character, like a dollar sign or an ampersand."

"That sounds unguessable."

"Right, Phoenix. That's the point. You're not supposed to be able to guess passwords. An easy one is like leaving a key under the welcome mat."

I slid the keyboard back in place. "All right. I suppose you won't be able to help."

"There is an exception, though."

"What?"

"If there are two levels of passwords, the first one is a standard that allows access to rudimentary functions. For example, we had a computer in the office waiting area. People walked in and looked at things like our appointment schedule. The password to enter that system was a formality. In fact, it was on a sheet of paper taped to the monitor. But if someone tried to do something like change the schedule, the system asked for another password. The second one conformed to the parameters I just mentioned."

I slid the keyboard out again. "What was your easy password?"

"We used *guest*. Another office I know used *visitor*. You could try those."

"Upper case? Lower case?"

"For our system, it didn't matter."

"Here goes." I entered *guest*. The screen cleared, and a diagram of the room appeared. Several slider switches ran down the right side of the screen—Power, Speed, Cooling Fan #1, Cooling Fan #2, and Cooling Fan #3.

"That did it. I see a Power controller. It's a slider, and

it's set halfway between maximum and minimum. I'll try to slide it to zero."

"Go for it."

I picked up the stylus and touched the slider bar. A window popped up asking for a password. "You were right, Albert. I need another password."

"You might as well try guest again."

I typed *guest*. The password window disappeared, replace by a message—Access Denied. System Locked for Ten Minutes. A digital counter displayed 10:00 and began counting down—09:59, 09:58, and so on.

I set the stylus back in place. "It locked me out. I'm stuck."

"Which means the architect isn't stupid. But every computer-controlled machine has an emergency shutoff switch somewhere. You could look for that."

"Good idea." I closed the panel doors. Guided by the flashlight, I walked to one of the machines. A low hum emanated from its surface, one voice in the midst of a humming choir. I set my hands on the front and shoved, but the box wouldn't budge.

I squeezed my body between it and the box next to it, using the flashlight to check the sides and backs of both. No switches anywhere. Not even a power cord. Checking the other machines resulted in the same.

"Negative, Albert. The computer's the only way to turn them off, short of smashing them with a sledgehammer. I couldn't even find a power cord to cut."

"Maybe the power cords run through the floor under the units."

"Could be, but they're too heavy to move. The computer's the only way to power them down."

"Trust me. There's a shutoff switch somewhere. Probably in another room."

I swept the beam around the perimeter. Nothing but machines and plaster. "Maybe, but I don't see an access anywhere. When I get back to the top, maybe I can find something heavy to hammer them with. I'd have to drop it into the abyss and then swim down here in ghost mode, but it might work."

"Sounds like your only plan. I'll be thinking about other options."

"Good." I looked up and imagined the tormented souls. Even if I could stop this torture, was the timing right? They would be sucked into eternity in their emaciated states. When they reached their destinations, maybe they would be restored, but... I finished the thought with a whispered, "How can I be sure?"

A woman said, "You cannot be sure based on what you know."

I spun toward the voice and shifted the beam. The Sancta stood next to the control panel, the flashlight's glowing circle resting on her chest. A hint of a smile graced her lovely face. "You seem surprised to see me."

I unplugged my cloak. "Uh... yeah. It's been a while."

"I mentioned that I am unable to enter the Gatekeeper's abode. Powers are in place there that prevent my entry. Since this room is inaccessible to those powers, it is an exception."

"What kind of powers?"

"Evil powers. Spiritual forces of darkness. Since they are many, and I am only one, I am vulnerable. But I will say no more about them. Dwelling on darkness leads to further darkness."

"But shouldn't I know more so I can watch out for them?"

"You need not worry. They are selective about whom they accost. Since they do not sense that you are in the service of the Highest Power, you are safe."

"Why don't they sense it?"

"Because you are not."

"Not what?"

"In the service of the Highest Power."

"Isn't the Highest Power good?"

She nodded. "Of course."

"I'm trying to conquer the Gatekeeper and rescue all the souls. Isn't that good?"

"Again, of course."

"Then why aren't I in the service of the Highest Power?"

She chuckled. "Oh, Phoenix, you are so much like your grandfather."

"You know Maxwell?"

"Quite well. He came to the Gatekeeper's abode seeking to do good, as you do, but he refused to take off his blinders, so he failed."

"Blinders? I was told he had a weakness that made him a slave to a woman. Somehow that led to a heart attack while he was trying to learn the secrets of the Gateway."

The Sancta nodded again. "All true."

"What has that got to do with blinders?"

"He did whatever the woman told him, but he was blinded by his unwillingness to believe her warnings to properly prepare for his quest. When he set out to do her bidding, his lack of preparation led to a fatal heart attack." She looked upward, sadness bending her features.

"Now he is among the wasted souls swirling in the cauldron above."

I joined her gaze and imagined Maxwell, whom I knew only from photos, spinning among the listless souls—another one to save. I turned back to the Sancta. "Who was the woman who controlled him?"

She lifted her chin. "I am that woman."

"You?" I drew my head back. "You controlled Maxwell and drove him to a heart attack?"

Her voice stayed as calm as a gentle breeze. "Not so, Phoenix. I merely told him what he had to do in order to conquer the Gatekeeper. He would not have suffered a heart attack if he had prepared appropriately."

"Why wouldn't he prepare? I mean, preparation is crucial, especially if you're trying to take down the most powerful being in the world."

Her smile withered. "I see that you wear the same blinders."

"Me? Why? How?"

"Oh, Phoenix, if I told you directly, you would become overly confident that you could strip them off, but you would fail. Only by perceiving the blinders yourself will you be able to remove them."

"How do you know?"

"I made the mistake of directly telling Maxwell how to prepare. He thought he was doing my will by trying to remove his blinders, but one cannot remove what one cannot see. It would be like you telling a normal human about the presence of an invisible ghost. He would believe the ghost is in the room, but he would never be able to catch it. He might triumphantly show you a glass bottle, claiming that the ghost is inside, but he would be oblivious to the fact that he had captured only air. In the same way, Maxwell was blind to his blinders, so he was unaware that he did not successfully remove them."

"Phoenix?" Sing called from above, her voice barely audible over the hum. "Are you okay?"

I shouted, "I'm fine. Are you and Peter holding out all right?"

"We're just waiting. There's nothing else to do."

"I'll be there as soon as I can." I refocused on the Sancta. Her gaze never altered—calm, peaceful, patient. "If I'm blind to my blinders, how can I hope to take them off?"

"Allow me to demonstrate. Kindly turn off your flashlight."

I did so. The room darkened to pitch black.

"What do you see?"

I shook my head. "Nothing. Nothing at all."

"Why nothing?"

"There's no light. No one can see in complete darkness."

"Is that so?" She grasped my wrist. "Hold your hands up, display however many fingers you wish, and I will tell you the number."

I held up all ten digits. She wouldn't be likely to guess that.

"Phoenix, I find your gesture interesting. Five on each hand. It reflects your personality. You never do anything at less than full speed." My pewter ring wiggled. "You are still wearing the ring Misty gave you, though she is no longer in your life. Why?"

"If Alex sees me, I'm hoping the ring will keep her

thinking she controls me. I might be able to work that to my advantage."

"Interesting."

I flicked the flashlight back on. The Sancta's expression had turned skeptical.

"Alex doesn't control me."

She blinked. "I did not say otherwise."

"No, but were you thinking it?"

"Does that matter?"

"No.... I mean... yes."

"Why?"

"I guess... well... I guess because I want you to believe in me."

"I see." Her brow lifted. "You believe my faith in you will spark a greater passion to succeed."

"Is that bad?"

"Not at all. Faith is always a motivating factor, as it should be. Faith provides energy, even if you think you are depleted and cannot take one more step. And faith in the Highest Power will infuse you with energy if your reserves have run dry." She tapped her chin with a finger. "Tell me, Phoenix, in the room above us, which of the two souls believes in you more?"

"Sing. Definitely. She was a close friend. Peter conspired to murder Sing and Misty."

"Which of the two are you more motivated to sacrifice for?"

I resisted the urge to roll my eyes. "I'm sure you already know the answer."

"And if you learned that Peter has become contrite and now believes in you wholeheartedly, would your motivation toward him change?"

I nodded. "Most likely."

"There. You see? For you, faith is the deciding factor. Why should you act sacrificially for a person who doesn't believe in you? It would be ridiculous to suffer for someone like that, and even more ridiculous to do so for someone who hates you."

"Right. Exactly."

She covered my eyes with a hand. "And that is why you still wear blinders."

"What?" I grabbed her wrist and pulled her hand down. "Peter helped Alex murder innocent people. Am I supposed to sacrifice for someone like him?"

"Not only for him, but also for Alex."

"Alex? That's insane! She's pure evil. Nobody would sacrifice for her."

"Nobody?" The Sancta's eyes brightened, as if kindled with passion. "Phoenix. Hear me. Most warriors of the light are called to battle evil with physical force. They wage war with weapons of flesh, fire, and foundry. Like a radiant storm, they destroy the sons and daughters of darkness in order to set slaves at liberty. To them, sacrificing for their enemies would be foolishness. Incomprehensible. Madness."

"Exactly." I tilted my head. "Are you saying they're wrong?"

"Not at all. The Highest Power marshals such warriors for service at the right time and in the right place. But not until another kind of warrior has finished his service."

"Another kind?"

The Sancta set a hand on my shoulder. "You, Phoenix, are one of the precious few who march in front of the storm. When death surrounds you, you always choose life. While others surrender to the darkness, you shine a light of hope. You are an emissary of mercy even as the tempest boils on the horizon—the storm of righteous retribution waiting at the doorstep. You are the final opportunity to turn away from darkness. This mercy is woven into your very being as surely as your hair is woven into your cloak. Inseparable. Inextricable. Immutable. It is who you are."

I let her words soak in. Mercy. A light of hope. Maybe that was why I couldn't bear to sit and watch my district dwellers die, why I had to smuggle medicine to them even if it meant my own death. Still, they were decent people. Innocent victims. They were not Alex. "What if someone stomps on the mercy and slaps me in the face? I'd look like a fool."

"Yes, you would. To almost everyone, especially those charging to battle behind you. In fact, you would look like a traitor for giving comfort to the enemy. But shouldn't everyone benefit from a final chance? Even someone who doesn't deserve it? Some are cruel because they have never seen mercy's open hand. That hand must first be offered before vengeance can be justified." She set a finger against my chest. "You are that offering, and only the most insightful of your allies will understand. Such is the nature of your lonely outpost."

"And if the offer is rejected?"

"Then the storm will come. Whether or not you join the war of retribution will be up to you."

"What about the Gatekeeper? Should someone offer him mercy?"

"Maxwell already did so, and the Gatekeeper spurned the offer. Now vengeance prowls at his doorstep."

We stared at each other, neither of us blinking. Her eyes, deep pools of sepia, pierced my mind far more deeply than could Alex's steely grays. I had to turn away. "I have a lot to think about."

"Indeed. And perhaps not much time to do so."

"But first I have to get out of here." I looked at the room's walls again. Maybe she could help me with the shutoff-switch mystery. "How did you get in? Did you pass through a wall from another room?"

"There is no adjoining room. I traveled through the energy field that surrounds the abyss. When I reached the bottom, I passed through this ceiling."

"Strange." Since the energy field didn't encompass this room, if Sing and Peter were to try to join me here, they might be sucked into the sky. The only other option was to swim to the surface with them in my cloak.

I refocused on the Sancta. "Listen, thank you for the talk. I'll definitely consider your cryptic words. Maybe I'll be able to take my blinders off since no woman is controlling me."

"So you say."

"So I say? What do you mean?"

She set a palm on my cheek. "You look fresher than I anticipated. You were more haggard at the outpost. How is it that you appear stronger and haler now after your arduous journey?"

"We got an energy recharge. Shanghai and me. We decided we couldn't possibly do what we have to do in a weakened state."

"That much is true." The Sancta's expression sagged. "You said you would consider my cryptic words, but I fear that you are on the wrong track." She turned and walked into the darkness. "Just take note of one truth you already know. The woman who controls you is the one for whom you violate your principles."

I shifted the flashlight in her direction, but the beam hit only a gray machine. The Sancta was gone.

I shouted, "But I didn't kill Sing! I didn't violate my principles for Alex!"

The machines' electronic hum swallowed my words.

As I grabbed the stepladder and set it up, I murmured, "Sing said the Sanctae would be cryptic, but she didn't say they would be so frustrating."

I stepped up to the door, pushed it open, and climbed into the room with Sing and Peter. Electricity again burned across my skin, more painful than ever. I transformed to ghost mode, even slower this time. Fortunately, the pain dwindled as the phantom part of me spread.

When I crouched with Sing and Peter, they stared at me with worried expressions. "What did you find?" Sing asked.

"Machines that control the abyss, but I couldn't figure out how to turn them off." I looked at her and Peter in turn. With him listening, mentioning the Sancta probably wouldn't be a good idea.

After giving them details about the machine room and the password issue, I concluded with, "So you two will have to ride in my cloak. I can take you to your bodies, and maybe you can help me figure out how to put you back inside them. We'll also try to find the password and maybe where they store energy so we can give it to the souls in here."

"I say find the energy first," Peter said. "If you can

restore the souls, then you can come back with an axe and destroy the machines. You won't need a password."

"Good point." I looked Peter over. His crouch, arms supported on knees, communicated readiness to help. "Listen." I extended a hand. "Bygones are bygones. Okay?"

"I'm all for that." He shook my hand. "And I'm sorry for what I did. I could blame it on a domineering mother, but that's no excuse. I shouldn't have let her control me like that."

I concealed a shudder. The control issue again. I had no idea how to respond.

Grasping an edge of my cloak, I spread out an arm. "Sing first?"

"Sure." Sing stepped close. I draped the cloak over her and began drawing her in. Starting with her head, she elongated and melded into the fibers. With my energy level still high from the recent boost, absorbing her took less than a minute, but the process was painful, more like it had been before the infusion of the purified energy.

When she disappeared, I spoke toward a new shimmering spot at my shoulder. "How does it feel?"

"Strange, but not uncomfortable." She let out a soft laugh. "So you're Crandyke?"

"Yes. Call me Albert. It's good to have some company here."

"The pleasure's mine."

I spread my cloak toward Peter. "Ready?"

He reached out and unplugged my clasp, then leaned close. "Listen carefully," he whispered into my ear. "I know you're still suspicious of me. You have every right to be. Like I said before, I have no excuse. But here's the deal. I have the same weakness you do. I couldn't resist obeying my mother. She controlled me. Sometimes I felt like a robot, and every time I helped her do something terrible, I died inside. I just thought you'd like to know, but I didn't want Sing to hear. I don't want to look like I'm making excuses." When he drew back, tears sparkled in his eyes.

I nodded. So that was why Erin preserved his body. She knew about Alex's control and hoped to give him a second chance. I grasped his wrist, and he grasped mine in return. I spoke in the same low tone. "So we're allies."

A tentative smile broke through. "I'm not sure what I can do to help you, but I'll do my best."

"What if Alex finds out? Will she be able to control you now?"

He shook his head. "I don't think so. Now that I'm dead, I feel better. It's like Erin set me free by killing me."

I looked into his eyes—deep, sincere, passionate. Who was I to doubt his sincerity, especially since I might be vulnerable to the same influence? I plugged the clasp into my valve. "Let's go, then."

Peter slid closer and hunched low. I draped my cloak over him and began the reaping process. His position, humble and subservient, again spoke volumes. I could trust this fellow Reaper. He might prove to be a powerful ally.

After finishing, I gazed at the new shimmer in my cloak. Peter, Sing, and Albert began chatting, but I tuned them out. A seemingly impossible chore awaited. I had to get going.

I leaped into the blockade above and pulled myself into the spinning mass of limp bodies. As before, they pressed on me, making the going tough, but I squirmed through and broke out of the clog.

Now spinning along with the others in the liquid-like blackness, I pulled on arms and legs to propel myself until I made my way into a clearer section. At this point, I could no longer use the others as ladder rungs. Swimming was the only option.

Paddling with arms and legs, I beat against the current. As I inched upward, the downward suction dragged against my cloak. It was so far to the surface, a seemingly impossible distance. But I had no choice. Maybe I could take my mind off the enormity of the task.

I spoke into my cloak. "Sing," I gasped. "Albert. Peter."

"Yes?" Sing said.

"I'm right here," Albert replied. "We're getting a stinging sensation. Not too bad, though."

"I'm... I'm swimming against... the current in the abyss."

One of the souls bumped into me from above, halting my progress. Beating my arms, I dodged it and swam on, still spinning as I struggled upward. "It'll take a while."

"You can do it," Sing said. "I've seen you overcome obstacles worse than this."

I pushed another soul out of my way. "Worse than this? Name one."

"Well... how about when you..." Her voice trailed off. "Um... I guess I can't think of any."

"That's what I thought."

"It doesn't matter, Phoenix. So what if this is the highest mountain you've ever climbed? You've scaled every other mountain you've attempted, so you can scale this one."

"That's not necessarily true," Albert said. "Just because he scaled one—"

"Stay out of this, Albert." Sing's voice grew passionate. "Phoenix, listen to me. I haven't known you for very long, but ever since that day you smuggled medicine into the Fitzpatricks' home and stood up to Alex, I knew you were special. You could've let them take the blame, but instead you were willing to die to save that precious family."

Her words infused my phantom muscles with strength. My upward speed increased. Relative to my own progress, radiant souls drifted downward, though many also struggled to move higher. Still, I had a long, long way to go.

"Phoenix," Sing continued, "you infiltrated the corrections camp and helped the family escape. Even though you accomplished your quest, you went back in there to save everyone else, knowing Alex would set a deadly trap. Your love is a life-giving stream. Your courage is a forging flame. Your will is a granite mountain. I know it. The Fitzpatricks know it. Shanghai knows it. And Misty knows it."

"I know it, too," Albert said. "You really are a hero."

"I agree," Peter added. "After I met you, I admired your courage ever since."

My momentum surged. Light came into view above. Maybe I really could do this.

The other souls thinned further. Only a few determined battlers remained. When I passed the last one, I shouted, "Shanghai! Get ready to grab me!"

When the light came within reach, I materialized an arm and thrust it upward. A strong hand grabbed my wrist and pulled. As I lifted out of the abyss, I forced the rest of my body into physical mode, starting with my protruding arm and running down my frame.

My feet settled onto the floor. Blinded by the light, I blinked to clear my vision. Alex stood before me, her arms crossed. "You never cease to amaze me, Phoenix."

CHAPTER FIFTEEN

I SUPPRESSED A GASP. Disoriented from being in ghost mode, I tilted, but I couldn't be sure which way.

Alex grabbed my wrist again and forced me to sit. "Rest."

She sat in front of me, wearing gray pants and a matching jacket as well as a partially unbuttoned shirt that exposed the top of a sternum valve.

I averted my eyes. Was Alex still an active Reaper?

"If you don't mind," she said, "tell me why you were in the abyss."

My dizziness clearing, I glared at her steely owl eyes. "I do mind."

"I see." She opened her jacket further, revealing a holstered sonic gun.

"If you think you can scare me with that gun—"

"Of course not, Phoenix. I know you don't fear death." She withdrew it from the holster and laid it in my hand. "I'm giving it to you."

I stared at the gun. "Why?"

"Why?" She laughed softly. "To defend yourself, of course. I heard you call for Shanghai. Since you expected her to be here, I assume she would be if she could.

Therefore, I suspect that the Gatekeeper has her now, and his minions are probably searching this building high and low trying to find you, but they haven't searched low enough." A second laugh sounded like a purr. "Who could have guessed you would hide in the abyss?"

"I wasn't hiding." I pushed against the floor and climbed to my feet.

She rose with me. "Then what were you doing?"

Anger boiled within. This murderer had no right to ask me anything. "What do *you* think?"

"I assume you were searching for Singapore." She brushed a hand along my cloak's shoulders. "You have a shimmer. Are you carrying her?"

"If I were carrying her, I wouldn't tell you. And if I couldn't find her down there, I wouldn't tell you that either. But I will tell you that I'm carrying a file clerk from a DEO office. His name is Albert Crandyke. I can ask him to speak if you want proof. Since you're a Reaper, you'd be able to hear him."

"No need for that. I believe you." Alex leaned close and whispered with a stern tone, "Phoenix, I sent you here on a mission. You know the purpose, and it wasn't to go swimming in a hellhole. You're the first person in all of history to emerge from there. No sane person would go voluntarily, even to try to rescue the soul of a girl he is smitten with. If you intend to complete the mission, you can't follow your passions. You have to stay the course."

As my anger spiked to fury, I took a deep breath to quell it. "Listen, Alex. I plan to finish the mission, but I'm the one risking my life, so let me do it my way."

A growl spiced her voice. "You have no idea how powerful the Gatekeeper is, so you'd better do exactly what I say. If you slip in the slightest, he'll kill you, drain your energy, and throw your scarecrow soul back into the abyss. In that condition, you'd never return."

I forced my facial muscles into an acquiescent façade. "All right. Tell me what to do."

She gestured toward the seven chairs lining the abyss. "The Council will convene in this room quite soon. Since the Gatekeeper will be preoccupied, you will have some freedom to search for Shanghai. You will need her for a task I have in mind."

I eyed the center chair, the seat of the world's tyrant. "Do you have any idea where she is?"

"I can only guess that the illuminaries have her. I told you about them yesterday."

"Where would they hold her?"

"Since the Gatekeeper likely plans to use her to coerce you, she is probably being held on a pedestal in one of the two drainage rooms. Have you seen those?"

I nodded.

"Then you know what a pedestal can do."

"I know it can drain a disembodied soul. What can it do to a living person?"

"Inflict pure torture. Slow and excruciating. She will wither, as if someone were leeching her vitality. Eventually she will become a living skeleton, and she will beg to die."

"Then I have to go."

I took a step toward the door, but Alex pulled me back. "She'll be guarded by a dozen illuminaries. You can't face that many. When the meeting begins, there will be fewer. The Gatekeeper is convinced that one of the Council members wants to assassinate him, so he protects himself during every meeting. When we convene, he will call most of the illuminaries in as bodyguards."

"How do I fight them?"

"They can be knocked around by physical blows, but they will always rebound and continue fighting, so hand-to-hand combat is ineffective." She touched the sonic gun she had given me. "A blast from this in the usual place will disrupt their electrical brain center. That's why you must wait until the meeting starts. You can't take on too many at one time, because the gun needs to recharge after each use. Wait ten seconds for a stun, twenty for a kill. Also, since their bodies flash at regular intervals, you can time them, usually one second of brightness, six or seven seconds of darkness. Don't let one touch you during the flashing phase. The charge will paralyze or kill you, depending on how much of the jolt you absorb. Also, a split second before an illuminary flashes, it emits a slight buzz. You have to be pretty close to hear it."

I imagined Shanghai inside one of those enclosures. Since the glass lifted so easily, either they kept her in a paralyzed state or they anchored the glass in place. In my mental image, her Reaper's uniform hung like baggy rags on her emaciated frame.

I hissed, "I can't wait for the meeting. I have to go now."

She waved a hand. "Sure. Run straight to the drainage rooms into a mass of illuminaries. You will die. Shanghai will die. And all will be lost."

"But I can't just sit around knowing she's suffering."

"It is true that you can't sit around. While you're waiting for the meeting to begin, I will let you in on my plans to regenerate a body."

"Regenerate a body?" I cocked my head. Did she know about Sing and Peter after all? "Whose body?"

"You will see." She set a hand on my back. "The Gatekeeper and the other Council members are in the outer room. I will take you through another passage to avoid them."

We walked to the eastern perimeter of the circular chamber, ninety degrees separated from the main entry. Alex pushed on the wall, forcing a door open. "Your flashlight, please, Phoenix."

I detached it from my belt, turned it on, and handed it to her. She closed the door and, shining the beam in front, ascended a steep, narrow stairway. As I followed, she spoke in a hushed tone. "Erin and I need you to retrieve a person's soul, but we think the soul might have passed beyond the Gateway."

I mimicked her quiet voice. "Isn't coming back from the Gateway possible only in theory? No one's ever done it, right?"

Alex stopped and shone the flashlight just below my eyes. Above the beam, her dim features bent downward. "A few have tried and failed to return. Others have volunteered, such as your weak-minded grandfather and my impotent son, but they proved themselves incapable, so I canceled their attempts. However, I think you will succeed for two reasons. You are more powerful than those who actually traveled to the Gateway, and you will be going there alive, in ghost mode instead of as a dead soul. It's the perfect test to prove whether or not you can conquer the Gatekeeper, because if you are too weak, I don't want to stick my neck out to support you if you appear to be failing."

I blocked the flashlight with a hand. What might Peter be thinking after hearing his mother insult him? In any case, this might be a good chance to learn more about the Gateway. "Bartholomew showed me a computer tablet. Mex's icon was on the eternity side of the Gateway icon but closer to the Gateway than some souls we had reaped. He said a Reaper could retrieve Mex while he was at that spot, but then Bartholomew sent him along with the others where he couldn't be retrieved."

Alex lowered the beam to my chest. "Bartholomew is ignorant. His knowledge of the Gateway is limited to glowing icons and the lies the Gatekeeper tells him."

"Then you'd better explain more. Bartholomew said if a Reaper retrieves a soul from beyond the Gateway, the Reaper has to stay behind. I don't want to rescue a villain ghost to help you conquer the Gatekeeper and then get stuck, thinking for all eternity what an idiot I was for letting you use me like that."

Alex raised a finger. "First, when you see whom you will be retrieving, you will instantly change your mind." She raised another finger. "Second, allow me to correct Bartholomew's mistaken view. The Gateway icon is just a representation of the depot. When Mex's icon was close to that icon, he was still in the energy line at the depot while the others had already traveled through the line and had arrived within these walls. When Bartholomew sent Mex along, he merely pushed him through the line to this place.

"Since Bartholomew is ignorant of reality, he melded his knowledge of the icon positions with rumors he has heard. No one truly goes beyond the Gateway until they are released into the sky from the collection point under the dome. Such a release was once a common occurrence, but as you have likely guessed, nearly all souls are now collected for harvesting and tossed into the abyss when no more energy can be squeezed from their withered phantoms."

A new mental picture arose—thousands of souls crying out for release from torture, many of whom I casually knocked to the side in my haste. I had to get them out of there... somehow.

Alex grasped my wrist. "Let me show you what I have in mind. You will soon set aside your hesitation."

Again guided by the flashlight, we walked the rest of the way up the staircase. At the top, Alex opened a narrow door and guided me into a room. Radiance ran along the ceiling, floor, and all four walls, illuminating the area. The only other entrance appeared to be a black door on the wall to the right. Based on my understanding of the building's layout, we were now on the east side of the upper level, and that door likely opened to a hallway that led north to the balcony above the stairway room.

A few paces away at the far wall, a coffin-like box, similar to the ones Sing and Peter lay in, sat on a long table. As with their boxes, an energy hose led from the coffin to the wall. Glowing meters displayed a zero heart rate and a temperature of 37 degrees.

Alex closed the door, turned off the flashlight, and handed it to me. "Come."

We walked to the coffin and looked through the glass cover. A woman wearing typical Reaper garments and bearing Asian features lay within, her face familiar. Unlike Sing, she wore only dark socks on her feet. A pair of black ankle-high leather boots sat near one of the table legs, unusual for a Reaper. Most of us wore athletic shoes.

Alex ran a hand along the coffin's edge and whispered, "Takahashi Fujita."

My legs stiffened. "Tokyo?"

Alex nodded.

I stared at her smooth skin, jet-black hair, and trim frame. She appeared to be no older than thirty-five, but she had to be in her late forties or early fifties. "You've kept her body preserved this long?"

"This is Erin's doing. Since Tokyo's death, she has been the leader of the Resistance, and their efforts to conquer the Gatekeeper have failed dismally. I recently offered to combine our forces, and she joined with me in what you might call an unholy alliance to defeat a common enemy. Our relationship is tenuous, of course, and we each wonder what the other is planning behind the scenes. I assume one of us will eventually stab the other in the back, so we are constantly on guard."

I clipped the flashlight to my belt. "Getting cozy with the Gatekeeper probably gives Erin the upper hand."

Alex nodded. "I'm sure she believes that, but she is unaware of some, shall we say, aces in the hole I have."

I studied her expression, cocksure and condescending. Erin surely also had some aces in the hole as well, such as the bodies of Sing and Peter. "But you won't let me in on what your aces are."

"Of course not, Phoenix. I'm sure you realize by now that I'm no fool. I tell you only what you need to know. And now you've learned that I am not calling you to retrieve a villain, but the greatest Reaper the world has ever known."

"But I thought her Reaper days were over. Didn't she finish her term and retire?"

"She did, but even after her sternum valve was removed, freeing her from slavery to energy infusions, she was able to reap. She could still absorb souls into her cloak, though she could no longer dematerialize. This proved her long-held theory that the energy wasn't really needed for a Reaper's duties, which contradicted the Gatekeeper's assertions and undermined his control of the system.

"As you can imagine, the Gatekeeper had to destroy the living evidence that he had constructed a system based on lies. Tokyo had become a Reaper who was not under his whip, so he arranged to have her murdered. As a martyr, she energized the Resistance leaders. And that led to this bold scheme, a brilliant plan, I must say. If Tokyo can be resurrected and show the world the Gatekeeper's treachery, and also teach other Reapers how to ply their trade without being enslaved to his energy reserves, his system will begin to crumble from the foundation."

"She could do all of that, but then you wouldn't need me to face the Gatekeeper. I would be expendable."

"Not so, Phoenix. Even if his foundation crumbles, he will not topple easily. There is much more to his power than energy distribution to Reapers. No one but you will be able to pry loose his stranglehold on the world."

Alex lifted the hose running from the wall to the coffin. "Let's get to the bottom line. There are many energy outlets such as this one throughout the building. Since Erin has detected no activity in the lines within these walls, we believe Tokyo escaped through one of the outlets. But she likely didn't know a crucial fact. Any soul that emerges in an unshielded room will be instantly transported up to the Gateway."

I glanced at the radiance surrounding us. Since it didn't shock me like the abyss energy field did, maybe it wasn't as strong. "I assume this is a shielded room."

"Correct. Therefore, Tokyo is either still hiding in the energy network and has somehow avoided Erin's detection, or she has chosen the wrong room and flown into eternity. First, you should search the network. If Tokyo is there, then bring her to this shielded room. If not, then we will move to the more dangerous step of sending you to the Gateway, though, as I mentioned before, I am confident you will not have to stay behind since you will go there alive."

I again maintained my conciliatory mask, though I didn't trust her for a second. "I'll do whatever it takes to retrieve Tokyo's soul."

"Good. I must say, Phoenix, only a fool would ever doubt your courage."

I let the obvious attempt at inflating my ego fly by without comment. As her confidence in her control over me heightened, her manipulation techniques were getting more transparent.

"In order to ensure your safety, you will need someone to act as an anchor." Alex slid off her wristwatch and set it in my palm. The hands pointed toward me, then drifted away. She picked it up and shook it. A second later, the hands pointed at me again. "That's better."

I nodded at the watch. "How will an anchor use that?"

"I will explain in a moment." She again set the watch in my hand. "This room is your launch point. In ghost mode, you will be absorbed into the energy lines and begin your search for Tokyo. I suggest looking for her in the collection bowl under the dome. Since that point is the terminus of the two incoming depot lines, the junction creates a lot of energy sparks, much like two electrical power lines coming together, so a soul can hide in an energy pool that forms under the dome. But there is a danger. As I told you yesterday, during every Council meeting the Gatekeeper sends an energy surge through the lines, which flushes all souls into the pool. Then he opens the dome and releases them into the sky."

"Why would he do that at every meeting? Do souls ever get past the illuminaries that put them in the drainage rooms?"

"Once in a while, which prompted the Gatekeeper to set them free. He considers it a magnanimous gesture to reward their struggle to escape, but he is merely grandstanding and waits for a meeting to free them all at once in front of the Council." Alex gestured with her hands as if illustrating an opening dome. "You see, before the soul-drainage system came into existence, the Gatekeeper opened the dome more often. He stole enough energy from the souls to supply his needs as well as what the Reapers require to do their jobs. Now he stockpiles much more energy for reasons I have not yet determined, but I assure you that his purposes are not benevolent."

"That I can believe." I looked toward the dome, though it was out of view. "So the danger is that I could be sent flying with the souls if I'm still searching when the Gatekeeper opens the dome."

"Exactly."

I slid the watch into my pocket. "Okay. What about the anchor?"

"If you'll recall, the watch monitors your connection status to the physical realm. When you go into the grid, someone on the outside will follow you around and give you updates about your status. You will be able to hear that person, but he or she will not be able to hear you. If your level gets to zero, for all intents and purposes, you will be dead. Your life would be over, and your soul will be unreapable. You will be a wraith-like being who is doomed to wander eternally in a phantom state."

I concealed a shudder. "I guess since I have a blend of the purified energy and the stuff I got from the supply here, my connection level will drop faster than it did during my journey to this place."

"Considerably faster. Eventually your ability to transform will be as difficult as it was before you received your first infusion of the purified energy."

"So who on the outside will follow me around?"

"Shanghai, of course. I endorsed her travel with you for this very reason. I assume you would trust no one else with making sure your eternal life stayed intact."

"That's true."

"Then we're agreed. The moment the meeting starts, you will rescue Shanghai, and the two of you will work together to search for Tokyo."

Although I didn't trust her at all, I gave her an enthusiastic nod, hoping to mask my suspicions. "Let's do it."

Alex bent her brow and stared at me as if trying to read my mind. I resisted her penetrating gaze by mentally replaying the moment she shot Misty. The image built a brick wall, my best defense yet.

She murmured, "Interesting."

"What?"

"You're fighting me, which is futile, but your stubbornness might delay completion of your mission, so I need to make sure you are properly incentivized."

She opened my clasp and removed my cloak. "Your cloak is more precious to you than ever." She swung it around her shoulders, slid her arms through the sleeves, and closed the clasp. "Your efforts to hide Singapore never fooled me, of course. The idea that you might leave the abyss without her is laughable."

"Maybe you should try going down there and see how long *you* want to stay." I grabbed the cloak's sleeve. When she pulled away, I lunged at her. With a quick spin, she swept a leg into mine, making me topple face first and land with a thud.

She stomped on my back. "Don't move. Just listen. I took you by surprise, but I know your skills, and I don't relish the thought of fighting you on equal terms. If we battle, we lose time—time to restore Tokyo and time to save Shanghai. If you acquiesce, I will teach you how to rescue Shanghai, and I will do all I can to delay the dome opening."

Heat surged through my body and burned in my cheeks. Letting this witch think that she had control over me felt like polishing her boots with my tongue, but I didn't have much choice. "You're right, Alex. I'll do what you say."

"That's better." She lifted her foot and helped me up. "Now about the illuminaries. Use the element of surprise, as I just did to you. Strike hard and fast. They are able to disappear, but they stay visible while at their stations to let Erin and the Gatekeeper know they are on duty. When you attack, they will likely vanish, unaware that you can see them in their invisible states. Use that knowledge to your advantage."

I continued my subservient mode. "That's good information. Thank you."

"You are quite welcome." She touched a wall valve similar to the one connecting Tokyo's supply hose to its energy source. "This is your access port. Once you are inside the network, it will be essential that you orient yourself and remember where it is, because if you exit the network in an unshielded area, you will be sucked into the sky."

She shifted her hand to a nearby rocker switch. "This has three settings—input on the left, output on the right, and neutral in the middle. When you return with Shanghai, transform into ghost mode and ask her to press the switch to the left for suction. You will then let yourself be absorbed. Then Shanghai will switch it back to neutral, and you will begin your search. I have no idea what you will see or how long your mission will take, but when you return, Shanghai will switch the valve to output, and you will come into the room, we hope with Tokyo's soul. Since Erin monitors activity in the grid, she'll know you have returned, and she'll meet you here to regenerate Tokyo's body."

I eyed my cloak. "If Tokyo is too weak to come with me, I'll need to reap her with my cloak and carry her out."

"A poor attempt to mask that you are still besotted by your traitorous, drug-addicted lover."

"Traitorous? Drug addicted? What are you talking about?"

Alex laughed through her nose. "Oh, Phoenix, I can never decide if your ignorance is charming naïveté or blind loyalty. How many times do I have to tell you that Singapore is a conniving, deceitful vamp? When I found her cloak, I also discovered a bottle of medicine that—"

"It was cough medicine. She had a bad cold."

"You didn't let me finish. Yes, the medicine was a cough suppressant, but it also contained hydrocodone, an addictive narcotic. Illegal, of course, but not uncommon among the gutter dwellers who seek an escape from the painful rigors of life."

"You're lying. Sing wasn't a drug addict."

"Yet you are addicted to her deceptions." Alex rolled her eyes. "Very well. She is of little consequence. When you return with Shanghai, your cloak will be here." She strode to the door and opened it. "Quietly now. Follow me to the balcony but stay out of sight."

She exited the black door and turned down a hallway to the right. I stayed close behind. As I had guessed, we were heading toward the lobby overlook, this time on the eastern side.

Chattering conversation rose from the lower level. When we approached the area where the passage opened to the balcony, Alex took off my cloak and signaled for me to get down. I lowered myself to hands and knees and crawled to the waist-high wall.

As Alex strutted down the stairs, she swung my cloak in dramatic fashion. "All is well, my friends. I found Phoenix and killed him. We don't have to worry about him any longer."

I risked a peek over the wall. The Gatekeeper and five others looked up at Alex and applauded. The five, two of whom appeared to be women, wore masks of various sizes and shapes that looked like accessories to ancient tribal costumes. The masks seemed familiar somehow, but I couldn't put my finger on the reason.

Four illuminaries stood guard, one stationed at each corner. The Gatekeeper, now wearing a white robe with scarlet satin trim, stood near one of the sentries, as if the closeness provided a sense of security.

Standing almost out of sight on the south side of the room, Erin stared at a computer tablet, maybe monitoring grid activity, as Alex had mentioned.

When Alex reached the floor, she tossed the cloak to Erin. "Extract any souls you find in there and put them in the drainage farm."

CHAPTER SIXTEEN

A SENSE OF DREAD knifed into my heart. Did Alex really mean that, or was it for show?

"Where's his body?" Erin asked as she draped the cloak over her arm.

"Upstairs in the control room. Dispose of it however you wish."

"We have no active Reaper here to extract his soul for drainage. Unless you want to—"

"No need." Alex waved a hand. "We'll let the poor, misguided boy's soul self-detach. He'll be sucked into eternity in seconds."

Erin nodded. "As you wish."

"Also, Phoenix told me something that aroused my suspicions. I am concerned that an attack is at hand."

"From the Resistance?" the Gatekeeper asked.

"From within our ranks. We have traitors among us." Alex's owlish stare shifted from one masked Council member to another. "I will soon find them out."

The Gatekeeper gave each masked person a long, hard look. "Unless I find them out first."

Alex set a hand on his elbow. His glow ran up her arm and across her shoulders. "There is no need for a touch test of loyalty. Phoenix could have been lying to save his skin."

"Still, since Phoenix is dead, we no longer have to worry about him trying to rescue Shanghai." The Gatekeeper nodded at Erin. "Summon the other illuminaries to the meeting. Leave two in each drainage room in case Phoenix has allies we don't know about."

"Right away." Erin strode toward the front of the building, the cloak still over her arm.

The Gatekeeper picked something up from the floor and handed it to Alex. "Your mask."

When Alex put it on, I locked my stare on her. That mask—white with black lines, bearing no clear expression—seemed familiar, an image from years gone by. The memory combined with an aroma, something sweet. A montage of images flashed, running backwards— a masked woman sucked in a breath, making a powder stream from my face to a small cloth bag. She then set a cold finger on my lips while standing in my house with my father and Misty looking on.

I swallowed hard. She was the Council member who took me from my home almost four years ago. Had she been monitoring me ever since that day?

The Gatekeeper walked into the meeting room, followed by Alex, the five other Council members, and a single-file line of illuminaries, now numbering at least ten. I focused on the last one in line and timed its flashes—six seconds of darkness, then one-second of light. The others appeared to flash in similar intervals, though not in sync with each other.

The moment they disappeared inside and closed the door, I hustled to the stairs and down to the first floor, withdrawing the sonic gun along the way. When I reached the hall leading to the two drainage rooms, I stopped near the Gatekeeper's statue and looked toward the west wing, then the east. No sign of illuminaries.

I marched to the eastern wing, stopped at the end of the corridor where it opened into the drainage farm, and peeked around the corner. Shanghai sat inside an enclosure in the middle of the closest row, her legs folded underneath her body as she leaned against the glass.

An illuminary stood at each side, their hands on the glass. When one of them flashed, arcs of electricity raced around the enclosure. Shanghai twitched and grimaced, her mouth open and her eyes closed.

I counted the seconds until its next flash. After a few sequences, I had them both measured. The closer one displayed six seconds of darkness, and the farther one seven. Both illuminated for exactly one second.

The moment the closer one lit up, I ran from the corner, wrestled it to the ground, and set the sonic gun at the back of his dark head. When I pulled the trigger, a sickening pop pierced the air. Arcs of electricity shot from the sonic wave's entry point and crawled around the creature's head and shoulders. I lunged to the side, rolled, and looked back. The illuminary burst into crackling flames.

The second one skulked toward me, as if cautious, likely thinking I couldn't see it. A buzz emanated from its body. When it flashed, I jumped to my feet and backed away, counting the seconds. I needed at least ten for the gun to recharge to stun level. It would probably attack in less than seven.

I wagged my head from side to side and growled, "Show yourself, freak!"

It straightened and strode toward me. Three seconds till its next flash. I sidestepped, pointed the gun toward another glass enclosure in the second row, and shouted, "Freeze!"

The illuminary flashed and lunged at me. I leaped out of the way, pretending to head toward my fake target, making it miss. "Where are you?" I hissed.

My count continued. Less than two seconds to a stun-level charge. Ten more after that to a kill. I pivoted toward Shanghai's row. The illuminary stood next to her enclosure, its shining red eyes trained on me, apparently waiting for its next flash. Shanghai blinked. She, too, looked at me, though dazed.

Aiming the gun toward the exit hall, I growled, "I see you now." I quick marched in that direction without looking back. The illuminary was probably following me, but I couldn't check. Five seconds more to a kill-level charge.

When I reached the corner, two illuminaries leaped from the hall and bowled me over. The gun flew from my grasp. Pinned to the floor, I punched and kicked. Both creatures stayed dark, but that wouldn't last. With a burst of strength, I flipped to my stomach and thrust with all four limbs. I broke out from under them, but one grabbed my ankle. It buzzed, then flashed. Electricity shot up my leg and spine.

I jerked free and crawled on shaking arms and legs. Ahead, the third illuminary stood in my path. The other two hauled me to my feet while the third reached toward me. Its body buzzed. Then, it sizzled and burst into flames. As it crumpled, Shanghai came into view, teetering, the gun tight in her trembling grip.

Calling on another burst of strength, I broke loose and

ran to Shanghai, dodging the burning illuminary. I steadied her and whispered, "Can you run?"

Her eyes wide, she nodded. "From them I can."

"On my word. And stay quiet."

One of the remaining illuminaries buzzed. As the pair drew closer, I guided Shanghai toward her enclosure. The glass shield lay on the floor. I picked it up with both arms and heaved it at the illuminaries. "Now!"

We sidestepped into the next row and sprinted toward the hallway. I glanced back. The illuminaries gave chase with surprising speed. Keeping our footfalls quiet, we dashed to the statue and turned north toward the meeting-room lobby. I spoke in halting gasps. "Have to search… the energy lines… for Tokyo. You guide me… with Alex's watch."

"Don't talk. Just run."

We ran up the stairs and down the hallway. Erin stood next to Tokyo's room, wielding a sonic gun in an extended hand. She growled, "I finally have you." Her face was stoic, unreadable.

We halted and looked back. The illuminaries, now at the top of the stairs, glided closer at a cautious pace.

"Phoenix." Erin extended her other hand. "Your gun."

I whispered to Shanghai, "We're trapped."

"We can fight." Shanghai set a hand on her weapons belt. "Us two against these three shouldn't be a problem."

I backed toward Erin, my focus on the approaching illuminaries as I pulled Shanghai along. "Fighting's too noisy. We'll get lots of company. Let's hope the Eagle's really on our side."

Shanghai's shoulders sagged. "You're right."

Heaving a resigned sigh, I turned and handed Erin

the gun. She gestured with her head toward the room. "Get inside."

I opened the door and waited for Shanghai to enter first. When I followed, I stopped just inside and looked back. Only Erin stood in view in the hall.

She smiled at the illuminaries. "Well done. Report my capture of these two intruders, then return to your station."

I peeked down the hall. The illuminaries had turned and were walking toward the stairs.

A sonic gun in each hand, Erin marched forward and shot each illuminary in the back of the head. Pops rode the air. Electric arcs flared. Fire erupted and spread down their bodies. Within seconds, they burned into piles of smoking ashes.

Erin spun and waved a gun at me. "Get going," she said with a hiss. "Follow Alex's instructions. I have to clean up this mess before someone notices."

I closed the door. The radiant shield along the ceiling and walls illuminated Tokyo's coffin, now draped by my cloak. As I put it on and plugged in the clasp, I gave Shanghai a quick summary of what we had to do and how to manipulate the port. I also explained why I had to explore the dome area and get out before it opened.

When I finished, I withdrew Alex's watch from my pocket and handed it to Shanghai. "Let's agree on a drop-dead point. I have to be back at the port before the connection level gets down to three percent."

"Which means you might have to turn back at five or six percent if you're far from the port."

"I'll rely on you for the timing."

Shanghai touched my cloak's sleeve. "You'd better

check your passengers. It might be safer for them if you leave them behind."

"Good point." Touching my clasp, I spoke into the fibers. "Sing? Peter? Albert? Are you in there?"

Silence ensued.

"Hello? Sing? Anyone?"

Again, no one answered.

"Erin must have extracted them."

"We'll find them later. You need to get going." Shanghai strode to the energy port and set a finger on the switch. "Ready."

I stood next to her and summoned the energy. My arms shifted right away, but the ghost boundary crawled across my shoulders and down my torso like a listless turtle. It took almost a full minute to completely transform. "Done."

When I set my head against the port, Shanghai flicked the switch. A sucking sensation drew me off my feet. Darkness followed—deep blackness, empty and silent. Then a river of radiance appeared. I rushed toward it, unable to resist its pull.

A moment later, I dove into the river—an expanse of motionless sunshine. As if I were submerged in water, I was able to shift my body by paddling with my arms and legs, though the light felt thinner than water, making my strokes less effective. Unlike being in water, however, I could breathe. The radiance warmed my insides as if I were inhaling air rising from a fire.

From my left, a shimmer of light hurtled my way, looking like a radiant log rolling down a hill. It slammed into me and caught my body in a network of electrical fibers that adhered to me like an electrostatic web. The shock paralyzed every muscle. I tumbled with the momentum, urging my numbed arms to fight.

After a few seconds, feeling returned to one arm. I grabbed a handful of electric fibers and tore through the web. My body fell through the hole and floated again in the river.

As the numbness eased, I watched the shimmer roll on—a horizontal wave that was probably an impulse designed to carry souls from a depot to this place. Most souls, being dead and confused, likely didn't fight back. They just sailed along, stuck to the web, until the flywheel spun them out into the holding tank.

If Alex told the truth, in the past, an impulse probably took souls all the way to the dome where they would eventually be set free to the sky. That was how the original system might have been designed to work.

In any case, if I hoped to maintain control of my movements, it would be best to avoid impulses if I could, but when might the next one come? Impossible to guess. My only choice was to swim in the direction the impulse traveled. If my assumptions were correct, that would lead me to the terminus.

Now that my limbs were again working properly, I swam toward the terminus. After about a minute, I had established a good rhythm and ventured a look downward. Shanghai walked across the floor of one of the farm-drainage rooms, glancing between the watch and the ceiling. "Your connection level is twenty-three percent, Phoenix." Her voice sounded far away, like a distant echo.

Something sizzled. I stopped and looked around. Shanghai halted directly under me, lines etched deep in her brow. "Are you stuck? You're not moving."

Far behind me, a new shimmer appeared. I swam as fast as I could and followed the river's right-hand turn. Below, Shanghai broke into a jog. "You're at twenty percent, Phoenix. I don't like how it's dropping. When you move faster, the meter drops faster."

I stopped swimming, though I drifted forward as my momentum carried me at a slow rate. Now it seemed better just to let the impulse take me to the terminus. I would get there quickly and save energy.

Below, Shanghai slowed to a walk. "Phoenix, you're heading for the Council meeting room. I can't follow you in there."

The impulse drew close. In seconds it would carry me out of Shanghai's reach. She stopped and looked at me, now quiet, maybe concerned that those in the meeting could hear her. With her free hand, she raised a single finger, then all five fingers—fifteen percent.

The impulse crashed into me and swept me along. Shanghai pivoted and ran toward the front of the building and out of sight.

Two seconds later, the impulse dispersed and released me, as if something in the system obliterated it now that it had completed its delivery function.

Below, the Council meeting room appeared. Melchizedek perched on his chair while the masked Council members sat in a semicircle to his left and right, three on each side. With the flashing abyss at the center, the chairs looked like a crescent moon trying to embrace glittering stars.

My body glided into a slow swirl that made the room seem to rotate. Melchizidek stood and pointed at the abyss. "We can no longer deposit souls here. It is time to flush them out and use this pit as we did before, as a punishment for rebellion. Let's send these spent souls into eternity."

A male member on his far right rose, his mask bearing narrow eyes and an elongated chin. "Have you confirmed that they will be restored there?"

Melchizidek glared at him for a moment, but his scowl quickly transformed into a smile. "Sydney, perhaps you would like to volunteer as an emissary. We could drain your energy and send you skyward. When you return, you can provide a report." His voice then boomed like thunder. "Of course I don't know if they'll be restored. And what do I care? Let God deal with them."

Sydney folded his hands at his waist. "I only wish to avoid charges of cruelty."

"And who would bring these charges? You? No one outside of this room knows what takes place here." His head rotated as he eyed each Council member. "Or has one or more of you leaked information?"

"Not I, Exalted One." Sydney returned to his seat, his hands tight on the armrests.

As the meeting continued, I scanned the swirling energy. It seemed void of souls, though the radiance made it difficult to see beyond a few feet. Sparks flashed somewhere toward the center of the swirl, most likely the terminus where the lines joined.

I swam around, glancing back at the meeting every few seconds. With my connection level dropping so quickly, I couldn't stay long.

A groan emanated from somewhere in the swirl, weak and feminine. I swam toward the source, but the swirl scattered my sense of direction. If only she would groan again.

I hissed, "Tokyo? Are you here?"

No one answered. In spite of my declining connection to the physical world, I had to keep looking.

Alex rose and faced Melchizedek. "Exalted One, perhaps it is time to end all doubts about your beneficence. Among the citizens, rumors abound about what really happens to the souls of their loved ones when Reapers collect them and deliver them to the depots around the world. Many doubt that the souls go to a place of freedom and contentment, that the process provides an escape from their troubled lives. In order to ease their worries, let us make a video recording. First, we release the souls from the abyss."

She pointed upward. "They will fly into the energy pool where they will be partially restored, though viewers of the recording will not be able to perceive that this is a faux simulation. A narrator with a cheery voice will explain that these rising souls are a daily occurrence here, then joy and hope will make everyone believe that they have seen what really happens beyond the Gateway."

The Gatekeeper stroked his chin, staring at Alex. While he pondered, I continued my search, paddling faster now while calling for Tokyo. I was running out of time.

"Phoenix?" The voice came from above, tiny and muffled. "I hope you can hear me. I'm on the roof. Your connection level is down to eight. You'd better start back soon."

Knowing Shanghai couldn't hear me if I answered, I stayed quiet and pushed deeper into the swirl. Still no visual sign of Tokyo. But now that Shanghai was on the roof, I could count on her updates to let me know how much longer I could search.

"Call for Erin to bring in the tripod camera," the Gatekeeper said. "Then we will turn off the abyss engines and do as you suggested."

"I will get it." Alex hurried toward the door.

When she exited, Sydney rose again. "Events unfolded exactly as I predicted. She insinuated that there are traitors among us, while she is a traitor herself. She hopes to rescue her son from the abyss and make an attempt to usurp your seat of power. You saw that she now has a Reaper's cloak."

"She took that cloak from Phoenix," the Gatekeeper said. "It won't work for her."

"So she says. Yet we know that Tokyo's cloak worked for Singapore. We all assumed that a close genetic match allowed it to function, but doesn't one exception prove that more exceptions are possible? Also, if Alex really killed Phoenix, why would she take his cloak? As a memento?" Sydney huffed. "Ridiculous. Either she knows she can use it herself, or Phoenix is still alive and hiding until she can summon him for help."

"If she planned to use it against me," the Gatekeeper said, "why would she show it to us?"

"To build up your confidence in her by showing off a hunting trophy, if you will. She has always displayed a flair for the dramatic."

The Gatekeeper stroked his chin. "I must admit, that kind of flair does fit her character."

"As does theatrical deception. While we are watching the upward exodus from the abyss, she will use the cloak to capture Peter. He will be easy to pick out of the mass of souls since he has not been drained." Sydney pointed toward the door. "At this moment she is retrieving the cloak and will likely hide it in the camera bag. You will see."

A man sitting in the chair next to the Gatekeeper's rose. "If I may, Exalted One. We have all long wondered why Alexandria chose to keep her valve. No Reaper who has finished a twenty-year term wants to continue dragging the ball and chain."

Sydney nodded. "Unless she has grandiose plans to use it for her benefit. The potential reward has to be supreme."

"True." The Gatekeeper touched his chest. "I once asked her why she retained her Reaper valve. She said she thought maintaining her ability to reap might be useful someday. It seems that her forward thinking is bearing fruit of a rotten variety."

"What will you do?" Sydney asked. "She is powerful. Even if we five were to try to subdue her, she might escape."

"Don't worry. I will take care of her personally."

"What about the abyss? And the dome?"

"We will keep the abyss intact and open the dome, but we must first flush Tokyo in case she is lurking somewhere in the system." The Gatekeeper gestured toward a wall. "Station yourself at the switch and be ready for my signal."

"My pleasure, Exalted One." Smiling, Sydney walked toward the wall. The Gatekeeper and the four remaining Council members sat quietly, apparently waiting for Alex to return.

"Phoenix," Shanghai said. "You're down to five percent. You have to get out of there."

Tokyo was still nowhere in sight. I had to make a decision now—save my own skin and leave her behind to get sucked into the sky, or keep looking for her and risk almost certain death.

I swam deeper into the pool. She had to be here somewhere.

Something glimmered to my left, then winked off. I turned that way and entered a stagnant area I had missed earlier. A female in Reaper attire floated upright in the radiance, her eyes closed and her arms spread. *Tokyo!*

"You're down to four," Shanghai said from above. "Phoenix, if you don't get moving soon, I'm going to tear this dome open and get you out of there myself."

I draped my cloak around Tokyo and began the absorption process, but being nearly fully ghost myself and almost disconnected from the real world, how long might it take? I concentrated on the process, but nothing happened. It didn't seem to be working at all. The only remaining option was to manually carry her while swimming, but could I battle against the impulse waves with her in my grasp?

"Three percent. Phoenix, please hurry."

I wrapped an arm around Tokyo's waist and swam toward the exit with the other, kicking hard.

"Finally! You're moving. As soon as you're out of that room, I'll run back inside."

When Tokyo and I neared the stream's entry point into the dome room, an impulse burst in and threw us back. We tumbled through the swirling soup until our momentum died. I righted myself, repositioned Tokyo, and swam again, but with one arm occupied, I couldn't move fast enough. Another impulse was bound to overwhelm us before I could get back to the port.

Below, Alex entered, carrying a suitcase-sized bag. When she arrived at the semi-circle, she set the bag on the floor and stood in front of the Gatekeeper. "Shall we proceed?"

"Most assuredly." He rose and set his hands on her shoulders. Radiance erupted at the contact points. Alex gasped and tried to back away, but he held on. Her entire body quaked. Light shot from her eyes, and she dropped to her knees, moaning.

"I sense rebellion," he roared, "resistance to my influence."

Alex forced out a labored, "No... Exalted One.... I resist... only the pain... you inflict."

"Liar!" He pushed her into the abyss. She screamed, and her voice faded in the depths.

"Two percent, Phoenix!"

The Gatekeeper nodded toward the wall. "Sydney, open the dome."

I swam as hard as I could, now a foot from the hole leading to this room. We just might make it. Something clicked. The hole narrowed, closing rapidly. Another impulse blasted through the gap, knocking Tokyo and me back into the swirl again. The energy line had been cut off. There was no way out.

A mechanical groaning sound knifed in. The energy pool slowly lifted. The swirling action accelerated, and the radiance curled into a tight cyclone of light, sweeping Tokyo and me into the vortex. After all of my efforts, I was too late. I had failed.

I wrapped both arms around her and whispered, "Hang on, Tokyo. This might be a rough ride."

CHAPTER SEVENTEEN

STILL RISING, I threw my cloak around Tokyo and held her close. I had to absorb her, then transform to physical mode to avoid ascending to the Gateway, but if I failed to do so in a few seconds, I would rise too high to survive the fall.

As I concentrated, the swirling energy seemed to fight against my efforts. Try as I might, I couldn't get the fibers to draw Tokyo in.

The upward pull strengthened. We had to be higher than the dome by now. Only one option remained. Go physical first and then absorb her into my cloak while falling.

I focused on transforming, but I couldn't mentally force my inner energy to move in the right direction. It seemed that I had no anchor to physical reality. Maybe my connection level had bottomed to zero.

Tokyo gasped, then looked at me with blinking eyes. "Who are you?"

I grunted. "Phoenix... trying to transform... from ghost mode. We're getting... sucked into the sky."

As we continued rising—how quickly, I couldn't guess—she kissed me on the cheek. A tingle raced across my phantom body. "You can do this," she whispered, her accent tinged with an Oriental flavor. "Concentrate on your cloak. It is the easiest part to transform. When it becomes physical, I will go into it. Then transform from your valve outward. Your weight will compete with the upward pull. Our hope is that you will fall slowly and hit the ground without breaking your bones."

I nodded and focused on the cloak, still partially wrapped around Tokyo. After several seconds, she disappeared into its fibers. The upward suction eased. Seconds later, the cyclone of radiance lifted away, revealing my surroundings. I floated in midair, the dome below, maybe fifty feet down, closed now that the system had been flushed.

As I transformed further, I sank, my weight overcoming the suction. Now that the transformation had started, I couldn't reverse it or I might again risk losing connection with reality. I just had to slow the process enough to enable a soft landing, as Tokyo had said.

My chest turned solid, then my head and arms. The upward draft pulled my ghostly legs higher, elongating them and turning me upside down. Pain throttled the boundary between ghost and reality. If I didn't hurry, the competing forces might rip my body in half.

I rushed the process. The moment my legs solidified, gravity pulled me into a full plunge. When I passed the dome's level, a line looped around my torso, binding my arms against my sides. The line tightened. As my velocity slowed, I swung into an arc and fell at an angle.

Above, a woman screamed. The line gave way, and I slammed into the ground, shoulder first, and slid through grass and leaves.

When I stopped, I turned to my back and stared skyward. The spin of radiance had spread out into a flat, swirling cyclone, wider than the hole in the radioactive shield. As the swirl rose, its extremities brushed against the shield's boundary. Tiny explosions of light erupted at the contact points, and the shield retracted, expanding the hole. Soon, the swirl disappeared at a higher level, and the hole contracted to where it was previously, though the shield seemed thinner than before.

Pain jerked my attention away from the sight. My arm throbbed, immobilized by the binding rope. My back tingled. I tried to move my legs, but only my toes responded.

From the dome, Shanghai descended a line, touched down, and sprinted toward me. When she arrived, she dropped to her knees and laid a hand on my cheek. "You're alive! I *did* slow you down enough!"

"You did great. That was an incredible line throw." With the words, pain ripped across my skull. I grimaced, but kept my gaze on Shanghai. Although sweat dripped from her smudged forehead, she looked like an Asian angel. "Thanks for saving my life."

"Glad to do it." She whipped out a knife and sliced through the line, freeing my arms. "Did you find Tokyo?"

"Got her in my cloak." I touched my clasp. "Tokyo, are you all right in there?"

"I am well, Phoenix. A bit confused, though."

"Give me a minute to recover, and I'll explain everything."

"Of course. Take your time."

I lifted my good arm. "Let's see if I can get up." Shanghai grabbed my wrist and eased me to my feet. The right side of my body ached, and I couldn't lift my injured arm, though I could bend it at the elbow. "I might have separated my shoulder."

"Let's hope it's just a bruise." She massaged my shoulder. Her strong fingers pushed deeply into my muscles, spiking the pain. "Does that hurt?" she asked.

I grimaced. "Quite a bit. I'm not sure it's helping."

"Wait a second. I see what's wrong." She gave my arm a shove. Something popped. Pain knifed through the joint and down my spine, but it soon eased.

I rotated my shoulder, raising only a twinge. "It feels a lot better."

"You dislocated it. I popped it back into place."

I continued exercising my shoulder. With each rotation, the pain eased further. "Who taught you how to do that?"

"My trainer. It happened to him a few times. He showed me how to pop it back in."

"Well, thanks for the fix, Doc." I lifted my legs in turn. The right one throbbed, but it worked. "I think I'm ready to go now."

Shanghai pointed toward the building. "I came out the front door. It's probably still unguarded."

As we walked in that direction, I limped, though the pain lessened with each step. "Tokyo," I said into my cloak, "I found you in the energy grid in the Gatekeeper's building. You were under the dome where the depot lines terminate."

"Thank you for the information, Phoenix. I will comment on that in a moment. First, do you have any word on Abigail?"

"Abigail?"

"My daughter. Perhaps you know her by Akua, her Ghanaian name."

"Oh. Right. She told me about her multiple names. Her Reaper name is Singapore. I call her Sing for short." I looked at Shanghai. She winced, apparently realizing that I had to tell a mother that her daughter was dead. "Tokyo, I have bad news. Sing died while trying to find your soul in the Gateway system, but we have her body, and we're hoping to rejoin her soul to it, just like we hope to do for you."

After a moment of silence, Tokyo sighed. "Thank you for your efforts. Perhaps God's purposes will be accomplished in ways I could not predict."

Her words stuck in my mind—God's purposes. More God talk. A topic that once seemed odd had grown in frequency. "We'll keep doing the best we can," I said. "Maybe soon you and Sing will be alive and together again."

"What about my husband, Kwame? Have you heard anything about him?"

Again I glanced at Shanghai. She patted my arm and whispered, "Just tell her. No use hiding anything."

"Tokyo, Kwame is dead. We heard Alex say his soul was going to the abyss, so I still have to rescue him. I don't know how he died, but it seems clear that he hid his death from everyone he knew, including Sing... I mean, Akua. Abigail."

"And from me." Tokyo's voice lowered to a pain-streaked whisper. "Allow me some silent meditation, if you don't mind."

"Of course. Take all the time you need."

As we continued at a slow pace, I focused on Shanghai. "Big news. The Gatekeeper pushed Alex into the abyss."

Shanghai's eyes widened. "Why?"

"He suspected her of being a traitor." For the next couple of minutes, I gave her a blow-by-blow of what I had seen and heard. By the time I finished, we had come within sight of the main door. "So, assuming Alex got fried by the electrified souls, only Erin knows I'm alive. I don't know how she'll explain your disappearance. Maybe she'll say you were killed trying to escape."

"Let's hope she'll be waiting for us in Tokyo's coffin room. I'm sure she didn't expect you to retrieve her soul this way."

"Nobody did." We walked into the building as fast as my gimpy leg would allow, breezed past the statue, and hustled up the stairway, past a pair of dark spots on the carpet, then to the room where we had started.

Erin stood next to Tokyo's coffin with a computer tablet in hand. A dark container similar to a foundry crucible sat on the table next to the coffin along with a pair of tongs and a white bag with a red cross emblazoned on the side. A lid covered the crucible, shielding its contents from view.

When we entered, Erin looked up from the screen and gasped. "Phoenix! You made it!"

"Yeah. I guess this isn't the way you thought I'd come back."

"Yes. I mean, no." She looked at her tablet, then at me. "I saw that the system flushed, and I didn't see you on the grid afterward. How did you get back?"

I gave her an angled stare. Had she ever been this flustered before? "We took a different route. I'll explain later. I have Tokyo's soul in my cloak, so—"

"You do?" She glanced at the crucible, then put on a

stoic mask. "I mean, of course you do. You wouldn't have come back without her."

"Well, it wasn't easy, but I managed." I eyed the crucible. I could ask for an explanation, but too many other issues demanded attention. "We figured out that you're the Eagle."

"As I expected you would, but I have no time to discuss my alliances or defend the actions I took to ensure our success." She extended a hand. "Give me your cloak. We need to get started right away. Time is of the essence."

I glanced at Shanghai. She gave me a nod. We had come this far without confronting Erin. We could wait a while longer.

I whispered into the cloak's fibers. "Tokyo, we're starting the process."

"Thank you, Phoenix." Her voice sounded stronger now. "I hope to see you with my real eyes soon."

"And I'm looking forward to seeing you." I unplugged my clasp, removed the cloak, and gave it to Erin. "How did Tokyo die?"

"An assassin used a sonic gun. Since that time, a surgeon repaired her brain. I also had Sing's brain repaired, though I have not yet had time to do the same for Peter. Not that his situation matters now."

"His situation? What do you mean?"

Erin waved a hand. "Never mind. It's not important."

"Where are the souls who were in my cloak when Alex gave it to you?"

"In Sing's coffin room. It's shielded now, and they're comfortable. No one should find them there."

"How do you keep the Gatekeeper from entering?"

"He thinks this room and Sing's room are labs for

purifying the energy, such as what you received at the portable depot. He has no interest in the particulars, so he never enters. In fact, he never even ventures up the stairs."

I nodded. "That sounds as safe as we can hope for."

"Let's focus on the job at hand. We have much to do." Her manner reflected businesslike disinterest as she neither smiled nor frowned, though a tremor in her hands gave away fear. "First we put Tokyo's soul in the coffin with her body. To do that, we infuse your cloak with a stream of electrified energy, which will force her out of the fibers. The process might be painful for her, but it shouldn't take long."

"Considering Tokyo's power," I said, "why can't she just come out on her own? She was able to go in without my help."

"Perhaps she can, but I need to follow the procedure to make sure I get it right. This is all new to me." Erin opened the hinged top of the coffin, draped the cloak over Tokyo's body up to her chin, and closed the lid. She reached for a dial on the wall and turned it clockwise. "I'm maximizing the energy influx. When we see Tokyo's ghost emerge, we'll move to the next step."

I kept my gaze fixed on Tokyo and the cloak. "If this is new, how do you know what to do?"

Erin stared at the wall meters. "Melchizidek has been in power for two hundred years. As you might expect, there have been a number of assassination attempts. When one attempt succeeded, a team of his worshippers captured his soul and devised this restoration process. When he resurrected, he reassumed power with great force, which made his opponents hesitant to try again."

Shanghai touched the coffin. "I think I see her."

Inside, a ghostly form eased out of the cloak, like fog rising from the ground. When her face clarified, it matched the corpse perfectly. Her ghostly eyes darted, apparently looking at each of us, though the rest of her features stayed calm.

"She's ready." Erin turned the dial back to its former position. "Now I remove the cloak and let her settle." She lifted the coffin's lid a few inches, reached inside, and pulled the cloak out from under Tokyo's soul, as if sliding a tablecloth from under the place settings. After a few seconds, her soul sank into her body and faded from sight.

Erin handed me the cloak. "Next comes the most delicate step. Like I said, I've never actually done this myself. I'm just following a set of instructions." Erin directed her voice toward Tokyo's corpse. "Tokyo, you now must reattach yourself to your body. I have no idea how to do it, so you're on your own. I will give you some time to figure it out."

Erin closed the lid. "Normal humans are unaware of how the attachment works, but Reapers are intimately acquainted with it, so they're better candidates for success."

"What about the Gatekeeper?" I asked as I put the cloak on. "How did he know what to do?"

"Trial and error. Four pain-filled attempts, I am told. The process left his heart weak even to this day, which is why you will never see him exert himself. As I mentioned, he hasn't climbed the stairs in years. He has an elevator that takes him to his bedroom suite."

"Why doesn't the energy heal his heart?" Shanghai asked.

"The energy reverses degenerative damage from

aging, but the resurrection process left a burn scar on his heart that surgeons have been unable to repair. I could explain more, but we need to get back to Tokyo." Erin set a finger on another wall switch. "This will send an electrical shock through her body to restart her heart. I set a power level that's lower than what they used for Melchizidek. Tokyo is smaller, and I don't want to inflict a similar burn on her heart."

Erin turned on the switch. Tokyo's body jerked. Her limbs twitched. Then, she lay motionless. The heart meter on the wall displayed 40, but it changed to 36 and rapidly dwindled.

Shanghai clasped her hands. "Is she dying again?"

"We'll see in a moment." Erin opened the coffin and spread the top of Tokyo's shirt, revealing a valve embedded in her sternum. A flexible hose ran from a disk-like adapter that had been plugged into her valve and then led out of the coffin to the wall where it attached to an outlet.

Erin grasped the hose and pulled. The hose and valve came out as a unit along with wires that ran into Tokyo's chest cavity. Blood oozed from the edges of the opening and trickled across her skin. Erin inserted a finger into the hole, her lips pressing together. After a few seconds, the heart-rate meter showed 45 and increased until it rose to 54 and stayed there.

Exhaling, Erin set the hose-and-valve combination at the bottom of the coffin, withdrew her arm, and closed the lid. "I didn't have a chance to put gloves on. I hope she doesn't get an infection."

"So you did it." Shanghai pumped a fist. "Great job."

"We're not out of the woods yet. According to the instructions, a heart rate means only that the body has restarted, not that the soul has attached. If she fails to attach soon, the heart will stop again."

I kept an eye on the meter, now fluctuating between 52 and 53. "What did you do to stabilize her heart?"

Erin opened the medical bag and rummaged inside. "In order to preserve Tokyo, we installed a valve so we could infuse her body with energy and keep it from decaying. The connection to her heart was temporary and easily removed, as you witnessed. I think her heart rejected the connection to the valve, most likely because she became accustomed to its absence after she finished her term as a Reaper, so I disconnected it."

From the bag, Erin withdrew a pliers-like tool, surgical gloves, an ointment tube, a tiny spray can, and a sternum valve sealed in a plastic bag. After putting on the gloves, she nodded at me. "Please open the lid and lean it against the wall."

When I did, she pointed the can's nozzle at Tokyo's chest and sprayed a clear liquid around the opening.

"She's still out cold," I said. "How long till she wakes up after she attaches?"

"*If* she attaches, probably immediately, which is why I'm worried. The delay is troubling." Her hands shaking, Erin squeezed paste from the tube and ran it around the edges of the chest opening. "If her heart fails now, we have only one more option, but I'm not going to describe it unless it's necessary." She fitted the valve into the chest hole. "This is a cosmetic valve that will seal her chest. She'll need plastic surgery later to patch her up permanently."

"A cosmetic valve?" Shanghai said. "It looks real. Could it be used to disguise someone as a Reaper?"

Erin's eyes darted from Shanghai to the meters to

Tokyo. "Actually, the Resistance once employed that deception in order to infiltrate the death industry. We used a real valve, and the implantation required every surgical step that Reapers go through except for attaching the wires and energy-infusion tube to the heart. We even inserted a bag behind the valve and inflated it with energy so the fake Reaper could pass an energy-level test or even give energy to another Reaper, but the mission ended in the death of the fake Reaper. Let's hope we never have to try that again."

When she finished, she stepped back from the coffin. "Now we wait."

I checked Tokyo's heart rate again—50. "It's dropping."

"I noticed." Erin set her tools in the bag and peeled off her gloves. "If it gets below thirty-five, I'll have to take the next step."

The desire to ask about that step nearly burst from my lips, but I swallowed down the urge. It probably had something to do with the crucible. "Did you hear what happened in the meeting room?"

Erin tossed her gloves into a waste can. "No. I've been cleaning up the mess from the illuminaries and waiting here for you."

"Melchizidek threw Alex into the abyss."

"What?" Erin's cheeks flushed fiery red. "Why?"

The Gatekeeper shouted from somewhere outside the room. "There was no cloak in the bag! You accused her falsely!"

"Uh-oh." Erin hurried to the door and opened it.

"Exalted One..." Sydney's voice sounded feeble, contrite. "You said yourself that you felt her rebellion."

"More likely just her stubborn, independent spirit. I need Council members who will speak their mind."

"But I'm sure she had a scheme to usurp you. I just guessed wrong about her method."

"Perhaps you are the one with the scheme. Perhaps I should send you into the abyss to get her out."

All three of us walked down the hall to hear better, though we stayed out of the Gatekeeper's view.

"Surely she is dead, Exalted One. The electrical shock alone—"

"You know nothing. Alex is an Owl. She has powers you cannot hope to possess. If anyone can survive in there, she can."

"Very well, Exalted One. If I can have a protective suit, I will go at your bidding. I will risk my life and hope you will think better of me."

"I will think better of you the moment you are out of my sight."

"Out of your sight? But I have been nothing but loyal to you. My motivations have always been—"

"Motivations?" the Gatekeeper roared. "Motivations are proclaimed from rooftops by men who hide their real intent behind masks. Facts are facts. You accused Alex of treason without sufficient grounds and incited me to punish her."

"I grant that my accusation was premature. What can I do to earn back your trust?"

"There is only one way to regain my favor. Before I tell you, I must summon Erin."

Something beeped back in the room. "My tablet," Erin said as she rushed that way.

I edged closer and sneaked a look. Sydney and the five

remaining Council members stood between the staircases, all still masked as they waited for Erin to respond to the Gatekeeper's call.

Erin rushed into the hallway, her tablet in hand. She stopped at my side and whispered, "Phoenix, I fear that Melchizidek has murder on his mind, and I might not be immune. Whatever you do, don't interfere. You must save Tokyo and escape this place."

"What about the abyss? I have to rescue the souls there. I need the password to the computer system to stop the machines."

"If you must, you must. I am not certain of that password, but I know the one Melchizidek uses on his tablet, so it might work. It's a colon, then Melchizidek spelled backwards, then a seven, then an exclamation mark. Do you know how to spell his name?"

I nodded. "I've seen it plenty of times in the propaganda posters."

"Good." She slid her hand into mine. "It has been an honor working with you, Phoenix, even though you didn't know it until now." She then ran down the stairs and chirped in a cheery voice, "Yes, Exalted One?"

I whispered to Shanghai. "Keep an eye on Tokyo and come get me if her heart rate falls below forty."

"Will do." Shanghai skulked toward Tokyo's room.

I crept closer to the balcony wall. With everyone focusing on the Gatekeeper, they weren't likely to notice me.

The Gatekeeper held out his hands. "As a sign of loyalty, the Council members will form a circle with me while Erin records this event with her tablet."

Erin aimed her tablet's camera lens at him. "I am ready."

Sydney grasped the Gatekeeper's hand on one side, while one of the women did so on the other. The remaining three completed the circle.

A bright glow streamed from the Gatekeeper's hands to the two Council members at his sides. They stiffened as if locked in place. As the radiance flowed to the other three, they, too, stood like statues, an aura surrounding each one.

The Gatekeeper released their hands and backed away. "Erin, they should stay paralyzed for a few minutes. Have the illuminaries throw them into the abyss right away. Then report to me in my private chambers."

Erin lowered the tablet. "Of course."

When the Gatekeeper walked away, I turned and hurried to Tokyo's room. Shanghai stood near the wall, her eyes locked on the heart meter, which now read 42.

"Too low," I whispered. "I'm not sure what Erin's going to do or even if she'll make it back."

"What happened out there?"

I gave her a quick rundown on the Gatekeeper's treachery and the concern that Erin might be his next victim. Melchizidek seemed to be in the mood to murder.

Shanghai sidled to the table and plucked the lid from the crucible. As vapor rose from the opening, she picked up the tongs. "If he kills Erin, we'll have to figure out the next step she was talking about."

I eased closer. "You'd better not. She'll probably get the illuminaries to dump the bodies and then come straight here. She'd be a fool to go to the Gatekeeper now."

"What are you doing?" Erin barked as she stormed into the room.

Shanghai set the tongs down. "Just looking. I didn't take anything out."

Erin looked at the heart meter and sighed. "Thirty-six. I suppose it doesn't matter. You'll have to see it soon enough. Kindly give me a bit of room."

As Shanghai backed away from the table, Erin picked up the tongs and inserted them into the mouth of the crucible. "This container holds six crystals, the only ones in the world. Melchizidek's scientists invented them when they sought to restore his soul to his body. I hoped Tokyo would be powerful enough to allow me to bypass this step, but it seems that no one is able to reattach soul to mind without help, not even her."

When Erin pulled the tongs from the crucible, the ends pinched a ball the size of a fingernail. Tiny spikes protruded from the surface, spikes that bent under the tongs' pressure. She dropped the crystal into her opposite palm, then set the tongs down and rolled the crystal from hand to hand. "It will cool in a moment."

"What does the crystal do?" Shanghai asked.

Erin stared at the heart meter, now at 32. "You know how difficult it is to detach a soul from a body."

Shanghai nodded. "It can take a lot of effort. Sometimes the attachment points feel like they're glued to the brain."

"That's what many Reapers have told me." Erin let the crystal settle in her right palm. "It's clear now that reattachment takes much more than just effort. It takes the spark of life, which this crystal will carry."

I shook my head. "I don't understand."

"And I won't explain it. Just watch and learn." The crystal still in hand, Erin climbed onto the table, lay on top of Tokyo chest to chest, and looked at me. "Phoenix,

I am deeply sorry for my part in the deaths of Misty and Sing. I wanted to restore Misty, but her brain damage was beyond repair. I don't expect you to forgive me, but I need to let you know that my heart broke with each senseless loss of life. Now I am doing what I can to atone for my sins."

"For your sins?" I stepped close and grabbed her wrist. "What are you doing?"

She jerked her arm away, pushed the crystal into her mouth, and swallowed it. "I'm afraid you're on your own. Whatever you do, stay away from Melchizidek."

"Erin, no!"

I reached out again, but Shanghai pulled me back. "I think it's too late," she whispered.

A glow emanated from Erin's face. "I am leaving my tablet for your use. All passwords are entered, so the systems are open to your access with the exception of the abyss engines, and I provided a password that might work there. With the tablet, you can control almost everything in the building, even the physical wall switches." The glow strengthened. "Now if you would be so kind..." Her voice fractured. "Please... please send my wretched soul directly to the Gateway. And... and pray for a merciful judgment for me." A trembling smile graced her lips. "Farewell."

Shanghai clutched my hand and whispered, "Farewell, Erin."

Her face now shining like a miniature sun, Erin opened Tokyo's mouth, set her lips on Tokyo's, and exhaled. The glow eased away from Erin and drifted into Tokyo. Then Erin fell limp over Tokyo's body.

CHAPTER EIGHTEEN

I LEAPED TO THE table, rolled Erin out of the coffin, and shifted her toward the floor, my wounded leg throbbing. When I laid her on her back, I checked for a pulse at her neck. Nothing. I set my ear against her chest. No heartbeat.

I lifted away and sighed. "She's dead."

Shanghai looked at the wall meter, her eyes sparkling with tears. "Tokyo's heart rate's back to fifty. Whatever Erin did seems to be working."

I whispered, "A crystal that transfers life. Somehow it channeled energy from Erin to Tokyo."

Shanghai set the lid back on the crucible and crouched with me next to Erin. "I guess life is more than heartbeats and soul attachments. Like Erin said, life needs a spark, and only living people have it. She gave her spark to Tokyo."

"Does that mean one of us can give our spark to Erin and bring her back to life?"

"Probably, but I don't think she wants to come back. She made that pretty clear. Besides, the Gatekeeper has Erin on his kill list. She wanted to go out this way instead of by his hand."

"I guess I'd better grant her last request." I pulled my cloak's sleeve over my hand and covered Erin's eyes with my palm.

Shanghai pinched the sleeve. "Let me take her out to the hall. She can fly away from there."

I slid a hand under Erin's back. "I'll carry her out there for you."

"With that bad leg?" She shook her head. "Not a chance."

"Well, then wait a few minutes and I'll help you. Don't you want to be here when Tokyo wakes up?"

Shanghai bit her lip. "Actually... no."

"Oh. Right. The infamous comment you made about her."

"Yeah." She clenched her eyes nearly closed. "Do you think you can smooth that over for me a little before I get back?"

"Sure. I'll see what I can do."

"Thanks." Shanghai touched my cloak. "Do you still have the bottle of pills?"

"Right here." I pushed a hand into my pocket and withdrew it. "Why?"

"I'm going to make Erin's death look like a suicide." Shanghai opened the bottle and dumped the pills into the medical bag. "I'll be back soon." She slid her arms under Erin, lifted her into a cradle, and carried her into the hall with a staggering gait.

I rose and stood next to the coffin. The heart meter stayed constant at 58—somewhat low, but not surprising for someone who hadn't moved in a year or so. Tokyo's eyes shifted under their lids, a good sign of brain activity. Maybe she was ready to wake up.

"Tokyo?" I whispered. "Can you hear me?"

Her eyes opened. After blinking several times, she smiled. "Ah! There is the brave young man who plucked me out of oblivion."

"It was my pleasure, Tokyo." I grasped her arm and helped her sit upright. "How do you feel?"

"No pain, I think." Tokyo ran a hand through her dark hair and scratched her scalp. "But I feel like I haven't had a bath in years."

I laughed softly. "That's probably true."

She looked at her chest and touched her valve. "Why is this here?"

"It's just a cosmetic filler. To preserve your body, the Eagle installed a different one that hooked to your heart, then she took it out while she was infusing your soul and replaced it with the filler."

"You mean Erin?" Tokyo looked from side to side. "Where is she?"

"Well..." I picked up the crucible and gave her a quick explanation of the life-spark transfer process. I finished with, "She gave her life so you could live."

Tokyo's expression drooped, for the moment making her look closer to her real age. She glanced around again. "Where is her body?"

"Another Reaper carried it from the room to release her soul."

"Another Reaper? How many Reapers are here?"

"Just two who are alive... three if you count yourself."

Tokyo reached for my hand. "I would like to get up, please."

I helped her climb out of the coffin and down to the

floor where I kept a grip on her arm. "Do you think you can stand on your own?"

She shook her head. "I feel so weak. My muscles have atrophied."

"You'd better sit." I guided her down to a sitting position. When she settled with her back against a table leg, I sat in front of her. "I can't stay here with you for long. I know where your daughter's body and soul are. I have to revive her as soon as possible."

"Of course you do, and I want to come with you. Please give me a moment to gather my strength."

"Sure." I glanced at the open door. Shanghai was nowhere in sight, but she might be listening. "Tokyo, do you know how I survived the fall from above the dome?"

She shook her head. "My faculties were compromised. I was barely conscious."

"Another Reaper standing on the roof shot a line around me, shifted my fall into an arc, and slowed my downward momentum. I hit pretty hard but not hard enough to break anything."

Tokyo lifted her brow. "That is a remarkable feat. This Reaper must have incredible prowess."

"She does. Her name is Shanghai. Have you heard of her?"

"Heard of her? I'm her biggest fan."

"Really? Did you hear what she said about you in an interview?"

Tokyo nodded. "I love her swagger. From your description, it sounds like she's well on her way to fulfilling her confident self-assessment."

"I'm sure she'll be glad to hear that. She was worried—"

"I did hear it." Shanghai walked in, her gait lively.

When she sat next to me, she extended a hand toward Tokyo. "It's an honor to meet you."

"The honor is mine." After shaking Shanghai's hand, Tokyo smiled. "I have heard marvelous stories about you. When my strength recovers, it would be a delight to stage a competition with you. I would like to see your talents with my own eyes."

Shanghai bowed her head. "That would be the greatest honor of all."

"Not to break up this mutual-respect thing," I said, "but we should get back to business."

"Of course." Tokyo took in a deep breath and let it out slowly, as if relishing the ability to do so. "First, thank you both for what you have done. Just the fact that you're here proves your courage and willingness to sacrifice."

"Second," Tokyo continued as she picked up her boots and set them near her feet, "from what I could gather, Phoenix, it looked like you pulled me out of the energy pool under the dome. Yet, earlier I was certain that I had entered a room like this one, but then I ascended to heaven, as if drawn by a vacuum." She blinked. "Or was I dreaming?"

I gestured toward the wall and explained how the energy shield works and that she probably emerged in a room that had no active shield. When I finished, I added, "Erin said she couldn't detect you in the energy network, so you probably did come out, at least for a while."

Tokyo slid one of her boots on. "I remember that I rose swiftly and came upon a bright light. A voice that sounded like a sweet cello sang to me. It said something like, 'Welcome, champion of the oppressed. Come with me.'"

She breathed a delighted sigh. "Then I saw the speaker,

a tall, winged man with eyes of fire. I assumed he was an angel, like the ones in the old stories. He took me by the hand and led me through a gateway made of a pearly substance, I believe. We stood on a street paved with gold that led to a city on a hill that sparkled like glittering gems in sunlight."

"That sounds beautiful," Shanghai said. "What happened next?"

Tokyo began tying the boot's laces. "I think he told me to wait there. Something about events transpiring in the sphere of mortals that might have a bearing on my future. So I waited. How long, I don't know. Eventually, a young man wearing a Reaper's cloak appeared at the other side of the gateway. He asked the angel if I could return to earth. The angel said I could, but only if this bold visitor had the power to pass through the gate while pulling me out. And even if he could perform the feat, he would have to stay there."

I whispered to Shanghai, "Bartholomew's theory. It's true after all. Just not the way he expected."

Shanghai nodded. "I wonder how he knew."

I refocused on Tokyo. "Then what happened?"

She slid the other boot on. "The angel and the young man discussed where my soul would be taken, somewhere that I wouldn't just immediately fly back up, a place where I would be safe from those who would do me harm and where I could be found by my allies. Then the young man flared his cape and walked toward the gateway opening. Just as he crossed the boundary, he stopped and extended his hand toward me. I approached him and said that I couldn't let him take my place, but he grabbed my hand and said something cryptic. I remember the words, but I didn't understand what they meant.

"Then, in a brilliant flash of light, he pulled me back through while leaping to the other side himself. The angel warned me not to protest this Reaper's act of loving sacrifice, so I acquiesced. Then I blacked out, and I assume the angel transported me to the dome room."

"It's odd that the angel put you there after saying he wanted to make sure you wouldn't just fly straight back to the Gateway."

Tokyo began tying the second boot. "Perhaps it was the safest place available. I'm not sure what would have happened if I had gone back to heaven. Perhaps the angel would have sent me to the dome again. One principle I have learned is that sacrificial love is never wasted, and I will never forget that young man's sacrifice."

Shanghai raised a finger. "You mentioned something the Reaper said. Something unforgettable."

"Ah, yes. Tears streamed from the young man's eyes, though they seemed to be tears of joy, tears of relief. He said in a trembling voice, 'Tell my mother that I'm finally free.'"

Shanghai glanced at me before looking at Tokyo again. "Did he have blond hair and a muscular build?"

"Yes." Tokyo finished tying the boot. "I assume you know him."

"Peter. Alex's son." Shanghai touched my sleeve. "Are you sure his soul was in your cloak when you gave it to Alex?"

"I'm sure. When Erin removed him, he must have gone to an unshielded area." I tapped my chin with a finger. Erin said something about Peter. What was it?

Her words drifted back to mind. *I also had Sing's brain repaired, though I have not yet had time to do the same for Peter. Not that his situation matters now.*

But his situation did matter at the time she said that. We had both his body and his soul.

"When Erin extracted the souls from my cloak," I said, "she must have seen Peter come out."

Shanghai shook her head. "Not if he was invisible. But we won't know what happened until we get to the other coffin room and see what's going on."

"Right." I rose to a crouch in front of Tokyo. "Feel up to seeing your daughter?"

"Without a doubt." She spread her arms. "If you two will help, I'm sure I can make it."

Shanghai set the crucible in the medical bag and tucked it under an arm while I picked up Erin's tablet. We each grasped one of Tokyo's arms and walked her through the doorway and into the passage leading to the balcony. After checking the lower level to make sure it was clear, we slinked along the balcony's south wall.

When we reached the western side of the upper level, we turned south toward Sing's coffin room, Tokyo now needing only to set a hand on our shoulders. Ahead, the door to the room stood ajar.

The tablet still in hand, I hustled into the room. As before, Sing's and Peter's bodies lay in coffins. Three pedestals sat near an adjacent wall, but two of the glass enclosures were empty. Albert's ghost stood in the other, his eyes wide as he laid his palms on the glass and shouted noiselessly.

Shanghai walked in and looked around. "Strange. The room's shielded, but the door was open."

"Where's Tokyo?" I asked.

Shanghai gestured with a thumb. "In the hall adjusting her boots. Her feet aren't used to them. She also said she needed to rest a minute."

"Being dead so long takes a toll, I'm sure. She's probably also preparing herself to see her daughter's body." I looked at the walls and ceiling. As Erin had said, an energy shield now covered every surface. "Let's see if Albert can get us up to speed."

I set the tablet on the coffin table. When I lifted the glass enclosure a few inches, Albert's voice pierced the gap. "Phoenix? Is that you?"

"Yes. Bend over so I can slide this thing off you." As Albert bent his hefty body, I pulled the enclosure sideways until it cleared him. After laying it on the floor, I brushed my hands together. "I guess you haven't seen me before."

He straightened to his plump, five-and-a-half-foot stature and pushed his hair over a bald spot. "No, but your gender, age, and Reaper's garb made it an easy guess."

"Can you tell us what happened?" Shanghai asked.

Albert pointed at the door with a thick finger. "A woman brought us here and extracted us from a cloak. Singapore called the woman Erin. Anyway, Erin and Singapore engaged in a whispered conversation, which I thought rather rude considering that Peter and I were in the same predicament as Sing. In any case, Erin set up these pedestals and asked me to stand on one. I complied, of course. What choice did I have?"

"Did Sing and Peter do the same?" I asked.

"Patience, Phoenix. I'm getting to that." Albert nodded toward one of the other pedestals. "After Erin enclosed me, Singapore made ready to stand on that one, but she turned back to Erin and whispered to her again. After they agreed on something, Erin just walked out and left the door open. She ignored Peter completely. Never said a word to him. A few seconds later, Peter followed her. Then… whoosh… he lifted straight up and disappeared."

I gestured toward the ceiling. "Any soul outside that energy shield gets suctioned straight to the Gateway."

"Well, since no one told me that," Albert continued, "Peter's sudden departure left me in quite a shock, but then Singapore stepped close to me and said, 'Peter is making the greatest sacrifice a man can make. He is laying down his life for another, someone whom he once considered an enemy. There is no higher love than that.'

"I retorted that Peter was already dead, but when she explained that he was giving up his chance to be regenerated, I felt pretty stupid. Then she said the glass around me would soon become soundproof, but not to worry. I would be rescued in a short while. My temporary prison was there to protect me. After that, she got into her coffin, settled into her body, and disappeared."

"Then she must still be there." I strode to the coffin and set my hands on the lid.

"No, Phoenix," Albert said. "I don't think so. A few minutes after she entered, a hissing sound came from the wall, and I saw a blur, like maybe she got sucked somewhere. That was the last thing I heard before my sound got cut off."

Tokyo walked in and closed the door. "Then she must be in the energy lines."

Albert gasped, wide eyed. "Tokyo?"

She nodded. "How do you know me?"

"Who wouldn't know you? You're the most famous

Reaper ever to walk the earth. If I were alive, I'd ask for your autograph."

Tokyo bowed her head. "You are kind to say so."

"Kindness is easy. Courage is not. Now I realize that Erin stuck me in that glass cage to keep me from running out of here like a scared puppy. And she stifled my voice to make sure I didn't yell my head off when everyone left me here alone."

"Erin set everything up," Shanghai said. "Sing's in the energy lines for safekeeping. Erin waited until after the flushing was finished and then used her tablet to control the coffin valve. She wasn't taking any chances that someone might come in and see Sing on the pedestal."

I nodded. "And Sing asked Erin to leave the door open."

"Do you think Sing told Erin that Peter wanted to retrieve Tokyo from the Gateway?"

"Maybe. But if she did, Erin doubted it was possible. That's why she was so surprised when I showed up with Tokyo's soul."

I leaned my back against the coffin table. "So what do we do now?"

"We're in pretty good shape in some ways," Shanghai said. "Alex is out of the picture. The Gatekeeper thinks you're dead. My guess is that Erin told him I'm dead. I put Erin's body on the floor near the bottom of a staircase and set the empty pill bottle next to her. I took the bottle's label off so the Gatekeeper wouldn't know what was in it. I hope he'll think she killed herself to escape getting thrown into the abyss with the others."

I picked up the tablet and held it out for everyone to

see. "Can the Gatekeeper track this? We don't want it to lead him to us."

"That's easy to remedy," Albert said. "That model has a privacy setting that turns off its beacon. The signal was designed as a way to find the tablet if you misplace it, not as a way to spy out and find a tablet user."

"Perfect." I gave Albert an angled glance. "How did you run across that setting?"

He shrugged. "I misplaced things a lot. I was a busy man."

Shanghai took the tablet. "I'll find the setting."

While Shanghai searched the system's menus, I explained to Tokyo and Albert everything I knew about the building and its dangers. I also provided a summary of what we had accomplished and where we stood.

When I finished, Tokyo squared her shoulders and looked at each of us in turn. "Since Erin is dead, I will resume my leadership of the Resistance movement and take command of our ongoing mission. That is, if there are no objections."

"Not from me," I said. "It will be an honor to serve under you." Shanghai and Albert each gave an affirming nod.

"I appreciate your confidence in me." Tokyo folded her hands at her back and began pacing in front of us. "So our goals are to conquer the Gatekeeper, find where he keeps the reservoir of energy, turn off the abyss machines, and somehow feed the reservoir energy to those souls so they can escape with their phantom forms refilled and intact."

"Or use the energy to break down the shield," I added. "They might be restored on their own when we send them to the Gateway."

Tokyo stopped, her lips firm as she nodded. "Good thought. I will have to ponder that one. At some point we will retrieve Abigail... Singapore... and regenerate her. If the procedure fails as it did with me, then I will be the one who ingests a life-spark crystal. Since I am her mother, and since my work here will be done, I assume no one will dispute my right and duty to do so."

Tokyo again looked at each of us in turn. I gave her a resigned nod. How could anyone argue with a mama bear like her?

Apparently satisfied with our silence, she returned my nod. "Phoenix, you will dive into the abyss and prepare to stop the engines. Shanghai will take the tablet and search for the reservoir. I am confident that the tablet will be able to communicate with the computer below the abyss, so Shanghai will keep you up to date with messages. We'll leave it for you to decide how to best use the stored energy once Shanghai learns more about where it is kept and how it can be distributed."

Albert raised a hand. "Since Phoenix has the passwords he needs, my skills are better used if I accompany Shanghai in her cloak." He gave me a timid smile. "No offense, Phoenix, but I would like to avoid another spin in that whirlpool."

"None taken. But now that we know that the Gateway is real and safe, don't you want to go there and get out of this place?"

"Everyone around me is risking their lives to save the world." He shrugged. "I'm already dead, so why not help? I'll get to the Gateway eventually."

I clenched my fist. "That's the spirit."

He grinned. "Literally."

"Tokyo, how about you?" Shanghai asked. "What are you going to do?"

Tokyo touched the tablet. "We'll use this device to shut off the drainage from the soul farms. Then I will set all the intact souls free."

"And the souls in the holding tanks," Shanghai added. "I can show you where they are. But someone will have to deal with the illuminaries. They're sure to be guarding the farms."

Tokyo pointed at herself. "I will keep the illuminaries distracted so you can search freely. I hope they will summon the Gatekeeper so I can deal with him personally. He is our ultimate target."

I raised a hand. "According to Alex, I have the power to resist him. Maybe you shouldn't battle him until I get out of the abyss."

Tokyo gave me a long, hard look before offering a tight-lipped nod. "I will consider your appeal, but if the illuminaries interrupt Shanghai's search, I won't have any choice but to draw them away from her, perhaps by threatening the Gatekeeper. Just hurry as much as you can."

"I will."

"You'd *better* hurry," Shanghai said. "You have to dive in while in ghost mode, and your connection's probably going to start out near rock bottom.... Unless..." She stepped to the control wall and lifted a supply hose attached to a valve. "Unless you get another infusion."

I shook my head. "No. Definitely not."

"But you need it. A lot more than I do, that's for sure."

"Listen..." As I raised a finger, my entire arm shook. "I'm not going to take a single molecule of any energy that's been sucked out of those pitiful souls. Molly's out there. Mex and Colm. And my parents are somewhere in this warped excuse for heaven's gate."

"But you did it before when they were out there."

I firmed my jaw. "Well, I'm not going to do it again."

"If you asked them, they would gladly donate their energy for this cause. They wouldn't think twice." Shanghai looked at Tokyo. "Right?"

Tokyo crossed her arms. "This is an ethical issue that Phoenix must decide for himself. I don't want to influence him."

"I don't care if they'd donate," I growled. "They're not the only ones suffering out there. Consuming their energy is wrong. It's evil."

Shanghai dropped the hose and clenched her fists at her hips. "The eternal lives of millions of suffering people hang in the balance. Are you going to turn your back on them? If you don't get more energy, you'll run dry, and everything we've worked for will fall apart."

I locked stares with Shanghai. Tears trickled from her reddened eyes down her flushed cheeks. She was so sincere, so filled with determination. How could I counter her reasoning? Should I even try?

Then, as if whispered in my ear, the Sancta's words returned. *Faith in the Highest Power will infuse you when your reserves have run dry.*

I swallowed past a lump in my throat. Faith? What did I know about faith? I had always been like Shanghai, just doing what I had to do to survive and help others the best I could. Neither of us knew anything about faith.

"Phoenix?" Shanghai asked as she lifted the hose again. "You know you have to."

Once more the Sancta's words flowed. *The woman who controls you is the one for whom you violate your principles.*

I whispered, "My principles."

Shanghai raised her brow. "What?"

"I'm not going to violate my principles." I twisted the pewter ring from my finger and dropped it. It landed on the floor with a hollow thud. "I'll look for an update on the computer screen when I get down there."

"Well, *I'm* going to get an infusion," Shanghai said. "One of us has to be ready to fight the Gatekeeper."

"You do that." I strode from the room and down the hall. There was no need to look back. Shanghai's face pulsed in my mind—angry, perplexed, disappointed. But I couldn't do anything about that. I had a hellhole to dive into.

After skulking down the steps, I scanned the chamber outside the Council meeting room. Erin's body was nowhere in sight. Apparently the illuminaries had collected her. The Gatekeeper probably believed he was alone now, so security might be lax, at least until Shanghai and Tokyo started the purge of the farms.

I strode into the meeting room and walked straight to the edge of the abyss. Leaning over and allowing the downward pull to catch my cloak, I began the transformation to ghost mode. Because the process had slowed so much, I had to let it get further along before entering. Otherwise, I would stay physical too long, and the shocks would end this journey in a hurry.

When my body became more than half ghost, the upward suction battled the suction below. I couldn't risk waiting any longer.

I jumped into the abyss. As before, I plummeted

through the open area in the center, surrounded by the swirling blackness. When the swirl absorbed my phantom form, I swam with the downward pull as fast as I could until I reached the clogged souls.

Using both hands, I plowed through the obstruction and emerged into the open space, my head, torso, and arms protruding from the clog. Below, a pile of humans covered the trap door, taking up most of the area. Apparently their physical bodies had plunged right through the immaterial bottleneck.

I wriggled the rest of the way and dropped onto the person on top of the pile, though my weightless form had no impact. Being immaterial, I had no way to check for a pulse on any of the Council members. Even in a physical state, I wouldn't be able to stay long enough to check. The electrical jolts would paralyze or kill me. I just had to open the door and get out.

I peered at the bottom of the pile. Alex lay there, her mask still in place. Although her eyes were closed, the fingers on one hand moved as if she were clawing at the floor. The other Council members stayed motionless.

Setting my hands close to the person on top of the pile, I began shifting out of ghost mode. As soon as my forearms became physical, I grabbed that person's arm and urged the rest of my body to hurry. Pain shot through my hands and crawled up my skin along with the progressing transformation boundary.

When my head returned to normal, electrical jolts crashed from one side of my skull to the other and back again. The moment my legs formed, I threw the top person off, then one after another until I reached Alex.

As shocks stiffened every limb and pain blinded my

vision, I dragged her off the trap door. I jerked the door up and, holding on to the edges of the opening, lowered my feet to the top of the ladder.

Once I gained my balance, I reached for the door. Alex murmured, "Help me," though her eyes stayed closed.

I grabbed the door, pulled it shut, and stepped down two rungs to allow room for my head. Now in darkness, I looked up. White spots spun in my vision. Alex lay up there, suffering incredible torture. Yet, why should I care about her pain? She deserved it. And now she was out of the way. She wouldn't be around to hurt anyone ever again.

Too dizzy to climb down the ladder safely, I unfastened the flashlight from my belt and flicked it on. The spots in my eyes stayed in place, nearly filling my field of vision. For all practical purposes, I was blind.

"Blind," I whispered as I turned off the flashlight and refastened it to my belt. Once again, the Sancta's words returned. *There. You see? For you, faith is the deciding factor. Why should anyone act sacrificially for another person who doesn't believe in him? It would be ridiculous to suffer for someone who hates you.*

I spoke my response out loud. "Right. Exactly."

Her blistering rebuke followed. *And that is why you still wear blinders.*

The words scalded my heart. How could I be so filled with bitterness that I would leave Alex up there to die? Yet wasn't my reason practical rather than the product of bitterness? Saving her would not only bring about my own suffering, she could continue her crusade to take over the world. And she would probably be crueler than the

Gatekeeper ever thought of being. Even my saving act of kindness wouldn't soften her heart.

I sat on the ladder's top step. But how could I be certain of what she would do? Surely many people have changed their ways because of a loving sacrifice. But Alex? I shook my head. Impossible. No one could penetrate her callous heart. She was a controller—a cold, calculating controller.

I caressed my ring finger, now bare. Years ago, my father thought Misty controlled me. Then Alex thought she did. After that, it seemed that Shanghai held my reins. At times, I had given in to their influence, buckled under pressure, but no more. Now I was free.

Yet, was I really? Had hatred for Alex blinded me to another kind of chains? Was I now being controlled by my own fears and malice?

The Sancta said I wasn't in the service of the Highest Power. What did she mean by that? Whom did I really serve? Didn't I always try to do what was right?

The questions rose again. What was really right? Or wrong? Who decided moral boundaries?

I touched myself on the chest. I did. I chose what was right or wrong. I was my own moral master. I just did whatever seemed best at the time, and fears, doubts, and duties often pushed me one way or another. How could that be a trustworthy standard?

And now I faced a dilemma that tested every aspect of my nagging questions. My moral compass said to let Alex die. She deserved it. Even if I rescued her, she would betray me at her first opportunity. Evil turned her compass needle. Saving her would be folly.

Yet letting her die still felt wrong, as if another

compass demanded my attention. A moral standard had risen from the dead and raised a red warning flag. A quiet voice seemed to call from the depths. *Don't let fear control you. Never underestimate the power of a loving act.... Mercy is woven into your very being as surely as your hair is woven into your cloak.... It is who you are.... Shouldn't everyone benefit from a final chance? Even someone who doesn't deserve it? Some are cruel because they have never seen mercy's open hand.*

Again I shook my head. Not Alex. She was cruel from her very core. If I extended an open hand of mercy, she would just spit on it and callously kill again. I had to leave her there for the sake of those she would murder in the future. She would be gone for good, and I would be free to prepare to face the Gatekeeper.

The word *prepare* ushered in another memory—something I said to the Sancta.

Preparation is crucial, especially if you're trying to take down the most powerful being in the world.

Then she said, *I see that you wear the same blinders.*

What could she have meant? Since my statement prompted her retort, the answer had to be in my own words.

I whispered, "The most powerful being in the world." I was referring, of course, to the Gatekeeper. Obviously the Sancta took offense. Since she talked so much about the Highest Power, she probably thought I meant that the Gatekeeper had more power. Yet, I wasn't thinking about the Highest Power at all, which meant that I didn't have regard for any power other than what I could see.

Was she right about my blinders? Did I really think the "Highest Power" wasn't high enough? Was I turning my back on Alex because I believed no invisible power could conquer her? At this moment, she lay at the bottom of the abyss, conquered by the Gatekeeper, a visible force of evil. What would be wrong with letting her stay there?

More words whispered to mind. *You are an emissary of mercy.... That hand must first be offered before vengeance can be justified.*

I clapped my hands over my ears and shouted, "It makes no sense to save a murderer!"

In spite of my covered ears, words continued to flow. *Only the most insightful of your allies will understand. Such is the nature of your lonely outpost.*

I clenched my eyes shut. Allies understand? I didn't understand it myself. The Sancta was right. I didn't believe the Highest Power could stop Alex. My blinders were dark. Too dark. After all the cruelty I had seen, how could I believe in a virtuous higher power? The world was veiled in shadows. Evil ruled every corner. Cruelty consumed the souls of the innocent. Little girls like Molly died because a monster seated at the center of seven thrones denied her the means to survive, all the while gazing upon shriveled souls swirling at his feet, precious people upon whom he had fed, engorging himself with their vitality.

I shouted again. "How can anyone believe in the Highest Power when there's so much suffering in the world? What has he been doing while the children in my district strangle in their own mucus?"

I buried my face in my hands. I couldn't believe. I just couldn't.

"What has he been doing?" the Sancta whispered. "He has been preparing you for such a time as this. The

Highest Power reaches out to you, but you must also take a step... one step of faith."

I unhooked my flashlight, flicked it on, and swept it across the room. Now that my vision had cleared, every abyss machine was easy to see, but the Sancta was nowhere in sight. Her voice entered my ear as if she had been standing inches away, but that was impossible. I was sitting at the top of a ladder.

"You have identified your blinders," she continued, the words swirling around me like wind-blown mist. "Will you refuse to take them off? The Highest Power has chosen you to give breath to the little Mollys of this world. Will you turn your back because you cannot see how an apparently foolish act might fit into a larger picture? Are you so wise that you know what course a merciful act will take? A river often splits into many streams, paths you cannot guess."

"Just tell me," I called out. "What will happen if I save Alex?"

"A second step cannot be determined until the first one is made. This is where faith comes in. You must trust in the Highest Power to guide the steps that follow."

"But what if she doesn't stop killing?"

"Then you must keep trusting. The fruit of faith sometimes takes a long time to ripen." A whoosh passed by my ear. "Until we meet again, Phoenix."

The sound faded and vanished.

I doused the flashlight and returned it to my belt. A black void again shrouded my vision. I stared at it, trying to see beyond the emptiness, but darkness prevailed. And the longer I sat here, the greater its victory. Every moment I waited, the more Alex suffered, and the higher the probability that she would die while I delayed making a decision.

I couldn't let that happen. I couldn't let darkness win. I had to decide now. The answer was clear. I had to step out while in darkness and act like I believed in the light. Then maybe I would be able to see the light for myself.

Still, showing mercy to Alex would be the hardest thing I had ever done in my life.

My legs trembling, I rose, pushed the trapdoor open, and reached for Alex. Again electrical pulses sent shock-waves across my head and shoulders. After gathering her into my arms, I carried her down the ladder one slow step at a time, my path illuminated by light from the abyss.

When I reached the bottom, I laid her on the con-crete floor, took her mask off, and threw it aside. She moaned, but her eyes stayed closed. Above, the energy shield leaked into the room and began spreading across the ceiling.

I climbed the ladder, reached through the opening, and grabbed the door. Once again, jolts assaulted my body. As I climbed down, pulling the door behind me, a new wave of dizziness flooded my brain.

My foot missed a rung. The ladder toppled, and I dropped next to Alex. My head slammed against the floor, and everything turned black.

CHAPTER NINETEEN

SOMETHING COLD PATTED my face. "Phoenix. Wake up."

I opened my eyes. Alex straddled me, one knee on the floor at each side and my flashlight in her hand. Anxiety lines on her face softened, and a genuine smile appeared. "You had me worried."

My head throbbed, like someone was pounding my skull with a sledgehammer. "I feel terrible."

"It's no wonder." Alex rose. When she stood upright, she teetered before gaining her balance, making the flashlight beam sweep back and forth. "I think I figured out what happened. We both suffered enough electrical shocks to kill an elephant."

"Maybe two." Every part of my body ached, and much of it tingled. "But I had to come down here."

"Not to save my life." She extended a hand. "I was shocked, if you'll pardon the expression, that you did so anyway. Although I control you, I didn't ask you to save me. You did that on your own."

I locked wrists with her and rode her shaky pull to my feet. As she steadied me, I looked into her eyes, now less lustrous than usual. To this point, allowing her to think she was in control had provided some benefits, but the deception gnawed at my gut. It was time to come clean and stay that way, even if doing so skewered my advantage. "Yes, I did it on my own, but you don't control me."

"Phoenix, I thought you decided to accept that." She ran a hand along the back of my head and stopped at a painful spot. "That's quite a lump."

I batted her hand and stepped away, my legs ready to buckle. "Alex, I pretended to accept it. You don't control me, because I didn't kill Sing. She killed herself. She reached back and pulled the trigger while you were distracted. I just let you think you controlled me so I'd have more freedom."

She stared at me for a long moment with the light shining on her chest, allowing the beam's outer edges to wash over her face. At times, an eyelid or a cheek muscle twitched. Soon, she blinked and shook her head as if casting off a web of thoughts. "I..." She licked her cracked lips. "I don't know what to say. I should be furious at you for deceiving me, but I feel... grateful, I suppose. After all I've done to you, after all of my scheming to coerce you into this mortally dangerous mission, you still saved my life." She gave me a nod. "Thank you, Phoenix. Obviously I owe you a debt of gratitude I'll never be able to pay."

The standard answer—you're welcome—wouldn't rise from my throat. She wasn't welcome. Like the Sancta said, showing mercy toward Alex made me look like a fool, a traitor. And I felt like both.

I returned her nod and whispered, "Don't mention it."

Alex picked up her mask. As she looked at it, she whispered, "Never again."

"What do you mean?"

"Oh, nothing, really. Just that I won't need to wear this mask again. But that's not your concern."

"Why did you wear it?"

"Short answer, the Gatekeeper's superstitions. He believed that seeing our expressions during our discussions might distract him or influence his decision-making process. He also wanted us to wear them when making public appearances. Anonymity has its advantages."

"Like generating more superstition."

"And fear." Alex tossed the mask to the floor and set a fist on her hip. "Now to the matters at hand. I deduced that we are in the machine room under the abyss. I have heard about it, but I have never seen it."

"Yes, we're under the abyss. My main reason for coming down here was to shut the system down."

She set the flashlight beam on one of the machines. "If you shut down the abyss, the souls will fly out. In their emaciated states, that could be a horrific tragedy."

"We're working on that." I took the flashlight and walked to the control panel, Alex following. After setting the flashlight upright on the floor, I entered *guest* as the first password, then picked up the stylus and touched the power control. When the second password prompt appeared, I typed:*kedizihclem7!* and waited.

A message flashed on the screen—Password Accepted. Full Access Granted.

"Well done, Phoenix. Where did you get the password?"

"Long story." I searched the screen and found a flashing Messages box in the upper left-hand corner. I touched it with the stylus and dragged it to the center of the screen.

When I lifted the stylus, a list box containing one message appeared.

I tapped on the message and covered the screen with a hand. "Alex, I'd like some privacy."

"Of course. You have no reason to trust me." She turned her back and folded her arms over her chest. "Proceed."

I lowered my hand and read the message silently. *Phoenix, your connection dropped to 3%, but you recovered, so I guess you're physical now. But your energy reading is 14%. I will keep monitoring. Erin's tablet showed me the location of the reservoir, a huge tank below the farms. Those pedestal stations drain into the tank. I found a way to reverse the lines and feed the souls that are partially drained. Not sure how long that will take, but when they look healthy, Tokyo will set them free. While we're waiting, I'm searching for a way to channel the energy to the abyss. I'll let you know if I find something. One more thing. Before I set up Erin's suicide scene, I took the sonic guns. Now I have one, and Tokyo has one. Reply as soon as you can.*

After sliding out the keyboard, I typed, *I am in the room under the abyss. I took a beating, but I survived. Alex is with me. I will wait on further word from you.*

When I sent the message, I closed the dialogue box. "Done."

Alex turned toward me. "Can you tell me your plans? Surely we can't stay here."

"Maybe I can tell you. Let me think about it." My head still pounding and my vision spinning, I leaned against one of the machines. "I will say that your advice on how to fight the illuminaries worked perfectly."

She smiled. "Good to hear. I had full confidence in you."

"Well, maybe you can give me hints on how to face the Gatekeeper. You've been telling me for a while that I'm able to conquer him, but you haven't said how."

"An excellent question." She stepped to my side and leaned next to me. "I had hoped to prepare you under different circumstances, but that's not possible."

I nodded. Her manner and tone had changed so much. She wasn't being her usual arrogant, domineering self. "We'll just do what we have to do."

"Let's sit. Preserve your strength." Alex slid down to her bottom. When I joined her on the floor, she looked at me with her metallic eyes, though they no longer carried a piercing effect. "As you know, the Gatekeeper uses his overpowering energy to influence minds. It is a paralyzing force that incapacitates anyone, including me, and a large dose is fatal. Unfortunately, he pours it directly into the brain, so the victim cannot capture and use it. So when he attacked me, he first knocked me out with his energy, then he employed a secondary tool. He used my own strength against me."

"Your power as an Owl?"

She nodded. "I was born both a Reaper and an Owl. I have a Reaper's birthmark and an Owl's telltale irises. By simply looking into someone's eyes, I am able to detect moods, feelings, lies, and fear, as well as other aspects. The power is enhanced when I am touching a person, so much so, people often swear that I can read minds. I am also able to absorb a great deal of pain without succumbing."

"I suppose that's why you survived and the other Council members didn't."

"The other Council members? Are they in the abyss as well?"

I provided a quick summary of Sydney's accusation and downfall, as well as the Gatekeeper's circle of betrayal, though when she asked me how I knew the stories, I declined to answer.

"In any case," Alex said, "the Gatekeeper is able to temporarily absorb an enemy's power, strength, energy, or whatever you wish to call it, and reverse it so that it attacks his opponent. First, he paralyzed me with his primary weapon, then he absorbed my defensive shield and reversed it so that my own armor pummeled me into unconsciousness. Fortunately, when he let go, my armor returned in time to protect me from the abyss's hostile environment."

"So after I resist his energy surge, what do I do about his second ability?"

"That depends." She looked at my pocket. "Where is my watch?"

"Shanghai has it. Like we planned."

"Do you know your energy level?"

"It's low. Real low."

"No surprise. You look like a junkyard wreck."

I smirked. "Thanks. That's a confidence builder."

"I am just being realistic." Alex stared at me and let out a long hum. "Considering your condition, here is my advice. When you face him, act as if you don't want him to touch you but allow it to happen anyway. I'm sure you can devise such a scheme. Then he will infuse you with his purified energy, which you will be able to resist. But don't let him touch you after that, because his next weapon will be to use your energy against you. Yet, I suspect that he will be confused about your resistance, which will make him vulnerable. When you see that moment of doubt, that's when you strike."

"Strike with what?"

"With the sonic gun. Do you still have it?"

"No. Shanghai has it. I'll have to get it from her."

"What is she doing now?" When I glared at her, she rolled her eyes. "Oh. Right. You don't trust me."

"I'll let you know if that changes." I averted my gaze and imagined a standoff with the Gatekeeper. He approached with hands extended, ready to touch me, but with which power? "Is there any way to tell which weapon the Gatekeeper's going to use?"

"Watch his hands. If they glow, he plans to infuse you with his energy. At that moment, he is practically invulnerable. His energy becomes a force field that can deflect opposing forces. If his hands are normal, he plans to absorb your power and use it against you. That's when he is open to attack."

"Good to know." I refocused on her. Her expression seemed sympathetic, even thankful. For once it seemed that I had the upper hand, but how far should I push my advantage? I had an ace in the hole, as she had put it— her son's freedom. I could test the waters without giving it away. "Do you want to know why I can't trust you?"

"I'm sure I already know. If a mother can have her own son put to death, who in his right mind would trust her? He would be a fool."

I kept my face slack. Somehow she knew that I was thinking about Peter. "And how do you respond to that?"

"Obviously I am guilty, but you lack understanding. Peter, like you and your grandfather, had the same weakness. I controlled Peter without limits. He was more robot than human, and he knew it. The chains tortured him to no end. He begged to die, but I refused to allow it, so he had to live on as my lapdog as he so ruefully called himself. I tried just releasing him, but the attachment was too powerful. He kept coming back to me."

"But you finally did have him killed."

"For good reason. When he failed the test to determine if he could conquer the Gatekeeper, he said, 'What good am I now? Please, please let me die.' Of course I didn't want him to die, so I gave him jobs to do, such as helping me at the corrections camp, as you witnessed. But when his torment reached a boiling point and it seemed that he had nothing else to live for, I gave the order to put him out of his misery. I thought it better to give him an honorable death than to allow him to commit suicide as he often requested."

Nausea churned in my gut. Her smug, self-righteous rationalization made me want to vomit. "So if you controlled me, would you have killed me if I failed?"

Alex let out a humming laugh. "Of course not, Phoenix. I don't love you enough to kill you."

I glared at her again. She didn't deserve to know that Peter had found freedom and peace. "You disgust me." I climbed to my feet and stalked toward the computer. As I drew near, it beeped. I pulled up the message list and opened a new entry—from Shanghai.

I looked back. Although Alex stayed seated out of reading range, I blocked her view with my body and read the message. *Phoenix, I found your parents in the tank where the souls enter from the depot. Tokyo and I stopped that revolving-door device. Now every soul comes out of the line and flies straight to the Gateway. We also emptied the tank and a twin tank on the opposite side of the building. Since the souls were in good shape, we released them to the sky, except for your parents. They asked me to shoot a video of them and put it on a photo stick. More in a minute.*

Tears crept to my eyes. My parents' souls had been up there all along, and I didn't get to see them, not even to say good-bye. My hands trembling, I typed *Tell my parents that I love them, and I always will. I hope I'll make them proud.*

I sent the message. Biting my lip, I stared at the screen, trying not to imagine their souls standing inside that tank while Shanghai made the recording. But the effort made it worse. Their phantom figures might as well have been standing in front of me. I couldn't shake the vision.

I glanced at Alex again. She stared at me in silence, apparently smart enough to stay quiet for now. Maybe chatting with her for a minute would distract me. "What's on your mind?"

"You are, of course. I can tell that you are deeply conflicted about something crucial, and that conflict is keeping you stuck in this room. You need to gain more knowledge before you can act." She climbed to her feet and dusted off her pants. "Perhaps I can offer some advice. I know much more about the Gatekeeper's abode than you do. Since I want to get out of this pit with my skin intact, you should trust me at least as far as it serves my survival instinct."

"All right. The options won't be a surprise to you. When we were in my apartment, you gave me an assignment, to find the reservoir and release the energy into the atmosphere to dissolve the radioactive shield around the world. That's one option. The other is to feed that energy into the abyss so the shriveled souls will absorb it. We found the reservoir, but we don't know how to do either option. Shanghai is working on it."

Alex stroked her chin. "Has Shanghai asked Erin about channeling the energy where you need it?"

"Erin is dead."

Alex's brow shot upward. "Oh? What happened?"

"I'll keep that to myself."

"As you wish." She scanned the ceiling, slowly rotating in place. When she stopped, she focused on me. "I have a solution that will address every issue."

"What is it?"

She gave me another humming laugh. "Phoenix, you know me better than that. If I come right out and tell you my idea, I will have no leverage to ensure my survival."

"But you have a way around that problem, don't you? Otherwise you wouldn't have mentioned your solution at all."

"'Tis true." She half closed an eye. "Will you submit to a challenge of principles?"

"Let me guess. If I make some sort of promise, you'll tell me your solution. If I go back on the promise, then you'll control me because I would have violated my principles. Right?"

She flashed a smug grin. "You have a gifted intellect, as always."

"Cut the posturing and tell me what you have in mind."

"Very well. Let's say you use my idea, and at least one of your goals is accomplished. Then if you face the Gatekeeper and defeat him, you will leave me in his abode to do as I please."

"One of our goals? You mean either to restore the souls

or disperse the shield. If we achieve at least one goal. Not necessarily both."

"Correct. Because we don't know if enough energy is available to do both."

"And only if your idea does the job."

"That is correct again."

"But if I conquer the Gatekeeper, then you'll have access to everything here, including the means to stop Shanghai and me from leaving."

Alex nodded. "You will be free to go. I will not accost you or Shanghai in any way."

"If you do, then the deal is off. I can do whatever I want."

"Agreed."

I mentally recounted each detail. Every item seemed in place. The part about Alex controlling me was a legitimate concern, but I had walked away from Shanghai's control, hadn't I? Maybe I had overcome the weakness. In any case, I wouldn't go against my word, control or no control, so it wasn't an issue. "All right. Let's hear your solution. But I'm not making any promises unless I use your idea."

"Very well." Alex stooped and used a finger to draw an invisible box on the floor. "This is the energy reservoir, a rectangular metal tank. It feeds a number of pressurized supply vessels throughout the building so the Gatekeeper can turn on a valve and feed from anywhere."

"You told me you didn't know where the tank's stored."

"I didn't then. I do now. Erin gave me a schematic." Alex drew a line from the box to a point several inches away. "One feeder line runs from the reservoir to the point where the depot energy lines enter the dome room.

When the Gatekeeper shuts off the flow in order to open the dome, the lines that enter the dome are cut off by a check valve, and the energy runs into the reservoir so that it's not wasted."

She drew a new line in the opposite direction. "The key is to reverse that flow and send all of the reservoir energy into the dome, which will flood the collection pool at the terminus. Once that's done, then we stop the abyss engines. The souls will fly into the pool and stay there until we decide if they are sufficiently restored. If the energy doesn't begin restoring them right away, then there is no reason to expect that it will. If it does restore them, then they will be ready to go to the Gateway."

"Does the reservoir tank have enough energy to restore so many souls? Since the Gatekeeper has been using the energy to rejuvenate himself, and Reapers use it to stay alive, hasn't it been depleted?"

"I have no way of knowing."

"Okay. All we can do is give it a try, I guess."

"And after the souls have absorbed as much energy as possible..." Alex set a fist over her drawing and raised it, splaying her fingers. "Then we open the dome and release the souls to the sky. The energy pool will naturally spread out and cover an area much bigger than the Gateway access hole. Then we will see if it can dissolve the shield."

"It does dissolve the shield temporarily. I saw it contract when some energy touched it, but it just expanded again. The release was on a much smaller scale, but the shield is so big." I shook my head. "Probably way too big."

"Then we'll hope for a chain reaction." Alex set a hand on my shoulder. "The plan allows for both options to work. What the energy can and cannot do is not up to us. We just have to give it a chance to succeed. If the souls are not restored and the shield remains intact, you are free to do with me as you please. I won't be able to overcome both you and Shanghai."

I studied her eyes—more piercing than before. The old, manipulative Alex had returned. Yet, her explanation made perfect sense. If it worked, what harm could she do if we left her to her own devices? If I defeated the Gatekeeper, his rule would be over. One way or the other, the souls would be free. And if the shield dispersed, no one would ever have to come to this place again. The fear and manipulation would end. If Alex tried to set up a throne here, her only subjects would be the electrified cats in the forest.

Still, one nagging assumption remained. Somehow Alex would try to betray me. How and when? Impossible to guess. I just had to be ready for anything.

"Are you satisfied with our arrangement?" Alex asked.

"Let me think another minute." I imagined the procedure—the emaciated souls rising into the energy pool, their phantom frames filling out, and the dome opening to release them. In theory, it all looked reasonable, but when they lifted into the sky, my mental image drew Sing being flushed out with them. Before we opened the dome, we would have to get her out.

"All right. But I call the shots on timing. We won't open the dome unless I say so."

Alex crossed her arms. "Fair enough. I am in no position to demand otherwise."

"Good. Now help me explain the energy rerouting to Shanghai."

"Of course."

The computer beeped. I turned to the screen and opened the new note. *I gave them your message. While I shot the video, I cried. A lot. Phoenix, we have to defeat this monster and set all the souls free. And we will. But I still haven't found a way to channel the reservoir energy anywhere.*

A sob rose from my gut, but I fought it back. No time for grief. I cleared the message and sidestepped to give Alex room at the keyboard. She set her hands on the keys and typed with lightning speed and perfect accuracy. When she finished, she stepped out of the way. "I suggest that you add something personal so she'll know it's from you. The details are too specific to have come from someone who doesn't know the system intimately."

"Right." I scanned the message. Nothing appeared to be sinister. Alex wanted to get out alive, so she wouldn't double cross us, at least not yet.

At the end of the note, I typed, *Shanghai, the above message is from Alex. This is Phoenix now. When you get the energy channeled to the dome, let me know, and I'll stop the abyss engines. I'll see you in a little while.*

I glanced at Alex as she looked over my shoulder. When I cleared my throat, she spun and stepped away. I typed *I'm still looking forward to that kiss* and sent the message.

"All clear."

Alex turned back. "The only sticky point is how you and I will get out of here. When the abyss clears, perhaps we can climb the walls, but that remains to be seen."

"True. I have a spool line I can shoot, but it might not be long enough to—

The computer beeped again. When Alex pivoted away,

I read the message. *I'm on it, Phoenix. Results soon. And I'm looking forward to it too.*

I cleared the screen. "Let's see what we can do." With Alex again looking over my shoulder, I used the stylus to open a help screen that explained how to turn off the engines and shut down the energy shield around the abyss. After practicing with the stylus by easing the slider control a tiny fraction and verifying that the sounds emanating from the machines diminished at the same time, I set the stylus down.

The computer beeped once more. When Alex turned, I read the message. *Energy ready. Get up here! Hurry!*

CHAPTER TWENTY

"I HAVE TO SHUT everything down!" I pushed the spin-power slider to zero. A prompt appeared that read, "Shut Down All Systems? Y or N." I tapped the Y key, then snapped up the flashlight and fastened it to my belt, the beam still on.

As the machine noise faltered, the computer screen blinked off as well. I touched it with the stylus, but the system failed to respond. "I guess the computer shut down, too. I don't know how to turn it back on."

"No matter," Alex said. "Let's go."

I set the ladder in place, climbed to the top, and pressed my hands against the trap door. The moment the machines silenced, I pushed upward and heaved myself into the abyss. The bodies of the five other Council members still lay motionless on the floor, their masks scattered about.

Above, the souls had dislodged and rose in a slowly spinning vortex, like shimmering leaves caught in an updraft. The entrapping blackness had vanished, leaving behind a sheer metal wall—an impossible-to-climb cylinder.

When Alex's head appeared above the door, I helped

her climb to my level. As we both looked up, I tried to see past the blinking lights. Far above, a swirling mass of radiance under the dome caught the souls, raising tiny splashes of sparks.

I nodded. "So far, so good."

Alex crouched and checked the pulse of each Council member. When she finished, she nudged a mask with her foot. "They're all dead. Since the Gatekeeper decided to purge the Council, he must believe that he no longer needs them to maintain control of the various regions. That means he has dangerous plans."

"Probably something to do with storing way more energy than he needs."

"Exactly." Alex touched the surrounding wall. "Can you throw your spool line to the top?"

I mentally measured the distance, maybe two hundred feet. Not only was it too far for throwing, my line maxed out at a hundred. "No way. And I can't send a message to Shanghai to call for help."

Alex crossed her arms. "Well, then, it seems that we have rescued the souls only to leave ourselves in dire straits."

"Give me a minute. I'll think of something." I scanned the floor from one side to the other—maybe eight feet across. Since I stood about five-foot-ten and Alex was only about an inch shorter, we could try to span the floor and climb in tandem. Teaming up with her using close physical contact would be distasteful, but I could manage.

I turned off the flashlight. "In your Reaper training, did you ever do a barrel climb with a partner?"

"Of course." She looked up. "But it was twelve feet, fifteen at the most, not this insane distance."

"If you have a better idea, then let's hear it." I sat with my feet against the wall. It had been years since I had done this myself, back when Shanghai and I were kids, but I had done it enough times to remember the technique. "I'm willing if you are."

"I guess it's the only choice."

She copied my position, her feet against the opposite side of the wall. Our bodies met in the middle with our shoulders pressed together. "I need an anchor once we get near the top," I said. "Are the meeting chairs heavy enough to support our combined weights?"

"They're bolted to the floor. The Gatekeeper wanted to make sure no one could alter the arrangement. Another superstition."

"Perfect." After reeling out a couple of feet of spool line and attaching a grappling claw to the end, I reached back with both arms and interlocked them with hers, one hand holding to the claw. Then we pushed with our feet and began a slow upward march. Before each step, I called out which foot to use, trying to maintain a consistent rhythm.

As we rose, my legs throbbed, especially the injured one. Pain knifed into my wounded shoulder. More hammers pounded my head. We still had a hundred ninety feet to go. But if Alex could do it, I could do it.

With every footfall, Shanghai's last message shouted in my brain. *Energy ready. Get up here! Hurry!* Although the call tortured me with every repetition, the urgency in her voice spurred me on. I focused on the call. It was the fuel I needed.

The top loomed closer. One hundred feet to go. Eighty. Fifty. Soon I would be close enough to throw the line, but

I had to be sure. I lowered my marching orders to scant whispers. Alex groaned softly. I swallowed hard to keep my own groans silent. Although every muscle burned like fire, and my calves cramped into screaming knots, the worst was yet to come—getting over the edge without falling.

When Shanghai and I attempted it, we succeeded only once. Our failures resulted in drops to a cushioned floor twelve feet below. Alex and I had no such luxury. A two-hundred-foot fall would kill me and maybe her as well. Her armor couldn't take that kind of pounding too many times.

When we came within three steps of the top, I grunted, "I'm going to throw the hook. Get ready for a jolt and then a climb."

Her reply came in a gasp. "Just say… the word."

Since my arms were still locked with Alex's, I could move only my forearm, wrist, and hand. I spun the claw at the end of a foot or so of spool line and tossed it, letting more line reel out. It sailed toward the chairs and thunked somewhere out of sight. As I pulled the line and let the spool draw in the slack, I hoped for a sudden stop, but it ran easily back to the abyss and dropped to my side.

"Missed." I reeled the line in. "I'll try again."

Alex groaned. "Hurry. My legs are cramping."

"Just another second." I threw the line again. This time metal clanked on metal. Just as I began pulling to test for a hold, Alex's feet slipped. She fell and took me down with her. The line screamed as it zipped from the spool, still attached to my belt.

When the line reached the end, the spool locked. My plunge stopped, nearly jerking my hips out of their sockets. Now upside down, my arms stayed linked with Alex's and halted her fall as well. We swung back and forth next to the wall of the abyss, almost a hundred feet from the top.

My biceps throbbed. I couldn't hold her for more than a few seconds. "Alex! Climb over me and grab the line!"

"Easier said than done." She slid an arm from our lock, turned herself, and muscled up by using my body, cloak, and clothes as a ladder. With every move, the pressure on my hips spiked, and the belt slid toward my legs. Within seconds, it would likely slip off.

When she reached the spool line, she grabbed it and hung on, her feet against the wall. Gasping, she turned her face toward me. "Just rest while I climb." She heaved a deep breath, sweat dripping from her chin. "When I get to the top, I'll pull while you climb."

I nodded. But would she? Now that I had saved her, she could easily cut the line and be done with me.

Her feet still against the wall, Alex climbed hand over hand. When she reached the top, she hoisted herself up and rolled out of sight. Seconds later, the line began inching upward. She called out, "Start climbing, Phoenix! I can't do this by myself!"

I grabbed the line, copied her climbing pose, and pulled myself upward, summoning every atom of remaining energy. My hamstrings strained to the breaking point. The burning felt like acid on raw skin. A scream surged from my gut. I bit my lip hard to stay quiet, but I couldn't stop tears from seeping past my clenched eyelids.

When I neared the top, Alex grabbed my collar and heaved me over the lip of the abyss. We rolled together and flopped to our backs side by side. As we caught our breath, I tried to move my arms, but they were completely numb, limp appendages I could only drag.

I looked up. The pool of energy had swelled to a massive sea of radiance with hundreds of flashing forms within. The surface seemed to be only a leap away, maybe eight feet up.

Shining faces streamed by, most displaying smiles. A man filled out even as I watched. "The idea is working."

"So our covenant is active," Alex said, her voice quiet, exhausted. "We won't do harm to each other."

"You didn't know it was active while you were pulling me up. You could've cut the line."

"Merely returning the favor. I understand the value of reciprocation, even between rivals."

"Okay. I can accept that."

"Are you able to get up?"

"Not yet."

"What do you think your energy level is?"

"I don't know. It's never felt this low."

"I started the day at one hundred percent," Alex said, "so mine is likely in the forties or so. My problem is muscle fatigue, not low energy."

"Okay. Why are you telling me that?"

She turned to her side and propped her head with an elbow on the floor. With her free hand, she pushed her valve stem. The inner spring made it protrude. "I can transfer some energy to you."

The mere mention of energy ignited a reflexive desire, a deep hunger, as if a chef had brought a tray of food to a starving man. The sight of sizzling steak, potatoes and gravy, and hot bread along with their savory aromas would incite ravenous growls in his stomach. Such were the cravings in my body. It demanded the energy. And it was so close. Offered freely.

Then a new mental image appeared—Alex crawling on top of me and linking our valves together. As she pushed energy into me, her rapid breaths chilled my skin. A fresh round of nausea boiled inside.

I chased the image away. If I wouldn't listen to Shanghai and take stolen energy from a hose, I certainly couldn't listen to Alex, link up with her so intimately, and come under her control. The cost was way too high.

"Phoenix?" Alex waved a hand in front of my eyes. "Stay with me, now. I offered you an energy transfer."

I shook my head. "I'll manage without it."

"Suit yourself." She pushed her valve stem back in place. "But you look like you're under five percent. You'll be lucky if you can walk."

"I'll crawl if I have to." I sat up, let my legs dangle over the abyss, and dragged my arms into my lap. As blood returned to my limbs, hot tingles ran to my fingers and toes. Cramps tightened my thighs, but I couldn't massage them. I just had to endure the pain. "Give me a minute."

"Of course." With the anchor claw in hand, Alex crawled to my side and sat next to me. She detached my spool and began drawing line into it. "I offered because you seemed to be in a hurry. But if you think we can afford to wait, we'll wait."

Once again, Shanghai's message blared in my mind. *Get up here! Hurry!* The mental voice sparked a new flame. With control returning to my arms, I pushed back from the abyss and climbed to my feet. "I'm ready."

Stumbling and staggering, I made my way to the door. From above, sighs of relief and joy filtered down, but I kept my focus forward. We would set the dome-bound souls free soon. I had to get Sing out of the system first.

With Alex close behind, I hobbled out of the Council room and through the lobby. A woman's shouts pierced the air, coming from the drainage farm on the left. Urging my stiff legs to hurry, I jogged into the room. Shanghai and Tokyo stood in the midst of toppled glass enclosures, surrounded by a circle of at least a dozen illuminaries. Three smoking piles of ashes lay here and there on the floor.

As the illuminaries closed in, one flashed, then another, then a third, each cloaked form gliding slowly. Shanghai extended a sonic gun, as did Tokyo, but two slow-to-recharge guns against twelve shock-injecting creatures seemed like impossible odds.

I called out, "Throw the guns to me and do a propeller-kick drill."

Shanghai and Tokyo each tossed a gun underhanded. I snatched one out of the air with my right hand, but when I reached for the other, Alex stepped in front of me, grabbed it, and spoke with a cocky tone. "It'll take two of us to clean up the trash."

"Let's do it. I'll go left. You go right."

Alex and I parted and limped toward the collapsing circle. The moment the illuminaries moved within striking range, Shanghai and Tokyo set their palms on the floor and kicked outward in opposite directions with both feet. Two illuminaries flew backwards and bowled through fallen glass enclosures. Then, rotating while thrusting their feet, the two Reapers kicked another pair of attackers.

When the first illuminary slid to me, I shot it with the sonic gun. Alex shot another on her side of the circle.

While they burned, Alex called, "Just keep shooting. Stun will have to do."

Bracing on the floor and thrusting their feet, Shanghai and Tokyo kicked one illuminary after another into flight, moving too quickly for the standing illuminaries to flee. One crashed onto a glass tube and cracked it. Another slammed into a pedestal, making it career into two others.

Alex and I hurried around the circle and shot the fallen illuminaries where they landed. Vibrant pops sounded with each trigger pull, and electricity arced across their bodies. After an initial jerk and a moment of writhing, they lay motionless.

Shanghai and Tokyo rose from their kicking stances. As they walked toward me, Shanghai glared at Alex. "What are you doing here?"

"Saving your life." Alex strode to me, snatched my gun, and bent close to the nearest illuminary. After waiting a few seconds, she shot it in the back of the head. When it ignited, she sidestepped to the next one and shot it with the other gun, then repeated the cycle as she hurried around the circle.

Shanghai embraced me and laid her head on my shoulder, whispering, "It's dangerous trusting her."

"I know, but we have no choice. If not for her, I'd still be stuck in the abyss. And she also gave you the energy-channeling instructions. I couldn't have done that."

Shanghai pulled back and scanned me from head to toe, wincing. "You look terrible."

"I *feel* terrible."

Tokyo touched my cheek with her palm. "He's flushed and feverish. Signs of severe energy deprivation."

Shanghai withdrew the watch and read the face. "Oh, Phoenix! You're at three percent. You're practically dead."

"Better than two percent." I looked around the room. "Where's the tablet? The souls will be ready to go soon. We have to get Sing out of the system before we flush it."

"Over here." Shanghai jogged to a corner of the room and picked up the tablet from the floor. As she walked back, she studied the screen. "Give me a minute," she said as she slid her finger along the surface. "I'm checking the network for her."

I grasped Tokyo's wrist. "I wish I could've been fighting with you, but that was the most amazing propeller-kick cycle I've ever seen."

"Shanghai's kicks were stronger than mine." Tokyo stretched her back, making it pop. "My joints need a bit of lubrication."

I scanned the room. Every pedestal sat empty. "Did you free the souls in the other drainage farm?"

Tokyo nodded. "Hundreds of refreshed and happy souls rose to the Gateway. Actually, it was rather fun knocking down the glass enclosures while illuminaries chased us around the room. Invigorating."

When Alex finished igniting the illuminaries, she slid the sonic guns behind her waistband and extended a hand toward Tokyo. "Greetings, Tokyo. I am—"

"I know who you are." Tokyo looked at Alex's hand. "Your reputation precedes you."

Alex drew back, an eyelid twitching. "It seems that gratitude is lacking. I was instrumental in your restor—"

"Save me the self-applause. I know why you restored me, and it wasn't for my benefit." Tokyo nodded toward

Alex's waist. "Give me those sonic guns. I don't trust you with them."

Alex set a hand on each gun. "And I don't trust *you*, a Resistance leader who once pledged to rid the world of the Gatekeeper and his Council members."

The women stared nearly nose to nose—two immovable mountains daring each other to blink. After what seemed like a full minute, Alex withdrew one of the guns and pushed it into Tokyo's hand. "Now we can distrust each other on equal terms."

"That is acceptable." Tokyo stepped back and slid the gun behind her waistband. "But I'm going to keep an eye on you."

"And I will give you no reason to do so." Alex turned her gaze to the illuminaries. "The stench will soon be unbearable. Let's reconvene in the meeting room. We can talk strategy and check on the souls from the abyss at the same time."

Shanghai tucked the tablet under her arm, then pushed her shoulder under mine, while Tokyo did the same on the other side. Together the four of us made our way through the halls, past the staircases, and into the Council chamber.

My helpers hoisted me into the Gatekeeper's chair and took seats next to me. Alex stood at my side, looking up at the energy pool. Since it hovered so low, plenty of light flooded the area.

Shanghai set the tablet on her lap and touched the screen. "Okay, I see a strong signal here. A human form. And it's moving."

Alex stepped to Shanghai's chair and looked on.

"That's the Gatekeeper's signal. He allowed Erin to track his location for security reasons."

"So he's in his bedchamber in the underground bunker," Shanghai said, "but it looks like he's leaving."

Alex nodded. "He's heading for the elevator. My guess is he's on his way here to confront us, but he'll likely stop at a feeding station before he arrives. We have a few minutes."

"Any idea why he's stayed away all this time?" Shanghai asked.

"Only that he is preparing to face whoever the survivors are. Trust me. He has his reasons, and he will be ready for us."

"How do I look for Sing? She's not in Phoenix's cloak anymore. She's somewhere in this place's energy network."

Alex touched the screen and slid her finger a few times. "Here's the energy grid. See those dots?"

Shanghai nodded. "There are hundreds of them."

"That's the energy pool over our heads. The dots are the souls."

I looked up. The glowing soup swirled in a slow rotation as if stirred by a tired cook. Radiant souls swam within. They all seemed healthy now.

Alex tapped on the screen. "Here are the magnitude readings for the souls. Highest is one hundred percent. Lowest is eighty-two percent. Average is ninety-four. The increase rate is here—one percent per minute. So the average should reach maximum in six minutes, unless the rate slows. Once we see that, we can release them."

Shanghai nodded. "After we get Sing out."

I eyed Alex's confident stance. She knew much more

about the systems here than she had indicated earlier. Probably one of her aces in the hole.

Alex squinted at the tablet. "I'm not sure how Erin conducted her searches, but you can scan every network channel for a glowing dot that isn't in the dome area."

"Will do." Shanghai slid a finger across the screen. "This might take a while."

I looked up at the pool again. "Alex, is there any way to release the souls without flushing the system?"

"Perhaps, but I don't know of one." She nodded toward a wall. "The Gatekeeper has a switch over there that controls the process. I don't think the tablet has a similar function."

Tokyo looked on. Her deeply furrowed brow gave no room for doubt. She was definitely keeping an eye on Alex.

"Here." Shanghai touched the screen. "This dot is a hundred percent. Probably Sing."

"She's close to the Gatekeeper's signal," Alex said. "He's at a feeding station next to the elevator."

Shanghai's eyes widened. "His percentage spiked to one-fifty."

Alex nodded, tight lipped. "As I said, he's preparing for battle. He knows something's wrong."

I leaned over the chair arm. "Let me see."

Shanghai angled the screen. A bright, human-shaped figure stood in what appeared to be a hallway on a floor-plan grid. A glowing circle drifted along a bordering wall, closer and closer to the Gatekeeper. "Can the Gatekeeper detect Sing?" I asked.

Alex crossed her arms. "Without a doubt. Whether or not Sing can detect him, I don't know."

Tokyo pointed at the screen. "She probably can't. Floating around in those lines can be disorienting. It takes a while to get your bearings."

"The depot lines have impulse waves," I said. "Can you create one that sends her in the opposite direction?"

Alex shook her head. "Not in that line. It's part of the building grid, not the depot feed. It is pressurized, so it has a flow component. You might be able to reverse the flow, but the Gatekeeper has manual controls on that wall. He can override the tablet."

"I'll try anyway," Shanghai said. After tapping the screen several times, she shook her head. "It's not working."

I pushed up from my chair and squeezed next to Tokyo. She braced my arm while I looked on. When Sing's signal reached a point directly behind the wall where the Gatekeeper stood, it stopped.

Shanghai swallowed. "That can't be good."

"He found her," Alex said. "Since he knows who she is and her importance to the Resistance, I don't want to imagine what he'll do to her."

I tried to read Alex's expression—fearful, alarmed. "What *can* he do to her?"

"Consume her energy. Make her into a withered skeleton of a soul. Then send her into eternity in that state."

Sing's signal crossed the wall and melded with the Gatekeeper's. His icon brightened even further.

"He jumped to a hundred-sixty percent." Shanghai let out a lamenting moan. "Sing's signal is gone."

Tokyo gripped the back of Shanghai's chair and whispered, "My precious daughter. She'll suffer for all eternity." As her body shook, she set a hand on her sonic gun and growled. "I'll crush that cockroach with the heel of my boot!"

"Save your energy," Alex said. "You'll need it. When he arrives, his power will be terrible to behold. And if his skin's glowing, that gun will do you no good. The shot will send a concussive jolt back to your body."

"How does he know to come here?" Tokyo asked.

Alex touched the side of her head. "I have a tracking chip embedded in my scalp. He knows where I am."

"Shouldn't we take cover?" Shanghai asked. "Not to retreat, of course, but to plan an ambush."

"Or I could leave and lead him away," Alex said.

"No." I shifted over to the center chair and sat. After taking a deep breath, I summoned my strength, straightened my body, and set my arms on the rests. "We will not run. We will not hide. We will not set an ambush. I will meet him face to face, and his own chair is the perfect place to issue a challenge."

Tokyo stood in front of me and leaned close. "No one doubts your courage, Phoenix, nor your resolve. But Abigail is my daughter, and I will avenge her if it's the last thing I do."

I looked into her sad but determined eyes. "I'm the one who can resist his power. No one else can. Even if you could, he'd turn your power against you."

"Phoenix speaks the truth," Alex said. "But he's too weak to stand up to the Gatekeeper now. We all must do what we can to defeat him."

Tokyo reached for Shanghai's hand. "You and I together again?"

"With pleasure." Shanghai set the tablet on her chair, locked wrists with Tokyo, and bounded to her feet. "We'll be a double-trouble tornado for that snake in the grass." They skirted the abyss, jogged to the door, and stationed themselves, one at each side, crouched as if ready to pounce.

Alex looked at me and shook her head. "I fear for them. Their spirit is marvelous, but it will take more than spirit to defeat the Gatekeeper." She picked up the tablet and ran a finger along the screen. "The souls above are ready. Perhaps I should release them now."

I raised a hand. "Wait till the Gatekeeper arrives. I want him to see his captives fly from his grasp."

"Ah. Shake his confidence. A distraction for our courageous front line can't hurt." She walked toward the door. "I'll let them know your plan, then station myself at the dome-control switch."

As she walked, my mind drifted back to the moment she slammed me against a wall and set a sonic gun at the back of my head. Her words still echoed. *You're dealing with someone who could jerk your soul out of your skull and hurl you into the abyss without a second thought.*

And now I was trusting this evil woman to release the souls when the Gatekeeper walked in. Of course she could betray us at any moment, but it was too late to worry about that now. We had passed the point of no return.

When she stationed herself next to the wall switch, I lifted a hand, my elbow on the armrest. I didn't have the strength to do more. "On my signal."

Alex nodded, the tablet in hand. "Ready."

"How close is he?"

She looked at the screen. "He is passing the stairways now. Three seconds. Two. One."

CHAPTER TWENTY-ONE

I STARED AT THE double doors, still closed. The Gatekeeper likely knew we were monitoring him. Maybe he planned a surprise that—

The doors exploded toward us. Wood shards flew everywhere, some falling into the abyss in front of me. Beyond the shattered doorway, the Gatekeeper appeared, his hands extended. A brilliant aura pulsed from his body, as if he had consumed a sun.

Shanghai and Tokyo stayed crouched at either side of the door, ready to attack the moment he stepped in.

He pivoted for a moment as if picking up something behind him. When he turned back, a radiant energy field hovered between his hands. Sing's ghost floated in the midst, her expression pained as she looked straight at me.

When the Gatekeeper walked in, Shanghai and Tokyo lurched but then recoiled and flattened themselves against the wall, apparently trying to stay hidden until they could figure out how to attack this blinding monster. Our only hope might be the planned distraction, a way to dim his inner furnace.

I lowered my hand. Alex hit the switch. At the ceiling, the energy line pouring into the room surged for a moment, then shut off. A creaking sound emanated from the dome. Barely visible through the radiant soup, the apex opened. The energy lifted, and sparkling souls streamed through the widening rift.

The Gatekeeper looked up. His cheeks reddened, and his lips thinned out. When he faced me again, he spoke with an even tone that belied his furious expression. "You have done quite a lot of damage for someone who is supposed to be dead."

Shielding their eyes with their hands, Shanghai and Tokyo sneaked behind him and conversed in a huddle.

I took a deep breath and forced a calm reply. "Release her now, and I will stop the opening of the dome."

"From where you sit?" He looked at the wall switch. "Where is your accomplice?"

I glanced that way. Alex was gone. But where and why? Was a betrayal in the works?

"Perhaps I can incentivize you," the Gatekeeper said as he lowered his arms. The energy around Sing contracted, and the edges withered into sparks. Looking straight at me, she set a hand on her heart, then on her lips, and blew a kiss. Her shield dissolved, and she rose into the energy pool.

I gulped and looked at Shanghai and Tokyo. Had they seen what just happened? I tried to shout, "Run to the switch," but only a breathy whisper came out. I pushed up and dragged my feet toward the wall, glancing at the Gatekeeper while searching for Alex.

Tokyo ran, sprang into a flying kick, and slammed her feet into the Gatekeeper's spine. The moment she made contact, her legs flipped up. She shot backwards in a double somersault and smacked against the wall face first. Her limp body slid to the floor and lay motionless.

Shanghai whipped out a dagger and slung it at him. The blade pinged against his skin and bounced away. She charged in a full sprint. When she collided with him, she locked her arms around his waist. The impact sent him lurching to the side for a moment, but he regained his balance and braced his legs.

Still hanging on to him, she gritted her teeth and moaned, as if she were holding a live electrical wire. Jerking with her body, she appeared to be trying to wrestle him to the ground. Although he staggered to maintain his balance, her efforts seemed hopeless.

My legs buckled. I dropped to my knees and whispered, "Alex. Where are you?"

"Enough of this." The Gatekeeper reached back toward Shanghai, his hands glowing.

I forced out a weak call. "Shanghai, don't let him touch you."

"Touch me?" Her voice quaked. "I'm clinging to him like wet socks."

"I mean with his hands."

As he stretched to touch her, she slung him down. They rolled over and over until Shanghai halted the motion and straddled him, her knees on the floor and a fist raised to punch. He grasped her throat with both hands. Her eyes clenched shut, and her arms dropped to her side. Radiance flowed from his body to hers. She jerked violently, like a ragdoll being shaken by a dog.

I looked up. The energy pool had risen to the sky. It was too late to save Sing, but I could still save Shanghai. Summoning all of my strength, I pushed to a standing position and dragged myself toward the battle. At my energy level, I might die in five seconds, but it would be five seconds to remember.

Something grabbed my hood and jerked me backwards into strong arms. "No. I won't let you commit suicide."

I craned my neck. Alex held me, my back against her chest. I struggled to break free, but she was too strong. My muscles were spent.

The Gatekeeper's hands darkened. Light drained from Shanghai's face. She jerked and thrashed, but he kept his grip on her throat.

"He's absorbing her power," I said, my voice nearly gone. "She still has a lot."

"A handicap for her. When he reverses it, she'll be in trouble."

In a burst of light, Shanghai flew off the Gatekeeper and toward the splintered door. As she jetted through, a protruding spear slashed her side. Her shirt ripped. Blood splashed. When she hit the floor in the anteroom, she slid across the marble and stopped halfway to the next hall. She lay on her back, motionless.

I exhaled in a whisper, "Shanghai."

As the Gatekeeper climbed to his feet, Alex loosened her grip on me, her voice barely audible. "You're our last hope, Phoenix. Since you have no energy, he can't absorb and reverse it. Play along with my rhetoric and watch for when he is vulnerable."

The Gatekeeper brushed off his clothes. "Well, Alex, it seems that you're the traitor after all."

"Nonsense, Exalted One. I feigned allegiance with this fool in order to escape the prison to which you condemned me, though I am innocent." She helped me walk, guiding me around to the front of the abyss. "Now I have him in my clutches, and he is yours to destroy."

When we stopped within reach of the Gatekeeper, facing him and the main entry, she helped me balance myself. Pain throttled my body and thoughts, but I was too weak even to cringe. Her rhetoric sounded convincing... too convincing. Whose side was she really on? Was she playing both sides to see who would win?

The Gatekeeper set a glowing hand on my shoulder and spoke with a genial tone. "Phoenix, since you are a misguided pawn, I will be lenient and kill you quickly. You are already near death as it is."

I growled, "I'm no pawn."

He chuckled. "Pawns rarely realize that they are sacrificial lambs doing the bidding of a power-hungry king." He looked at Alex. "Or queen."

"Exalted one..." Alex touched her chest. "Me? Power hungry? I delivered him to you."

"Then who opened the dome if not the woman who told me this Reaper was dead?"

"I... I thought he was dead. He lay motionless. Erin checked his pulse. Apparently she deceived me."

"So Erin is the deceiver? I find it interesting that Erin is unavailable to dispute your accusation. Someone who commits suicide isn't in a position to usurp a seat of power. And my guards are missing. Are you saying this ignorant Reaper figured out their weaknesses and how to exploit them without guidance from someone who helped develop them?"

"Develop them?" I whispered through a gasp. "Alex... you... said—"

"That I didn't know much about them and then teased

you with more information later." She laughed. "So I lied to get you to cooperate with me. More proof that I am not your ally."

The Gatekeeper's energy ran across my shoulder and up my neck. Soon it would invade my brain and incapacitate me. It was time to fight back, but my mind felt as wasted as my body. And with new information storming in, it seemed ready to burst.

"In any case," Alex said to the Gatekeeper, "Phoenix had help from Shanghai and Tokyo, whom they were able to raise from the dead. And I had no idea that Erin killed herself. As you know, I have been in the abyss."

"You conspired with Erin. She was the only person besides me who knew the password to the abyss computer."

"Believe your theories, or believe my deeds." Alex released me. "Maxwell is dead. Peter is dead. And now I give Phoenix to you, the last Reaper capable of overthrowing your rule."

"I'll deal with him first. If you are truly loyal, then you will neither interfere nor run for your life."

She bowed her head. "Yes, Exalted One. I will stay and bear witness. Let your righteous anger be appeased."

The Gatekeeper set his free hand on my other shoulder and looked me in the eye. "Phoenix, relax and let my energy flow. You are too weak to resist. Make it easy for yourself and face the truth. You have lost. Give up the fight and settle into the peaceful slumber of death."

His energy drifted into my brain. I steeled myself. I had to fight. This was the moment I had prepared for. Maxwell wasn't able to defeat him, nor was Peter. Only I remained standing, but my trembling legs begged to give in and collapse.

As the energy coursed, an image of Misty flowed—her twelve-year-old self holding hands with me while I was the same age. We walked through a meadow of knee-high grass and tall daisies. We each plucked a daisy and lay in the midst of the grass, hidden from view. As a warm breeze bent the blades, I touched my daisy to her cheek and twirled it, letting each petal caress her lovely skin. Her smile lit up the meadow—warm and inviting.

"Come and be with me," she whispered, her accent as melodious as ever. "Death is the only escape from the cruel world that enchains you to its sorrows. Let us be together in bliss, at peace always. Here you will never have to fight again. We will be lovers at last and for all eternity."

Shanghai's voice broke through. "Fight, Phoenix! You have to fight!" Was it her ghost?

I swept Misty's image away. *Shanghai. I'm trying.* I had to resist. But why? Misty was dead and gone. So was Sing. Shanghai and Tokyo were probably dead as well. Even if I miraculously survived this onslaught, what then? I had no way to escape.

I shook my head. No. The Gatekeeper's influence planted those seeds of doubts. I couldn't let him win. Since Alex seemed to be knuckling under, I was the only one left to do battle. Millions of people all over the world needed to be set free.

His mesmerizing voice blended into my thoughts. "If you resist, Phoenix, your death will be excruciating. Either way, you'll be dead. Why take the road of torture?"

Dimness flooded my vision. My heart fluttered,

skipping beats. My energy level had to be below one percent. I was dying.

Again I shook my head. I couldn't die. I had to check on Shanghai. And Tokyo. I might be able to save them.

The Gatekeeper looked at Alex. "His resistance is extraordinary. I will go ahead and kill him with his own reserves."

Alex nodded, showing no hint of fear, compassion, or anger. She was a blank wall, completely callous, or perhaps she hid her feelings with extraordinary acting.

The Gatekeeper's body darkened, including his hands—signaling a shift to absorption mode... and his temporary vulnerability. Since I had no energy to reverse, what would happen? How could I attack?

As he stared at me, his brow wrinkled. "What is this magic? No Reaper can survive with so little energy."

He pressed on my shoulders. Pain burned down my arms and legs and deep in my brain. I bit my lip hard. I couldn't run. I couldn't even crawl. I had to stay put and resist his leeching touch.

Although the staredown continued, Tokyo stayed in view behind the Gatekeeper. She crawled toward us, her limbs trembling and her face bruised. Since the Gatekeeper kept his eyes locked on me with his back to her, he couldn't detect her approach. But in her condition, what could she do?

I resisted the urge to glance at Alex. She could see Tokyo. Maybe Alex's alliances would finally be revealed.

When Tokyo reached Shanghai's dagger, she picked it up and tossed it toward me. It flew past the Gatekeeper, missing him by inches. I caught the hilt, plunged the blade into his gut, and pulled it out. Warm liquid poured over my hands. He released my shoulders, stumbled back three steps, and glared at me. Tokyo withdrew her sonic gun, but she collapsed on top of it, her eyes still open.

Blood spread across the Gatekeeper's shirt and dripped to the floor. Radiance returned and streamed across his entire body, concentrating on the dagger's entry point at his solar plexus. Sizzles erupted, and the flow of blood stopped.

His face now almost too brilliant to view, he sneered. "An insignificant pawn cannot topple this king."

I said nothing. I couldn't speak a word or will myself to run.

"Somehow you have resisted my power, but as weak as you are, you cannot resist strangulation." His hands reaching out, he stomped toward me. I had only one hope, to use his force-field against him.

I dropped to my back. When he dove at me, I lifted my legs, thrust my feet into his stomach, and used his momentum to send him flying behind me with far more power than I delivered.

I twisted my body to watch. As he sailed across the abyss, he flipped completely over and fell across the far edge, his arms over the lip and his legs dangling.

Still glowing, he clawed at the floor, but he slowly slipped. He would fall in seconds. "Alex! Help me! Prove your loyalty!"

"Of course, Exalted One." Alex ran around the abyss and knelt at the Gatekeeper's side.

I grimaced. I had him! If not for Alex, I would have beaten him! But now all would be lost.

Alex grabbed the Gatekeeper's arm, then jerked back. "I can't touch you. Turn off your energy."

When he darkened, Alex reached down, grabbed his belt, and dragged him out. He lay on his stomach, panting. "You will be greatly rewarded for this, Alex."

"I know." She pulled her sonic gun from her waistband and set it against the back of the Gatekeeper's head. "Checkmate, Exalted One." She pulled the trigger. A pop sounded. His head jerked, then fell limp along with the rest of his body.

Moving with cool precision, Alex slid the gun away, grasped the Gatekeeper's ankles, and, walking backwards, dragged his body around the abyss. As she passed me on her way toward the door, she said, "Stay there. Rest. I'll see about Shanghai and Tokyo. And remember to honor your promise."

I closed my eyes. My heart thumped in an uneven rhythm. Dizziness washed in along with darkness. I floated in a black medium, similar to the ghostly liquid that spun in the abyss, only this felt like a gently flowing stream, sweet smelling and warm.

Something cool touched my hand. I opened my eyes. I sat against a tree, the same tree where I rested when coming out of ghost mode after leaving the depot grounds. Shanghai slept next to me, as before. How could this be? Hadn't it been only moments since the Gatekeeper sent Shanghai flying through the broken doors?

"Sancta sum." The familiar voice sounded like a song.

I turned my head toward the source, unable to move my body. The Sancta sat in a patch of grass at my side with her legs curled under herself. She smiled, her face lovelier than ever. "I get the impression that you're surprised to see me."

"I am." I glanced around. "Did I die? Is Shanghai dead, too?"

She let out a soft laugh. "No, you are not dead. You are unconscious, and the Highest Power saw fit to give you this vision so I could visit you again. It was my decision to include a phantom Shanghai so you wouldn't be startled."

"Good idea. I think it helped."

"It also seemed fitting, seeing that she has been so loyal." The Sancta slid her hand into mine and pulled it into her lap. "I asked for this visit to tell you that you will not see me again in this world."

"Why not?"

"My role here has ended. You are now on a path of light that will lead you to the Highest Power. You are not quite there yet, but I am confident that you will arrive as long as you stay on the path."

"How can I be sure to stay on it?"

"You need not concern yourself with that. Once you are on the path, you have to consciously choose to depart from it. The path is light; all other choices are darkness. You will know."

"How did I get on it in the first place?"

Her eyes twinkled. "Oh, I think you know that answer."

I absorbed her infectious smile and let it dress my own lips. My principles. I had to stick to them no matter what. And the greatest principle was offering everyone a hand of mercy, even Alex, and believing that the Highest Power really is the Highest Power. "Yes. I think I know."

"Although I must depart, I trust that you will always have a guide. Perhaps it won't come in the form of a Sancta, or perhaps it will. In any case, there is always a guiding light to follow."

"You said your role here is over, but I still don't understand why you have to leave. It's great having you around."

"Here is why." As a serious countenance darkened her face, she pressed my hand against her chest. "Do you feel my heartbeat?"

I concentrated on the pressure point. Nothing pressed back. "No."

She released me. "I have no heartbeat because I am dead."

"Dead?" I drew my hand back to my own lap. "Then how can you—"

"Visit you? Talk to you?" Her beautiful smile returned. "How is that so surprising to a Reaper?"

"You mean, you're a ghost?"

"In a manner of speaking. I can take physical form or become a phantom. We Sanctae were once alive on the earth, but now we are like angels, commissioned with special assignments to care for those whom the Highest Power has selected. When the Power gave me a list of assignments to choose from, I chose you."

"Why? Weren't there easier assignments than me?"

She laughed. "Oh, to be sure. But you occupy a special place in my heart. You are uncommon in so many ways. You have never been taught the Highest Power's principles, yet you instinctively follow them. That proves that the Power's laws and precepts were indelibly written on your heart, and you rarely cast them away."

I laid a hand over my own chest. Her kind words infused inner warmth. "Can you give me any final advice before you go?"

"I can leave you with a few questions to ponder." She

nodded toward Shanghai. "What other woman would have stayed as loyal to you as she has? Faced nightmarish dangers? Endured horrific pain? Her warrior spirit is willing to suffer for the greater good of all mankind, but there is more to her loyalty than that. She longs to be with you, as your friend, your fellow warrior, and your lover. No amount of suffering can thwart her dedication to the cause of helping those who cannot help themselves. She also longs to be with a young man who has shown her nothing but the purity of selfless love and a desire to keep her safe and strong in body, mind, and spirit."

I nodded. "She definitely made it clear that she wants us to be together. I'm not sure how to handle it. I mean, we're supposed to live in the same condo. It would be hard not to... you know."

"Hard? That is an understatement. To this point, your principles have protected you—dedication to Misty, memorialized by a pewter ring. But Misty is gone. The ring has been cast aside. Yet, Shanghai remains, and her desires for you are unabated. She has, indeed, been forward, but she has merely reacted to her longings without the inner guidance that has been nearly lost to this world. What will you do in response? How will you ensure that her virtue, and yours, are maintained as you continue your journey, living in the same condo, traveling together day and night? Holding fast to Misty's phantom will never last. That is a chain that will bind you."

The Sancta's words settled into my mind, too deep for quick analysis. I needed time to ponder them, figure out how to apply these newfound principles.

"I must go," she continued. "Your courageous acts

freed my husband from the abyss, and now I will stay with him forever. I hope to see you again beyond the Gateway."

"Hope? You mean it's possible that we won't see each other again? Doesn't everyone travel beyond the Gateway?"

"Everyone passes through the eternal gate, but not all go to the same place. There is a path of darkness as well as a path of light. Each soul chooses the destination before he or she arrives at the Gateway."

"What happened to Peter's soul? Did he go to darkness or light?"

"I have no way of knowing. I did have a chance to speak to him before he died, so I have hope." She waved a hand. "That is all I will say about this subject. I have already delayed too much."

As she faded, I reached out, but my fingers passed through her phantom hand. "Wait. If you were once alive, you must have had a name."

"I do. I am Maxwell's wife, your grandmother." Just before she vanished, she whispered, "Sarah sum... I am Sarah."

I echoed the whisper. "I am Sarah." The sound of the name expanded the warmth inside. My grandmother had come from beyond the Gateway to help me rescue her husband and teach me the ways of the Highest Power. A gift. A legacy. Far too wonderful to fully comprehend.

As I tried to remember her face, her voice, her words, I continued whispering, adding names to the list of beloveds. "Sarah. Sing. Shanghai." The three sounded wonderful together, like a breeze passing through high branches in a forest. Then I added, "Misty." The S in her name blended in with perfection.

I closed my eyes and lay on my back, still whispering the names in turn. With each repetition, the warmth grew. Maybe this visit from the Sancta was a dream. Maybe I had died and now drifted in limbo. Either way, it didn't matter. Peace reigned. I was no longer in control of any situation. And that felt wonderful.

CHAPTER TWENTY-TWO

"PHOENIX? CAN YOU hear me?"

I opened my eyes. Shanghai lay over me, chest to chest, her valve connected to mine. "You're awake!" She quickly unplugged, closed our valves, and lifted away.

Now on her knees, she pressed a hand against her side. Blood stained her fingers, but it looked dry. "I'm sorry, Phoenix, but you were unconscious, so I couldn't ask your permission. I tried to wake you up earlier, but you didn't respond. I saved this as a last resort."

I whispered, "Saved what as a last resort?"

"Giving you energy. I know you're against it, but I thought since there aren't any souls left to give it back to, it might be all right. And I didn't give you much."

She pulled the watch from her pocket and looked at it. "You're at eleven percent. That's enough to survive for a while. And I think I'm at about thirty-five. We'll both have to get the surgery to remove our valves soon, or we'll die."

"So will every other Reaper," Tokyo said.

I shifted my eyes toward her. She stood at my side with her arms crossed. A purple and green bruise marred her face from one eye down to her chin. "Did the energy get rid of the cloud shield?" I asked.

Tokyo shook her head. "Only part of it. I climbed to the top of the dome and could barely see the shield's edges, so we have a much bigger hole. It goes well past the canyon walls, and if it extends beyond the most radio-active areas, maybe it won't be too dangerous to transport souls to the Gateway."

"Without our valves, how can we reap souls and trans-port them?"

"Before I explain..." Tokyo crouched close. "Let's check on how you're doing."

She and Shanghai pulled me to a sitting position, allowing me a better view of my surroundings. We were in the coffin room where Sing's body still lay, though Peter's was now gone. The computer tablet, the life-spark crucible, and the tongs lay on his empty coffin. "How long was I unconscious?"

Shanghai slid her hand into mine. "About an hour."

"What did you do with Peter's body?"

"Tokyo hauled him outside while I kept watch over you. We needed the coffin for extracting a soul from a cloak, but I'll explain that later. We didn't have time to bury him, and burning him might attract Alex's attention. We assume she'll eventually find him."

"Where is Alex?"

A worried look darkened Shanghai's expression. "We don't know. After she checked on Tokyo and me, she dragged the Gatekeeper's body away. I was conscious, so I watched her until she moved him out of sight somewhere beyond one of the staircases, but I haven't seen her since."

"That has to mean trouble. She'll exploit every remain-ing secret in this place."

Tokyo nodded. "So we should finish our business here and leave as soon as possible."

"What business is left? The souls are free."

"This evil system can be rebuilt, so we have to destroy what we can. We'll work on a new soul-delivery system later."

I looked at Sing's coffin. "We should take Sing's body with us. Give her a decent burial."

"Trust me. I have not forgotten her." Tokyo straightened and, with Shanghai's help, hoisted me to my feet. "First," Tokyo continued, "allow me to address your earlier question about reaping souls. I gave Shanghai a crash course in how to reap without using energy from her valve. Fortunately, Albert acted as a willing guinea pig, safe in this shielded room."

I glanced around. The shield still covered the ceiling and walls. Obviously enough energy remained in the lines to keep it active and to supply Sing's coffin.

Shanghai smiled. "I must have reaped Albert ten times, and each time we had to strip him out of the cloak using the electrical surge in Peter's coffin. He got tired of the repetitions, but he stayed in good spirits."

Tokyo touched the tablet where it lay on the empty coffin. "We recorded the training session so we could send the procedure to every Reaper in the world. Since no one will be able to receive energy, time will be of the essence."

I gave her a doubtful look. "We're assuming they'll continue reaping. Once they have the surgery that gets rid of the energy ball-and-chain, I think most will quit. Reaping can be torture."

Shanghai's smile thinned to a tight line. "We'll just have to come up with a way to encourage them."

"That'll be a challenge." I adjusted my cloak sleeves and pushed my hands into the pockets. Sing's photo stick, Kwame's watch, and the radiation-detection band still remained along with the key to the condo. "Any other unfinished business?"

"Finding Alex," Shanghai said. "We can't get out of here without that flying machine she talked about. The canyon walls around this place are too high. And we can't go into ghost mode to climb. Like Tokyo said, the heavenly suction hole extends past those walls now. It would gobble us up."

"Not to mention that Tokyo can't transform to ghost mode. Even if you and I could go, we couldn't leave her stuck here with Alex."

"Don't worry," Tokyo said as she looked at Sing's body, her head low. "I won't let that happen."

Shanghai picked up the tablet. "Back to finding Alex. The only energy signal is in the reservoir tank, remnants that didn't get pushed into the dome room. It's showing five percent full, but that's still quite a bit."

"Enough that Alex might want it," I said.

"Exactly my thinking. So we'll shut off the output from the tank to keep her from accessing it, and we'll go down there to see if she shows up to claim it."

Tokyo set a hand on Shanghai's arm. "Can you keep a feeder going to Sing's coffin?"

Shanghai scrunched her brow. "Why?"

"Well..." Tokyo looked up as if searching for the right word. "It might be a while before we can transport her. I know it sounds crass, but she will begin to stink. The longer we can keep her intact, the better."

"I'll see what I can do."

I raised a finger. "There is a problem."

Shanghai and Tokyo turned my way. "What?" Shanghai asked.

"I made a deal with Alex. Rerouting the energy to the dome was her idea. We decided on a trade—her idea to restore the souls in exchange for a peaceful split. We don't bother her; she doesn't bother us."

Shanghai traded glances with Tokyo, then looked at me. "We were wondering why she hasn't bothered us. We've been able to go wherever we wanted."

"So she's keeping her end of the deal. We need to keep ours."

"It wasn't my deal," Tokyo said, pointing at herself. "Or Shanghai's. It was yours. You have no authority to make such a bargain on my behalf. We have to find Alex and kill her. She is more dangerous than the Gatekeeper ever was."

Shanghai nodded. "Tokyo's right. We can't leave without dealing with Alex."

I spread out my hands. "But I gave her my word. I can't go back on it."

"Or else Alex will control him," Shanghai said to Tokyo. "That's a genetic weakness Phoenix has. If he violates his principles in association with a woman, he becomes a slave to her."

"I'm not worried about that. I'm hoping the weakness is gone, if it ever existed."

"Good," Tokyo said. "Then we will hunt Alex down and—"

"No. Don't you get it? Fear of being controlled isn't why I keep my word. It's just the right thing to do. If I break a vow when it's convenient, why would anyone ever trust me again? You couldn't trust me. Shanghai couldn't trust me. I wouldn't be able to trust myself."

Tokyo crossed her arms. "But you still have no right to expect us to voluntarily join your vow. You made it for yourself, not for us. If I have to hunt Alex down myself, I will, and I suspect that Shanghai will join me."

"She's right, Phoenix," Shanghai said. "We have to stop Alex whether you help us or not. We're not bound to your promise."

"I understand. Just give me a second to think." While they stared at me, each with a concerned expression, I probed my mind once more. I was trapped. I couldn't break my vow, and I couldn't let these two march into danger without me. Besides that, Alex hadn't done anything evil since I rescued her from the abyss. She even helped me out of it when she could have cut the line. Maybe she had responded to my hand of mercy. The likelihood seemed microscopically small, but I had to consider it and watch for more signs of change. In any case, Shanghai and Tokyo wouldn't believe it, so it was best to keep the idea to myself. "I'm coming with you. For defense. Not to kill Alex."

"Fair enough." Again looking at the tablet, Shanghai strode out the door. "Everyone follow me."

We walked single file, Tokyo trailing. Although my legs still hurt, they no longer cramped. In the past, a ten-percent level would have incapacitated me, but now it felt like a new lease on life. At least I could walk without fear of collapsing.

After descending the stairs and entering the former drainage farm on the east side, we dodged the scattered pedestals until we reached the northeast corner of the room and faced a wall where seams outlined what appeared to be a door.

Shanghai tapped on the screen. The door slid open to darkness. She unfastened her flashlight and shone the beam on the first few steps of a descending staircase. "Quiet now," she whispered as she looked down the stairs. "Alex might already be there."

With Shanghai leading the way again and Tokyo following me, we tiptoed down the stairs. Shanghai kept the beam close, just a stair or two in front. A musty odor rose from below along with a gentle hum, maybe a small motor running.

The stairs continued downward at least forty vertical feet. When we reached the bottom, Shanghai swept the beam slowly. It landed on a wall just a step to our right, then on a narrow corridor leading into darkness to the north, then on a head-high metal container to our left. That was likely the reservoir tank.

Staying quiet, Shanghai walked along the corridor and gestured for us to follow. We passed the northern end of the tank and kept going, now bordered on the left by a plaster wall, interrupted only by a closed elevator. A few seconds later, we reached an open door at the corridor's end.

Shanghai aimed the beam inside and waved it around. "Looks safe," she whispered.

When we walked in, Shanghai tapped the tablet screen. Ceiling lights flashed on, revealing a rectangular conference table with a world map under glass. Inch-high statuettes covered by dark cloaks and hoods stood at various locations, the densest concentrations atop the larger cities. Black circles covered the burned jungle cities—Moscow, Phoenix, Shanghai, Mexico City, Saigon, and many others. All but one of those spots had no statues standing on them.

Chicago was the only city with a black circle as well as hooded statues. At least twenty stood there facing away from the city center. I touched the glass near the outermost statue and whispered, "The next city to burn?"

Shanghai nodded. "But why the little Reapers?"

"Maybe they're not Reapers." Tokyo tossed a stack of photos on the table. "Maybe they're illuminaries. I found these in a drawer."

I stepped closer. The first photo showed an illuminary, and a caption at the bottom described it as A:1— a prototype, a model that was never built because of its inadequate size. Wearing a black cloak and hood and bearing red eyes, it resembled the illuminaries we faced. A man who looked like Sydney posed next to it, standing two heads taller than the illuminary.

I flipped to the next illuminary photo and read the caption. Model A:2 was the first unit to be put into service as a house guardian, though it proved to be too vulnerable to energy surges. The next seven photos revealed more illuminaries that were obsolete and no longer existed, having been mothballed after extensive testing revealed their flaws.

The tenth photo displayed a currently working model, the kind we battled upstairs, the first unit to have the ability to become invisible. The caption described them as slow, lacking intelligence, unable to adapt to attacks, and vulnerable to sound waves, so the inventors relegated them to defensive duties.

I skipped to the last model—F:3. The description

sounded like a marketing ad, touting this illuminary as the perfect soldier, highly durable under physical punishment and invulnerable to radiation, electricity, and fire. Artificial-intelligence processors endowed it with decision-making abilities surpassing those of most humans. It was able to learn while battling and could devise countermeasures to defeat any enemy.

Not only that, a single charge from the Gatekeeper's energy supply would keep it fully operational for a year. Its internal motor ran with such efficiency, it emitted only a quiet purr, which also made it a good candidate for stealth approaches. When the Gatekeeper gave his final approval, the inventor put the design into production.

I whispered, "The Gatekeeper was building an army."

"But why?" Shanghai asked. "He already ruled the world."

Tokyo picked up one of the photos. "To squash the Resistance once and for all. You can bet he had an inkling that we were getting close to taking control of some of the major metropolitan areas. Before I died, we had uprisings planned in Budapest, Johannesburg, and Baltimore."

"I never heard about any uprisings," I said.

"We were waiting for a trigger, my journey to the Gateway. If I returned with news that it's a real place to look forward to, then our supporters would be willing to die for the cause."

"So now you can go back and tell them. The uprisings can begin."

Tokyo let out a heavy sigh. "Yes, that was my plan."

"Was? Is something wrong?"

She gave me a weak smile. "Don't worry about me. I'm conflicted between my warrior side and my grieving-mother side. Tears can wait for tomorrow." She gripped my hand and interlocked our thumbs. "Today we will be warriors. We will find these illuminaries before they are activated and sent to the cities, and we will destroy them… that is, if your vow to leave Alex alone allows it. These machines are not Alex."

I studied Tokyo's expression—intense, piercing. This commander of the Resistance wasn't pleased at all with my vow. I released her hand. "Maybe I can. I'll think about it. But like I said, I'll help on defense. If the illuminaries try to hurt you or Shanghai, I'll be all over them."

"That's better than nothing, but I must confess that your ethics balancing act is frustrating. Alex is a devil, and you're dancing with her." Tokyo punched her palm with a fist. "You need to hit a woman like her square in the nose and rejoice at the sight of her blood. Otherwise, you'll never be a good soldier in this war."

I kept my tone calm but firm. "Look, Tokyo. Here's the bottom line. The deal with Alex worked. The energy went to the dome, the souls were set free, and the Gatekeeper is dead. I have no regrets, and I will keep my word."

"Very well." Tokyo crossed her arms. "Let's just hope your principles don't become a handicap."

Although her words bit harder than she likely intended, I gave her a genial nod. "I understand."

"It's all making sense now," Shanghai said, apparently hoping to change the subject. "Alex knew everything about the illuminaries from the start, and her plan has always been to gain access to a robotic army. Phoenix, she just used you to get the Gatekeeper out of the way."

"And we were wondering why the Gatekeeper needed

so much energy. He didn't want it for himself; he wanted it for his soldiers."

"But maybe they're not already energized." As Shanghai swiped a finger on the tablet, her eyes darted from side to side. "According to this histogram, the reservoir tank was half full this morning, which is a pretty consistent level until three days ago when it was..." Her mouth dropped open. "Ninety-eight percent full. They drained almost half of it in a single day."

I looked over her shoulder. A graph with vertical bars ran across the screen. "So they energized their soldiers three days ago. They already have a battle-ready army waiting somewhere to deploy and take over."

"But where?" Shanghai asked, looking at me. "Are they here, or have they been transported somewhere else?"

Tokyo looked at the ceiling. "It's possible that Alex doesn't know where they are, and she's searching as we speak."

Shanghai refocused on the screen. "I'm sure she checked the Gatekeeper's bedchamber for clues, but maybe she missed something. Let's have a look." She walked out of the conference room and into the corridor. "Follow me."

We tagged along, this time with me at the tail end. When Shanghai stopped at the elevator, she tapped on the tablet screen. The door opened to a lighted compartment with dark green carpet and mahogany walls, its size perfect for one person but not for three.

Once we had crowded in shoulder to shoulder, Shanghai closed the door. While we rode the car up, she showed me the floor plan. The staircase we had walked down bypassed one level—the Gatekeeper's personal suite—lower than the meeting room's level and higher than the reservoir tank room. This elevator was the only access.

The car eased to a stop and opened. We exited onto plush blue carpet in a wide, marble-walled corridor and turned left, Shanghai again leading the way. The corridor ended at an enormous bedroom. Drawers lay on the floor with clothes and papers scattered everywhere. A bed sat with its ornate headboard against the far wall. On the mattress, the Gatekeeper rested upright, his face white, his eyes closed, and his torso propped in place by pillows.

"Obviously Alex has been here," Shanghai said.

Tokyo strode to the body, pried one of his eyes open, and peered in. "I can't tell if his soul's still there." She turned to us. "Shanghai?"

Shanghai grimaced. "All right. I'll check. But it'll be like sticking my hand into a jar of maggots." She pulled her cloak's sleeve over her hand and covered the Gatekeeper's eyes. As she probed, she looked away with a second grimace, as if disgusted. Soon, she withdrew her hand and pulled her sleeve back up. "He's gone. I guess Alex reaped him."

I scanned the ceiling and walls. "I don't see any energy shield. Maybe she just sent him skyward."

"Don't count on it," Shanghai said. "His body's here, but that doesn't mean she reaped him here."

Tokyo picked up a stack of papers. "At least we know she was looking for something, maybe the location of the illuminaries."

"But we can't tell if she found it." I stared at a tall mirror that stood in a corner. A pale, smudged face stared back at me. My bent form made me look like a decrepit old man. An odd gap divided my hair at the side of my head. I brushed through it with my fingers, but it stayed in place. "Shanghai, did you notice this gap in my hair?"

"Sure." She walked closer, squinting. "You didn't?"

"Last time I looked in a mirror was at the condo, but I was in a hurry. We had to get to the train station."

"I thought maybe some had gotten pulled out in a fight at the camp."

I brushed through the gap again. The shorter ends seemed uniform. "No, it's been cut, like with scissors."

"That's strange."

As I bent over so I could see the hair at a better angle, my medallion slipped out and dangled from its chain. Of course Alex couldn't track me because Shanghai still had the watch... or did she?

I turned toward her. "You still have Alex's watch, don't you?"

She withdrew it from her cloak pocket. "Right here."

"I wonder if she has a second one. She might be tracking me now."

"I suppose it's possible since she didn't mind giving you the original tracker."

I slid the medallion's chain up over my head and hung it over a bedpost. "I'm wondering about the device the Gatekeeper uses to keep tabs on her and the other Council members." I looked at Tokyo. "They all have tracking chips in their scalps."

"Maybe that's what she was looking for," Tokyo said.

I walked to the bed, slid my hand into the Gatekeeper's pocket, and withdrew a watch on a chain. "Maybe this is it."

As I opened the casing, Tokyo and Shanghai closed in.

On the face, five hands pointed toward the room where the deceased members drew their last breath. The sixth, bearing a tiny "Alex" label, pointed south. A meter embedded in the hand flashed 84.

"Eighty-four feet?" Tokyo asked.

"I assume so. Alex said these devices use the ancient units."

Shanghai looked at the ceiling. "But on which level?"

"No way to be sure."

She put on a skeptical frown. "The watch was way too easy to find. I smell a setup. She wants you to track her."

"It can't hurt just to read the watch." I pointed toward the exit. "Let's move. If she's tracking me, she'll think I'm here, at least until my medallion conks out."

Shanghai looked at the tablet screen. "We'll head for the main floor while you keep an eye on Alex's signal. If we can zero in on where she is, we'll stop and decide what to do next. With any luck, maybe we can pluck an Owl."

CHAPTER TWENTY-THREE

WITH SHANGHAI AGAIN leading the way, we trooped to the elevator. "The car goes up to the lobby," she said as she looked at the tablet. "And it exits through a hidden door under one of the staircases. It's a good shortcut."

"I'm all for skipping the stairs." I lifted my sore legs in turn. "Right now, any shortcut is a good shortcut."

We entered the elevator and rode up to the next level. When the door opened, we walked out from under the east staircase. From there I followed Alex's watch hand southward to a point a few steps north of the hall that joined the two drainage farms. When the hand reversed and pointed north, I halted and turned the watch to a vertical position. Alex's hand shifted until it pointed downward.

Shanghai and Tokyo joined me. "What's her distance now?" Tokyo asked.

I squinted at a tiny 41 on the hand. "Forty-one feet straight down."

Shanghai studied the tablet. "The only thing directly below us is the reservoir tank. The signal must be coming from somewhere inside it. I guess it's a good place to hide."

I looked at the screen. A glowing haze, most likely particles of energy, filled a square representing the tank. "Alex wouldn't cower. She's got something up her sleeve."

"So we proceed cautiously," Tokyo said. "But first, allow me to visit my daughter's body and leave something with her. If you survive, I want you to see it before you carry her home. I assume our encounter with Alex might end in death for one or more of us."

I studied her sad expression. It seemed that the grieving mother had usurped the confident commander, at least for the moment. "Sure. Go ahead."

Tokyo limped up the west-side stairs, her body bent and head drooping. Climbing to see her daughter's corpse again had to feel like a funeral march.

With a quiet groan, I lowered myself to the floor and patted the space next to me. When Shanghai sat, I took her hand and looked into her eyes. Having her at my side felt so good, I had to let her know. "I just wanted to say you're really fantastic."

She tucked a strand of hair behind her ear, her smile weak and tired. "I guess you're not too mad at me for giving you a dose of energy."

"Not at all. It was an act of love. Who could get mad at that?"

"You're right, Phoenix. It was love." She lifted my hand and kissed my knuckles. "No matter what happens, know that I love you. Everything I have done and everything I will do is because I love you."

I grinned. "Even if I don't like it?"

Her smile freshened. "Even then."

"I'll remember that." I looked at the watch again.

Alex's distance meter stayed constant. "I guess we'd better come up with a plan. Alex will be ready for us."

"If she's drawing us to her on purpose, she's probably loaded with energy. She'll be tough to beat in a fight, even with all three of us combining what's left of our strength."

Shanghai looked down as if she could see through the floor. "If Alex isn't in the tank, are there any other reasons her signal could be coming from there?"

"It's possible that someone cut her chip out, but it would shut off if it's not close to her DNA. She has to be there." As I joined Shanghai in a downward stare, the hum of a motor returned to mind. Had it come from inside the tank? It carried a repeating quality, like fan blades gently pushing air, almost like a…

I finished the thought out loud. "Like a purr."

"What?" Shanghai asked.

"The photo said the newest illuminaries have quiet motors that sound like a purr. I heard something like that at the energy tank."

"Do you think the illuminaries are inside?"

"It's the perfect place to store them. They can get charged up. Stay out of sight. Who would think to look there?"

Shanghai gave me a tight-lipped nod. "I wonder how many she has."

"If the map showed an exact number…" I resurrected a memory of the conference table and mentally counted the statuettes. "Maybe a hundred and fifty."

"How are we going to fight a hundred and fifty of those souped-up cyber monsters?"

"We can't fight them. We'll have to neutralize them. Maybe lock them inside the tank."

Shanghai looked at the tablet screen. "I see something that might be an access panel, but even if we could lock them inside, it would just delay them. They'd eventually break out."

"Does the tank have a cleaning cycle? Do they ever flush it with anything?"

"I'll check the help screen."

As she tapped with both thumbs, the sound of footsteps drew my attention to the stairs. Tokyo walked down, now wearing the cloak that was on Sing's body, actually her own cloak since Sing had borrowed it. With the hood up and the cloak trailing, she looked regal—a Reaper divine, as so many called her.

When she arrived, she sat on the floor in front of us. "I put a note in her pants pocket. If I die and you survive, please read it before you remove her body from this place."

I nodded. "We will, but we're not going to think about failing. Shanghai and I have a battle philosophy. If you plan to die, you will die."

Tokyo looked away and whispered, "That is a wise philosophy."

After I updated Tokyo on our discussion about the possible number and location of the illuminaries, Shanghai spoke up. "I found something. The tank can get an acid wash, but it's manual. A maintenance worker attaches a hose to an adapter on top of the tank. Then he turns a valve that sends a spray inside."

"That has potential," I said.

Shanghai's eyes widened. "Well, this is a great find. The help menus led me to other devices not controlled automatically. I found where Erin parks her vehicle. It's in the forest. We passed pretty close to it on our way in. Of course, that doesn't mean it's still there. This information could be old."

"Make a mental note. That might be our escape route once we're finished here."

"Will do." Shanghai pointed at the box representing the energy reservoir. "Okay. I found the exact dimensions. Looks like the tank is big enough to fit a couple of hundred soldiers. But Alex just sitting inside with them makes no sense. I'm thinking she didn't find the control device, so she hasn't activated them, or maybe she has to activate each one manually. That means every minute we're sitting here, she's making progress. An acid shower would put a stop to it."

I nodded but kept my mouth shut. Saying that I needed to get Alex out before the acid wash might start a new argument. I just had to bide my time and wait for more evidence of her presence in the tank.

Shanghai climbed to her feet, grabbed my arm, and hauled me up. My legs trembled. I was as weak as a kitten, and Shanghai knew it. I just had to swallow my pride and accept her help.

Skipping the elevator to avoid making noise, we walked abreast to the stairway in the farm room, descended without a sound or a light, and arrived at the east side of the reservoir tank. I listened for the purr. Only my thumping heart disturbed the silence.

I plucked the flashlight from my belt, covered the end with a hand, and turned it on, careful to deaden the click. The glow provided enough light to see a foot or so ahead.

After a few moments of tiptoeing around, I located a plastic hose about the same diameter as my arm. It led to darkness somewhere above. I aimed the flashlight that way and spread two fingers apart to let a sliver of the beam through. It shone on a faucet valve and ceiling connector labeled *Acid*.

Shanghai picked up the hose's loose end, while Tokyo set her hands in a cradle at knee level. Shanghai planted a foot there, braced with a hand on the tank's side, and rode Tokyo's boost to the top.

Prowling like a cat, Shanghai pulled the hose across the tank's roof toward the center and out of sight. Soon, she reappeared at the edge and dropped to the floor. She whispered, "Acid hose attached."

I extended the flashlight to Shanghai, withdrew the Gatekeeper's watch, and held it in my palm while she set the beam on the face. Alex's hand pointed toward the tank. The meter indicated twenty feet away, roughly the tank's center.

Shanghai leaned close and whispered directly into my ear. "I don't hear the motor. Do you think Alex is alone in there?"

I listened to the sounds in the room—again nothing but my own heartbeat. I glanced at Tokyo. Her stern face said that we should just execute Alex and be done with it, but I couldn't let that happen. We had no right to act as judge and executioner, especially since she still hadn't shown any evil toward us since the abyss rescue, at least nothing we knew about.

Still, I couldn't just walk into the tank to see if she was there. If Shanghai's suspicions were right, the watch might be leading me into a trap. I had to take one careful step at a time.

"Let's find the way in," I whispered.

Tokyo frowned but said nothing.

"I saw the access over here." Shanghai led the way to the south end of the tank's east wall and stopped near the corner. She shone the beam on a head-high metal door that stood closed with a deadbolt latch turned to the unlocked position. Blood covered the door's handle, and a bloody handprint emblazoned the wall to the side. I touched the blood on the handle with a fingertip—tacky… recent.

The three of us exchanged glances. Alex was the only person who could have placed that print. Maybe the illuminaries turned on her and she was hiding in the tank, injured and bleeding. Or maybe this was all a ploy, though that seemed doubtful. Shedding her own blood didn't match her style.

In any case, I couldn't just walk away and leave her to die. "I'm going in."

Shanghai tugged on my cloak sleeve. "Blood or no blood, it could still be a trap."

"I know. You two can stay out here and stand guard. Shout if you hear or see anything unusual."

"No way. I'm coming with you. Tokyo can handle it out here. She still has a sonic gun."

I gave Tokyo a respectful nod. "If you're willing, of course."

"I am willing." She grasped my wrist and looked me in the eye. Although the flashlight's dim glow allowed only a faint view of her face, her expression was clear—sincere and somber. "We have different ideas about what should be done, but I honor your courage and integrity. You are an extraordinary young man, and I apologize for any comments I made that could be interpreted to the contrary."

I grasped her wrist in return. "Thank you. I honor you as well."

Shanghai gave Tokyo my flashlight, withdrew her own, and turned it on. With my sleeve pulled over my fingers, I turned the bloody handle and opened the door quietly. Shanghai aimed her light inside and shifted it from side to side. The tank appeared to be empty, though a blanket of radiant fog covered the floor, deep enough to conceal a body.

We stepped in and padded toward the center, our movement stirring the fog up to knee level. Shanghai aimed the beam into the space ahead as I silently counted off our paces. When we reached about the twenty-foot mark, I stopped. Shanghai swept the beam around. As it passed across the floor, an object appeared in the light.

"Wait." I grabbed her wrist and guided the beam back to the spot. A small mass of bloody skin and hair lay on the floor with a tiny metallic disk on top.

I hissed, "Let's get out of here!"

Just as we turned to run, a shout erupted from the access door followed by a thud and a metallic clank. We dashed in that direction and found Tokyo sitting on the tank's floor, rubbing her head with one hand and clutching the sonic gun with the other. "Two illuminaries ambushed me. I didn't see them until it was too late, and I couldn't get in position to shoot."

I grabbed the door handle and tried to turn it. Locked. I rammed my shoulder into the door, but it wouldn't budge. The purring sound reached my ears. Either Tokyo didn't hear it in time, or we forgot to clue her in on what caused it. Too late to worry about that now.

"Phoenix." Alex's voice penetrated the wall. "It is

tragic that I have to end your life. If you had been under my control, I would have kept you alive to serve as ruler of the world, but now you're a liability. I cannot allow news of my plans to spread beyond this building."

"Don't answer," Shanghai whispered. "She wants to gloat. While she's waiting, maybe we can plan an escape."

"Escape?" I helped Tokyo to her feet, also whispering. "How?"

Shanghai pushed the flashlight into my hand, whipped the tablet from her pocket, and tapped on the screen. "No idea yet. Maybe an output channel big enough to crawl through. Stall her."

I aimed the flashlight at the ceiling and shifted it around. A few valves appeared, but they were much too small to enter. "Alex, what happened to your promise? You said you would let us go free."

"And you said you wouldn't interfere with me."

"I wasn't interfering with you. I came in here because I saw your chip's signal on the Gatekeeper's watch, and then I saw blood on the door handle. I thought the illuminaries might have hurt you."

Alex laughed. "Phoenix, do you expect me to believe that your only motivation was to save my life, that you had no thought of sabotaging my plans?"

"You should believe it. I could have left you unconscious with the other Council members at the bottom of the abyss, but I didn't. Think about it. What motivation could I possibly have had other than to save your life?"

Everything fell silent except for Shanghai's fingers tapping on the tablet screen. After a few moments, Alex spoke up again. "I cannot deny your life-saving heroics, nor can I explain why you chose to risk your life for me, but your kindness has bought you one more chance. Join me and become the leader of a new world system. Together we will establish a system of order and justice that reflects the compassion that you showed me.

"You will be the face of our rule. When people learn that you conquered the Gatekeeper and freed the oppressed souls, they will flock to you, and when they see for themselves your magnanimous character and self-deprecating charm, their loyalty will be unshakable. Your service as a new kind of world leader will far surpass anything you have ever done, and you will be able to help people in more and greater ways than you could if you decline my offer."

I glanced at Shanghai. As she continued searching the tablet for information, she rolled her eyes, obviously unimpressed by Alex's pie-in-the-sky offer. Yet, I had to act interested, to keep Alex talking to buy more time.

"If I agree, will you allow Shanghai and Tokyo to go free?"

"Shanghai, yes. She can be your wife, lover, mistress, whatever. The Resistance doesn't consider her to be one of them. Tokyo is another issue. Now that the Gatekeeper is dead, I have no need of her, and she is too dangerous to be allowed to live."

"Killing her is harsh. Could we keep her in prison instead?"

"That would be a risky proposition," Alex said. "What prison could hold Tokyo?"

"I'm sure you could think of something. Who has ever outwitted you?"

Her tone sharpened. "I think you're stalling, Phoenix. It won't work."

"I'm just trying to strike another deal. I can't let Tokyo die."

Her humming laugh drifted in. "Your appeal is ironic in a way, because your tactics have hastened her death. As I said, I can't trust any prison to hold Tokyo, not even the one you're in now. She has likely been planning her escape while you kept our conversation going."

Silence ensued. I looked at Tokyo, then at Shanghai. The flashlight revealed a worried expression on each face. Alex's words sounded ominous.

Tokyo slid the sonic gun behind her waistband and guided us back until we were a few steps away from the door. "Shanghai," she hissed. "Any luck finding an escape?"

Shanghai lowered the tablet and whispered, "I searched every possible outlet, but they're all too small. I also looked for something I could operate from here to distract her, you know, create an emergency, but everything dangerous has automatic countermeasures." She pointed toward the tank's northwest corner. "There is an outlet over there that leads to Sing's room, but it's as narrow as a broomstick. We could go in ghost mode, but we might get sucked up to the Gateway before we could reach the outlet."

Tokyo stooped and stirred the energy fog with a hand. "Maybe if we scatter it, we could create our own shield to protect you."

"Is energy still running through the line?" I asked.

Shanghai slid the tablet back to her pocket. "Just the trickle needed to keep Sing's corpse intact. I don't know if it would be enough to shield us."

The tank's door opened. I jerked the flashlight beam

that way. An illuminary stepped inside. Its eyes glowed scarlet, brighter than any we had seen. Alex appeared behind it, a bandage around her head and another illuminary standing next to her. Her expression calm, she looked at me. "You had your chance. It seems that I will have to bring order to the world without you."

I stepped in front of Shanghai and Tokyo and squared my shoulders, though every muscle ached. "A warning, Alex. You're breaking our deal. One way or another, I'll break *you*."

She laughed. "And as always, you can't fool me. You can barely stay on your feet." She turned toward the illuminary. "Kill them." She then slammed the door. The click of the deadbolt echoed throughout the tank.

CHAPTER TWENTY-FOUR

THE ILLUMINARY LUNGED at us. Tokyo leaped into a flying kick. Her foot slammed into the illuminary's face and sent it staggering. It crashed upright against a wall and stared at us with blinking red eyes, easily visible through the swirling energy gas.

I waved a hand. "To the center. More room to maneuver. It's probably learning and coming up with a counterattack.""

As we backpedaled, the flashlight trained on the illuminary, it glided toward us, accelerating. Tokyo charged and leaped again. It raised an arm, blocked the kick, and sent her flying to a wall.

I dropped the flashlight. The beam spun as I called out, "No kicks. Use wrestling moves. Go for the throat." I surged forward, collided with it chest to chest, and body slammed it to the floor. The radiant fog splashed and rose toward the ceiling. As I straddled the beast, I wrapped my hands around its throat and squeezed.

Shanghai stomped on the illuminary's arm and stabbed at its eyes with a dagger. It threw me off with a single hand. As I slid on my bottom, the illuminary snatched Shanghai's hair and slung her away. She bowled into me and knocked me flat on my back.

I rolled to all fours. Shanghai struggled to her feet, while Tokyo rose and braced herself against the wall.

The illuminary leaped up and stood straight, no sign of injury except for one dimmed eye as the redness pulsed once more.

"It's calculating again," I said as Shanghai helped me up. "If it gets even smarter, we're dead."

Tokyo withdrew the sonic gun. "Let's see how smart it is after I scramble its brain."

A click sounded above. Something stung my cheek and hands.

"She turned the acid on!" Shanghai shouted.

Tokyo shoved the illuminary, making it backpedal for a moment. She whispered to us, "You two go to ghost mode. I'll create an energy shield." She ran in circles around the illuminary, stirring the fog higher and higher as she accelerated.

Shanghai cried out, "But you'll die."

"Just do it. Obey your commander." With the gun still in hand, she kept running while the illuminary swiveled its head, apparently devising a countermeasure.

"Why don't you shoot it?" I called.

"I plan to! At the right moment!"

I took a hard step toward them, but Shanghai grabbed my arm. "No!" she hissed. "I won't let you!" When I took another step, she blocked my way, whispering, "Stop it, Phoenix. You're too depleted to get past me." She withdrew the tablet and looked at it, tiny acid droplets gleaming on her cheeks. "I have to send more energy to Sing's room and turn the shield back on. It's our only chance."

The fall of acid strengthened from a sprinkle to a downpour. Burning streams ran down my face and hands, forcing me to draw my hood lower and tuck my hands into my sleeves. With the moisture soaking through the cloak, we would be dead in moments, and I had no energy to do a thing about it.

Smoke rose from the tablet along with sizzles and pops. Shanghai dropped it and shook her hands.

"Did you get it done?"

She pulled her sleeves over her exposed skin. "I'm not sure. I hit the right control, but the screen wouldn't respond."

While Tokyo continued running, the illuminary lunged at her, grasping, but she dodged its hand time and again. She glanced at us once more, her expression desperate as she shouted, "Do I have to tell you again?"

With radiance swirling everywhere, I pulled Shanghai into my arms and held her close. She looked at Tokyo and gave her a trembling smile as we edged toward the outlet. "Good-bye, Reaper divine," Shanghai said. "No one will ever match your greatness."

She stopped, folded her hands in front, and bowed. "I have no doubt that you both will."

The illuminary stormed toward her. Tokyo dodged, leaped onto its back, and set the sonic gun against its head. When she pulled the trigger, the usual pop echoed. The illuminary showed no reaction. It reached back with both hands, grabbed her head, and slung her to the floor, snapping her neck as if it were a toothpick. The illuminary then slammed a fist against her temple, crushing her skull.

Shanghai gasped. "Tokyo!"

I shouted, "No!" My stomach knotted. Tokyo was

dead. And my stubbornness was the reason. She tried to get me to listen, but I wouldn't.

Shanghai whispered into my ear, "It's too late to help. Let's go. Make it sound like we're dying."

While Shanghai screamed, I let out a wretched moan. Concentrating on my depleted energy, I willed it to flow through my head and hands first to protect them from the burning rain. As the process continued, I watched the illuminary over Shanghai's shoulder. It rose from Tokyo and looked our way. Acid soaked its cloak and drew its hood back, exposing its smoking, skull-like head. It would perish soon. The fact that Alex didn't mind sacrificing one indicated that she had plenty more.

When we fully transformed, we silenced our cries. The Gateway's upward suction pulled us, lifting our bodies several inches from the floor. The swirling energy acted as a dragging influence and kept us suspended in midair. Another suction drew us toward the corner valve. Using a wall as a traction surface, we crawled with the flow, found the valve, and stretched our bodies toward it.

I grabbed Shanghai's hand, poured myself into the hole, and emerged into a stream of energy, much narrower than the one I had navigated earlier. Still in my grasp, Shanghai floated behind me. Since the current carried us in the right direction, we just rode with it in silence.

After a few seconds, the channel narrowed, and we squeezed through a series of valves until we expanded into Sing's coffin, passed through the glass, and floated to the floor. As we had hoped, the energy shield ran along the perimeter, illuminating the room and keeping us from flying skyward.

We rose to our feet and began the transformation back

to normal. When we became physical, dizziness returned, but not severe. I shrugged my cloak from my shoulders and let it fall to the floor. As it lay there, tiny ribbons of mist rose from the fibers.

I stared at the vaporous streams, my heart thumping, my throat tight. A mental image of Tokyo's body pulsed— her broken neck, her shattered skull. The Sancta said if Alex kept killing, I would have to trust in the Highest Power for the next step. The fruit of my faith might take time to ripen. But it seemed that the entire tree had died. How could any fruit come from this disaster?

As vapor rose from Shanghai's shoulders and sleeves, I gestured toward her cloak. "You'd better take that off," I said, my words squeezed to a high pitch. "That acid will strip your skin raw."

Sobbing spasms rattled Shanghai's voice. "I have… have to get Albert out." She set the medical equipment and the crucible on the floor, then shed her cloak and laid it in Peter's coffin. After closing the lid, she turned a wall valve. Energy rushed into the coffin and pushed Albert out in a matter of seconds. He lay at the bottom of the glass box with his eyes tightly shut.

Shanghai lifted the lid and leaned it against the wall. "It's safe now." She sniffed and brushed a tear from her cheek. "You're all right."

Albert opened his eyes and sat up, shaking his head. "And I thought riding in Phoenix's cloak was rough. You're the princess of pain."

A weak smile crossed her lips. "Our cloaks are drenched with acid. I'm not sure how to carry you anymore."

"Don't bother." Albert climbed over the coffin's walls and down to the floor, half floating through the effort.

When he stood upright, he bowed his head toward us in turn. "If you don't mind, I would like to take my leave now. The adventures have been... well... stimulating."

My throat loosening, I nodded in return. "Albert, you've been a... a godsend. Thank you for everything. I'd shake your hand if I could but... you know."

"But I'm dead." He winked. "Now if you will open the door, I will be on my way. I believe the energy field would prevent me from walking right through it."

I opened the door a crack. Without another word, he slipped through the gap and rose into the ceiling.

Albert Crandyke was gone. He started as an annoying ghost I could hardly wait to get rid of and transformed into a trusted ally. As I stared upward, I whispered, "Bon voyage, my friend."

When I closed the door, Shanghai strode to the wall and flipped another switch. "I have to stop the flow to Sing's coffin. Gas from the acid will mix in, and there's not much energy left in the tank anyway."

Shanghai brushed more tears from her cheeks. "Phoenix, this is so hard. Tokyo is dead. We couldn't do anything to stop that monster."

"We couldn't save Tokyo, but we can get her daughter's body out of here." I lifted the lid to Sing's coffin and leaned it against the wall. "We'd better hurry. No telling when Alex will check the tank for our bodies."

"Wait." Shanghai dug into Sing's pocket and withdrew a folded piece of paper. "Tokyo's note." She unfolded the sheet and read out loud.

"Phoenix and Shanghai, since you are reading this, I assume I am dead. This is no surprise, because I am ready to sacrifice my life to stop Alex. Why? Simple. I hope to rise to the Gateway and send my daughter's soul back to you. I am sure she will protest, but she will not be able to counter my strength. I will request that the angel deposit her in this coffin to make it easy for you to resurrect her. My hope is that since she has not been dead for very long, the procedure will work without need of giving her the spark of life. If it doesn't work, then please send her back to the Gateway. I do not want one of you to sacrifice your life for hers. One more item—remove her valve first. It should come out fairly easily. It is important that you learn the truth. Yours in the Redeemer's blood— Takahashi Fujita, aka Tokyo."

Shanghai folded the page and stuffed it into her pocket. "The greatest Reaper who ever lived."

The image of Tokyo's smashed body again flashed to mind—this time surrounded by radiant gas, a shield blocking the upward suction. "Do you think the energy in the tank will trap her soul there?"

"I don't know. Maybe the gas will settle to the floor."

"Her corpse is on the floor. We have to purge as much as we can." I stepped to the wall, turned on the energy line leading to Peter's coffin, and closed its lid. Shanghai activated the feeder hoses that we had used to energize, the gas likely contaminated now by acid. A slight hiss emanated from the wall valves and hoses, but would the drainage be enough to set Tokyo free? We had no choice but to stay and wait.

Shanghai looked at the ceiling. Gaps cut through the radiant shield. "It's breaking down, so maybe the energy drain's working, but Sing's not getting energy. Her body will start deteriorating."

"What was that about her valve?" I leaned against the

coffin's side, grasped the feeder hose leading into Sing's valve, and pulled. Although a slight suction held it in place, a bit more effort pried it loose.

I shifted my fingers to the valve's edges and lifted it away. As it rose, a flexible tube followed. After it pulled out a few inches, it snagged. When I pulled harder, a white balloon-like bag popped out, but no wires ran from the valve to her heart.

Shanghai gasped. "Phoenix? What does it mean?"

I dropped the items to Sing's side. "I don't know." The sight of the valve and bag brought Erin's words to mind in a rapid-fire series. *We used a real valve. Every surgical step that Reapers go through. Inserted a bag behind the valve. Inflated it with energy. The mission ended in the death of the fake Reaper.*

The final words spilled from my lips. "The fake Reaper."

Shanghai clutched my arm. "Sing wasn't a real Reaper?"

"It's… I… I don't know."

"If she was fake, we wouldn't have been able to track her. Alex said the device worked only for Reapers."

I pinched the chain around Sing's neck and pulled the medallion up. Something hairy was wrapped around it. I peeled back the mass—hair held together by dried blood—revealing the medallion underneath.

Shanghai ran a finger along the hair. "Phoenix, tell me what's going on."

"I'm not sure." I touched the gap in my hair. Had Sing cut it? When did she have time to do that without me noticing?

My mind drifted back to a morning I woke up in the corrections camp's visitor's building—the Hilton. Sing had groomed, folded, and laid out my cloak. The image morphed to Sing sitting in my room cutting material with scissors while making the disguise she wore to become a prisoner at the camp.

I whispered, "This is my hair. Sing cut it. And the blood probably came from the sample I gave to Erin at the depot checkpoint. This covering kept the medallion from shutting off."

"So that's why Alex's watch got confused. The hand was trying to point toward Sing's medallion. It had your blood on it all along."

"Which means Kwame's watch was programmed to follow me instead of Sing. The Resistance has been planning to use me for a long time."

"Sing wasn't sure about how to operate the watch," Shanghai said, "but she knew enough to cut your hair."

More thoughts flooded in, like revelations from above. Sing passed by Miriam, that ghost near the alley, because she couldn't see her.... Sing didn't recognize her father, Kwame, because she couldn't see him either. He stayed invisible to keep his identity a secret.... Because Sing could no longer reap without her mother riding in the fibers, she "lost" her cloak to hide her inability.... At times, she couldn't hear souls talking from within my cloak.... She didn't want to do a soul-through-valve transfer because it wouldn't work, and her valve might have come loose. Later, on the roof, she was able to give me energy because of the bag behind her valve.

And finally, in the executions chamber, she held the end of her sleeve to hide her inability to dematerialize, counting on Tokyo to reap Gail's soul into the cloak. Then Sing chased me out of the executions room, not because she didn't want me to strip Gail naked; she wanted to take the tracking medallion from her without my knowledge. Shortly after that was when I first noticed it dangling from the chain around her neck.

I heaved a loud sigh. "No doubt about it. Sing being a Reaper was all an act. A dangerous, brilliant act. It was the only way she could get her mother to the depot."

Shanghai whispered, "And it worked."

I looked at the wall thermometer—36. "Her temperature's dropping. We'd better get everything ready. If Tokyo escaped the tank, Sing's soul might show up at any second." I set the medical bag, crucible, and tongs on top of Peter's coffin.

Shanghai grabbed the bag and rummaged inside. "We'll need a cosmetic valve to plug the hole."

I walked to the wall and found the switch to send a shock to Sing's coffin. In mere moments, it would be up to us to bring her back to life. My entire body shook, half from excitement and half from being ready to collapse.

Shanghai withdrew a valve in a plastic bag. As she opened it, Sing's soul appeared in the coffin. Her eyes confused and frantic, she sank into her body.

My legs quaked. "She's here. Let's do it."

"We'll secure this later." Shanghai slid the valve in place. "Sing, listen to me. You need to attach to your body. Do it as quickly as you can. We have to hurry and get out of here before Alex shows up."

Something sizzled above. At the ceiling, gaps in the energy shield widened. It wouldn't be long before the suction would jerk Sing's soul out. "We can't wait," I said. "Shut it. I'll send the shock."

Shanghai closed the coffin's lid and stepped back. I hit

the switch. Electricity arced across Sing's body. She jerked hard, her head nearly hitting the glass.

Sing's heart-rate jumped to 65. I turned off the power. Shanghai bounced on her toes, her fists clenched as she watched the meter.

The number dropped to 60... 58... 56.

I swallowed hard. "It's falling."

"It'll be all right," Shanghai said. "Sing's a trooper. She'll get it done."

54... 52... 50.

I looked at the crucible on Peter's coffin and eased toward it. A life-spark crystal might be Sing's only hope. Since I caused Tokyo's death, I had to be the one to take it.

48... 47... 46.

"It's not dropping as fast." Shanghai looked at me, then at the crucible. Alarm in her eyes, she leaped to the side and blocked my path. "Oh, no you don't! Tokyo said not to."

"It's not her choice anymore. Sing will die without a life spark."

"Then you'll die. What kind of trade is that?"

"A good one. Reaper or not, you'll get a better soldier for the cause."

"Better than you? Why?"

"My principles are a handicap. If not for my stubbornness, Tokyo wouldn't have died. Alex will never stop using that strategy against me."

Shanghai frowned. "That's ridiculous. Your principles are the reason I trust you more than anyone in the world."

"But what if I have that weakness? I'll be vulnerable. Alex will come up with a way to trap me. She always gets the upper hand."

Shanghai shook her head. "I don't believe it. You're strong now. You won't give in."

I looked again at the meter—42... 41... 40. "Sing's close to the point of no return. I have to do it."

Shanghai set her feet and fists in battle stance. "I won't let you."

"You'll fight me?"

"If I have to." She shoved me with both hands. "Don't come a step closer."

38... 37... 36.

I charged. She jumped into a 360 and kicked me in the chest. I staggered back a few steps before catching myself. Pain stabbed my ribs, but I refused to grimace.

She reset her stance. "Phoenix, don't. My energy level is triple yours. You can't win."

I curled my hand into a fist. "I can't beat you in a fight, but I can win if you'll let me restore Sing. Then she'll be alive, and I'll be with Misty."

Shanghai lowered her fists. She glanced at Sing, then at the meter. It now read 34 and continued dropping. When she turned back to me, tears streamed down both cheeks. She whispered, "You really love them, don't you?"

"Of course." My voice shattered. "But... but I love you, too."

Her lips quivered. "Misty... Sing... Shanghai." A sob shook her body, but she stifled it. "I'm... I'm third choice."

32... 31... 30.

"There's no ranking. We just can't all be together. It's impossible."

"True. It is impossible." Shanghai picked up the crucible. More tears flowing, she lifted the lid. "But I can make sure you get your second choice here on earth.

Then sometime in the future, you'll get number one beyond the Gateway. Your third choice will become a distant memory."

"No!" I lunged.

Shanghai dodged. I crashed into Peter's coffin, bounced back a few steps, and fell to my bottom. My arms and legs tingled. My heart fluttered. I had to be under three percent again.

27… 26… 25.

Shanghai returned the crucible to the coffin lid and crouched in front of me. Leaning close, she kissed me on the forehead. As she drew back, she caressed my cheek, her eyes filled with tears. "I guess I'll never get the kiss I hoped for, but at least maybe I can watch over you from above."

I grabbed her wrist, but she broke free with ease. "Shanghai… you can't… please."

"Tell Sing to give the rest of my energy to you. I'm sure the two of you can figure out how to get home." She straightened and stood in front of me, her sad eyes fixed on mine. "Good-bye, Phoenix."

Gathering what remained of my strength, I struggled to my feet and set myself in my own battle stance. "Get out of my way."

"I guess I'll have to write a message to Sing." Shanghai heaved a sigh. "I'm sorry to do this, but I love you too much not to."

She leaped and spun another 360. Her foot swung around and flew toward my face. When it smashed into my cheek, I fell straight back. Pain ripped through my head. My eyes snapped closed. Darkness swamped my mind and carried me into oblivion.

CHAPTER TWENTY-FIVE

LIGHT ASSAULTED MY senses, though my eyelids were closed. Music flowed from somewhere, and the aroma of bacon tinged the air. Soreness and aches ran from my toes to the top of my head, and a tender spot at the back of my thigh pulsed with heat.

I opened my eyes. I lay in a double bed with sheets and a comforter pulled up to my chest. A night table stood to the left and a dresser to the right, neither of which looked familiar. With varnished wood and no scratches or missing drawer knobs, they were nicer than any furniture I ever owned.

A partially open door led to what appeared to be a hallway. New carpet covered every inch of floor in sight. How had I gotten to such a fancy place? Was this the bedroom in the new condo? It certainly seemed so. My time there had been short, and memories of its appearance were fuzzy at best.

My gaze drifted to an IV pole standing in a far corner, recognizable by an empty plastic bag dangling from its arm. Had I been hurt that badly?

Somewhere in the distance, a female sang, probably whoever was cooking the bacon. The lyrics seemed foreign—a language crooned in a sing-song way that created a harmony of its own. The accent raised reminders of Misty's Scottish lilt.

As I listened, her recent words returned, as clear as if she were standing next to the bed and speaking them with the same passion she had while trapped on the pedestal.

Since your heart truly reflects that of the creator, a heart that weeps over the evils perpetrated in this world, you can be his instrument to bring this suffering to an end so that all souls will finally go to the glorious place he has prepared for them. You can sing the creator's song and fill their hearts with new hope.

Her lovely image came to mind, though merely a phantom as she set her hands on the glass enclosure and said, *You have been guided here to liberate the song. The creator knows you can do it. I know you can do it. Let that confidence seep into your own mind. Embrace it, and let it strengthen you for the task ahead.*

And now someone nearby sang with fullness of joy, a sound that had been so long lacking in this world of toil and tears. Her voice sounded familiar, deeper and older than Sing's, Shanghai's, or Misty's. Maybe I would soon learn the singer's identity.

As my friends' names came to mind, a more recent memory flowed—the brief fight with Shanghai in Sing's coffin room. I touched the cheek where Shanghai landed her lights-out kick. Pain made me wince. Probably a nightmarish bruise darkened my skin.

I blinked. What was that fight all about? As memories flashed by in a blur, the answer seemed just out of reach. Two facts I did remember—we had killed the Gatekeeper and purged the energy reserves. But how could I have recovered with no energy available? I was probably down to two or three percent when Shanghai knocked me out.

I raised a hand and felt for my sternum valve but touched only skin. The valve was gone? Had I been unconscious long enough to have surgery? Apparently so, and the surgeon probably grafted skin from my thigh, explaining the soreness there.

My fingers brushed across something metallic closer to my throat. I picked it up and squinted at it cross-eyed. A photo stick?

After sitting up against the headboard, I folded my hand around the stick. Azure light rose and hovered over my chest. A hologram formed—ghostly images of my parents standing within the soul-collection tank. My father spoke first. "Ariel, we don't have much time, so I will keep this brief. While your mother and I were on a business trip in Chicago, eating at an Italian restaurant, a hooded man burst in and shot us with a handgun. Although I don't know his identity, I suspect that he worked for Bartholomew. It's a long story, but Bartholomew and I were business partners until he began working for the death industry a couple of years ago. He continued playing nice to me on the surface, but as he advanced up the ladder, he began worrying that information I have about him might ruin his career and his plans to take control of the industry. The information itself isn't important now, because I'm not alive to bear witness to it. Just stay as far away from him as you can. He can make life miserable for a Reaper if he so chooses."

My mother stepped forward. "All I can say, Ariel, is that I love you, I'm proud of you, and I'll miss you. Since you're a Reaper, we lost so much time we could have spent together, but I don't regret the loss for my part. Shanghai told us about your courage, your sacrifice, and your dedication to integrity. I can see in her eyes how much she loves and honors you, and that reflection helps me to go to eternity in peace, knowing that my son has a strong, vibrant, loyal companion at his side as he works to ensure that life is better for everyone." She blew a kiss. "Goodbye, my beloved son. I will see you beyond the Gateway."

The hologram dissolved. I opened my hand and set the photo stick at my side. As tears welled, I sucked in a deep breath to quell a sob. My parents were gone. For almost four years I had longed to see them and Misty, and they were all swept through the Gateway.

A morbid memory returned—the reason for the fight with Shanghai. We were battling to see who would die to restore Sing.

My heart sank. If I had fought harder, I could have won, taken the life-spark crystal, and revived her. Then I would have risen to the skies and joined my loved ones. Yet, that wasn't possible. I had lost nearly every atom of energy, and Shanghai was too powerful. Her foot to my face ended my plan in the bat of an eye.

A new thought lurked, as if sneaking out from a corner where I had hidden it away. What happened after Shanghai kicked me? Did she swallow a crystal and pass her life spark to Sing? Or did someone or something thwart her plan? Who was alive, and who was dead? And who carried me from the Gateway building in time to escape Alex and her new army?

The singing drew closer. A woman carrying a tray stepped into the room. Although strikingly familiar, she seemed out of place. It took my frazzled brain a few seconds to identify her. "Fiona?"

"Phoenix!" She scurried to the bed and set the tray on my lap. Folding her hands at her chest, she chattered in her distinctive Irish accent, thicker than usual. "Ah, the hero awakens from his slumber after recoverin' from his near-fatal wounds. Straight from the storybooks in the old country. And here I am to witness yet another miracle."

I gave her a weak smile. "Right. I did wake up, but—"

"I thought you might, because you've been stirrin' and mumblin', so I made this nice breakfast for you." She adjusted the tray. "If it's too heavy on your legs, I can—"

"No. No. It's fine." I looked the tray over—five strips of bacon, a heaping pile of scrambled eggs, four slices of toast, an orange sliced into sections, a fried red tomato, and a cup of tea blended with milk. The delightful aromas filled my nostrils, making my stomach growl. I hadn't eaten a meal like this in years. "Where did you get this great food?"

"The bacon was in your refrigerator. The rest was donated by people in your district."

"Donated? But they're so poor."

"They gave what they could, and Noah's mama cleans house in a nicer neighborhood. She came up with the orange and tomato. I didn't ask for details."

"Why is everyone being so generous?"

Fiona's expression turned grim. "Well, *some* are being generous. News of your return from the Gateway has spread far and wide, but not everyone is happy about it, I'm afraid. Many think you've brought disaster upon us. Doom is sure to come."

"But you don't believe them."

She blew through flapping lips. "Bunch of rawmaish. Fear mongerin'. Here we have a young hero who liberated countless souls and all they can do is gnash their teeth about doomsday." She laid a hand over her chest. "But I know this in my heart. The Gateway is real. Our departed loved ones are safe, and we have hope for their future."

I nodded. "We have to spread that word."

"I've been shoutin' the news from the rooftops. That's why you have medical care. Colm's sister is a nurse, and she's been visitin' twice a day to wash you and help you with... well... other bodily needs. Also, a doctor has joined the Resistance and is performin' valve-removal surgeries on the Reapers to free them from energy dependence. He removed yours two days ago."

Fiona took a deep breath. "Well, I've talked long enough, and I need to be headin' on." She pointed at the tray. "And you'd better eat before it gets cold."

I gave the bacon a longing stare. My taste buds said yes, but my stomach offered a weak maybe. "I'm not sure I can eat such rich food so soon."

"It's up to you." She grinned. "I'll let you decide between this and some plain broth I have in the kitchen."

"I'll see how my stomach handles it." I grabbed a strip of bacon and popped it into my mouth. It tasted so good— sweet and savory. When I finished, I winked. "Just what the doctor ordered."

"Speakin' of doctors, your surgeon said he knows you. I suppose he heard me shoutin' from the rooftop, and he came callin'. His name is Dr. Rubenstein."

"Ruby," I whispered. "Albert's friend." I again touched the skin where the valve used to be. A ridge of stitches ran in a circle—a symbol of liberty. Making friends in the city and in my cloak had set me free. "So what's it like out there? On the streets, I mean."

Fiona's cheeks flushed. "Lots of folks're fearful. They're so used to being in cages, they're not sure what to do now that someone opened the cage's door. And lots of whisperin's in the breeze. Maybe Phoenix is lyin'. Maybe the Gatekeeper's still alive and he'll pounce on us like a ferocious tiger if we step out of line. Not to mention all the ghosts. Other Reapers have already found out no one's runnin' the depots, so they stopped reapin'. But that doesn't explain why ghosts are wanderin' around like someone opened the sheep gate."

"How many are out there?"

"Hard to tell. I saw three this mornin' on the way over here, and I never saw that many in a month before the Reapers quit."

"How long was I unconscious?"

"Counting this mornin'?" Fiona rolled her eyes upward for a moment. "About five days."

I echoed in a whisper, "Five days."

"A long time to be unconscious, to be sure, but not long enough to sprout so many ghosts."

I shook my head. "You're right. It doesn't add up."

"Indeed. So many questions."

"I'll try to figure it all out, but my biggest question is who brought me here?"

"Ah. Of course. Liam carried you from the door to the bed. You're much too heavy for me." A faraway look came over her. "He is such a fine man, strong and courageous. He and his lovely wife remind me of Colm and myself when we were younger." She patted my arm. "You see? Because of you I can think of Colm and even Molly without fallin' apart. I know they've gone to a better place. My faith has been restored."

"Right. That's all true, and I'm happy for you. But who brought me back from the Gateway? Was it Sing or Shanghai?"

Fiona pointed at me. "She said you'd ask, but I'm afraid I'm not allowed to say. She wants to tell you the story herself."

"I can guess. Sing didn't know where the condo is, so it had to be Shanghai." I shook my head. "No, Sing's smart enough to find it. I still had the Fife Tower key ring in my pocket. Shanghai probably sacrificed for Sing. When she sets her mind to something—"

"Just… just stop." Tears sparkling in her eyes, Fiona fanned her face. "Phoenix, the story is tragic, and your guessin' is breakin' my heart."

"I'm sorry. I wasn't thinking." While Fiona composed herself, I bit my lip hard. A beautiful young woman was dead and here I was playing a guessing game. I had to shake myself back to reality.

I looked at the bedroom door. "Where is she?"

Fiona gestured with her head toward the hallway. "In the sittin' room. She sleeps on the sofa, but she's visited you countless times."

"I have to see her."

When I picked up the tray, Fiona pushed it back down. "Eat first. You need your strength. And your stomach's handlin' it fine."

"But—"

"No buts. I'll not hear another word about it." She walked to a closet and slid a door open. "You also have to get dressed."

I looked at my clothes—pajamas, black with white stars. I hadn't worn real pajamas since I was three.

Fiona returned with Reaper trousers and tunic as well as my cloak draped over an arm. She laid them at the foot of the bed. "All washed, mended, and pressed. Gettin' the acid out of your cloak was a chore, but it's not much worse for the wear."

I pinched one of the pajama sleeves. "Where did these come from?"

"A seamstress I know. The pattern is the same as on the new flag we designed for the Resistance movement— a clear, star-filled sky such as the world has not seen in centuries. It is a symbol of reality and a future hope. You have opened the skies for us, Phoenix, and someday we'll remove the shield altogether."

I looked at the pajama top again and stared at one of the stars. In many ways, it was true. The skies had opened. We could all live without worry, fight without fear. The final enemy, death itself, had lost its bite. "I like it, Fiona. I like it a lot."

"Good. Now eat, get dressed, and come to the sittin' room. No need to shower. The nurse bathed you earlier this morning."

"Bathed me?" I laughed under my breath. "I feel like a newborn baby. I need to catch up on everything. And fast."

"Don't worry. You will. Liam and I will visit soon, and perhaps Colleen as well. Then we'll all sit for a long chat. Right now I have to check on my girls, so I'll be gone before you come out." Fiona kissed my cheek, walked to the door, and stopped. With new tears in her eyes, she smiled. "Thank you, Phoenix. Thank you for takin' care of Molly, Colm, and all of us. You are truly a hero in every way." She walked out and closed the door.

I pushed the tray to the side while sliding my legs from under the covers and down to the floor. When my feet touched the carpet and took on the weight, pain ran up my legs—annoying, but nothing like the torture I endured when my energy had drained.

While I changed clothes, I grabbed pieces of the breakfast, gobbled them down, and slurped the tea. Every bite and sip sent bursts of flavor through my senses. I had never tasted anything so good.

When I draped my cloak over my shoulders and slid my arms through the sleeves, I looked at a full-length mirror hanging on the wall next to the dresser. Although my face was still pale and bruised, it was clean and shaven, and the freshly washed garments looked great, though they hung a little looser than usual. It would take some time to regain lost muscle.

A few raw welts marred my cheeks, though nothing severe enough to develop a scar. Years of being exposed to acid rain provided one benefit; it forced my skin to thicken and adapt to the abuse.

I opened the door in silence and padded down the hall of the new condo unit, recalling the layout as I walked. This corridor would open to the foyer on the right and the sitting room on the left. In only seconds I would learn who had lived and who had died.

After reaching the hall's corner, I stopped at the edge of a room furnished with a sofa at the far wall, an adjacent loveseat, and a coffee table in front of them. Someone wearing a hooded cloak knelt on a sofa cushion, leaning with elbows on the sofa's back and looking out a window.

Far below lay a park with trees and a playground void of children.

I trembled. The hood and billowy cloak made it impossible to tell the person's size. The cloak looked like Shanghai's, but if Shanghai died to resurrect Sing, Sing could have taken it from Shanghai's corpse as a keepsake. So I still didn't know who this was. Whom did I hope for? Shanghai or Sing?

Images of each young woman flowed through my mind. Every mental photograph of Sing showed her at a distance, raising reminders of her mission, her dogged pursuit of truth. Her goals were admirable, essential, life-saving. She would do anything to ensure success, including deceiving me. Which was fine. Now that I could see the end result and her methods, it all made sense. Her single-minded purpose required her to divide her loyalties. The mission came first. Although she loved me, I was always a distant second.

Images of Shanghai, on the other hand, showed her next to me, her arm curled around mine as we walked side by side, whether physical or phantom, through forests surrounded by electrified cats, across fields populated by guard dogs, or into wilderness zones assaulted by lethal radiation. She was always there. Her love seemed boundless.

My recent words returned to mind. *I can't beat you in a fight, but I can win if you'll let me restore Sing. Then she'll be alive, and I'll be with Misty.*

I cringed. What a fool I was! Such a stupid thing to say to Shanghai, far worse than her Mount Everest moment. My words probably stabbed her heart. Yet, she didn't stab me back with cruel words of her own. She never stopped loving me.

I raised a silent prayer, the first in my life. *Highest Power, if it's all right with you, let it be Shanghai. She's the one I really love.*

As I stepped into the room, I cleared my throat. "Hello?"

The cloaked figure turned, lowering the hood at the same time. Shanghai's face appeared, her shining black locks framing her beautiful features. She stood and offered a trembling smile. Her eyes searched with a longing probe as if hoping to find a priceless treasure. Today there was no need for a shot of purified energy to make her shine like an angel. She was stunningly beautiful.

Finally, she spoke with a shaking voice. "Hello, Phoenix. Are you glad to see me?" She bit her lip. "Or were you hoping to see someone else?"

Tears erupted. I stumbled forward and threw my arms around her. "Shanghai! You're alive! Thank God you're alive!" I pressed my cheek against hers and ran my fingers through her silky hair. "It's you I wanted. Not Sing. Not Misty. Not anyone else. You are my beloved, my one, true beloved."

Shanghai sobbed against my shoulder. As we held each other, she kneaded my back with strong fingers. "Oh, Phoenix, I love you so much.... *So much.*"

After a few moments of quiet weeping, she drew away, holding my hand while touching her chest. The plackets of her V-neck tunic lay open farther than usual, revealing a circle of stitches where her valve used to be. "I have a lot to tell you. Come sit with me."

She pulled me to the sofa where we sat hip to hip and

shoulder to shoulder. Her smile seemed to shine like the morning sun. "I guess you're wondering what happened after I kicked you." She touched my cheek, grimacing. "I hope it didn't hurt too much."

I shook my head. "I don't remember any pain, just your foot flying toward my face."

"At least I didn't break your nose." Her smile turned sheepish though still lovely. "Well, here's what happened. After I wrote a quick note telling Sing how to take you home, I climbed into the coffin and got on top of her corpse chest to chest, holding the life-spark crystal. Just as I got ready to pop it into my mouth, Sing's soul spoke to me from inside her body. She said, 'Don't waste your life, Shanghai. If you save me, I'll be dead in a matter of weeks.'"

I drew my head back. "What? Dead?"

Shanghai nodded. "She didn't have much time to explain. Supposedly a surgeon repaired her brain from the sonic-gun injury, but he didn't know about a secret problem. Soon after her mother died, Sing became sick, so her father took her to a doctor." Shanghai set a hand on my knee and lowered her voice. "Sing had lung cancer. Not even Tokyo knew about it."

"Lung cancer?" My mouth dried out. "But... but she was so young."

"Still fifteen when they discovered it. That's when she and her father cooked up the idea to make her a Reaper, complete with a fake valve and birthmark. That was the only way they could get her any medical care, and even then it wasn't much. No radiation. Only oral chemo, not even enough to make her hair fall out. When they decided her case was terminal, she stopped the treatments and became a Reaper on a mission to learn the truth about the Gateway. And you know the rest."

"If she was dying, wouldn't we have noticed something? She showed no symptoms."

"Not so, Phoenix. Remember her cough? Didn't you see the bottle of cough suppressant she carried around?"

"I saw it. And Alex told me she found it while searching your room at the Hilton. According to her, the suppressant also had hydrocodone in it."

"Hydrocodone." Shanghai looked up as if searching for a definition. "That's a pain killer, isn't it?"

I nodded. "It's all coming together. Sing was hiding her pain. She wouldn't let anything stop her from learning about the Gateway."

Shanghai brushed a tear from her cheek. "I can't imagine how much she suffered."

"And now her willingness to die makes a lot more sense."

"Definitely." Shanghai inhaled deeply. "Anyway, when Tokyo tried to pull Sing back through the Gateway, Sing told her about the cancer, that she didn't want to come back to life just to suffer a horrific death. Tokyo and Sing decided that they should just stay together in eternity with Kwame, but the attending angel intervened and ordered the transfer to take place. Sing needed to return to deliver a message from the Highest Power."

"What message?"

Shanghai's face contorted, and her voice broke. "She said… she said…"

I slid my hand into hers. "Take your time. There's no hurry."

She took in another deep breath. After composing

herself, she looked me in the eye. "Sing says she loves you with all her heart, and she's sorry for all the deception." A spasm made Shanghai quiver. "She said when you refused to take the energy, that time when you dropped the ring, your vulnerability to being controlled by a female was destroyed forever. So don't fear Alex. She can never control you. Also, the Highest Power will send us a helper. Sing didn't know when that helper would come or what kind of help we would get, but it should be soon.

"Oh, and one more thing, Tokyo knows you're feeling guilty about causing her death. She says to stop. That's an order." Shanghai smiled. "Sing had a big grin on her face when she said that. She and Tokyo are thrilled to be together with Kwame, so they're hoping you'll stop beating yourself up over it."

Warmth flowed throughout my body. The release from bondage was sweet indeed. "That's great. Really great. I feel a lot better."

"There's more." Shanghai compressed my hand. "Sing said, 'Tell Phoenix to love you without reservation, without worry that I or Misty will take offense. The Highest Power will bless your union if Phoenix is willing.'"

"Union? Do you mean…"

Shanghai pulled her hand back. "If you'll have me." Words began spilling from her lips without a pause. "I mean, I know I called marriage quaint, but I'm all for it. And Reapers grow up fast, so our age really isn't an issue. Since we'll both be seventeen next month, it will be legal then. And since we've kind of been thrown together in this condo, it's the perfect arrangement to keep us from violating any principles. When we're traveling, we won't have to decide who sleeps on the floor and who sleeps on a cot or a bed. We'll be free to do whatever we want."

"Shanghai?" I gazed into her eyes. "Is this a marriage proposal?"

Her sheepish smile returning, she folded her hands in her lap. "Well, since you said you hope nothing ever separates us, I suppose it is."

I let her confession hang in the air like a perfumed mist. Her words were true. I did hope that nothing would ever separate us. But marriage? That called for a lifelong commitment. I had been warned multiple times about emotional entanglements. Since district hounds were never allowed even a close friend, we were vulnerable to being taken in by the first come-hither flirt that came along. Yet, Shanghai was nothing like that. She had proven her incomparable selfless character time and time again. No one could be a better wife.

"My answer is yes." I retrieved her hand and kissed it. "Without reservation."

"Oh, Phoenix!" She threw her arms around my neck. "I'm so happy!"

After we embraced for a moment, I drew back, our faces still close, our lips inches apart. Her delicate scent—a hint of spring flowers—and her longing eyes called me even closer. We both knew what we wanted, the big kiss we had promised each other, intimacy, ultimate togetherness. But that moment would come, as we had said, when all of this was finally over.

I withdrew farther and held her hands. "When do you want to get married?" I gave her a smile and a wink. "As soon as possible, I hope."

She nodded with vigor. "On my birthday next month. The moment we're both legal."

"That sounds perfect."

Shanghai withdrew something from a pocket and held it out in her palm—my pewter ring. "I saved it for you. Just in case. If you want to use it as a wedding ring we can—"

"No." I closed her fingers over it. "That was the past. You and I are the future."

She smiled and slid the ring back to her pocket. "That's exactly what I wanted to hear."

"So we'll get married in five weeks. In the meantime, I'd better stay at my old apartment. Even with a sofa available, it's still too close for comfort."

"I understand, but let me stay there. You're still weaker, so you should have the comfier place."

I shook my head. "You agreed to take the better bed the next time we had a choice. You can't wiggle out of it."

She sighed. "I did agree to that, didn't I?"

"Yep, but considering what Alex probably has in mind, I don't think I'll be spending much time there. We might be fighting day and night." I tilted my head. "Speaking of Alex, any word about when she might strike?"

"Nothing. I made contact with Bill and gave him the information about the illuminaries and the map we saw. He said a Resistance leader will get in touch with us soon. In the meantime, everyone is on the alert, but since the city's in an uproar because of the Gatekeeper's death, I'm thinking Alex's move will be disguised as a law-and-order crackdown. Liam's keeping an eye on the corrections-camp gate. If it gets repaired, we'll know the crackdown is coming soon."

"Good thinking. We should also watch for activity at the crematorium. They'll need more attendants if they're planning a lot of executions." I looked out the window. Midday light bathed the park. No rain in sight. "Let's walk to my apartment and check out the camp and the crematorium on the way. I need some exercise."

Shanghai rose from the sofa. "I'll pack your clothes." She winked. "Including those cute new pajamas."

After we gathered my few belongings in a duffle bag, we put on our weapons belts and left the condo. As we walked toward the corrections camp, most passersby frowned and looked away, though a few offered tentative smiles. One driver honked and flashed an obscene hand gesture. Later, an elderly woman walking with a cane kissed us both on the cheek and spoke kindly in a foreign language. It seemed that the citizenry's opinion of us was sharply divided.

As we walked, fatigue set in. My legs weren't ready for such a long hike. When we arrived at the camp, we stopped, and I leaned against a parked car. A man wearing a DEO insignia on his sleeve ran a tape measure across the fallen gate and wrote on a clipboard, ignoring us as we looked on. Apparently repair planning had begun.

An engine rattled nearby, the telltale sound of Liam's van. We followed the rattle and found the van parked in an alley, Liam in the driver's seat watching the worker.

He gave us a ride to the apartment, taking a long route to pass the crematorium where at least a dozen cars and trucks had parked, twice as many as usual—the second sign that the crackdown would come soon, and it seemed that Alex wasn't trying to hide preparations.

Along the way, I told Liam some of our story, skipping

most of the minor points. Shanghai added details I didn't know—how she carried me out of the building and through the forest, dodging the electrified cats. When she found Erin's transport, it took her a while to learn how to fly it, and she had several mishaps along the way, but she made it safely to Chicago, hid the vehicle under the cover of darkness, and found a cart to wheel me to the Eggs & Stuff restaurant where she contacted Liam. From that point, Liam knew the rest of the account, so Shanghai promised to tell me more later, including details about her heartbreaking decision to leave Sing's body behind.

When Liam dropped us off at my apartment, he gave me a nod and said in an accent similar to Fiona's, "We're all in this together. Now we have hope, thanks to you and Shanghai. And Singapore, of course." He laughed as if trying to conceal a sob. "I loved that little squirrel. She could climb thin air, I'm sure."

We bade him good-bye, rode the elevator to the second floor, and walked to my apartment. After unlocking the door's deadbolts with the three keys I kept on my belt, I entered to the sound of squeaking hinges, followed by Shanghai.

I set the duffle bag on the floor. Daylight from the window illuminated the apartment—no need to light the hanging lantern next to my reading chair. Everything seemed to be in its usual state of relative order except for one oddity. My copy of *1984* lay over the arm of the chair. Holding the open spot with my thumb, I picked it up and scanned the pages. A few lines had been underscored in ink.

I read the words out loud. "One does not establish a

dictatorship in order to safeguard a revolution; one makes the revolution in order to establish the dictatorship."

"Alex is the dictator," Shanghai said.

"And I was her revolutionary puppet." I threw the book across the room. "She's always a step ahead of me. She even knew I'd come back here. She planted the book so she could gloat."

"Actually you coming back here wasn't hard to guess." Shanghai crossed her arms. "Let's face it. As long as you're principled, you're predictable. That's not as crippling as being controlled, but it's something we have to deal with."

I stared at the book, now lying on the floor next to the wall. "What are you suggesting? That I not be so principled?"

"Not at all. In fact, I joined the principled parade, and we're not backing off a fraction of an inch. We'll just have to think of a way to use her strategy against her."

I gave her a smile. Her vote of confidence felt good. "Got any ideas?"

"I'm working on it." She walked to the window and locked it. "Just making sure you're safe. Alex won't think twice about sending an assassin here."

"Or to the condo."

She raised a finger. "Now that's a thought."

"What?"

"I'd better make sure it's secure. I'll go to a locksmith and schedule getting our locks changed there and here." She extended a hand. "For now, give me your door keys. I'll get copies made for myself."

I plucked the three keys from my belt and laid them in her palm. "Then what?"

"It depends on how long it takes." She slid the keys into an insert on her belt. "If it's not too late, I'll come back here to say goodnight, but it might be after dark."

Just as she turned, I grasped her wrist. "Wait. What about reaping duties? Do you know if we'll still get death alarms?"

"We will." She withdrew a photo stick from her pocket and handed it to me. "The training video is loaded on this. Maybe you can study it while I'm gone."

When Shanghai left and closed the door, the sweep of wind felt like a vacuum that sucked the air out of the apartment, at least any air worth breathing. She was such a part of me now, as if her presence kept my heart from sagging.

After locking the door, I sat in the reading chair with the photo stick in my curled hand. To be true to my Reaper vows, I needed to learn the new techniques, but weariness pushed the thought away. I didn't even have the energy to shed my weapons belt. This recovery was already taking longer than I had hoped.

I leaned my head back and fell asleep. Dreams took over—walking with Shanghai in ghost mode, staying silent as the sun sank to the horizon. After a while, darkness held sway, and cool, moist air wafted across my face. A siren pierced the peaceful vision, too real to be part of a dream.

I opened my eyes. The window had been raised, and twilight's dimness colored the alley outside. Multiple sirens wailed somewhere in the distance. Rain drizzled, raising metallic pitter-pats on the fire-escape landing. Shanghai had probably returned and lifted the sash to draw in some fresh air, but where was she now?

Staying as quiet as possible, I rose, walked across the darkened floor to my window, and looked out. Misty droplets splashed on my cheeks, delivering a slight sting. Across the alley, a hooded figure sat on the railing of the fire escape attached to Sing's former apartment.

I squinted. Darkness masked the figure's details, though her feminine profile was clear. I climbed through the window and stood on the landing. "Shanghai?" I called over the sound of the sirens. "What are you doing over there?"

"I am not Shanghai."

I grabbed the flashlight from my belt, flicked it on, and set the beam on the figure's head. A woman wearing a Sancta's red cloak with white sleeve cuffs sat on the railing, her hood raised, pulled down in front to conceal her face.

"Sarah?" I asked as I shifted the beam lower. "I thought you said—"

"I am not Sarah." She pushed the hood back. Dark curls spilled out, and the face of a young woman with coffee-and-cream skin appeared.

I gulped. "Sing?"

She nodded. "Surprised to see me?"

My legs trembled. "You're alive! How?"

"Actually, I am still dead." She touched her chest. "Sancta sum."

I whispered, "You're a Sancta now."

Her brilliant smile shone in the beam's glow. "Which allows me to sneak around and open a window while a certain someone is sleeping."

"What are you doing over there?"

"Reminiscing about living here, talking to you over the alley, fighting bandits with you."

A knot swelled in my throat. "Why did you come?"

"To bring counsel." She rose, stood on the railing, and leaped. I followed her with the flashlight beam as she flew across the alley, looking like a scarlet sail flapping in the night's breeze.

When she landed, she grasped my hand. Her hand was physical—warm and strong. She pulled me toward the window. "Let's get out of this rain."

After we climbed in, she found a box of matches in the kitchen and lit my hanging lantern. When the wick sprang to life and cast a soft glow throughout the room, she slid her arms around me and laid her head on my shoulder. "It's so good to see you again, Phoenix."

"You, too, Sing." I returned the embrace and buried my face in her soft curls. As a sob rose, I bit my lip to suppress it, but I couldn't stop the tears that trickled down both cheeks.

She pulled back and dabbed my face with her sleeve. "Someday you will shed no more tears. Joy lies beyond the Gateway." She gestured for me to sit in my reading chair. When I did, she knelt on the floor and laid a hand on my knee, merriment twinkling in her eyes. "The presiding angel presented potential assignments for the Sanctae to choose from. When yours came up, I volunteered. The angel advised me that this counseling assignment is far more difficult than most new Sanctae are allowed to take, but the Highest Power permitted it."

"What kind of counsel?"

"Counsel that will prepare you and Shanghai for

battle against Alex. You are woefully ill prepared to face the warfare she has in mind."

"She'll attack with the illuminaries?"

"Yes, but we'll discuss that once you're more rested. At that time, I also want to tell you everything the Resistance hid from you. Although I knew some of the plans, they were far more long-term and intricate than I realized. Now that I have spoken with my parents beyond the Gateway, I put it all together. In fairness to you, it's time for full disclosure."

"Let's hear it. I'm all ears."

"Like I said, when you're rested, but I'll give you a tidbit to think about." She looked upward in a thoughtful pose. "Let's see. What would show you how complex our plans were?" Her brow lifted. "Ah! I know. My father's watch."

"What about it?"

She returned her gaze to me. "Did you wonder why the watch always pointed to my medallion instead of yours? Your blood was on both."

I shook my head. "I guess after I discovered my hair wrapped around your medallion, everything went kind of crazy. I haven't thought about it since." I blinked. "But now that you mention it, why didn't the watch point at me?"

"Erin knew you would be wearing a tracking medallion, so she designed my father's watch to ignore any signal that came from a source less than a few feet away. It skipped your signal and focused on mine."

I blew out a low whistle. "So Erin was the mastermind all along."

Sing nodded. "With help from my parents and many

others. The plans have been in the works for years, and you have been a big part of them without realizing it. Being a depot attendant allowed her to keep track of you."

"I had no idea." The mention of Erin brought to mind her tragic expression the moments before she died—so torn, so conflicted. "Did you see her beyond the Gateway? I mean, did she make it? She seemed worried about what would happen to her soul."

Sing's lips thinned out. "I have not seen her yet, but I spent only a short time there." Her smile suddenly returned, as if refreshed by a new thought. "We need not worry. The Highest Power is a faithful judge, and mercy flows from his hands in generous streams."

"Can you find out if she's there? I would feel a lot better if—"

Sing set a finger to my lips. "Enough information for now. We have other business to attend to before you can rest." She turned toward the door. "And this business is close at hand."

I touched a dagger at my belt. "Is someone in the hall?"

Sing laughed. "No need for weapons, Phoenix. See for yourself."

I rose and looked through the door's peephole. Shanghai lay curled on the floor across the hall, her cloak wadded into a pillow and a hand on the hilt of a dagger, sheathed in her belt. "Why is she there?" I asked, still looking through the hole.

"Your condo's building is ablaze, most likely an arson attack designed to kill you both."

My cheeks grew hot. "Alex's claws are out. I wonder if she's going straight to burning Chicago instead of starting a crackdown."

"Time will tell, but right now Shanghai has nowhere else to go. When she came in here, she saw that you were asleep and decided to rest in the hall where she could guard your door. She suspects that this apartment is also a likely arson target."

"Why didn't she just stay inside?"

"Because of principles. She is one hundred percent committed to honoring your standards, which are now hers as well. She was concerned that the temptation might be too high for an engaged couple who love each other so much."

I shifted from the peephole and looked at Sing. Her peace-filled expression displayed no hint of jealousy. "So what's your counsel now? I mean, what should I do about Shanghai?"

Sing smiled. "Invite her in, Phoenix. I will stay with you all night as your chaperone and guardian. No one will accost you while you sleep in peace. I spoke to Shanghai in a dream, so although she won't be able to see me, she will believe that I am here."

"Why can't she see you? She's a Reaper."

"I am able to control who sees me. When dawn arrives, her blindness will evaporate. For tonight, believing without seeing is an important step for her, but that is her journey, not yours. Trust me to take care of it."

I unlocked the door, opened it, and stepped into the hall. I grasped Shanghai's arm and pulled her to her feet. Groggy and blinking, she allowed me to walk her into the apartment. "The condo's burning," she murmured. "Someone torched it."

"I heard. It'll be all right." After removing her weapons

belt and my own, I sat in the reading chair and pulled her into my lap.

She curled her legs and laid her head on my shoulder, nuzzling my cheek as she breathed a whispered, "Is Sing here?"

"She's here." I kissed the top of Shanghai's head. "She'll be here all night. Sleep now. We're safe."

Within seconds, Shanghai's respiration deepened and steadied. She was at peace. And so was I.

I looked at Sing as she walked toward the hanging lantern. Her brilliant smile communicated pure joy. She had fulfilled her passion. She had gone beyond the Gateway and returned to tell the world about it.

"You sleep, too, Phoenix. You'll need it. The fruit of your faith is ripening, and a door to aggressive action has opened for all of us." Her lips firmed, and her countenance turned to stone. She blew out the lantern's flame, darkening the room. "Alex had her chance to respond to mercy. Now she will face vengeance. Tomorrow we begin training for the battle to liberate the world."